Robert Fannin

The Path of Ashes

———Φ———

Spiritbound Chronicle: Volume I

GNARLED
ROOT PRESS

The Path of Ashes

Book one of the Spiritbound Chronicle

Copyright © 2025 Robert Fannin

ISBN: 979-8-9993230-0-2

Published by Gnarled Root Press, an imprint of Robert Fannin.

Cover Design by Emiliano F.

Character illustration by Ludmila V.

Section artwork by Bobooks

First edition, 2025

For my wife Lacey, who stood beside me every step of the way.

Contents

Prologue

Fire devours—or purifies.

It burns on the thatched roofs, on the dry grass, the floating timber on the water. The roars of the flames mimicked the din of grisly forms rending lifeless corpses scattered amongst the debris.

There were screams of those still alive being torn apart, though few and sparse. In the distance was the clang of metal on resilient surfaces. It echoed above the crackling fire.

A young man knelt in a distinct pile of ash, lit by the orange glow of the destruction. His face was mostly hidden by the curtains of wild, dark hair. His body muted by the glow, slumped in supplication as his tunic rippled from the fiery air.

His gaze was distant, lost in turmoil as he fixed on the silvery ash. A streak of the same silver coated his cheek.

He felt it in his lungs, on his fingertips. It should have felt like any other ash; foreign, smooth and soft. For him it almost hurt to touch—more like embers. Like a dying flame, one desperate to burn out.

1

But he couldn't let it go.

It came as a blur. Long claws came at him. And his reaction was instinctive. A sword lay beside him—then it disappeared.

The *clang* sounded high over the fire as it reappeared in his hands. His force knocked the form back, and his intense blue eyes shifted to it.

It seethed. Dark, thick scales covered the body of the beast. Black ichor coated the body and muted any other detail. Its eyes were bugged and mostly pupil. They twitched back and forth to return the gaze.

It let out air in a whistle, broken by the streams of blood from its maw. It ended in a cough, guttural sound.

"Seek the lady of the water," it croaked. Its tongue was not well suited to speech. Some words were lost to a clicking pattern.

"Lost one. Seek her—it will lead you to trail his abyss."

The man jolted and snarled as he threw the sword like a javelin. The tip shattered the skull, pierced between the brow of the beast. It slumped as the man did in return, returning to the silver ash.

A voice in the fire, fleeting. A scream cut short. A flicker of green, swallowed by the flames.

Was it a pair of eyes fading into the red? Or was it the fire itself that turned green? His head pounded with the flash and ached his heart.

Then he examined the mutilation around him. It felt alien in the aftermath, yet familiar too—the destruction in his wake. A distant memory faded, flashed and then he fell back to the emerald eyes.

He could not escape them even when he closed his own.

He opened his eyes and watched the ash fall through his hands. He tried to cradle it, but the wind scattered it into the encroaching darkness. The silver stained him—branded him—as he stood and retrieved his sword from the slumped mass.

He took one last look at the burning destruction before he walked away, swallowed by the thickening copse on the outskirts.

The Wooden Soldier

I

There was a wet gnawing sound—slow and rhythmic, like a malformed heartbeat. The tearing of flesh and the brittle breaking of bone echoed in the woods. It continued, monotonous and grating to the ear, as a scaly bipedal beast ripped flesh from a body.

It was a boy, either an adolescent or young adult, who laid as fodder. The features were undefined by the mauling. Blood bubbled from the corpse's mouth.

A soft footfall came from behind the beast that kept to the woods and close to a slope that turned rocky as it went upward.

From the thicket, a man emerged, fashioned in a faded red tunic adorned with armor. He was within arm-length of the beast when he unsheathed his blade: a claymore, its sheen dull with large, gash-like scratches embedded into the metal.

The raking of the blade being unsheathed caught the attention of the beast. It turned and snarled through clenched jaws. The corpse hung from its humanlike hands that ended in dagger-sized claws.

The man walked towards the beast with the sword at his side.

"Where is the sorcerer," the man demanded. His voice rasped and rattled, breaking the calm sway of the trees.

Its already bulging eyes popped out more as the beast roared a metallic screech with guttural undertones. It lunged with its claws in front of its face. The man sidestepped as the beast crossed its claws and separated them in a wide arc. Had it connected, the man would have been ripped in two.

He swung the sword in a hammer-like fashion with both hands on the handle. His arms flexed underneath his tunic and the force pulled the fabric taut.

It came down on the beast's back. With a crude *crack*, the sword tore into the beast's spine.

The creature let out a sharp exhale as blood flowed into its lungs. The force of the blade slammed it into the ground and its eyes popped out.

The swordsman paused briefly before he hammered the blade down again—and again.

His blue eyes burned with hatred. He panted slightly as he gazed at the corpse—the crude blows finally ripped the body in two. In his fervor, his hair, brown like the surrounding oaks and cascaded down to his shoulder blades, splayed out wildly and covered his face. He brushed it back with his free hand.

The man knelt and examined the wound and wiped the black ichor off his blade on the grass.

"Still no answers," he mumbled. "This is the fourth one and none have given me the answers about him like the first one did."

He pried its maw open and yanked out a large tooth. The squelching sound broke the sounds of nature as the tooth pulled away from the putrid flesh. The acrid stench of acid and rotten flesh rose from its mouth. The man wrinkled his nose as he examined the tooth.

So much time has passed and still no answers. What did he mean? 'Look to your past and you'll find me.' Nothing. I know nothing of my past. Just the things he took from me. And then there's the lady. What lady? No one else can give me an answer.

He coughed from the stench then spat into the distance. He wiped the tooth on the ground and stashed it in a pouch on his belt.

He twisted his sword in his right hand. It was well worn—far beyond what he would normally allow.

But time is not on my side. I can't stop knowing he's still out there.

He clutched the handle tight. The metal gave off a faint reflection that exhibited his eyes. Eyes the color of the deepest waters, but with the expression of a man far older than his young face should bear.

He sheathed his sword and walked over to a thicket of trees within the woods. Nestled in it was a horse, a roan, who gently whickered at his arrival.

"Easy, girl." He patted her snout, and she gleefully took it. "Nothing this time. Though the world is rid of another mutie."

He untethered her from a trunk and mounted the saddle on her back. It was packed heavily with a sleeping skin and pouches, bulging out from heavy use.

He clicked his tongue, and the roan set on.

The woods broke at some point to a small village nestled in the crevice of the looming mountain range. It was mostly huts, built from the wood of the nearby trees and stones from the foothills. There was a wall around the village twice the height of a man. The tower at this entrance was unmanned.

The clop of hooves echoed as the sunset painted the village in red. Kael grimaced.

Fire. And houses burning. And a burning feather.

He pushed the thoughts away. He nodded at several of the townsfolk, and they waved back.

He stopped his horse in front of a house that had a porch attached and a sign that had INN writ on it. He tied his horse to the porch and walked in. The inside was quiet, though there were a few men at the bar that took up one wall of the inn.

When he walked to the bar, the bartender waved. "Aye, Kael. Got any good news?"

"The mutie's dead, Aeron." Kael dropped the putrid tooth on the bar. "There was a traveler that wisnae so lucky, though."

Aeron seemed dismayed. His grey beard drooped slightly. "It's a dangerous world. I suppose that there's always a risk, right?"

"Mhmm," Kael replied and took the coin as payment. He eyed past Aeron to see if there were any other jobs available, but none stood out.

Harpies north of the town—I won't take another harpy job unless I absolutely must. some ghouls have been spotted near Reihl—specifically near the Reihl falls. Though, there was a whole field of graves that way, and ghouls are common. Someone else can take care of that, and not even a hunter. Just some silver will do the trick, or brute force.

It all muddled in his brain. Then he heard the drunkards' conversation.

"Aye, did you hear about the village up in the mountains?" The man slurred. He paused to take a gulp of his cider. A loud belch came out and he laughed.

"They say it disappeared—poof. The people gone."

The other man stared through glassy eyes. "Yer lyin'. They weren't gone. I heard they were killed. Probably sum monsters."

11

Kael leaned forward and nodded absentmindedly as Aeron spoke. He was focused on the drunkards' conversation. Their words stirred glimpses of fire and screams.

The other blew a raspberry and clicked his tongue. "Nah. There was some ashfall when people said it happened, but that's subsided since. I'd say it was magic. Fire magic. Then all these muties are popping up around here."

A third man was seated at the far corner of the bar.

"Aye, I heard there was one spotted down in Kiers a couple clicks away not long after that. There's been a few more since. Right up until the one that laddie took care of," he sloshed his drink towards Kael, who glanced at him and got back to his faux conversation with Aeron.

"It's been happening more since the news of that village," the first drunkard said. "Heard there's been strange activity amongst the monsters since."

"Ach, Rigges said he saw some woman sitting on the shoreline of Oquia in a white dress. Like she was waiting for someone."

"He went to talk to her, but she ignored him and kept muttering something about 'balaal,' and 'lost child,'. Poor thing."

The man jumped and spilled his drink on himself when Aeron yelled.

"Hey, Kael! Where you goin'? It's nearly nightfall!"

But Kael was already out the door and on his horse. He pulled the reins and into a gallop as he dodged a few of the villagers. He entered the forest as it turned to dusk and hoped to reach the shoreline by daybreak.

II

At the edge of the forest was a bend of the river Aquia. The sun creeped over the horizon, though it did not bring much light. The sky was bleak and grey, clouds awash and uninviting.

The crash of the waves broke the silence near the shoreline, followed by the crunching footfalls on the coarse sandbar. Kael guided his horse to the edge of the shoreline where the trees began. He paused to secure his horse before he walked onto the sand.

A large rock was positioned not far from the tree line. A woman in a long gown sat atop the rock, quietly murmuring. He walked towards the woman in a wide arc that maintained some form of advantage and stopped to her side.

Kael cleared his throat and when the woman turned to him, he bowed. He crossed his index and middle finger and placed them on his forehead. He fixed his gaze at her as he stood upright.

"This is no place for a woman to be alone. How fares it?"

"The days are short and the nights long, as I am sure you know, swordsman."

He noticed that her black hair was matted and wet.

"I am sure we are both here for the same thing. We are both prisoners of the past, it seems."

Kael narrowed his eyes. "What of it? What do you know of my past?"

"I know what he told me—what he showed me. And what he gave me."

She held out a small wooden object, but in a flash it was gone.

"My kind are dwindling. We once used to roam the seas, but a darkness pushed us in." Her mouth quivered. "Since then, we have been hunted, slowly dying off."

"Tell me, what would you give me? What does this mean to you?" She feigned a smile. She outstretched her arm, and he noticed a black band of script on her wrist.

"It is a key to you, right? But what door will it open? Will it open a door or a chest? Or is it a key to something else—memories, perhaps?" She smirked, but Kael could see it was full of pain.

Kael felt a burn on the back of his neck, like hot embers pressed into his skin. His hand covered it, but it did not soothe.

"Who are you?"

The woman came to him and pulled his hand off his neck. She placed it on her cheek and nuzzled her mouth into his gloved palm.

"I'm just like you—lost, desperate. I just want hope."

She kissed his hand, then his lips. He felt the burn spread and radiate, but it was accompanied by a different feeling.

Lust. He tried to pull away, but she bit gently at his lips to pull him back.

With every kiss his mind became cloudy: the warmth made him hesitate. She became more ferocious as she pulled his waist towards her. The strength was enough to pull the wind out of him. She chuckled, then the voice became distorted.

"The endless night is nigh, lost one. The door you shall open with this key that you seek is death."

She pulled him into the deepest part of the river. Her form changed into a dark, scaled horse and kicked him down to the depths. The blows knocked the air out of his lungs and immobilized him. The horse turned to resurface.

He brought on all his might and grabbed the long, black tail as it breached the surface. He gasped for air and straddled the back of it before he unsheathed his sword. Kael thrust his sword between the horse's shoulder blades as it descended again.

The kaelpie thrust them deeper underwater as he held tight to his handle, the momentum raking it from side to side. The waters turned black around them as the horse tried to shake him off her back, creating small currents that pulled him backwards. He held on with both hands as the current got stronger. But the force was too strong, and he was beginning to lose grip.

The air was heavy in his lungs as he fought the current, sure he would gasp involuntarily at any moment. But he forced his legs to pin against the sides of the kaelpie, who fiercely thrashed about.

The waters kicked up a storm and Kael felt his hands slip. His sword stayed in her back as he floated off. In a flash she was above him and kicked with her hooves. His back slammed into the riverbed and the air came out of him.

His lungs filled with water and choke him; panic set in and his eyes bugged out of his head. The onslaught of hooves did not stop and his strength was sapped from him. The horse cackled and neighed, then her elongated, equine face came down to his as he struggled.

"This key was death," she crooned.

Her eyes glistened dully in the water, then he saw it. The fires, the hooded man looming over him. A surge of strength came over him and he fought back.

He grabbed the sword handle protruding from her back and used riverbed as an anchor. The sword came out of her back with great restraint and a plume of blood. He struck the blade down into the kaelpie's skull and cracked the bone. He shoved the blade straight through.

The kaelpie snorted and kicked, but it subsided quickly. The lifeless body of the creature went limp and suspended. There were plumes of blood coming out of the wound as the wooden toy floated out of one of them. He grabbed it and heard another cackle.

"The key you seek opened the door of death. If not for you, then it will be for someone else."

"Tread carefully, for the keys you find will not open what you expect."

Kael's vision darkened around the edges. The water was heavy in his lungs and he panicked. He watched which way the body was ascending and swam viciously in that direction as he tried to reach the surface. His vision blacked as his body numbed.

The silence grew uneasy and the horse on the shoreline neighed softly. Then there was a break at the shore and Kael thrust himself on the shoreline and gasped for air.

In his left hand was his sword. In the other was a nondescript piece of wood. He knelt on the shoreline to catch his breath and examined the piece of wood for a moment.

He could barely make out the weathered shape of a man holding a sword, worn away by the water over time. He gazed upward to see the clouds were darkening. Then came the first few drops of the oncoming storm on his face.

He scanned the area and saw a small cave in a rocky outcrop before he retrieved his horse. He stashed it into his pouch and guided the horse to the cave.

The cave was quiet; the silence only broke by the footsteps of Kael and the horse. He made a small fire in a short time and sat in silence, staring at the fire, listening to the crackle of the timber for the night. The rain outside was pouring harder now, and he did not feel like he would be leaving the cave for the night. He glanced at his horse then sighed.

"Another day is gone, Jorunn. We are not any closer to our answers than we were yesterday." He leaned back and rested against the wall. The flames flickered and cast long shadows dancing around them.

He rummaged in his pouch and pulled out the wooden soldier. He ran his thumb over the worn surface, the deep grooves cast black by the dark shadows.

"A relic of my past... it's a key, you know?" He watched Jorunn for a response, in which she snorted. He snorted back. "Or so the sorcerer says. A breadcrumb, if you may. Enough to satiate but nothing more."

The horse watched at her owner in askance, but he did not say anymore, instead laying down close to the fire. The glare of the fires gleamed on the faded wood toy that he rotated in front of his face for some time. The toy pervaded his mind, raining down faded memories as hard as the storm outside.

He watched the river and his mind picked up one of the last things he saw in that riverbed. As his vision faded, he watched the body of the kaelpie turn back into a woman.

Why? Why was she bound to this place? Why was she cursed? He continued wondering why as he held onto the toy and drifted into sleep. The wooden relic began to warble and shimmer. Faint blue lines traced into the hand that held it.

The air distorted slightly as incoherent whispering came from the relic.

III

There was a blue haze in the dream. A pebble that danced upon the knuckle of a battered hand. He felt his eyes swim. He was just a scared boy. He watched as the pebble danced, so slowly he could see the skin ripple where it bounced.

There was a hoarse voice cutting through the haze. "You will forget the events of the massacre, child. Your new life will start now, and you will no longer be afraid."

It stopped. He glanced up to see a man, worn and tired, but there was warmth and sympathy in those eyes.

Ijos.

He knew the man well. There was an ache in his heart for a moment. The man stopped and observed upstream. He followed his gaze and saw a plume of smoke in the distance, far, far upstream.

He then gazed down and in his hands was the wooden soldier, albeit it was not worn at this point. He could see the details well, a soldier with a greatsword and shield. Then he watched himself trace two warriors on the ground and look up at Ijos.

The man smiled at him and his mouth opened, but he could hardly hear the words. Water drowned out the sound. He felt himself writhing in the water. Hearing the cackle again and the kaelpie whinnying in pain.

Then the dream shifted. The water disappeared and in its place there were blazing fires. He could smell it. Burning wood, burning flesh. The screams. His eyes focused on everything and on nothing; the people screaming as if they were being ripped apart.

The burning homes (*the castle, too, though there wasn't a castle then. Not in this village.*). He felt like a small child, lost to everything, but he knew better. He did lose everything, but he was a warrior by then. *Why do I feel like this had happened before? What were these dual memories, these dual set of eyes I am seeing through?*

His sword felt heavy in his hand, the terror in his heart heavier. And in front of him was the hooded face that started it all, the yellow eyes gleaming through that veil of darkness enshrouding it. He could feel hatred burning within him. Something deeper, too, was trying to claw its way out. He heard the snarl and bark, the gnawing at his insides. Those yellow eyes stared at him and he knew what they said.

Drown.

He awoke before dawn, his lungs feeling like they were drowned in water. He sat up sharply and coughed until he vomited up some leftover water from the day before.

Leaving the cave behind, he mounted his horse and rode to the east, following a faded path for some time.

It went through several thickets and over small fields. The dull skies invited him to abandon his task, but he ignored it, and crossed an old stone bridge at some point. The bridge crossed the narrowest bank of Oquia, one of the rivers of the northeast. The bridge itself was old, worn from weather and unstable from missing stones. The darkness had long come and went, too. The sunrise illuminated his path like a guiding light.

He continued this faded path, overgrown from disuse, until he came across an abandoned town. The winds whispered through the old structures, the black of some forgotten events still present on them. The gates were open and unguarded, the streets still vacated by lingering footsteps.

The center of town still held a half-burned bonfire and a weathered stone stature of a fallen man beside it. In his hands was a rusty sword. Kael rode past this, pausing briefly to examine the statue with some curiosity.

His path led to a castle. Its doors were wide open and clattered in the wind. He dismounted his horse and tied her to some debris beside the entrance.

The inside of the castle was dreary and dark. The unlit lamps were decorated with dust and the hallways felt crowded and empty at the same time. He walked through it, knocking up the decades of dust that had accumulated.

He entered a large dining hall still furnished with old food from an age ago. He walked along the table at the center of the hall and to a fireplace. The ashes were a reminder of a past forgotten.

A voice echoed in the hall. "These halls once held feasts and parties galore. It even held a feast on the last night this town was populated."

The voice quivered and warbled as it came closer.

"This town suffered a terrible end. Oh, sweet lost child, do you want to see how your home was lost?"

The voice came to him, and he felt a cold caress on his cheeks. The only thing he could do was nod.

The voice crooned and whispered in his ear. "Then come, sit down at the abandoned throne, and I shall show you. You will see how your path was changed."

He sat down at the large chair at the head of the table, leaning his battered sword beside him. As he sat down, he felt an invisible mist swirling around him, his eyes growing heavy and lulling him into a deep sleep. He could feel the familiar burn on the back of his neck, but he felt a chill to his bones as he felt dazed and paralyzed.

The wooden toy once again began to warble and shimmer, even from his pouch. The air around the chair distorted and wisps of fog engulfed it ever so slightly. Faint whispers began to recount memories and stories of old.

Incipient

Caede

I

Fire scorched the earth. The town is burning. *What do I do? These monsters are eating everyone. My family is dying in front of me. My wife, my children—I can't take their screams. What do they want? Why are these scaly beasts attacking Caede?*

The soldiers fell to these dark monsters, their scaly hides deflecting any weapon. Their dull eyes hold no sympathy. The bonfire burns in the background as a man watched his town massacred. In front of him is a cloaked figure with a face concealed by a hood, only yellow eyes cutting through the veil.

What do you want? The man screamed at the figure. He tried to swing his sword, but there is no sword. He has no clothes on, bare to the world. His hands are stained with blood.

The figure said nothing as it pointed to the man. The man could feel a burning sensation on his neck; a hot coal being pressed into his skin.

He grabbed his throat and yanked off a gold necklace that continued burning in his hand. The gold melted away and all that was left was a shard of stone, black in the night.

Stone. The figure whispered. *Boy.*

Then his mind flashed to the face of a young boy. The two words alternated in his head, spinning it around like a top.

He then stared into that shard and saw another set of eyes, a growl preceding a sharp, unhinged laughter. That laughter filled his head as his eyes were consumed by fire.

II

Caedmon awoke on a wintry morning to a chill spreading down his spine and his hairs standing on end. The events of his dream were beginning to fade already, the thought of his family's mangled corpses was replaced by obscure faces he didn't know.

The only thing that remained were the two words in his head: stone and boy. The boy's face stared at him. It appeared scared, but full of malice as well. That chill down his spine shook again.

He got out of bed and walked over to the window nearest to him, staring out at the town of Caede in the glow of the early morning.

The town of Caede resides in the Northeast, a small area that is often covered in snow. Caedmon watched the ports, where the two rivers Aquia and Oquia joined to form the larger Aqouia. There was a strip of land in between the two smaller rivers that was covered with trees, too small to be used for anything else.

On the other side of the larger river was the town Eid, a newer build. The king had sent him here many years ago to colonize the harsh conditions of northern Hera and in that time he had found his wife, who had already been part of Hera, though further south, than the snowy lands they inhabit now.

His morning routine was insignificant; he was dressed early in his fur and leather winter garments topped by a thick cloak, and he had already settled in the dining hall of his castle with his family, eating breakfast as he tended to documents that came via air or horseback. He peeked at his children in between the documents and smiled.

"Are you ready to visit Uncle Haskell in the Capital, Azalea?"

His daughter glanced up from her food and nodded. She was still a child, young enough to still have some childlike features, but puberty was around the corner. She was changing to look a lot like her mother.

A smile shone on her face and warmed his as well. "Yes, daddy. I especially cannot wait to see the market."

He nodded and his wife agreed with Azalea. Mynheir, the Capital, was known for many things, but the market and trade was central to the city's prosperity.

His eyes turned to his two boys, twins, which was uncommon. They were still young, but old enough the castle scholar was teaching them. That is, when the scholars can find them, as mischievous as they are.

"What says you, Gareth and Zareth? Are you excited?"

The boys nodded in unison, and both began to talk as fast as they could. Most of it was incoherent, but Caedmon caught the tail end of it.

Can you tell us stories about your time in the Capital?

He chuckled. "Another time, boys. There's plenty of that for the road. It'll take us some time to get there, and I can tell you about all the trouble me and your uncle got into."

The excitement of the stories tided them over until breakfast ended and they ran to hide from Elus, the scholar. For Caedmon, it came the time of morning for reports, which made him want to hide, too. It was mostly just townsfolk coming in with numbers for their livestock or the fish haul from yesterday. Then came in a man and son.

"Lukos," Caedmon set aside his documents. "How has the forests been?"

The man, Lukos, bowed and stood back up. "Quiet, m'lord. It's unusual. Wildlife is sparse and the ones there are flighty."

Caedmon nodded. "Maybe it's due to the war."

"Has it spread far, m'lord?" Lukos had a concerned expression on his face.

"I haven't received any news of it spreading near, but I find that animals are keener than man," Caedmon said reassuringly.

Caedmon noticed a young boy poke his head out from behind Lukos. His mind flashed to the nightmare earlier and the boy he saw. This was the boy from the dream he recognized. Caedmon gasped audibly.

"What's the matter, m'lord?"

Caedmon glimpsed at the man.

"Nothing," he smiled and gestured to the boy. "Is this your son?"

Lukos smiled brightly. "Aye, this is Kael." He turned to the boy. "Bow to the Lord, Kael."

The young boy mimicked his father's bow. "H-hello."

Caedmon smiled, nodding his head as he dismissed them, and the two exited. He watched as the man and child left; the boy's face still burned into his mind. He tried to shake it off and finish his morning reports, which dragged on after that.

Caedmon then left the castle and ventured to the town square, heading towards the blacksmith Sarreif. As he neared, he could hear the clanking of steel and the grunts of a man hard at work.

As he entered the blacksmith's shop, a burly, dark skinned dwarf with graying hair was bent over red hot iron, which was in a rough shape of an axe head. The dwarf had just placed the axe head into a bucket of water when he noticed Caedmon, stopping to wipe the sweat off his brow.

"G'morn, my lord. How fares it, today?"

"It goes well, Sarreif. I see you are beginning your work early, no?"

"Aye, some of your men need axes, so I have a sizable order to fill."

"And what about our order? Is the present ready?"

"Of course. I poured much of my time and skill into this piece, and I do think this is my finest work yet. Come, and I shall show ye."

Sarreif and Caedmon entered the adjoining house to the workshop and inside was a cozy place. It was not regal, nor would it befit a noble, but it had its own charm. Sarreif crafts some of the finest swords, axes, and shields, probably the best in the Eastern regions. They came to a box and inside the box was an ornate sword, made of Black Damascus, a material that was native to the mountains, a rare mineral that holds magical properties.

Damascus is said to be a scialytic blade—able to cut through darkness. But it is hard to find and even harder to forge from.

Sarreif, however, crafted such a fine blade, with a handle made to represent an unlit torch and the pommel an open basket design. The design was a symbol of the King as a guiding light. Caedmon planned to take this as a gift to King Alrich during his coronation.

Sarreif coughed and said, "Ain't she a beaut? I have created a many weapons and armor in my time, but this sword is by far my finest work. Hell, I think it's the finest work in the whole eastern kingdom."

"I would have to agree with you, Sarreif. You truly are valuable to this town. You're the gem of this province." Caedmon smiled and patted the dwarf's back.

Caedmon left the blacksmith's home and strolled around the town, interacting with his people, and ensuring they are happy. The town was awake and busy with daily tasks as well as hanging up banners and placing flower wreaths on various buildings. The town was holding a festival to celebrate both the coronation of the King as well as to bless the journey of the Lord and his family to the Capital.

Men were building a large bonfire at the middle of the town square, throwing wood to create a base and then there were various crafts made from dried crops or sticks that were designed much like various beasts to act as a ward for the journey ahead. This was to appease the

Goddess Aurelia, who resides over the sun and represented vitality and luck.

Children were running around, singing ancient poems and songs about the gods and goddesses, detailing the history of the world and how it came to be.

Caedmon would join in on occasion, smiling and laughing with the kids, and he would help the men throw firewood onto the pile. He was in good spirit after seeing Sarreif. However, he still felt a sense of dread deep down.

Caedmon walked towards the front gates of town, which peered west toward a larger dense forest. When he was at the gates, he stared at the forest. The wind whistled and whispered, as if trying to tell him something.

The gusts picked up more, much like yelling, and he had to stand fast to keep from becoming unstable. The gust then stopped, and when he glanced up, he saw an owl, its feathers dark and with piercing, yellow eyes.

The silence that fell was crushing; the presence of this bird was solemn and foreboding to Caedmon. It did not say anything, instead it just stared at him in silence before it turned and flew to the forest, disappearing amongst its tree line.

Caedmon tried to shake it off, explaining to himself that the owl was just a coincidence, and began to walk away. An old lady, sitting on a stoop nearby, spoke, startling the lord slightly.

"An owl in daylight 'tis a bad omen, my lord. Even more so one of dark colors, and golden eyes. It seems that the bird of death has paid you a visit. Are you so sure your journey will be a safe one?"

She cackled vehemently. Caedmon stared in bewilderment. The guards nearby tried to silence her.

He left the area in a hurry, heading towards the town square. In one of the alleys, he passed a family. He eyed the hunter Lukos, his wife and children. There was a daughter about the same age as his own, Azalea. Then there was the boy, his face still burned into his mind. The boy gasped in excitement.

"Look," he said. It was a small wooden toy, which had a little sword and shield much like the ones he brandished. The sister smiled and curtsied and the parents greeted him as well. He feigned a smile and hurried back to the town square, bypassed it unknowingly and ended at the port.

The waters of the river flowed gently; the sun glistened but the peace did not soothe Caedmon's worry. He turned and headed straight for the castle. He tried avoiding people as much as he could.

He arrived at the castle and nearly ran to his study, closing the door behind him. He sat at his desk, pulling out a pen and ink and began to write. He addressed his brother that he had concerns about his journey and detailed his route, stating that if he doesn't reach the capital to search this route.

He sealed the letter with his wax stamp and attached this letter to a crow and released it out his window. He still sat in his study for some time, even as the sun began its descent and came closer to sunset.

As the sun set and the people began to gather in the town square and around the castle, they lit the bonfire, dancing and singing as custom dictates. Caedmon was inside his castle in the main feast hall, sitting on his throne and observing the festivities. Although he had a smile on his face, his eyes seemed worried, and his wife, who sat beside him, noticed his feigned composure.

"Baldock, dear, what is wrong? This night is supposed to be joyous, but you wear worry on your shoulders."

"I cannot help but feel there is something wrong."

She placed her hand on his, stared intently into his eyes, and smiled. "There is nothing wrong, dear. It is just the worry of the journey ahead. I am sure everything will be fine."

Outside the castle, and beyond the town, forests surrounding the front were shifting, but not with the wind. Trees fell, toppled by such force that the townspeople were startled by the noises louder than the festivities.

The town stopped celebrating; the people came into the streets and focused past the gate, to the forests. Caedmon shot out of his throne, his forehead beaded with sweat and his stomach felt heavy, and he left the castle to see what the noise was, worried his suspicions were right.

Caedmon quickly crossed the town, standing at the gate alongside the guards when he spotted a large ball of fire flying in the air, arching over the walls, and hitting a house on the east side.

The townspeople ran frantically in any direction away from the front gates, as another fireball is launched at a tavern close to the market with debris hitting bystanders, some crushed under the crumbling building.

The Lord rushed towards the castle, occasionally getting shoved or imbalanced from the panicked people, screaming at the tops of his lungs.

"Run! Run to the port and flee on the boats!"

He felt winded and his eyesight pulsed with his quickening heart. His legs were numb but still moved forward to the castle. He reached it, running through the ajar door and rallying his men by yelling, his voice cracking from overuse and panic.

"Men! Get ready, we are under attack! Grab your shields, your swords, your bows! Protect the people at all costs!"

He gathered his family amongst the panic, his wife teary-eyed and his children scared. He spoke in a hoarse voice, but loud enough to be heard over the commotion.

"Follow me, and hurry."

He had them grab their cloaks and while they were readying themselves, he made a makeshift satchel out of burlap and string, throwing in quick provisions that would not spoil. Last, he grabbed a small sword that was light and motioned for his family to follow him once more.

At the end of the castle's banquet hall was a fireplace; the Lord pulled a torch on the right side and the fireplace shifted, revealing a secret passageway behind it. The Lord beseeched with his family to take this exit, explaining that it would go under the rivers and out the other side to the riverbank, close to Eird, where they can find help and refuge. He assured them he would meet up with them as soon as he could.

"Go, please. I will meet you again, my love."

He kissed his wife, embraced his children, and shoved them behind the fireplace with a torch. He closed the passageway, sealing it and protecting them. He then turned and grabbed his greatsword and greatshield from his throne nearby and rushed out joining his men to defend their home.

III

Caedmon ran out into the streets to see the town invaded by grotesque monsters. The townspeople were caught in the crossfire. Those who were too far from the port were surrounded by the beasts, claws and teeth ripping flesh from their bones, leaving mutilated bodies in their wake.

People who managed to reach the port risked leaving loved ones behind; some boats had left out of fear that they would be boarded, leaving many on the port screaming, some jumping into the water to avoid the beasts. Some people were snatched out of the water by the beasts, the lucky ones were killed immediately, as giant chunks were being chewed out of their bodies.

The soldiers of the castle clashed with the beasts; the lord fought with desperate fervor, thrusting at any monster he could reach, hoping to fell a few before being felled himself. As his family was evacuating, all he could do was give them time to flee through the passage under the castle.

The swords were not very effective; although the men could kill the beasts, it took several strikes to cut the scaly skin of the monsters, and for every one they slew, there was another ready to take its place. Caedmon stood with his men, using his greatsword to cut through the smaller beasts, his greatshield was the only thing between him and the creatures devastating attacks.

Caedmon had already seen these things cut through the armor of his soldiers, he had seen what that end would be like; while the man didn't fear death, he didn't invite it either. His equipment was becoming damaged though, his sword chipped and dulled, losing the razor edge he had honed. Large gashes in his shield threatened the stability; soon the thing would be useless.

An echo rang in his head as the word *damascus* repeated. Something about the rare metal gave him an idea and he was out of any other options. His shield, raked with gashes through was cast aside as he risked his life for any hope.

He instructed his men to follow him, leading them through the carnage, cutting down beasts as he could. He headed towards the town square. Upon reaching the town square, he made a path straight to the blacksmith's shop, which was empty. He had no time to find Sarreif. He ran into the dwarf's home, going back to the spot where Sarreif showed him the King's gift.

He found the sword underneath a broken window. He cleared the rubble and pulled the sword from its sheath. He left the house and was surrounded by the beasts.

They had a nasty growl that sounded like a dull, broken bell. They swiped at him with long claws and he dodged it. Caedmon countered with a swing of the ornate blade. The beasts shrieked as the sword cut them in two like nothing.

The beasts came charging at him and his band of soldiers. They flung their scaly bodies at him as he severed them midair. Blood coated the walls and the ground as they flopped to the ground. His men fell one by one as they protected him from the onslaught. He was the only one left standing.

He hacked away, and as he fought, he came to notice a man clad in a black robe, nearly formless as the ends of his clothing wisped like fog. The face was masked by a large hood. He had heard of a man who led the beasts that appeared like an apparition. It was as if death itself fronted the army that cut through the outer lands of the kingdom.

Caedmon did not waste any moment for the apparition to attack; he lunged at it and swung with the

Damascus blade, the swing slicing through the air with a ring. The man, though, disappeared in a cloud of black smoke. Caedmon stood bewildered, unsure where it went.

He turned, searching around the town square when he noticed a boy coming towards him. It was the boy, Lukos' boy, and his face stared back at him like in the dream. The child was alone, covered in blood with tears streaming down his face, stumbling across the square towards him. Caedmon knew the dream was an ill-omen, the boy the face of his own death, but still he rushed to the child.

"Help! M-my daddy—"

It was when he passed the large bonfire, roaring in the wake, that he was consumed by black fog. The fog itself began to condense and take shape, turning into the sorcerer, right in front of Caedmon.

He felt a sharp pain and warmth pouring from his chest. He had been stabbed by a spectral sword held by the sorcerer. The man in black leaned closer until his head was inches from Caedmon, his face indistinct except for glowing yellow eyes, and spoke in a deep, warbling voice.

"Where is it? Where is your piece of seven, Lord of the snowfields?"

Caedmon's face, once full of pain and anger, dispersed into one of fear. He then quickly changed his disposition, once again that of anger, and spat onto the sorcerer's cloak, his saliva tinged red from blood. His wounds were turning severe.

"It's not on me, and it is not in this village. Go to fucking A'hel, where you came from."

The sorcerer moved his free hand to rip at the armor covering the Lord's neck, revealing it bare. Caedmon cackled and smirked, which deepened as he peered at the sorcerer's free hand, scalded black and nearly rotted to bone. Caedmon cackled, blood running down his lips.

"What will you do when you find them? Can you even touch the artifacts you seek?"

The sorcerer hissed, twisting his blade, and shoving it even deeper into the Lord, all while reciting language in a foreign speech, and Caedmon could feel his body tighten.

Slowly, Caedmon began to yell, screech and moan, the skin on his face turning grey and hardening. *The boy.* He looked at the boy one last time to see the face was full of pain, but there was a malice in it as he watched the sorcerer.

Caedmon only stopped his anguish when he ended as stone, a statue forever frozen in pain. The sorcerer dispersed his spectral blade from the statue and turned around to view the frightened child. He then disappeared. The child stood still out of fright.

The sorcerer appeared behind the child, crouched to his height. His robes flowed endlessly. The sorcerer grasped the boy in his arms and leaned close to his neck. The sorcerer talked in an ancient language tracing a part of the boy's neck with his fingers.

The boy screamed in pain as the skin on his neck turned red. A scar was etched into his skin that resembled writing. The boy writhed in pain as the sorcerer disappeared once again. His shrieks of agony attracted some beasts ravaging the town, causing them to sprint towards the scent of flesh.

Fate will save you, for now, the sorcerer warbled in the air, his body hidden. *I can sense it within you.*

The strikes of the beasts were cut short, the bodies of each sliced in two by the air, a *whoosh* that seemed like something magical or divine came to bring mercy upon this child. The sorcerer then snapped, and four more beasts appeared, this time encircling the child.

Dirt mixed with blood and human remains flung in the air, creating a whirlwind of dust around the area, encompassing, and creating a shield that blocked the view. As the creatures surrounded the child and readied to attack, a man outfitted in a tattered robe, adorned with armor, had appeared beside the child. A phoenix was perched on his shoulder.

The man was tall, but thin—like he had not eaten for days. Dark eyes were pocketed in a hallowed face, circled by a mane of long, black hair, disheveled from the wind. Some of the hair was contained by a ribbon, but most had fallen out when he moved about. His movements were beyond an ordinary human's—his speed was extraordinary. The human eye could barely follow him.

In his hands was a long katana of Damascus steel, an extension of his body, and with it he danced elegantly in the night, amidst the flames of the bonfire and the massacred village, with swift lunges and slashes that the beasts could not keep up. The phoenix flew beside the man, engulfing the cut monsters with fire to burn them alive. So, the night entered a dance of conflagration, the creatures swarming a man and his bird that is as elusive as the wind, clawing at air that would not yield.

The monsters' screams were drowned in a river of blood, spewing from multiple wounds sliced into the necks, arms, backs, and legs of the army, burnt alive from the inside by the phoenix that tailed the man, the man winding his way through the wreckage of town, decimating the army to a meager band of few, but the few were the largest beasts.

The man returned to the Plaza and picked up the collapsed boy. He carried the child to a safe spot before confronting the last of the beasts. They flanked him and readied their own attack, their claws dripping with blood.

He then struck the tip of his blade into the ground. The blade was gone, deep in the ground to the hilt. The swordsman muttered an incantation and with it the wind began to swirl, pulling flames from the nearby debris and pulling the phoenix into the blade.

He pulled the sword out of the ground. A wind brought the flames and coated his blade in fire. It surrounded the man with embers in the shape of his bird. He lunged into the air.

He came down like a meteor, thrusting his blade into the ground again, and the flames dispelled from the blade. It created a vortex of fire that burned the beasts. Their skin and bone began to melt. The bird reappeared and fanned the flames. The beasts squealed, like metal scraping on metal.

They lashed at the man, with one cutting him deep on his right thigh. Amidst the flames, the man turned to a blur as he thrust his sword into each of the beasts.

The swordsman was then met with the man in black, the dark sorcerer, hovering the air behind him. He turned, staring intently at the dark sorcerer. He raised his blade in front of him and assumed a stance to strike.

The dark sorcerer did not seem to fear the man, but he did disappear. In a flash, the sorcerer was beside the man, chuckling slightly. The man would strike, but he had been rendered paralyzed, only his eyes able to move. The sorcerer cast a spell from his hand and green fog swirled around the man's body.

Inaudible whispering was passed from the sorcerer to the man, who kept a blank face. The sorcerer paused, and continued in one last breathy sentence, though his lips did not move.

The time is nigh for the endless night.

The sorcerer was gone again, teleporting to the air in front of the man like before.

The phoenix retaliated with a stream of flames from its wings at the sorcerer. The flames to hit an invisible shield around him. In the gleam of the flames, the man caught a glimpse of the sorcerer's face, and with a twinkle of a grin, the sorcerer left in a vortex of black dust, leaving only the man amongst the wreckage.

The village was decimated, leveled by the army of beasts led by the dark sorcerer. The man stopped to examine the wound on his thigh, gash that was profusely bleeding. He staggered, his balance weak as he shifted weight to pull out a flask with white powder. He sprinkled some of it on the wound, cursing slightly as it reacted and hissed. He then tore a piece of cloth from his cloak and wrapped his leg.

His bird perched once again on his shoulder, staring at his wound, and cocking its head. The man then took out a scroll and quickly wrote on it before attaching it to the bird.

"To Haskell. With haste," the phoenix seemed to nod and departed.

He then approached the nook where he hid the child. *Shock,* he examined as the boy did not move, his eyes glazed over. The only sound he made was the sniffling of choked sobs and a harrowed moan bubbling in his mouth. He picked him up and held him tight as he traversed the debris.

The man surveyed the village, searching for any life that could have survived. Homes were reduced to rubble and ash, the flames desperately licking the air to stay alive, space that were once taverns were empty and silent without the cheers and laughter of the folk.

The town was eerily quiet, broken up only by the ragged breathing of the man, the crackling of the fire still burning, and the choked sobs of the child. The roads through town were littered with remains, the smell putrid and suffocating.

The wind howled and the child shuddered from the cold. The man took his cloak and wrapped it strong around himself and the child. He traveled to the castle, stepping over the corpses of dead soldiers at the foot of the steps.

Inside the castle was dead, the wind outside riding the walls, creating a ghostly sound. He walked up the steps and searched each room. They were all empty.

He investigated the lord's chambers. It was empty, though there was a mess made in the chaos. He investigated the piles to find any clues. He found nothing and sighed.

They walked back downstairs with the echoes breaking as the man walked through a doorway. It was the hall, where chairs were overturned and food was left half-eaten, mead and spirits spilled. He grabbed one of the remaining drinks and took a long gulp. It burned, but it helped to dull his pain.

The flames flickered in the fireplace, the torches' flames swaying in the walls and in the elegant wood and bone chandelier. They walked to the fireplace and stood in front of the fire. He stared at the last few embers while the child writhed softly in his arms. As he stood, he began to feel a small breeze.

He examined the edges of the chimney and the sides of the fireplace. He noticed there was a gap. After he examined the wall he located the lever that the torch functioned as, cracking open the fireplace and revealing the passageway.

The passageway was dark, but he could see that the dirt on the floor was disheveled, indicating that someone entered here recently. With the town destroyed, the man had no path to follow except forward.

He may not be certain where this path leads. The path behind them may still contain stray monsters in the forest, and he was in no shape to fight. He shifted the child to one side of his hip, grabbed a torch from the wall, and entered the tunnel.

Echoes of the Fallen

I

Cold swirled and surrounded Kael on the abandoned throne. He felt like ice and was drained of energy. Behind him was a specter garbed in white, its eyes black and soulless with its mouth gaped open and he could feel that his life was being sucked in by it.

A Bánánach, I should have known. He struggled against the immense force holding him down as he fought to grab his sword, swinging it backwards towards the specter.

It released him as it dodged his attack, emitting a piercing shriek. The specter lashed out with its claws, narrowly missing its target as he sidestepped the attack. Seizing the opportunity, he lunged forward once more, his blade slicing through the ghostly figure's chest.

The specter wailed. The screech filled his ears and crept down his spine. To him it sounded like *memories* in a shrill voice.

He did not hesitate. He lunged forward and thrust his blade into the shrill being, his blade turning red. The being let out a faltering wail before turning to dust. Kael watched his blade cool. Intrigue and confusion sat on his face as he sheathed the sword.

Kael knelt and put the dust into a flask. He placed that flask into his pouch, brushing against the wooden toy, which was vibrating. He pulled the toy out and examined it, feeling the magic coursing through the relic. There was a faint blue hue to his vision as he held it, his mind flashing through a small home in the eastern part of town.

"This must hold some magic linked to my memories," Kael breathed.

Memories spliced through his vision more as he saw a man over him in a room. His face was familiar. Then he remembered seeing the face in the visions the bánánach used to siphon his health. There was the family that passed by the Lord. He looked like a hunter. The little boy with him—he remembered that family.

The warble subsided and so did the blue hue. This must be what enticed the Bánánach that began to consume his life force. He placed it back into his pouch then walked to the empty fireplace and examined the edges for the trace of the passage.

He felt the chilly air coming from the edges of the fireplace and searched for the sconce. He activated it and opened the passageway to peer inside, but he was met with the black of utter darkness.

His ears picked up the sounds of water deeper into the passage and assumed the tunnel finally caved in, so he turned around and exited the castle. The grey sky had subsided, leaving a clearer day. The sun was shining and near its zenith.

He untied his horse and went back to the weathered statue, kneeling to release the rusted sword from its grasp. He studied the weathered face and touched it with his hand. It was the Lord of Caede. His gaze then shifted to the blade itself, coated in the thick veil of brown and orange of weather and time. He tied this to his saddlebags and stood for a moment in the center of town.

He followed the alley, moving on a familiar instinct until he reached a charred structure. The door hung ajar, stuck to the floor with grime, and the windows were shattered. Inside, everything was covered in dust—the remnants of life long pilfered. It was a small house, forgotten like the memories it once held. He dismounted Jorunn and walked through the frame.

There was loose parchment on the floor and he walked over to them and picked them up. It was charcoal, and heavily smudged, but he could see the drawings for what they were. He remembered very poorly that he was the one who drew them.

The papers had different things; there was drawings of the goats that used to roam the forests, birds like snowy owls, even some cats and dogs. He flipped through them and then stopped at a picture he drew of the family, *his* family. A mom, a dad, a daughter, and a little boy. The little boy was him, and he had a family once. He absentmindedly stashed that picture away and then saw the next one.

It was the forest that flanked the town, but that was not the shocking detail. In the picture was a drawing of a fox, but more of an outline. There was small smudges, intentional it seemed, and somehow he had colored the eyes blue.

It resonated with him. It was a familiar thing he had seen mostly in his dreams. It would often say his name repeatedly. The picture picked at his brain and the feeling it gave him was unease, so he crumpled it up and threw it to the ground.

The rest of the house was covered in dust and grime, the food and clothes long pilfered. He walked through it, though it did not take long. It was small, with two adjacent rooms as sleeping quarters and then the largest room to function as a living quarter.

He peered into both adjacent rooms before returning to the main room. There was not much left in the structure, as it was not home anymore, and the memories were dull and mostly forgotten anyway.

As he left the structure he noticed a dark stain beneath the grime. It was an uneven stain, erratic and splattered. Flashes of a memory crossed his mind. In it was the face of the hunter (*dad*), splattered with blood as he tried to sound something.

His head throbbed as he saw it and felt a pain in his heart. He wanted to scream. *Dad, please dinnae go. Dad!* Was that him talking? He can't hear anything else.

It was his own yelling blocking anything else out. Then the memory faded to blue, but the only other thing he saw was those yellow eyes. *Those damned yellow eyes.*

He came back to as the pain in his head subsided. The wooden soldier vibrated in his pouch enough for him to notice, but it ebbed off too. He shook his head and realized he had fallen to the floor, pronated with his hands on the side of his head. He stood up and then heard Jorunn snorting wildly. He rushed out the door immediately.

When he crossed the threshold, he saw Jorunn surrounded by ghouls. They were vaguely humanlike, but their maws gaped open more than a man's and they walked on all limbs. They had a hoarse growl as they surrounded Jorunn, their forelimbs trying to stretch out and pull at her skin.

She whinnied and kicked. The ghouls dodged the blows and growled with a cadence of speech. They turned their attention to Kael when he came through the frame and back onto the road.

He unsheathed his sword, watching their coordinated movements. One lunged, swiping high, while another aimed low. The last tried to bite him, their attacks coming in an unrelenting pattern. He would take small windows and flick his sword, cutting the artery of the first. It screamed and rolled in the dirt until the pus-colored ichor stained the ground.

The other two became more sporadic in attack. They flanked him and did well in backing him to a wall, their strength pushing his sword back as he blocked. One bit his boot, which was fashioned of thick, durable leather with a steel cap.

He took the moment to flick his foot back and forth and crushed the jaw of that ghoul. It shrieked and grabbed at its broken maw, which flapped as it flailed.

He used the moment to swing his leg at the other, but it dodged it in one deft movement. It was distracted, though, from the shrieks of the other, pausing just slightly to glance back. That's when Kael attacked.

He swung his sword overhead, then pivoted the blade to swing it back down in a chopping motion. The blade tore through the ghoul's head as the bone cracked and pulled away from the socket of its eye. It couldn't even let out a sigh as it slumped to the ground.

The other ghoul cowered with its broken jaw on the ground as Kael walked over to it. In its last moments it sent out a flurry of kicks and swipes only for Kael to drive his blunted sword through it ribs and into its heart. The breaking bones echoed in the abandoned town.

Kael wiped his hair out of his face. It was warm and the fight has caused him to sweat. He wiped his sword on a small patch of grass and sheathed it. It took him a few moments to calm Jorunn down, including having to dodge cow kicks to get close to her. He patted her snout and shushed her some, quelling her fit in a few minutes.

"Let's go, girl," he tugged the lead more gently this time. Her eyes flickered a little and she was hesitant, but she followed him anyway.

He walked through the town some as he recounted the massacre decades prior. It was all hazy to him, though the 'memory' the bánánach showed him gave him a fresher perspective of it. He ended up at the dilapidated ports overseeing Aqouia.

The waters were calm and the scent of the water was refreshing after the putridity of the ghouls. The width of the river was quite large, forcing him to squint his eyes to see details on the opposing bank. There was smoke billowing from several buildings on that shore. He grimaced. It was a start to learn about Caede, but the memory ended in the tunnel and that was collapsed.

"*Dammit!*" He picked up a piece of rubble and chucked it into the river. He continued to throw rubble into the river until he was panting heavily.

Jorunn nipped at his hair and took him out of his contained rage. He patted her snout absentmindedly. The waves continued to gently crash on the shoreline. He glowered at the scene. All he wanted to do was give in to the anger again.

"Why cannae it be easy?" His voice came out as more of a whisper. Jorunn neighed softly in return. "Why cannae I just *remember*?" He yelled the last word, straining his neck as little as his face turned a dusting of pink.

Nothing answered back. Birds cawed, fish breached for a second, but nothing talked to him. It infuriated him. He strained his eyes more at the river and stared at the town again. Wisps of smoke continued to billow in the sky. *Wisps.* And that's all his life was, some cloudy wisp that he can't fully grasp.

He sighed. The anger ebbed a little and his head cleared. "Eird. I'm sure the tunnel leads there." He picked up a small piece of rubble and threw it in the river, more gently than before. "Maybe we stayed there back when."

He turned and patted Jorunn's snout one more time. He then mounted her and clicked his tongue, guiding her down the cobble and out the gate. He left Caede behind, retracing some of his path to Eird.

II

It took him about half a day to arrive in Eird. Kael saw the wall of the town through the thicket of trees long before he reached it. The setting sun painted those wooden walls with orange and pink. The gate to the town was guarded by a couple soldiers, likely employed by whatever Lord controlled this area. *Was it Estalin? Yes the crest—it was a raven. They had it on their tunic.*

He nodded his head as he passed and they returned the action.

The town was bustling, even in the twilight. The air was strong with brine and the men's voices carried from the docks as they hauled out nets of fish that flopped inside it with resilience. *Not for long,* he thought. He felt some sympathy for them, feeling like he was in a net himself.

The tavern was livelier than the rest of town, where twilight was the beckoning for workers to unwind after a hard day. Drinks sloshed and the sound of shuffling glasses filled the air as Kael walked in. The job bulletin was posted behind the bar, a custom that seemed to remain unchanged no matter where he went.

Hunters were not common, but common enough to have jobs posted in each town. Those who hunted monsters and other creatures risk their lives to make the life safer for others, and they paid quite a bit. Lately, though, the jobs had become more frequent and more dangerous. Few people take them, and of those who do, fewer return.

Kael walked passed the crowd enjoying their drink and leaned on the bar. He rapped his knuckle on the oiled wood to get the bartender's attention. He finished tending to some customers before turning his attention to Kael.

"Monster hunter, right? We've got a load of jobs posted for ye." The man started to pull down the papers when Kael raised a hand to stop him.

"I'm not here for that. Not this time. I need to know about Caede."

The tavern silenced, broken only by a glass tipping over or a muted gasp. The bartender leaned towards him and lowered his voice.

"We don't talk about Caede here. That was long ago, and I don't want to awaken any ghosts."

Kael sighed. "I see. I just need know about something that happened *after* it fell, if you ken."

The bartender shook his head and said no more. He walked to the other end of the bar and tried to clean up a mess, though Kael could see he was shaking. The tavern slowly resumed its raucousness, albeit more contained. Kael leaned on the bar for a moment before he ordered a drink himself, a tall glass of whisky. The bartender avoided eye contact with him as he handed his drink.

Kael went to fish out a couple of skells—a common currency in the lands, mostly in this eastern province—from his coin purse when another hand placed them down in front of him. He followed the hand up to see an older woman eyeing him intensely.

"I'll pay for that. That is, if you can entertain my intrigue." Her lips flowed as smoothly as her velvet voice.

He took a sip of his whisky and smirked. "I'm not really interested in going to bed with you, if that's what you want."

Her laugh pierced the air in an unnatural way. "No, I'm not looking for that. You're wanting answers about Caede. I can give that."

He raised his eyebrows. "Yeah? Then maybe I am interested then, if you ken." His playful smile faltered as she laughed again. It was grating to his ears.

She paid another drink for him and he downed them both. He was cautious enough to not drink too much, and he might have been buzzed. But his wits were still about him, even as she led him to a home on the far end of the port.

She opened the door to the home and lit a few lamps, mostly wick, but there were a few powered by crystals. The main room was barely furnished. He felt a little bit of caution when he walked into the room and she closed the door behind him. She crossed the room and leaned against the table.

"People don't talk about Caede around here. When it happened, people came in droves on the shoreline, shaken and weary. No one talked about what really happened, but we knew."

She laughed again. It was less trill this time, almost soothing. That made Kael more wary.

"There had been talk about a sorcerer guiding some mutated monsters and destroying towns. We thought it was safe here, and it was for some time. But when we saw the fire and heard the screams, we knew."

She stood up and walked slowly to Kael, who stood still.

"There was ashfall after that for some time. People who came across the river melded into this society."

Kael listened in silence, his mind turning over her words. The fire. The screams. It all sounded too familiar, a duality. Overlapping memories, the fresh one overpowering the faded. He tried to force himself to focus on the other, ignoring the open wounds of the other. He couldn't focus. The calmness in her voice felt wrong, like she was describing a distant memory rather than the horror of the past.

"But you, *you*, weren't here," she crooned. Her arms wrapped around his and felt a lull in his head. "I saw you further south with that man. Near the speaking stones. You came out of a rock wall, hidden by some vines. I watched as I was ensnared in a trap his kind did to me."

Her mouth began to brush his neck. It was cold, she felt cold. A short giggle and her eyes flicked up to him. They were red, cat-eyed pupils. He managed to smirk a little.

"Dearg due," his voice was hoarse and heavy with sleep. He was in her spell. He knew better than to let her trap him, but he wanted to know more. "So, we were near the speaking stones in the south?" *I can feel the veil of sleep. Just a little longer...*

A playful smile crept on her lips. "Aye," she moaned, her fangs becoming more prominent. "But that doesn't matter now."

She went to latch onto his neck. A swift blur came up and a hissing sound bubbled from her skin. The dearg stumbled back as Kael stretched a little, pulling the sleep from his bones. In his hand was a small dagger made of silver.

The dearg hissed and jumped at him. She swiped at him, her claws flashing. He blocked with his sword, but the force knocked him back into the wall, his head slamming hard.

The dearg stood over him as his head swam. She opened her mouth in a toothy smile, showing the fangs form over all her teeth. Her claws extended down and grasped him by the shirt, pulling him up.

"You're not ready for him," she hissed. Kael laughed through a cough. She grimaced and gasped as she glanced downward.

"I think I'm ready enough," he twisted the dagger and yanked it free. The Dearg Due shrieked and dissolved into ash, dropping Kael to the floor. He rolled backwards to mitigate the momentum.

The silence that followed was weightless, like a curse lifted. He walked over and put some of the ash into a vial. Then came a putrid, acrid stench. In the trap his senses were dulled, but not anymore. He crossed the room and opened a door to a wall of rotting smell.

The room was small—maybe it was a bedroom once upon a time. It was devoid of furnishing; the only thing in the room was a haphazard pile of rotting bodies— all men, mostly young—wrinkled and dry of blood. He closed the door and exited the cursed home.

He returned to the tavern and back to the bulletin board, beckoning the bartender over once more by rapping his knuckles on the counter.

"Look," the bartender said as he positioned himself in front of Kael. His eyes narrowed, but his skin was still paled from earlier. He took a deep breath. "Look, I've already said we can't talk about that—"

Kael reached around the man, who flinched. Kael leaned back after he pulled down a parchment nailed to the board and sat the vial of ash on it. The parchment had 'missing men' writ upon it.

"I found your missing men," Kael swirled the vial around. "It was a dearg due. A *vampyr*, ye ken?"

The bartender gulped and nodded. His pale complexion turned to ash. "A-a vampyr..."

Kael nodded. "Aye, specifically a dearg due. You'll find the bodies of her victims in a house on the north side of the port, close to dock nine."

The bartender said nothing as he handed Kael a pouch for the reward. He stashed it away and knocked on the counter before the bartender could walk away. "There's another thing. I need to find something called the speaking stones. It should be south of here."

The bartender nodded reproachfully. "Aye, it's a circle of stone that people say whisper to them. It's about a day south of the town, right off the path before you see Aquia."

"Thanks." Kael leaned himself upright and left the tavern. Jorunn was still at the entrance, drinking water from a pail. She observed him and neighed softly.

"Closer," he patted her snout, then checked the straps to make sure the saddle was secure. He climbed onto the saddle and rested one hand on the horn, brushing her mane with the other. "We're finally getting a little closer, girl."

He pulled the lead and led her out the gate. *It was a day's ride, the bartender said.* The speaking stones, where the voices whisper. "Maybe they will whisper something about my past."

Speaking Stones

I

The speaking stones were several large stones in a circle. At the center was a large slab. It was some sort of stone, but it was much lighter than the others.

Kael had traveled fast enough to reach the stones by early morning. The air was thick but the heat had not yet become unbearable as summer was starting. He entered the ring and immediately started to hear the whispers.

They were gentle whispers, inaudible unless you really focused on it. They overlapped and created a buzz effect in your brain. Kael picked out that it was almost choir-like, a chant of sorts in a forgotten language.

Kael stood by the slab for a moment before he sat down and leaned his back against it. The buzzing smoothed and became more of a purr. The voices then started to synchronize.

Bring out the artifact, it crooned. Kael did as they said, pulled the old toy from his pouch and sat it in front of him. He placed it so that the soldier was facing away from him.

In the deep, worn grooves a blue aura bubbled and filled them like a river. They coursed and shimmered, coming alive as he watched a bubble form around the speaking stones. Then there was shimmers, humanlike and gentle, that sat with him. One caressed his cheeks.

You are a lost child, it whispered. *We saw you enter the copse long ago. Our vision sees far and wide. Let us show what you have lost.* Then that blue hue took over him again, blotting out his vision and numbing his senses as he dropped to the past.

II

The tunnel was long, dark, and damp. It was reinforced with stone and steel, but the tunnel did not seem sturdy, like it could collapse any second. As the man and child descended deeper into the dark tunnel, the air became colder, his breath visible in the fire light.

His gait was staggered, limping from the wound he received in the battle, so his pace was slower. As time went on, he noticed water would drip from the ceiling, evident that the man had reached beneath the rivers, and he felt uneasy.

His body tensed as he readied to run if the tunnel walls began to fail. So far, he could not hear anything but the sounds in the tunnel. There was no swaying leaves, no wind, not even the bubbling of the river waves.

We must be far from the end, which made his soreness spike. He stopped for a second, but the tunnel began to shift slightly. He pushed himself on.

Time went on, and the man grew tired. He stopped once and sat on the damp ground, which he noticed was made of brick, surprised that the water did not make it slippery.

He was aching—his legs were tired and the wound had bled through the rag. It stung and tingled; a complex combination that made him unsure if it was infected. After some time, he slowly stood up with some struggle and started on his path again.

Hours passed by and he had used most of his energy fighting, using his magic to control fire always takes a lot out of him. The wound was beginning to feel less sore, evident that the powdered medicine was working. His breathing grew hoarse, though, resembling paper being ripped to shreds. His muscles were tightening up, cramping from overuse. His eyesight was beginning to blur, unable to focus as he was walking along the tunnel.

It was when he felt on the verge of collapse when he finally heard sounds of the surface: the wind brushing up against the leaves of a tree and the sound of the river. He felt a burst of energy, given to him by the relief that the surface was so close, he began to run.

The child in his arm, however, had finally fallen asleep, and he did not want to wake him. He walked quickly, but gently, and reached a slope that ended in steps which took him to a door.

The door had no handle or latch. Instead, it was a pure flat surface made of stone, embedded in a rough rock surface.. The man felt around, searching for a way to open. He was growing frustrated.

"A door must be able to be opened, dammit." He murmured, quiet enough not to stir the child.

It was when he searched the frame of rock around the door-like obstacle did he find a small loose rock that functioned as a button and he pressed it. The door popped, letting in a gush of fresh air, and the two exited. He noticed the other side was covered in vines to mask its presence.

Upon reaching solid ground, the man fell. He was exhausted, but he fell on his right side and dropped the torch, startling the child for a moment. The child gasped and opened his eyes momentarily but fell back asleep quickly.

They were both exhausted from the massacre, and the man was so depleted of energy he had no strength to take off his weapons. He fell out of consciousness quickly, unaware whether the area was safe at all.

III

The man awoke to a bright light, as day had creeped up on him, and his head was pounding. When he and the child exited the tunnel, it was still dark out, and they exited in a dense forest northwest of the rivers.

His eyes took a minute to adjust, but when he could finally focus, he found the child sitting next to him, staring at him—like he was studying him.

He glanced past the boy to see the morning light made the falling snow glimmer. In the distance he could see stones in a circle. He felt a drawing towards it and an evil whisper. He pushed it out of his mind and tried to stand.

The man was stiff, his muscles weakened from his techniques. It took time, but he finally mustered the strength to be able to stand and start building a small fire from fallen branches. He took time building the fire, placing the wood strategically.

Once it was lit, he began to pull items out of a bag he had on his back: a pan, some strips of preserved meat in salt. He was going to cook breakfast; he was starving, and the child probably was as well.

The man paused and glanced at the child again. He stopped tending to the fire and walked to the boy. He crouched and stared into the child's eyes. The child did not flinch or cower in fear. He still trembled, and his eyes red from tears. The man smiled and gently patted the child on the shoulder before he returned to his fire.

"Mister.." The child piped meekly while the man was cooking.

"Yes?"

"What's going to happen?" the child stared at him with big, watery eyes. "I want my mommy and daddy."

The man stopped cooking and went to the child. "I'm sorry child. I don't know what is going to happen," He patted the boy's shoulder gently. "But I will keep you safe."

The boy nodded. He shivered despite being beside the fire. *He has been through a lot,* The man thought.

"Do you have a name?"

The boy shook a little. "I'm Kael... da' said I was named after his da'." His eyes began to tear up. "Da'..." His tears started to stream.

Ijos sat down beside Kael for a moment. He wrapped him arm around Kael's shoulders and rubbed his back gently. Then he sighed.

"Kael... my name is Ijos. I'm sorry. I wish I could change what happened, but it is done. Let's focus on getting out of the wilderness."

Kael nodded slowly but continued to shake. Ijos got up and stared into the distance again. The stones were far off, but he could hear the whispering more intensely now.

There was silence. Kael was gone. Ijos flipped his head around and saw Kael heading towards the stones. A pit grew in his stomach.

"Kael!" Ijos tried to grab his shoulder, but the boy brushed him off. Ijos stood in front of him and looked at his eyes. They were puffy and vacant.

"Hey! Snap out of it!" he snapped his fingers to no avail. Kael's mouth was moving, but no sound was coming out. Ijos read the mouthing and got *dark* and *death* out of it.

Then came a horrible pain in Ijos' head. A set of red cat eyes pervaded his mind and caused him to double over. Ijos fought hard to get his vision back and then he lunged at Kael and picked him up. He pulled out an amber stone and placed it on his forehead.

Kael's eyes cleared but then showed worry. Ijos' smile faded as he turned serious.

"We need to go."

Ijos buried the fire remains, then they moved further downstream until the whispering was manageable. He built another fire and cooked food. Ijos glanced at Kael several times to make sure the voices were not entrancing him again. *He seems weak to magic. I need to be more careful.*

They ate breakfast, which was salted pork, and they hiked their way along the riverbank. Their direction headed primarily south, which would put them closer to the center of the Kingdom. Many towns were located near the center, so the man can find a place for this child. The man knew many people, he was sure one of them would help an orphaned child.

71

Darkness came as the two were closing in on a town, but the town was quiet. The man walked past the gates, and it was abandoned; this town used to be lively in the Autumn, where festivals of the gods would have people in the streets, dancing, and drinking.

All that was left now was dust dancing with the wind, no sign of life having been here in years. Time was relative to the man, so he could not remember when he was here last, but it did not feel like years had passed.

"What happened here?" Kael stared at the deserted town in shock.

"War." Ijos stated flatly.

"War." Kael repeated hollowly. Ijos noticed the boy's eyes becoming vacant.

Such observations were repeated in the next town. It was devoid of human life; it seemed like it was abandoned long ago. The two would randomly encounter beasts, but not that massacred Caede.

Ghouls lurked, banshees would be hiding in a corner, howling as if it were singing with the wind. A manticore, even, was perched on the steps of an abandoned tavern with a nice porch, yawning as it eyed the traveling duo. Ijos attempted to avoid encountering monsters, but they did not react to him. He thought about this during their journey.

At nightfall, the two made camp once again, nestled close to a giant tree by the river. Ijos remembered the name of the river was Oquia, named after the god of strength, who took the form of a bull with three horns. The river was wide and carried a strong current towards the sea to the south, and with that, it carried plentiful fish.

It was after they cooked and ate some fish from the river that Ijos watched as Kael was blankly staring at the river. He would not move, barely blinking, his breath slow but his heartbeat fast.

It seems the boy was still traumatized over the events and sad of his loss, but he has managed to travel with him well. For his age, he was resilient, but there are limits. It was then that Ijos had an idea. He got up and found three small rocks, no bigger than a marble, and sat cross-legged in front of the boy.

Kael snapped out of his trance and looked at him with sad, tearful eyes. Ijos did not say anything; instead, he took the three rocks in his right hand and began to juggle them with his fingers, at first in a circle, then figure-eight patterns.

The boy watched intently at the rocks, and in moments, he was entranced again, this time by magic of the rocks. The glow of the fire pulsed on the boy's face, mimicking the tempo of the juggling rocks. Ijos began to speak in a low voice.

"You will forget the events of the massacre, child. Your new life will start now, and you will no longer be afraid."

Ijos stopped juggling immediately, clasping his hands together over the rocks, breaking the boy from the trance. He smiled faintly at Ijos, giving him relief.

Ijos peered upstream, where Caede had fallen. His mind flashed to the massacre, the bodies that were mutilated and seeing the boy covered in blood. He observed the boy looking in the same direction, his eyes glossy and expressionless.

The boy then paused to play with the dirt. Ijos watched for some time, observing what he was doing. The dirt took shape into a tall man holding a sword, and beside him stood a child holding a smaller sword. He then realized that the boy was drawing them, so he gently clasped Kael's shoulder.

"I can teach you the ways of the sword."

The fire flickered and cast shadows on both their faces. Ijos pulled a short sword from his side, a wakizashi with a brown handle and bronze accents, and handed it to the boy. He then pulled his own sword out and stood up, assuming a stance with his right foot ahead of his left and about shoulder-length apart.

"Your footwork is important. A wide stand is strong, allowing you to withstand blows and put more strength into your own strikes. Let me see what you can do."

The boy stood up and looked at his own feet, moving them into position rather quickly. Ijos was pleased that he could assume stance, feeling that the way of the sword may come quickly.

"Good. Now, take your sword and place your hands so that you have leverage, using your right hand closer to the blade for power. Try it."

The boy held the sword naturally, wielding the sword as if an extension of his own body, and instinctively swung it down, hard. There was a small rock in front of him that split from the force, surprising Ijos. He then instructed Kael on various basic forms, all of which he got immediately.

They practiced until dawn, in which they packed up their camp and headed to the west, towards the Capital.

IV

The winter of the east province proved harsh for the travelers. Ijos and Kael traveled the wilderness alone, stopping sporadically to make camp and practice swordsmanship. Ijos watched as Kael packed up their stuff at their current camp before they resumed their travel.

"Make sure to cover the embers with dirt, Kael. We don't want to leave a trail."

Kael nodded with a slight smile. *He hasn't talked since I used the memory repression spell,* Ijos thought. He was worried that the spell may have affected him differently due to his young age.

He brushed the thought out of his mind as he watched a hawk fly overhead, thinking it was his familiar. *Nuria hasn't returned, either. I was hoping she would have come back with news.* He picked up a dead piece of grass and examined it mindlessly. Kael came over to him with both packs full and held out his. He dropped the piece of grass and shouldered his pack.

They had camped in a small bit of wooded area this time. After they set out, the thicket of trees cleared into a sprawling field. There were several empty fields that would have been filled with farmers collecting the last of their crops, but they were barren and there was no human life nearby. The field sprawled on for several miles before they came across a small home. The sun had not set, but it would before too long.

There were many abandoned homes on the frontier by those who fled from the impending war. They entered the house to see that the house was disheveled. The furniture had been shoved around in disarray, and a table was overturned on its side.

There was hearth that had not been used in some time. Ijos brushed some of the dust and debris away and began to make a fire. Kael sat down and rummaged in his sack. He pulled out the small wooden soldier toy. He stared at the toy blankly, as if looking through it.

His face shot up and connected with Ijos and he stashed the toy away. Ijos felt sad but suddenly had an idea. He pointed at the wakizashi on Kael's waist, which Kael unsheathed. Ijos unsheathed his own.

"Try your horizontal slash."

Ijos showed Kael once more how to properly leverage the blade to put more force behind it. The boy practiced this form several times, adjusting his hands to

76

provide a better grip and power each time. Ijos then had him practice other basic forms before he stopped.

Ijos walked over to Kael and smiled. "Knowing the forms is good, but to fight, you need to know the anatomy too. There may be moments where you want to kill, but there may be moments where you want to disarm or incapacitate as well."

Ijos sat down and pulled out a piece of parchment from a small sack that he kept on his back. The paper had a detailed drawing of the human anatomy, so the man began to point out the major organs of the body, then showed the skeletal structure and the musculature as well. He noted it was important since you can sever tendons and ligaments to slow down or stop your enemy without killing them.

"If you want information, they can't say much dead." He paused, then sighed a little. "Do you know any writing?"

The child paused for a moment before crouching down into the dust on the floor and marked two symbols in the shape of a straight line with a diagonal line and another with a few curves.

"'Ka' and 'ael'. So, you remember your name?"

The child just stared at him and nodded, but it seemed to give him discomfort. *The spell that I used should not have affected his long-term memory, but he is young, so it could have taken differently,* Ijos though again. *It seems remembering his past gives him discomfort, too. I need to figure out something to do to ease this for him.*

"Do you want to learn how to write my name? I can show you."

Kael's eyes glistened as he smiled and nodded. Ijos wrote his name in the dust, a two-character word as well. Kael showed interest in learning his name, so he traced it several times. Their camp at the house kept them out of the cold, but they were beginning to run low on rations after being on the road for some time.

He still seems to struggle to communicate, Ijos thought, grimacing slightly. He examined the child and noted that he must be closer to seven years old based on his stature, but he could be large for his age. He did not have any trouble moving and he was very good at listening. The wilderness bore threats that weren't present behind walls of town, and Kael would hold or hide at command. *I worry the spell may have taken effect more than I thought.*

Ijos then thought on how much time has passed since the massacre of Caede. It was hard to gauge the time since they have not interacted with any other people this whole time; the lands of this province were barren from the wars, not like they were well populated before, though. He stopped and watched Kael throw small twigs in the blazing hearth.

There was thud on the door. Ijos shot up and shot a glance at Kael, flicking his eyes to an overturned table. Kael silently scrambled to this cover as Ijos crouched beside the doorframe. Another thud hit the door, followed by a third before the door burst open.

A large man covered in furs walked through the frame and peered around. He could see the fire in the hearth, his eyes examining the house for any squatters. His breathing was ragged to the point it whistled. His face, what was not covered in an untamed beard, was red from the wintry night air.

"Aye, how about you come out and no one gets hurt." The large man said. He opened the door so hard that it hit Ijos, covering him from sight completely. The man inched closer to the hearth. He relaxed when no sound was made. He began to sit when he heard a shuffle behind the table. The man approached the table with an axe in hand.

He peered over the table to see Kael hiding behind it. The man smiled.

"Lookit you, little boy." He grabbed Kael by the scruff of the neck and yanked him up. "I'll make sure to keep you warm."

The man began to shift Kael and walk back to the hearth when Kael swung the wakizashi out. It clipped the man's cheek and over his eye. He let out a howl of pain and clasped the wound.

"You little bastard—" the man yelled as he slung his axe at the boy. Kael stepped back but not far enough; the axe connected with his shoulder and left a large gash. The man began to swing again but stopped as he saw a blade pierce his back and exit through his chest. Ijos stood behind the man, his blade dripping with blood. His face held malice as the man's body slumped.

Ijos pulled his bloodied blade out of the corpse, kicking the slumped body to the side. He knelt in front of Kael and examined his shoulder. The boy winced at the pain as Ijos pulled out the powder and coated the wound in it, which stopped the bleeding immediately. He tore a piece of his clothing off and wrapped the wound.

Kael stared past Ijos with an empty gaze at the corpse. The boy could feel the marks burning on his neck as he watched Ijos carry the corpse outside, the hate and bloodlust slowly filling inside him.

V

The whispers of the stones began to ebb as the blue subsided. Kael's vision came back slowly, blotting in one at a time. The glimmering silhouettes were still there when his vision returned, but the wooden soldier had returned to its blueless slumber.

"What was the whispering?" Kael's voice was hoarse. The sun had moved past its zenith. He tried to stand up but his muscles were stiff. He rubbed his legs as the silhouettes glimmered more intensely.

We are spirits. Once sorcerers long ago, we trapped our souls here when there was a need for protective rings. Your kind uses these rings to ensnare evil beings, and we try to help them. You heard one of them that day, calling to you. It beckoned a darkness within you, a darkness too dark for even us to suppress.

Kael stood, his legs less sore now. He scoffed at the notion. "A darkness within me? The only darkness in me is my lost memories." *But those feelings...*

No, there is darkness within you. A horrible malice. Beware, swordsman, as it can consume you... always tread the light...

The shimmerings were gone. The stones were empty, the magical properties and pressure lifted. They went to slumber, much like the toy.

"... do I have a darkness within me?" He gazed at his hands. His mind thought of the feelings he felt when Ijos killed the bandit. "Violence... it always calms me..." Does he enjoy it too much?

He leaned on the slab for a moment and watched the trees shift. *What is wrong with me?* His hands shook, but he clenched them tight. His face contorted into a grimace as he put his strength into pushing away the feeling. There was something rising in him. His neck began to feel warm. *It's rising...* His mind wanted to think of corpses and blood, but he tried to push them away. Then he thought of Ijos smiling and he calmed.

Kael watched Jorunn stomp the ground. She was staring at him and snorting. She snorted harder as he approached her, retreating a little. Then he patted her snout, and she began to neigh softly. "It's okay, girl." He patted her again. "I'm okay."

Kael left the stones behind, pulling Jorunn with him as he edged towards the rivers. There was a small stone shelf that dropped off into the river behind it. The rock wall had vines covering it and he examined it to conclude the hidden door was here. It held no use for him anymore, so he followed the river south.

He came upon the shoreline where he and Ijos camped. The large tree was much bigger now, tall enough to loom over Oquia. It cast a long shadow that almost reached the other side of the banks.

He stared at the bank. It was grassy, the snow from the memory not present due to the haziness of summer. He sat down on a fallen log. He tried to see the old fire, but those burnt twigs were ash in the wind. He then picked up some pebbles from the ground and tried to juggle them. He did well, but he wasn't like Ijos. *That speed, the hypnotizing shape... I can still see them.*

He wasn't sure, but he felt there was a red hue to the hypnosis. Maybe it was because he always associated Ijos with flames. But didn't he associate the sorcerer with that, too?

It's different. He watched the sky. *One is pure.*

The bank was nothing more than a memory. While it shed light on his past, it was really just a steppingstone. He stood up and left while riding Jorunn.

He eventually crossed through the copse and into the field. The old structure he and Ijos camped in was still standing. It was still abandoned, the door ajar but still in the windless sunset.

He didn't walk into the house at first. Instead, he walked down the hill to where Ijos had buried the bandit long ago. The mound was still there, but it had been long covered by grass and wildflowers.

"At least in death you had use as flower fodder."

A nasty sneer crossed his lips, but then he shook himself out of it. *Why did I say that?* The feeling dissipated quickly, and he left the mound to return to the home.

He walked through the frame and stood motionless. His eyes widened and his mouth went slack when he saw red writing on the opposing wall.

On it was writ 'CLOSER. YOU ARE THE WOODEN SOLDIER, BRAVING FORWARD.' Below it was an eye. Kael's hands shook and he quickly retreated and fled on Jorunn.

Whetstone

The Blacksmith

I

Kael rode far from the house, but the words burned in his mind, refusing to yield to the distance. Each stride put between him and that cursed place felt like an escape from more than just a forgotten memory. In his distraction he ended up at the entrance to a small thicket of trees.

The wall of trees caused him to stop. There was a weight hanging on the branches here, a soft weight, but enough for him to dismount and set up camp. The place had a familiar echo to his mind.

The sun set and he made a fire, bringing a small pot out of his saddlebags to cook a stew from nearby plants and some leftover meat he had. The stew was salty due to the preserved meat and did not fill his hunger too well, but he ate it all the same.

He stared at the fire for some time and heard a rustle behind him. He turned around and grabbed his sword that was beside him, ready to attack. Out of the trees came a large deer, grazing at the lush grass.

He placed his sword back down and instead pulled a crossbow from his saddlebags, quietly enough that the deer did not hear it. It only took one bolt to the skull for the deer to drop.

He dragged the corpse back to his campsite and began to dress it, but the feeling of familiarity persisted in his mind. It wasn't exact, but the rustling and presence of the deer was an echo of the past. He shook the feeling off as he finished his task.

After he finished preserving the meat he laid down for the night. His mind raced as he caught glimpses of Ijos traversing the wilderness, but he saw it through the eyes of a child. Was it when they were traveling? He watched as he followed Ijos, traversing these very woods and eating in this same area.

He then watched as ghouls sprung out of them from the thicket. He felt scared, but he felt something more. It was the burning on his neck. His eyesight had a dull vignette on the edges, swirling inward as he grabbed the sword Ijos gave him. But Ijos appeared tired, and his movements were much slower than before.

When the ghouls were dead, Ijos looked at him with pride, like a father to son. But wasn't there something else there? But there was a bit of worry in his face behind the pride. A calculating, watchful worry. Then it was gone, stashed away as Ijos led him through the thicket.

Beyond it was a fort in a lush field. He stared briefly before he felt a hand clasp his shoulder. He saw Ijos' stern, but loving, eyes staring back at him.

"Ijos."

Kael awoke at his own campsite to his fire burnt down to embers. Ijos' face still stared at him as the memory began to fade, though a pain in his heart persisted.

The night had passed, and the early tendrils of morning began to show in the sky. He felt the relic pulsating in his pouch, though it was beginning to slumber after its job was done.

He glanced around at the place one last time, remembering the ghouls and his relationship with the man in the dream. He cleaned up his camp before he continued his path and crossed the short span of forest.

Just like in the dream, the other side of the forest opened into a field. There was a town in the field replacing the fort of old.

The forest sloped down into the town and on the slope he noted there were small structures made of stone. These structures were gravestones. He knew this because he had seen them before in other places. He remembers well that he was once told that there was a war decades ago that decimated a lot of the population of the eastern lands.

II

The town nestled in the field well, not jutting out like a sharp rock, but rather like a smooth stone peeking out of the blades. There were shepherds tending to their flock on the outskirts and there were many women tending to their daily tasks outside their homes. Hunters traveled out to find game for their families, only glancing up at him to give a generic greeting or nod as he passed.

His sword was strapped to his back and clanked with each step of his horse's gait. The buckles of his belts holding his leather pauldrons in place gleamed in the sunlight. The wind whipped up and tossed his hair into his face, entangling it in his dark stubble, which had started to grow out. He pushed his hair behind his ears and moved on.

The town encircled a central barracks, both enclosed by a sturdy wall of logs. Another inner wall separated the barracks from the rest of the town. The gate was guarded by two soldiers, standing on alert when he rode up to them. He dismounted Jorunn a short distance away, but close enough to speak.

"I am looking for a blacksmith. Do ye tuigsinn?"

The soldiers glanced at each other, then the one on the right nodded.

"Aye, we 'ave one, w'at business do you 'ave 'ere?"

"I need to have some of my equipment repaired. Take a look if you must." He unsheathed his sword and showed the dullness of the blade. "It has seen much wear. I just need it repaired, and I will be on my way."

The soldiers waved him through without further resistance, pointing him towards a small building that had a chimney billowing white smoke. He led his horse over towards the building and tied her up to a post outside. The building had a large canopy covering a blacksmith's shop. The back held a building that he could assume would be the blacksmith's home. The shop was quiet, but as he rounded the corner, he saw a small boy tending to a fire. He knocked on a wood post to get the boy's attention. The boy jolted and turned around.

"Where is your master, apprentice? I need some work done."

The boy appeared sheepish amongst the multitude of weapons; he was lanky with unkempt hair, barely able to keep the fire going. "He went to the tavern down the way." He pointed out from the way Kael came. "I'm not sure when he will return, though. He tends to drink until he is in bed with one of the married ladies as their husband is away hunting."

Kael smirked at the comment. "I see. Thank you." He left his horse and walked to the tavern, a busy establishment with the discordant notes of a fiddle. The air inside was thick with the noise of off-duty soldiers drinking and talking. He made his way past the soldiers and townsfolk to the bar. Leaning on it, he rapped his knuckles on the counter to get the bartender's attention.

"How may I help ye?"

"I am looking for the blacksmith of this fort. I was told he was here."

The bartender nodded his head towards a booth at the back of the tavern. "Aye, he is back there. But he's not alone, and he has had quite a bit to drink—"

Kael left before the bartender could finish. He crossed the tavern and in the booth he noticed there were three middle-aged women around a small dwarf with dark skin. His face flushed from alcohol. He noticed the table was covered with large tankards that were empty. The dwarf examined him with glassy eyes.

"Aye, what do ya want? Came to kill my buzz, eh?" His words slurred together.

Kael smirked and sat down. The woman beside him eyed him and winked. "You are the blacksmith, right? I have something that needs repaired."

The dwarf snorted. "I am off for the day. If you ken, come back tomorrow afternoon when my hangover had subsided."

"I have a couple swords that need repaired."

The dwarf peered at him again, at the sword on his back. Then he noticed a katana on his waist. The hilt caught his attention—he had seen one like this before. "What's yer name, swordsman?"

"My name is Kael, blacksmith."

The dwarf straightened up when he heard the name. His eyes because less cloudy, sobering up a little in that instant. "Sarreif. Call me Sarreif." He stroked his beer-soaked beard. "Kael, huh. That's a name I haven't heard in a long time. Girls, go on and get!"

He shooed the women out of the booth, smacking each of their backsides as they passed him. Kael stood up and let the women out, each eyeing him with lust. Once they were gone Kael stayed where he was, expecting Sarreif to crawl his way out. Instead, he raised the only tankard that wasn't empty and smiled.

"Sit fer a moment, will ye? I'd like to finish me drink, if ye may."

Kael nodded and sat down. Sarreif in turn hollered at the bartender, who came over with another armload of tankards. "The usual, Sarreif?"

The dwarf shook his head. "Nay, only one this time. Fer this gentleman, too."

Kael eyed him for a moment. Sarreif cracked another grin and nudged him. "Come, now. Dinnae be so prude. It's gonna be sunset soon anyway. Ye might as well drink before you rest."

Kael reluctantly accepted the offer and drank his tankard slowly. The draft was strong enough to make his eyes water. He was sure it was closer to liquor than it was mead. He took a gulp and then sat it down. "So, why did you jolt at the sound of my name?" He wiped the foam from his mouth on his sleeve.

Sarreif glanced at him and then took a long drink. "Ye dinnae remember? Aye, we'll no matter. Stranger things have happened, but it would like to wait until we get back to the forge."

Kael nodded and finished his drink. He stomached two large gulps as he emptied the tankard as the dwarf finished his own. They stood up after the tankards were empty. Sarreif raised his eyes to Kael. He was about one and a half times the height of the dwarf.

When they exited the tavern the sun was already starting to set, glistening its shades of orange onto the town. People were retreating to their homes after a long day of work, some retreating into the tavern to quench their thirst. The pair passed by the women from earlier and they pouted their lips at them.

The dwarf grumbled. "Not today, girls. Ain't no reason to prey on a young man, either. Not unless he's willing."

He glanced at Kael, who responded with a slight shake of his head. The women groaned in disappointment, but the pair went on despite it. Sarreif pointed at another building a block down from the tavern.

"Ye might wanna stay there after our talk, you see? A fine inn, if you ken." Kael nodded and they continued.

They went back to the blacksmith's shop, where Sarreif reprimanded the apprentice for tending to the fire so poorly, throwing scrap metal at him as he scurried away. The dwarf muttered some slurred words under his breath, Kael catching few of them except for the colorful over usage of the word 'cunt'.

Once that was over with, the dwarf sat down on an old stool beside the furnace and lit a cigarette from a red-hot poker. He motioned the cigarette to Kael, who declined.

Sarreif took a long drag. "So ye dinnae remember us meeting, eh?" Kael shook his head. "Well, it was a long time ago, and ye were a wee lad then... I suppose it cannae be helped." He gestured at Kael's sword. "Let's take a look, here."

Kael handed him the sword. "It's been through a lot."

Sarreif examined the sword, touching the gashes and dull edge. "Aye... it looks like the blade has been through a lot. Like ye've been cutting logs with it." He glanced up at Kael. "Monster hunter, eh?" Kael nodded.

"That explains it. Well, I can sharpen it fer ye, and it will be good as new." The blacksmith turned around to begin his work when Kael stopped him.

"I also have another that needs looked at, if you dinnae mind." Kael disappeared for a moment and came back with the rusted sword from Caede. Sarreif's eyes could have popped from his head when he saw the blade, which he recognized immediately.

"By Gods, I thought this thing was lost forever! It has been rusted quite a bit, though... never mind that, I can fix it." He twisted the sword several times in his hands.

"Ye know, it really does bring up the day I met you with the swordsman. He came looking for answers."

95

Kael sat down and stared at Sarreif. "Can you tell me about our meeting? I'm also looking for some answers."

Sarreif nodded slowly and pitched the small remainder of the cigarette. He picked up the rusty sword and pondered on his own past. It started slow, but it was a cold day...

Ijos

Ijos and Kael came across a soldier barracks, a large fort situated in the field. The barracks were surrounded by a large wall made of timber. The outside of the barracks was crowded; Ijos could only assume that these were refugees from the war.

Many were tired and hungry; some were lying on the ground, and some were leaning against the wall. They passed the camp and arrived at the gate only to be stopped by two soldiers guarding it.

The soldier on the left put a hand out while the other spat off to the side. "Halt! What business do you have 'ere?"

Ijos bowed slightly. "We are just travelers, sir, but we have lost some of our group. I am hoping to talk to the general of this fort to see if he has taken any refugees."

The soldier spat snorted, then spat again, this time closer to Ijos' foot. "Why would the general know of any lowly refugees, eh?"

Ijos fished out a piece of parchment from his bag. On it was an ornate filigree stamped in wax. "Because they are nobility. It would be a woman and three children: two young boys a little older than this child and an adolescent girl. They were from the north, so I think they would have fur on as well."

The soldiers stared at the man in disbelief, thinking he was talking nonsense. They could not imagine why a noble family would be wandering around as refugees. Unsure what to do, so they did go get their general.

They waited outside the gate for a few moments before a short, burly man came outside and addressed them.

The man crossed his arms and bowed slightly. When he stood upright, his arms were still crossed. "I see you are searching for a noble family, and you had quite a description. Do you have an idea of their names?"

Ijos handed the man the parchment. "The family of Lord Caedmon, sir. I am sure you have heard that Caede fell?"

The burly general frowned at the mention of Caede. "Aye, several weeks ago, as had a few other towns. We have been busy with the refugees." He glanced at the katana on Ijos' waist and narrowed his eyes. "What is your name, swordsman?"

"My name is Ijos. I am a knight of the King's court, you see. And this child, he is....."

Ijos stopped for a moment. He had spent some time on the road with the boy, and he felt close to him after all this time. *He reminds me of myself when I was younger. He's quick and sharp for his age. But is he just another refugee?* The boy tugged at his sleeve and smiled when Ijos looked down. Ijos knew then what he really felt.

"This child's name is Kael. My son."

The general huffed and cocked his head towards the gate. They followed the general through the barracks and to a small shack off center of the busy quarters. He bent over his desk and read the letter Ijos had given him. When he was done he stared at Ijos with inquisitive eyes.

"So, you're looking for the Caedmon family? What of it?"

Ijos did not like telling many people his task at hand, but the general may have useful information.

"I was at the fall at Caede, sent from the capital to help escort the family there safely. I caught wind of the army about to attack the town and tried my best to intervene. I did not save the Lord, but I have been tracking family so that I can escort them back to the Capital for their safety."

The general scratched his stubbly face and stared at him, searching for any trace of a lie in his face. He could not find any, so he stood up and strolled towards the door.

"Follow me." The general had them go out to the yard in the fort where the men would practice their swordsmanship. They rounded a small corner to a covered area that had smoke billowing out of the roof and Ijos could hear the clanking of steel. As they entered this area they were introduced to a dwarf. The dwarf glanced at the men and then back to his work.

"Good evening, general. How fares it?" His voice was gruff, and Ijos noticed that the dwarf had many fresh cuts on his body.

The general smiled, but Ijos could see some contempt in his eyes. "Fine, dwarf. I brought this man here because you might be able to help him. He is looking for the family of Lord Caedmon."

The dwarf stopped and stared sharply at Ijos. "I see. So, I take it ye know that Caede fell, and with it, Caedmon?"

Ijos crossed the room and got closer to the dwarf. "I was there when it fell, blacksmith. I'm searching for the Lady and kids to take them to Mynheir, where they will be safe. This is orders from Haskell, Caedmon's older brother."

The dwarf put down the metal he was working with and held out his callused hand.

"Well, it would be an honor to help you, swordsman. The name's Sarreif. I was the blacksmith of Caede."

Ijos shook the dwarf's hand firmly. "Ijos, the name is Ijos. And this is Kael."

"Aye, I recognize that face from the town, though I did'n know his name. He's a spittin' image of his da', though. A fine man—his name was Lukos."

Kael did not react to this information. *He doesn't remember his family anymore. Maybe the spell was too strong for him...* Ijos put a hand on his shoulder and glanced at Sarreif.

"What of the family, then? I take it you know something."

Sarreif gestured towards the back of the covered area where a small hut sat.. "Come with me. This would be a talk better suited in my home, away from any wandering ears, do ye dig?"

Ijos nodded. The three exited the forge and wrapped around to the home.

II

Ijos took a swig of his bourbon. He felt the liquid burn his throat like molten lead as it hit his stomach, but he chased it with another swig just as quickly. The liquor helped his muscles ease after the strenuous few days.

He observed Kael as he remembered the fight with the three ghouls at the tree lines. *The child shows promise,* he thought. *While I struggled to move fast enough to dodge them, he picked up a sword and attacked their bellies. It was quick thinking.*

He rubbed his leg as he felt a throb of pain. *Though, the look in his eyes during was worrisome. He seems to revel in the violence and bloodshed. His anger was palpable.* Ijos watched Kael sit on the floor. The boy noticed, and Ijos feigned a smile.

Sarreif took a swig of his own drink and followed it with an exaggerated cough. "Aye, I was traveling with them for some time in the aftermath. I knew about a tunnel underneath the castle that led outside the town."

Ijos nodded. He knew the secret passageway, the one he and Kael traveled underneath the river.

"It was when I exited the tunnel that I found 'em, camped out right beside it. They looked so weary and afraid, but they were expectin' their da', I suppose."

Ijos eyed over his cup at the dwarf. "Caedmon is dead, Sarreif. I watched him turn to stone by a sorcerer." He followed the unwelcome news with a gulp of liquor.

Sarreif stroked his beard at the news. He sighed and spoke.

"Well, that explains why he didn't show. We waited for a day or two, then we left for the nearest town. We stayed there for some time, too, hoping he would show up there as well. But we left in a hurry because we did not have much money, so I told them we should head for Mynheir. We set on the Lyndis path."

Ijos knew of the Lyndis path. It was the most traveled road of the east, so it had the most towns and the safest route back to the capital.

Ijos then spoke. "So, why are you here now?"

Sarreif's eyes fell to the ground as he spoke. "We got separated, you see. I shouldn' have, but we decided to cut through a wooded area close to the Duris lake, and some kappas came out of the damned lake and nearly pulled the kids in. I bought 'em time so they could flee, and I fought 'em off with me axe," He motioned towards an axe in the corner, "but those damned shells are made of stone. By the time I was done with those bastards, the family was long gone. I cannae run too fast or long with me short, old legs."

Ijos pulled out an old map and placed it on the table. He traced down Duris Lake, which was a day or two from here, and found where the Lyndis path should be as well. He had a good idea where he should start.

"Thank you, Sarreif. This helps me immensely." He held out his hand. "Would you like to come with us?"

The dwarf shook the swordman's dirty hand but shook his head. "Nay, I've found decent work here for these men, and they are keeping me plenty a busy. But when you find them, can you tell the little rascals that Ol' Sarreif searched like hell for them?"

Ijos smiled and agreed that he would. He thanked the general as well for helping him, and he and Kael left the fort, heading west towards Duris Lake.

Haskell

I

Swords clashed, men screaming, grunting, and blood flying across the field. The grass was barely green, coated with the thick, viscous liquid of blood running from soldiers sacrificing their life on the line. Shields clattered against one another as the frontline pawns beat themselves to death, stabbing one another with spears and swords, hiding from the volley of arrows from the archers in the distance.

In the back of one side was a large man atop a horse, both plated in silver armor, the man holding a great axe into the sky.

"Come, men! We cannot let the Vralls take this land! Give your life for the good of the King! Let the harp of Dagda strengthen the strings of your heart!"

The men rallied their cries and charged, the fleets of soldiers behind the wall of shields, stabbing the opposing army. The two armies were a juxtaposition of one another: those with the man atop the horse were clad in silver armor with green and bronze surcoats. The Vralls—the opposing army—bore the idea of savages accustomed to the cold; clad in fur armor and bearing a similarity to wolves and bears.

The armies clashed, men fell from both sides by sword or arrow. The Vralls rode atop their woodsy steeds, eschewing the trope of horses and riding large deer, the size rivaling the horses the opposition rode.

The commander of the silver-clad army was in the back of his own faction, cleaving enemies in two that made it past his battalion. He would swing his large axe without so much as a grunt, the force obliterating the armor of the enemy. He would roar as each man fell, the sound rallying his men even harder.

He fought in a trance of bloodlust to the point that he did not notice the bird that perched on his shoulder until it squawked, jolting him from his focus.

"Nuria, what news?"

The general spoke to the bird as an ally, a bright red and orange phoenix, seeking an answer. The bird squawked once more, then peered at its leg, indicating a scroll wrapped there.

The general stopped to slice through an oncoming savage, the blood spraying the man, his horse, and the phoenix, but the man continued to unwrap the paper and read what was written. He reread it several times before he lapsed into a rage, causing the phoenix to fly off into the sky, and he began to violently rip apart any enemy he saw.

The battle tapered off as the sun set, both sides withdrawing to their barracks, multitudes of tents littered the sidelines. A large tent held the commander, who shed his armor and was wearing a dark tunic and cloth pants. He was sitting in front of a table, dimly lit by candles, rereading the scroll that was brought to him in battle, while he patted the phoenix that delivered it.

The flicker of the candles gleamed in his eyes, frozen orbs that were devoid of emotion. He was unsure how to react anymore; he knew Caede fell, but he did not know the news that the phoenix would bring would be so severe.

He was so lost in thought that he was shook back to reality when one of his men came into his tent.

"Sir, the King is here."

The commander stopped what he was doing and stood up, noticing that the king was behind his soldier.

"Your majesty, I did not expect you to be here." The man started while bowing. "You should not be out in the countryside let alone the battlefield—"

The young king held up his hand. He was in his early 30s, his face lacking any wrinkles and his long hair boasted voluminous, curly locks. He wore normal attire, though, to attain anonymity in the eyes of the enemy, no matter how far they were from here.

"I am not greater than you, commander, nor of the men here. Just because I was born of royalty does not mean I am bound to the golden halls of the castle, or the clean streets of Mynheir. I wish to see our troops and make sure their wellbeing and morale is intact."

The king stopped for a moment.

"And what of you, Commander Haskell? You look as though you lost this battle already."

The commander, Haskell, handed the king the parchment that he was so invested in. The king read over the parchment a few times, ensuring he understood the letter. He sadly returned the letter to the commander.

"Loss is hard, Haskell. I am sorry that your brother is gone. I feel like the expansion to the east was a mistake of the kingdom, especially when we have been warring with the border kingdoms and this new threat of the dark beasts. I feel the royal family is at fault for the casualties."

Haskell did not know what to say. He could not muster anything, but he knew it was not their fault. His brother chose to lord over the new province fifteen years ago.

He knew the risks, and he begged his brother to stay, but Caedmon was a stubborn one. He would always state that he knew what he was doing, that expansion was good for the kingdom, and the lands needed someone strong to govern them. He was lost in thought when the king cleared his throat and brought him back to reality.

"In all serious, commander, I came because I honestly already knew of the fall of Caede. I came to ask you if you still have your piece in your possession."

The tent seemed to dim at this statement and Haskell's attention was diverted to a more serious matter. He always kept this piece on him, instinctively reaching for his neck. In the glimmer of the candles did a soft, golden necklace shine, hidden mostly by his tunic.

"Let me make this clear: the safety of those pieces is the utmost importance in this world. I am afraid the times may be coming when we must guard these even more prudently. I ask that when this battle is over, you return to the Capital with haste."

The king raised his right hand once more, but in a more absolute manner than that of hush.

"I must make my leave, dear commander. Now that I know the status of this piece, I return to my own tasks. Once again, my condolences. May your flame never extinguish from the wind or rain."

With that, Haskell bowed and spoke. "May's yours as well. G'night, your excellency."

The king left, and with him the air seemed to leave with it. Haskell felt out of breath for a moment, sitting down in his chair for some time, digesting the gravity of all the news he'd heard today.

Kappa

I

Kael stared at the dwarf after their palaver that recounted the story of how they met years ago.

"So, you knew my father? What was his name?"

"Ijos? Ah, no, you mean your real father. Lukos were his name. He was a fine man. You really are a spittin' image of him, though you're a bit more of a brute," Sarreif grinned slyly and made a comical pose, pumping his chest with his arms.

"He was not part of the Lordship at Caede, but he helped hunt and obtain food for the town and sell the meat and pelts. He knew the area around the town well, and he knew animals and their behaviors like you and I know breathin'. It makes it even more strange that he did not sense anything odd about that day..."

Kael did not ponder it for long. *I mean I lived most of my life without him. Ijos is my father. But I still feel an ache when I think about my family.*

The two did not speak much more as the blacksmith repaired both weapons, the sparkle in his eyes growing brighter when his old sword was back to its former glory. "A weapon fit for a King but built for the battlefield." The dwarf was proud of the weapon and even more proud that it could be taken on a journey.

Kael took his swords and strapped both to his back using an extra baldric that Sarreif had. They formed a criss-cross pattern, their handles peering over his shoulders. Sarreif nodded and smiled. "It suits ye. The two swords, I mean."

Kael tried to give Sarreif money for the repairs and the baldric, but he refused.

"I don' need payment, youngin'. You bringing me that sword for me to repair was enough."

Kael did not protest, putting his coin purse back, but he still was not done. He sat for a moment longer before he asked Sarreif a key question.

"Blacksmith—Sarreif—is Duris lake on the Lyndis path?"

Sarrief shook his head. "Nay, it is about half a day's worth off it. They say the lake used to hold an entrance to some hidden temple at the bottom. Some say there were riches beneath the lake, but some said it housed a great evil, that's why monsters tend to flock to it. I would avoid it if I were you. The path itself can be crossed some ways down."

Sarreif pointed at a map he had tacked to the wall. "I advise ye to cross the field ahead of us and enter on the other side, on the outskirts of Liela woods. The path cuts through the woods and branches after the clearing."

Kael thanked Sarrief and left. He did not heed the dwarf's warning, though, as he mounted Jorunn and headed towards the lake. He dismounted Jorunn at the tree line and headed to the banks, bending down and searching in the tall grass intently.

The relic he had vibrated violently, almost bouncing out of his pouch. He knew that this area was a key to him, but he did not know where or why. His search became frantic, his actions more strenuous as he moved grass out of the way, pulling some from the root. He heard a splash from the lake and paused in his task, holding the handle of his sword as he turned.

A kappa was a couple of arm's length away from him, watching him with curiosity. The gills on its neck breathed, at first with desperation before it acclimated to the air. It let out a ducky wheeze before it took a step and then paused. It croaked slightly and smiled.

"It's been a long time since we last saw a human around here." It spoke with a duck-like quack. "We's don't care much for grown humanses, though. The tiny ones are much tastier and don't fight as much."

Kael stood up and drew his sword, swinging it in a wide arc at the kappa. It shrieked and withdrew into its shell, his sword bouncing back and leaving only a small scratch. He stood and stared at the shell.

"We's thinks you are too testy for our taste! Even if you do look like a small human from years ago! One that other big human put a spell under!" The kappa echoed within its own shell.

Kael sheathed his sword and stared at the shell. "What do you mean, spell?"

The shell did not respond, only shaking slightly.

"Answer me, or I will shove my sword down your windpipe."

"No! You are much too violent! We's don't like scary big humans!"

Kael sighed and turned around for a moment. He held his head in his hands before shaking it and turning back towards the kappa. "Look. I'm sorry if I frightened you. I winnae do it again." He paused and pulled a piece of dried meat from his bag. "I'll even let you have this."

There was a short silence before the kappa popped its head out of its shell and smelled the meat. "Wells, okay." In flash the meat was snatched out of Kael's hand by the jaws of the beast, enticing a monetary reflex from Kael to grab his sword, but he stopped himself and bit down on his tongue hard enough to make it bleed.

"You reminds me of the tiny human that traveled with a man in tattered robeses. The man was searching for something when a big scary monster came up and attacked the little one."

"It was a big scary battle between the two and after he killed it, he turned to the little one who was covered in

114

blood. He used a weird, shiny object on him and then they left in a rush. He even left the shiny behind when he was in a hurry."

Kael grabbed the kappa hard when he heard this. "Where is it? Do you know where this object is?" The relic in his bag began to vibrate even harder, and the kappa noticed there was a faint red glow coming from Kael's pouch. It shrieked and withdrew in its shell again.

"Too mean! You'se is being too mean!" Kael relaxed his grip and let go. He ground his teeth and pumped his fists for a moment.

"I'm sorry. It's just that this object is important to me. Do you know where it is?"

The kappa peeked put off the shell once more. "Of courses we do, we's has it hidden well. It is a shiny thing, not like anything we's seen before."

"It is very important to me. Is there anything you would like in return for it?"

The kappa pondered and pondered for some time. Its head peeked out of the shell as it did an inquisitorial purr.

"I remember once a human once came to this shore with a large stone that shone like a rainbow. He talked with a little human that he was with about how they were heading to a place called Keran. That stone was pretty. I would trade this for that."

Kael wanted to rip his hair out of his head. He should kill this kappa where it stands, but he did not think it had the object on its body.

"All right. I will find this stone and bring it back."

Kael whipped around from the kappa and walked away, heading to Jorunn to head towards the town of Keran. He urged her on swiftly as he moved further away from the lake that held another key to his past—even more so his future.

Corruption

Blackwood Estate

I

Keran was half a day on horseback from Duris lake. Kael rode hard towards the town, only letting off so that Jorunn could rest. He could not bear to let her tire too much. He converged onto the Lyndis path at one point, passing through the vast forest of Liela that Sarreif had talked about.

As he passed he felt the shadows pulling him down and a stink of rotting flesh pervaded the air. It all began to clear a little as he cleared the forest and the path opened to the outskirts of the town.

Before the town was a field with rolling hills. He crested one of the fields and immediately went on the defensive as a bandit flanked him from the other side, swinging with a curved sword. *A scimitar,* Kael noted. *Ijos said they were common further south.*

The bandit's blade was hard to deflect due to the curved edge, posing a risk of Kael being cut. The eyes of the bandit, the only thing visible above the mask it wore, gleamed red in the light. A chill ran down Kael's spine as he felt the wrongness of those eyes, but the malice it held was familiar. He quickly changed tactics to suit the scimitar and pulled out a small dagger. He threw it at the arm holding the sword, damaging the forearm. The scimitar fell to the ground as the bandit fled towards the rancid forest he exited.

There were no more incidents as he closed in on the town. The town was quiet, though. Much quieter than it should be in the middle of the day. The sun set high in the sky and loomed over the town.

Kael approached the town with caution on Jorunn, poised on horseback and ready to unsheathe one of his swords as needed. He felt eyes peer on him as he passed homes and businesses closed for the day.

The town did not boast much besides a central road and then a larger house than the others that acted as a mansion of sorts. The town felt tense, the air still in the middle of day. He dismounted once to knock on a door, but the whispers behind did not yield any information. His only other option was the large manor ahead.

He continued to hear the murmurs behind the walls of the buildings up until the mansion, where he stopped at the gates. Two thugs were positioned in front of the gate, blocking his entry.

"Aye, what do ye want?" The first thug placed a hand on Kael's shoulder firmly, stopping him.

Kael brushed the hand off. The man grimaced and placed his hand back on Kael's shoulder. "I need to speak to the head of the town about some matters."

"He don't speak to outsiders. He's plenty busy right now anyways, talkin' to our boss."

"Yeah, so shove off, you bugger." The second thug piped in. The first thug then clamped down harder on Kael's shoulder and shoved him, knocking him back a foot.

Kael stumbled, but did not lose his balance. He could feel his face get hot, the anger rising in him.

It's not worth it cause a scene. But the mark on his neck started to burn, too. He wanted nothing more than to beat the thugs unconscious.

It took all his willpower to walk away. He went back to Jorunn as the heat started to dissipate. Jorunn snorted and stomped her hooves at him, retreating slightly.

"Whoa, easy there," he tried to calm his horse. Jorunn didn't want to be touched by him, quaking as he put his hand on her.

One of the thugs laughed. "Got problem with yer horse?" The other joined in with his laughter.

Kael felt the heat rise again and Jorunn began to snort harder. He shifted his focus to her and tried to calm himself down. *Can she feel it? This feeling, does it make her nervous?*

He eventually got her to calm down enough to trot her down the main road for a bit. It wasn't a long stretch, but the trot calmed both of them down. His trot led him back to the main gate, which was desolate and empty. He stared at the lush field for a while as he pondered on his own state. *I'm getting too easily worked up. Even Jorunn is catching on it.*

He heard the clop of hooves behind him and turned. There was a band of three men riding towards him. As they got closer he saw the two bandits were flanking a rather large man.

When they passed the large man gave him a cruel sneer. Kael noted the man looked beastly with that expression. His long, red hair flowed behind him as they crossed the gate and into the field.

He watched them gallop across the field towards the forest before he turned his horse towards the manor.

II

The manor gate was left open and Kael walked straight through. The yard in front of the manor was cut close to the ground, the cobble stone walkway wide and polished.

The door itself was a large mahogany slab with gold ornamentation. The already ornate slab was embellished with a knocker in the shape of a lion. His mind immediately went to the large man on the horse as he hammered it on the door.

There was silence. He knocked again, then felt a chill on his neck and turned towards the front of town. His gaze lingered for a moment before he heard a squeaky voice from the mansion. He turned around to see a small, wiry man in the door frame.

Kael raised his eyebrows at the diminutive figure. The figure barely filled the doorframe in a way that was nearly comical compared to Kael's stature. But Kael could see a spark in the man's eye, however dulled and repressed.

"Who are you?" Kael asked, furrowing his brow.

"Who are you?" The small figure retorted, puffing out his chest. The façade the man tried to put on was betrayed by his shrill voice. Kael shifted a little, leaning down and holding out his hand.

"The name's Kael. I have come to see the head of this estate, and at that, the town, I assume." The man stared at Kael's hand with no intention of response. Kael dropped his arm to his side. "And who are you?"

The man puffed his chest out again. "I am the steward of this estate." The steward eyed Kael for a moment. "Are you a monster hunter?"

"Aye, I am. However, that's not what—"

"Maybe it is providence," The steward muttered, stopping Kael in his sentence. The steward looked down and muttered a few other things before looking back at him. "Come with me to Lord Blackwood."

The large foyer was dimly lit but elegant with the antique sconces cast flickering shadows on ornate tapestries hung on the walls and there was a faint scent of musty old books lingering in the air.

"What is this place?" Kael pondered his eyes on the large looms of books stacked in corners. Some had several layers of dust on them.

"Blackwood Estate," the steward led him past the foyer and through a hallway. "This home has been part of Hera for many generations, though it was only in the generation past that the Blackwoods occupied it. What you see is the accumulation of their wealth."

The steward led Kael through several doors, each moving them through a large corridor filled with various antique items. *Looks like old armor from the Bricht House,* Kael thought as he passed through a corridor with armor on stands. The ornate tree and filigree were the crest of that house. They passed through and the next had more armor.

This is from the Criech House, He paused, *and this is from the Irin House.*

He noted the different houses and crests, the floorboards creaking beneath their footsteps, but in his mind he noticed that each corridor was empty for its size. The volley of corridors seized, and they reached a set of grand double doors at the end of a long hallway. With a nervous glance at Kael, the steward knocked softly before pushing the doors open.

"My Lord, I've brought a monster hunter."

The doors opened to a study, and a very lavish one at that. The room was surrounded by walls of books and was filled with various display cases, cases where Kael figured held rare artifacts and other items. In the center there was a large, antiquated but lavish desk. Seated behind that desk was a bulky man with a worried expression.

"Thank you, Cisco." The man flicked his hand to motion the steward out, who bowed and left, closing the doors behind him. The man studied Kael, folding his hands in curiosity and suspicion. "A monster hunter?"

"Aye," Kael countered.

"Well, hunter, I do not have any jobs in our town, at least none posted." Lord Blackwood looked down at his hands for a moment.

"I'm not looking for any jobs, Lord. Not this time."

Blackwood raised his eyebrows. "And what are you looking for?"

Kael walked closer to the desk, stopping within arm's length and beside a chair positioned in front of it. "I seek a certain stone, one that was almost luminous. I was led to believe it would be in this town."

The Lord's eyes narrowed, examining Kael with scrutiny. "What business do you have with such a stone?"

"It is of personal importance," Kael replied, choosing his words carefully. He saw no need in revealing the reason behind his search.

The lord slumped and began to stroke his peppered beard. The dim candlelight reflected on his receding hairline as his eyes shifted from his desk to Kael a couple times. "This stone, is it about the size of a fist and shines like a rainbow?"

Kael hesitated. He was unsure of the size, but the kappa did say it was a rainbow stone. He might as well take the risk. "Aye, it is. Do you know where it is?"

The Lord drummed his fingers on the desk. "Ah, a stone... just a stone..." He then gestured towards a locked drawer in his desk. He produced a key, and with a very audible, antique *click*, unlocked the drawer and pulled out a leather pouch. He emptied the contents onto the desk: a luminescent stone the size of a fist.

Kael's eyes glistened when he saw the stone. *I need it.* The glow swam in his eyes. *I need this stone. I would kill for it. I would kill this man...* But then Kael snapped himself out of it. *What was that? That overpowering bloodlust.*

"This stone has been in my family for generations, my great-grandfather found it one day washed ashore. Since then, it has been passed down as a luck charm." Lord Blackwood gazed at the stone in awe, the rainbow patterns glowing on his face in the dim light.

Kael saw there was something sinister in the glow, pulling him towards it, too. Then Blackwood snapped his head up and stashed the stone away in its pouch. There was an ache that dissipated from his head at the same moment the stone retreated into the pouch. Kael unknowingly leaned over the desk and put his hand on the pouch. He felt the same need course through his hand.

"I need this stone," he began to pull the pouch towards him. Lord Blackwood kept a firm grasp on the bag, his eyes pulling expressing his intent to keep the stone.

"No," Blackwood seethed. "I do not know what you need such a stone for, but you will have to leave empty handed."

A sneer began to creep over Kael's face as the urge to kill the man and take the stone crossed his mind. The only thing that snapped him out of it was the crack of the doors opening and a child's voice filling the following silence.

"Daddy!" Kael turned to see a small boy, maybe eight, running towards them.

He took a wide arc around Kael and to the other side of the desk The boy jumped in the Lord's lap. Kael saw the man use the distraction to quickly stow the stone away. There was a gentle *click* as the drawer was locked.

The boy faced Kael. "Who is this?" The childlike eyes examined him and looked at the swords peering from behind his shoulders. "Is this a hunter, Daddy? Is he here to get rid of the lion man?"

Blackwood shifted a little at this notion, giving an awkward chuckle as he stood up. "No, Kinev. This man is just passing through." He glanced at Kael as he walked Kinev to the doors. "The 'lion man' is nothing to worry about. Now hurry along."

Kinev took once last glance at Kael as he turned and ran down the long hallway. The doors closed and Blackwood turned with an ashen face. Kael raised his eyebrows.

"Lion man, huh? Sounds like you might have a problem here."

Blackwood ambled clumsily back to his desk, passing as he steadied himself. He looked like a man shaken out of a nightmare. Or he was living in one now.

"Hunter, do you believe in demons?" his ashen pallor whitened. "Beings who look like men but must come from the darkest places?" He slumped into his chair.

Kael sat down in the lone chair on the other side. "There're many monsters who imitate, but it's all an illusion. I take it these bandits are the one your son is calling 'lion man'?"

Blackwood slowly nodded his head. "There's a man, you see, by the name of Dazlo. Him and his band of thieves came to the outskirts of our town a moon ago. It started slow—their presence I mean. There was talk of merchants being intercepted by bandits on horses; men with red eyes."

"Then one day people stopped coming here, wagons abandoned and horses roaming the fields with saddles. Then they came here. They pillaged the town, taking anything they wanted. At last, they came here. I had a small guard, but they were dispatched quickly." Blackwood paled again.

Kael leaned forward. *"How* were they dispatched?"

The Lord let out a long sigh and gagged a little. "They were dismembered. Slowly. The screams echoed through the halls as I hid Kinev and locked the study doors."

He began to sob, his belly rolling a little with the racking. "Then there was silence. No more screams, no thudding, nothing. Then the doors just opened. I don't know how, maybe my eyes played a trick when I saw a long claw swipe up the crack in between."

"But then it was open, and the hallway was dark. Too dark. What broke the silence was a dull, rhythmic thudding. And then I watched as the heads of my men rolled towards me like ninepins balls."

Kael watched as the man broke apart. His chest heaved with the racket of sobs and his eyes glistened with tears. In those eyes Kael could imagine the horror of watching heads roll from the darkness. But Kael needed to know more. "Then what?"

Blackwood straightened himself up and fidgeted with the collar of his tunic. "Then they came. The man Dazlo told me he would be taking over the town and to bend to his demands or more heads would roll. I had no other choice. No other choice..."

Kael stood up as the Lord repeated those words again. He noticed the display cases were empty. *This would explain the empty rooms, too. And the smell from the forest, the bandits heading towards it. I'm sure they are staying there. Something isn't right. If the man I saw was indeed Dazlo, then maybe...*

Lord Blackwood stood as well. "I'm sorry for wasting your time. You may stay here tonight; we have several guest rooms."

Kael looked at the drawer where the stone was locked, then turned his attention to the Lord. "I would much appreciate that, Lord Blackwood. Thank you."

There was not another word spoken as Blackwood ushered Kael out of the study, watching as he fumbled with the doors which did not quite lock. They returned to the foyer where the steward Cisco was waiting for them.

"Ah, Cisco. The hunter is staying here tonight, if you may see him to a room." He shifted his attention to Kael. "Have a nice night, hunter. I hope to see you leaving tomorrow morn."

Kael nodded crudely as Blackwood returned to the volley of corridors. Cisco cleared his throat and led him up an adjacent set of stairs. The second floor was a long corridor with many rooms. Cisco paused at a few before finally selecting one on the right side. He opened the door and gestured Kael inside.

The room had a large, elaborate canopy bed dressed in red. The floor had a large rug with patterns of red and gold and the walls were bookcases filled with books. Kael crossed the room and examined the bed, then looked at Cisco. "My horse is still downstairs. I need to make sure she is safe."

Cisco held up his hand. "Our stable boy will take care of it."

Kael nodded and sat on the bed. As he unbuckled his swords and leaned them on the nightstand. Cisco still stood in the doorframe. "Is there anything else?"

Cisco walked into the room and strode past him, towards one of the bookcases. He pilfered through the old, dusty books before he pulled a tome that was large and ratty. He handed this to Kael before he exited the room. As he passed through the door he paused and turned. "Read the story on page 104," then he left and closed the door behind him.

Kael turned the book over to the face, reading the title *The Amulon and Other Fairy Tales* before he opened the book. The dust plumed out for the book in a swirl as he sifted through to page 104, which started a story simple called 'The Manticore,'. The name had a ring to him, something familiar whispering in the back of his mind. It itched at him until he got a glimpse of a woman's smiling at him, then it was gone.

He began to read it when he heard the door creak. His head snapped to see the Lord's son peering through the crack. Kael flicked his hand at the door.

"Go away," Kael huffed. "It's late, boy. Go back to your father."

The boy opened the door more. Kael shrugged his shoulder and returned to the book. He began to read the first few words (*Legend goes that—*) but then he could feel the soft breathing of the child on his face.

He had climbed on the bed and was peering over Kael's shoulder at the book. Kael watched side eyed at the boy inched closer over his shoulders to read the book.

"The manticore," the boy breathed. "My ma used to read this story a lot when I was younger."

"Oh yeah?" Kael mumbled a little as he read more of the story, only partially tuned to the boy peering over his shoulder.

"It's all fuzzy, but ma used to say it was a story about even the most fearsome creatures have a weakness."

Something clicked in Kael's head as he finished the first page of the story (*mighty and fearsome—I've heard this before*). He glanced at the boy as he sat on the bed.

Kael turned to him and sat the book open on the bed. "What's your name?"

The boy smiled. "Kinev. You're a monster hunter, right? Did daddy hire you to beat the lion man? He's awful scary, like the manticore in the story."

Kael smiled at Kinev. "No, I'm not here for the lion man. But I'm sure things will work out. Remember, every monster has its weakness, right?"

The boy's smile faltered a little then he crawled off the bed. "Yeah, you're right. But I'm not sure if we can do it. Can you please talk to daddy? Please?"

Kael stood up and walked the boy to the ajar door. "I'll try to talk to him tomorrow and see what I can do. But it's late, Kinev."

The boy left in a shuffling motion and Kael's heart seemed to pang with hurt. *Am I doing the right thing? I mean I felt something odd about this Dazlo. But is he really a monster?*

Kael sat the book on the opposite side of the bed and laid down. He listened at the ceiling for some time and even picked up the book some, but he felt no desire to keep reading. It all felt familiar and distant at the same time. He drifted off to sleep as he held the book in his left hand.

The Manticore

I

Legend goes that there was a manticore who lived in a faraway mountain range. This manticore was formidable and fearsome, striking down all who opposed it. Many men came from all corners of the lands to fight this manticore, hoping to slay this invincible beast and claim the title of the greatest warrior. But all lost.

Ages past and the manticore was deemed invincible and immortal, unable to be slain by a mere human. It walked the mountain, the graveside of many warriors felled by the beast. Innis said that manticore skin is impenetrable, covered in thick scales, woven like chainmail. Even if a person were to get close, its razor-sharp claws would tear them apart and its serpentine tail could swipe them off their feet.

One day, a young hunter named Adan came to the mountain. Adan was from a village nestled in the same mountain range, having lived his whole life hearing of the invincible manticore. He came of age and departed his village to hunt amongst the lands for years until he was a young adult with knowledge of the lands. He came back to his home village and climbed the mountain to find the manticore of old.

His trek was fruitful as he found the den of the manticore nestled in a cave, far up the range. The rocky trail was perilous, but Adan knew how to traverse many landscapes. He, who traveled the lands, had heard rumors of a way to defeat the manticore. He searched and searched until he found the source of such rumor. And now he entered the manticore's den, wielding a bow and a dagger. Before him stood the manticore, mighty and fearsome.

"Welcome, warrior, to my den. It has been some time since one came to my home to challenge me. All have found their final resting place, as so will you."

Adan said nothing. The manticore grunted and lunged, swinging its tail wildly. Adan dodged and created distance. The manticore, invincible as it is, did not allow distance, crossing the space in a stride and stood before Adan. It let out a mighty roar.

Adan, though, did not pull his bow or wield his dagger. Instead, he brandished a single lilac flower, thrusting it onto the beast's chest, over its heart. The beast stopped, feeling frozen by the flower. The lilacs dissolved, disappearing into the body of the beast. It was then that the scales began to soften, turning to the fur of a normal lion. The manticore began to become less a monster, losing its strength and invulnerability.

Adan saw his chance. While the manticore struggled to stand, Adan brandished his bow and shot two arrows at the beast, striking it blind. He then pulled out a dagger and struck the beast's heart, exposed now that its armor was gone. The manticore could do nothing more than sigh, exhaling slowly as it stared at the hunter. A once immortal beast, slain like common prey.

Adan brought back the head of the manticore to his village, where he was heralded as a hero. Word spread of his valor and victory, about the man who slain the immortal manticore. When asked how he slain the beast, Adan would say:

"Every being has a weakness. It just takes perseverance and wit to find it."

II

Kael awoke early in the morning to a large crash underneath him. It was distant but loud, rippling through the manor. He shot out of bed and grabbed his weapons in his flight. When he entered the hallway it was empty, the silence following the crash palpable.

He retraced back to the stairs and down the curved case to the foyer. The door leading outside was open and shuddering from the faint wind. Outside he could see two men—bandits of the man Dazlo, he assumed. There was another large crash followed by several smaller ones deeper in the manor.

Kael crossed through the corridors and reached the study quickly. The doors were wide open and through them he could see the inside was trashed. Display cases were shattered, bookshelves toppled with the books sprawled on the floor.

The large desk was cracked in two directly over the top of the drawer where it held the stone. When Kael walked into the study he could see the drawer had been pulled out and thrown to the side, shattered into pieces.

Lord Blackwood was laying on the floor and over top him was a large man.

"Dazlo," Kael's voice filled the silence ominously. The man was facing away from him, his bulky frame only hinted by the dim candles spread in the room.

Dazlo turned his head. Kael could see the sinister smile cross his face. His maw opened and closed like he was chewing, but there was nothing. He turned around completely to see there was a tear in his black leather garb, barely concealed by a dark coat of sorts.

Kael's eyes widened in disbelief as he watched Kinev writhe in the man's grasp. Dazlo was holding him tight by the shoulder, the pain evident on Kinev's face. The man dug his fingers deeper into his skin then laughed.

"I knew we would cross paths one day. What did *he* call you? *Lost one*? An appreciable pet name."

Dazlo walked past the broken desk and towards Kael only to stop short. He used his other hand and rummaged in his belt pouch for a moment before he pulled out the rainbow stone. The expression on Kael's face made Dazlo howl with laughter.

"Only the strong get to survive, right? Only the strong get to *decide who survives.*" Dazlo shook his hand holding Kinev, making the boy squeal. "This runt came into the study as me and his dear old dad were negotiating over this," Dazlo held the stone up like he was looking through it, "when he took out a knife and stabbed me."

A cruel, nasty sneer plastered his face. "Then his dad refused the stone. So here we are."

Dazlo began to walk past Kael when he stopped beside him.

"I'll see you soon, *lost one.*"

Dazlo faded into the unnaturally dim hallway as Kael walked over to Lord Blackwood. He nudged the body with his foot until the man stirred. He sat up and looked around at the disheveled room. His face was purple with bruises and blood caked his nose.

"Where—where is my boy?" Blackwood stared at Kael. "Where is Dazlo?" Then he whipped his head to the vacant hole where the drawer used to be. "Where is the stone?"

"Gone." The look of contempt on Kael's face was apparent as Blackwood dropped his face to the ground. "You need to tell me what happened."

Blackwood inhaled and exhaled in a sharp, shaky manner. "Dazlo came in and demanded for the stone, and while I was trying to reason with him, Kinev came up with a large dagger..."

Then it dawned on Kael. His hand when to his thigh and felt the empty sheath. He ground his teeth. *That sneaky boy...*

"Listen to me," Kael hunkered down so he was eye-to-eye with Blackwood. "If you dinnae do anything, he will kill you son and take everything else. Do you want that?"

Blackwood shook his head violently, his eyes full of fright.

"Then you need to do as I say. You stay here. There's nothing you can do now and if you try to follow you can get yourself killed. I will save your boy, but it will come at a price. A *hefty* price."

Blackwood stammered and tried to stand up, but he only got as far as to slump back down in his chair. His eyes shifted a few times as he muttered before he stared at Kael. "What do you mean?"

Kael stood and stared down at the man. "The stone. I want the stone as price for Dazlo's head."

Blackwood's eyes widened in horror. "Oh please, anything but the stone. I'll pay you..."

"You have nothing left, nothing but your lineage. Dazlo has taken everything else. If you dinnae agree, he will take your son, too. Do you want to see his head rolling in here?"

Blackwood paled to a ghostly white and shook his head. Kael got close to his face. His eyes were alight with fury. "Agree to it."

Blackwood scooted his chair back and out of Kael's face, the fear etched on his face. "Fine! The stone is yours! Please save my boy, my Kinev!"

Kael whipped out of the study in a hurry, blasting past the foyer and out the open door as he whistled shrill. Jorunn came galloping from the side of the manor, a wiry boy hanging loosely to her reins. He fell off and tumbled on the ground.

Kael vaulted himself into the saddle as she strode past. He kicked her into a harder stride as the town blurred behind him, and he crossed the field in short time.

III

Kael retraced back to the entrance of the forest to where he smelled the pungent odors. The air felt still as he approached the tree lines, holding its breath in anticipation. Kael dismounted and tied Jorunn to one of the trees.

I should go on foot. It is much quieter.

He took the crossbow from his saddlebags and strapped it to his back, hanging the quiver on his side. The decaying scent tumbled out of the trees in waves as he readied himself in a small nook of bushes.

While he was examining his quiver buckle he noticed Lilac flowers growing from a small patch of loose dirt. The lilacs reminded him of the story, his mind forcing him to pluck a couple of the petals and stashing them in a small pouch on his belt.

He entered the forest. The light peeked through the canopy, illuminating enough of the forest that he could walk the faint path. There were obvious signs of the path to the gang, but that meant he would be spotted easily too.

He veered from the path enough that he could be concealed, but he could keep an eye on the path as well. The pungent smell became more intense as time went on, and as he went deeper into the forest, the less light was peering through the canopy, with sunset approaching.

It took time, but he came upon a campfire in the distance, and with that, he could hear the commotion of conversation.

"... can't believe the boss ain't killed the boy," Kael watched as the man raked a branch across a set of iron bars. In it was Kinev shaking uncontrollably.

"Aye, but the boss had the stone," another said as he poked a stick into the fire. "A twink in his eye, the boss had. But it was an onry twink, one I wouldn't want looking at me."

There was a wave of murmurs before another man piped up.

"The boss is downright scary sometimes, boys. I don't want to be on the other end of anything with him."

Kael watched as the man with the branch got down to eye level with Kinev.

"What says we have some dinner, boys?" Kael could see the toothy grin from his spot. It was a grimy, green mass of decaying stones. "I'm quite famished, 'specially since boss came back with the boy."

The other men were already agitating, their blood boiling. Kael could feel it, too. The air had a vibration to it; a dark cloud that pervaded your midnight and brought something out from within you. He felt the burn on his neck and the familiar heat rising within him.

Kinev shrieked as the man opened the cage, withdrawing into the far corner.

"C'mon now. I just wanna taste." The cracks echoed through the forest as the man's face contorted and broke, the skin falling off in sheets. What replaced it was fur, a snout protruding from the face in a grisly coat of blood.

The beast let out a howl before it created a hacking sound. Kael noted it sounded like laughter.

"Come and play, little boy—" the voice was cut off by a squelching sound and the piercing scream that followed. A silver-tipped bolt came out of its eye, piercing through the back of its skull. It collapsed and seized before stilling completely.

"Intruder!" the others began to stand and shake, that dark mist that Kael felt was conglomerating over them.

Their transformation was complete with some akin to wolves, but there was a variety of therianthropes that appeared bird-like and deer-like as well.

Lyncanthropes? No, they're different... No matter though. Kael snarled as he lunged out of his hiding spot with one sword in hand and crossbow in the other.

The flock of creatures jumped on him. He cut two deer-headed beings down with his sword, beheading them in one swift attack. Two raven men used their bloody beaks to pierce him, one hitting his shoulder and the other his forearm. He felt the warmth of blood pour down as he dispatched one with a silver bolt to the head and the other with a clean swing of his sword.

Then there was a pack of deer and wolves on him. They all tumbled back into the bushes and rolled. He fought blow after blow of hooves and claws, feeling the sting of wounds on his arms. The pelting was getting harder, and he could feel his heart quicken and a feat that he couldn't get out of this one.

He continued to block the blows as a voice nagged at his head. It was high, but it gave him comfort. It beckoned him and then a name came through: Kinaa. He then took a deep breath and whispered. *Kinaa, with your power may it come into me... give me the flames to cleanse and dispel darkness...* Familiar words as he had heard Ijos say something similar.

He swung in a wide, low sweep as his blade turned red. The creatures howled in pain as they were cleaved, the sword red and starting to alight with flames.

The creatures stared in fright for just one moment as Kael dropped his crossbow to wield his sword with both hands. He grunted and spun with blinding speed, pulling the beasts into him and severed them apart, the pieces burning to ash in seconds.

Kael stopped his momentum with difficulty, pausing as he felt a great fatigue cloud over him. He looked at his sword in awe as the flames dissipated.

"I did it... I finally did it." He muttered it a few times and then he snapped his head back up at the sound of a shriek. "Kinev." He cleared through the bushes and found Kinev still huddled into the corner. He entered the caged and passed over the corpse of the bandit he killed first. He saw it was still a wolf.

The boy flinched when Kael knelt. He paused and then held out his hand. "We need to go, Kinev. It's not safe here."

Kinev's eyes shifted in the growing darkness of the forest. "B-but the lion man is still here."

Kael nodded. "And that's why we need to get you away from here."

Kinev shakily grabbed Kael's hand and was led out of the cage. The campfire was still burning and Kael picked up the branch the first bandit raked across the cage. He tore a piece of fabric from the corpse and wrapped it around the branch. He strode across and lit the cloth from the fire and handed it to Kinev.

Kinev gawked at the makeshift torch. "I-I can't take this..."

Kael thrust it on him and then went to drop it. Kinev grabbed it midair. "You *can* and you *will.* I can hear him awakening further in." Kinev's eyes widened. "Dazlo. The lion man. And I cannae guard you while trying to guard myself. I would get us both killed."

Kinev gulped and turned. Kael grabbed his shoulder for a second, the boy jumping a little. "Follow the path out. It's getting dark, so the torch will help. At the treeline is my horse, Jorunn. Take her home."

Kael shoved him hard, and the boy began to run.

"Faster, for your father's sake!" Then it was all drowned out to Kinev. Even the roar was distant as his heart pounded in his ears.

IV

Kael watched Kinev run from the camp. He only stood for a moment, sword in hand, as a large serpentine tail swept low. He jumped to dodge, but a large paw slammed him back into the ground.

A lion's head stared back at him. No, it still had a human face. The lion's body was covered in scales, and there was a large, scaly tail. *A manticore.* Kael could feel the claws tearing into his shoulder. He could feel his neck burning again. He tried to instinctively cover his neck with his hand, but he could not move it. The manticore clicked a few times in its throat.

"I see you made it here quickly, and dispatched those under my command, traveler." The manticore exhaled. "I would not expect anything less from someone branded by *him.*"

Kael tried to look neutral at the beast. "I see, Dazlo. You were a manticore. Is your transfiguration to a human the work of the sorcerer?"

Dazlo the manticore grinned, its razor teeth glistening in the warm light from the campfire.

"Oho, intrigued? I am a manticore, indeed. But I was tired of the constant onslaught of humans who wanted to test their strength. I wanted to live my life more freely. So, the sorcerer made a deal with me. I can stay human and do as I please, but I was to retrieve a stone in this yonder town."

"Then he mentioned crossing paths with a man in a red tunic. I was supposed to kill him."

A click resonated in Dazlo's throat.

"Then I saw you at the gates. A man in a red tunic. More importantly, a man with a scar on his neck wearing a red tunic. The stone was merely an artifact to let me transform back."

147

Dazlo's smile widened when Kael's face contorted and a deep chuckle emanated from its chest.

"Did you really think it coincidence that you've faced so many beasts on your travel? The mark on your neck is like a beacon to us. A beacon of *darkness.*"

Kael tried to struggle against the paw, but the manticore pressed down. He felt a pang within his chest. "Why? Why me?"

"I do not know why he chose you, but we are here to test you. 'To see if you're strong enough,' he says. For what, I don't know." It clicked and exhaled again. Its double-lidded eyes blinked at him. "I suppose that won't matter, you end here now."

"Not to you, *beast.*"

Kael pulled out his dagger and thrust it into the manticore's eye. The beast roared, pulling its paw off him to flail. Kael slid out in a quick motion and rolling backwards, landing in a bush. He saw a glimpse in the sunset and saw his crossbow, still loaded from before.

The silver-tipped bolt gave him some hope, though Dazlo's words still resounded in his head. *A beacon of darkness. Is that me?* He stumbled as he crossed through the brush and didn't react in time to see Dazlo standing over him.

The eye healed quickly; the only memory of it was some dried blood underneath the socket. Kael was thrown across the campsite by a large paw, then was trampled by the beast before he could land on the other side. His sword went bouncing away from his body.

He had no time to react to anything. The manticore toyed with him, reveling as the darkness swirled around. The beast seemed to grow stronger, each lashing more painful than the last. He could feel his armor ripping, his skin tearing and the blood pouring.

But the words kept playing in his head, clouding him. *A beacon of darkness.* And he felt it himself. The darkness swirled within him and felt that low violent bloodlust fill him. It emboldened him, pushing away the lost, hopeless feeling and replacing it with the need for blood.

His hands reacted on their own, pushing the beast off him without any strain. His wounds steamed. *They're closing.* Dazlo was surprised, and so was Kael. But more than that, he felt fear. *I—I can't control myself.*

He moved, lunging at the manticore. It snarled and retaliated, swiping with his paw. But Kael aptly dodged; so swift it was nearly a blur. He unsheathed the other blade and swung it hard, but the manticore's flesh did not give to the steel. Dazlo howled with laughter.

"No mortal blade can pierce my scaly hide." A sinister grin spread across his maw. But Kael could see fear in his eyes. "You've run out of options."

Then he heard a voice in his head. It was low and deep. It felt like the darkness personified.

The flower. Use it. Then he felt some imaginary chains fall off his body. That feeling he had disappeared, the violent nature no longer controlling him.

He had no time to fester with the voice or the dissipating heat he felt; he reacted out of old instinct. It was the mind of a seasoned hunter that came forward, pulling out the flower like it was a weapon.

In a way it was. When the petals touched Dazlo's great, snarling head, it immobilized him. He stopped in his attack, paralyzed. Then Kael watched as the scales softened, turning to a tan fur. The wound in his eye opened back up and pushed blood.

The beast tried to pull away, but there were ethereal tendrils holding him down. The lilacs acted like a shackle. Kael held the flower to Dazlo as he stabbed the beast with his sword, plunging into the flesh with no resistance.

Dazlo moaned in pain from the wounds. His paw quaked as he tried to fight the lilac, but it was no use. Kael pushed his hand into the lilac and the lilac into Dazlo, the flower dissipating into his flesh.

A faint purple hue ran across Dazlo as the flower entered his bloodstream, his claws turned into ash. His eyes clouded and he thrashed weakly, his paw flopping on the ground.

Kael moved backwards for a second before he took a wide swing at the creature, severing the tendons in the paw. It collapsed on the ground and did not move again.

Kael knelt to the creature and stared. "It's over, Dazlo. There's nothing else you can do."

The weakened Dazlo snarled. "No! I cannot be defeated this way! I will not die here—"

Kael slit the beast's throat, it's snarls and growls drowned by the outflow of blood. Dazlo's had gone cold. They were black stones within the sockets of his skull.

He knelt and searched the body of the creature before he found the stone he needed; its rainbow hue still present in the dimming light of the forest. It gave off the sinister aura again, so Kael wrapped it in a cloth and placed it in a knapsack he found.

Lastly, he pulled a tooth from the beast's jaw, examining at it for a moment before storing it away. The shadows were darkening in the forest, casting the bright orange of the sunset through the canopy.

With the aura of the stone ebbing, slumbering in the knapsack, Kael staggered out of the copse. He felt drained since that darkness had dissipated; the wounds were still painful despite the surface having closed. When he exited the thicket of trees, he noticed Jorunn was nowhere to be seen, nor was Kinev.

"Jorunn did well," Kael breathed. His lungs felt heavy. He glanced back at the thicket of trees. He could hear a faint whispering permeating from the encroaching darkness.

Kael... it is almost time. It had a duality to the voice. One high and one low; one dark and one light. The words were the same, but was the meaning different? What was it almost time for?

He took a step backwards and tried to turn towards the village, but his vision blurred. The colors of the sunset melded with the ground as it engulfed his vision. Kael smacked into the ground hard, his sword bouncing from his grip. He faded in and out of consciousness, wincing with each breath from the faded injuries. It took some time before he could regain consciousness and stumble upright, grabbing his sword to use as a cane.

He walked slowly in the field, leaning on his sword for some time before he felt he was able to stand unsupported. He sheathed the dirty blade before he got to the town, reaching it as the sun was fully set and became night.

His walk through the town was on full spectacle; he felt tired and bruised, limping slightly through the main road. He could sense eyes peering through cracks as he walked, silent murmurs from behind the walls around him.

The mansion was a marbled corpse jutting from the ground; there was a stillness to the structure. As he limped to the door, it opened slowly, waiting for his return, but he stopped short.

Jorunn was alone in the front of the structure, grazing on some grass that was not clipped short. He patted her snout as he passed by her, stopping long enough to examine her for any wounds or signs of exertion. There was none, relieving some of the weight in his chest.

"You did good," He continued to put her, running his fingers through her black mane. "Take it easy for now."

She snorted, but he could sense some form of disquiet in her actions. A twitch, her jolting eyes. He knew she felt it. He finished patting her and ambled his way to the door, ajar like a gaping mouth.

"Through the mouth of A'hel," He remarked. He didn't think the inside would be treacherous, but there was a weight in the darkness behind the door.

He took a deep breath and passed through the threshold. Cisco was waiting for him on the other side, standing stiffly in the dimly lit foyer. The odor of the musty books replaced the fresh cut grass. The steward stayed quiet as he nodded his head sideways and began shuffling through the array of corridors again with Kael in tow.

The dark of night loomed over the artifacts; to Kael it was like ghosts of former possessors, holding on tight to their old belongings. The muteness of the travel and the dancing of shadows cast by wall sconces gave a cold chill on his neck.

Cisco stopped him at the double doors of the study, though the doors no longer closed together anymore. They were agape and Kael could see the silhouette of the Lord inside. Kael eyed Cisco, who nodded, and then passed through. He took a few small strides into the study before he stopped behind on the guest chairs.

Blackwood had been sitting cockeyed in the chair, his feet resting on an open drawer of the desk. He continued in this position as he craned his neck to look at Kael.

"I see you have made it back in one piece." When he spoke, it was no more than a whisper. Kael saw glimpses of Kinev's face nestled into his father's chest from the candlelight. "I assume Dazlo and his band are dead?"

"As was promised," Kael rasped, his voice barely a whisper too. "As well as your son's return." He gestured towards the boy in Blackwood's lap.

Blackwood shifted gently, moving an arm from beneath the slumbering child. The candlelight played its magic and made the boy seem much younger, clinging to his father like a toddler. The man's palm was upturned as he held it out. Kael raised his eyebrows.

"You have done a good enough job saving this town and my son. But the stone—I must have it. It is far too precious for someone like you."

Kael sneered. He pulled the knapsack from his back and held it out just out of Blackwood's reach. As the man tried to lean forward to take it, Kael pulled the bag away. Blackwood's face contorted into a grimace then flushed with red that was visible even in the dim candlelight as Kael did it again.

"You are nobody, you vagrant." Blackwood's voice rose just above a whisper as rage filled him. His voice cracked and broke, but he still cared enough not to stir his boy. "You're a monster hunter, and nothing more. Take some fucking gold and go back to wandering the roads."

Kael pulled the bag back and slung it over his shoulder. "No. Our deal was the stone for your boy's life. The life you put in danger in the first place."

A wave of violet flushed the Lord's face. His eyes bugged as he stifled himself from waking the boy, stopping himself from jumping out of the chair.

"My boy will understand one day when he takes this seat. Like you would understand. Your father probably died a nobody just like you will."

Some of the candles blew out as Kael swiftly danced over the chair and stretched over the table. A knife was held against Blackwood's throat. The sharp edge cut slightly into a fold of skin over the jugular. His breath quickened with the stench of death, his body still for fear that one wrong move could spill his blood on his son.

Kael's face was inches away from his. The sneer had disappeared and replacing it was the lines of a man who has seen more than Blackwood would ever see—with eyes that burned a cold flame.

"You are not half the man my father was. You will die a pitiful death, surrounded by your shame and regret."

The knife was pulled off Blackwood's throat and Kael swiftly left the study. He could her the man beginning to sob behind him, choking out any retaliation.

The steward met him outside the study and did not speak, despite Kael knowing the man saw everything. The passage through the corridors was quiet, the stillness gone, though, and it seems the shadows played more violently than before.

Cisco opened the final door to the yard basking in moonlight was a tired sigh. Before Kael could exit the manor, Cisco held out his hand. It was not upturned, but rather it was waiting for something else.

It was a handshake. Kael cocked his head but returned the gesture, the two hands locking in a firm shake. The final action took Kael off guard; the steward pulled him down and brought Kael's ear to his mouth. He spoke in such a breathy whisper, the words barely sounding at all, like he was afraid someone—or something—would hear.

Kael recoiled from the words. His eyes were wide with shock, and he stumbled out of the doorway and mounted Jorunn in a hurry. He spurred her quickly out of the town, away from the manor. He fled as fast as he could, but the words followed him regardless.

Those words resounded in his head all the way back to the kappa: 'The path of ashes you walk will consume everything you touch. It will burn all that stands in your wake.'.

Frenzy

I

Kael rode through the night to Duris Lake, reaching the body of water as light began to dispel the darkness, creating a bleak, grey landscape. He dismounted Jorunn and scanned the field for the kappa.

"Kappa! I have brought what you desired!" His yells echoed through the air. There was no response. "Kappa!"

Silence. He turned and cursed, sitting on the wet grass. He took the stone out and felt the warmth of bloodlust fill in him. He could feel a snarl form on his face, like the stone was enticing him to kill.

It pervaded his mind, like a whisper in his ear. *Kill. Conquer. Feast.* It would repeat. It emboldened him, feeding into his darkness that swirls within. He could just cut down everything in his path and all that would be left would be the sorcerer. The one who took it all away from him, and he could cleave him in two.

Didn't that beast say the sorcerer sent monsters to test my strength? Am I strong enough? I can cleave into the invincible manticore. I've severed the heads of many to get to where I'm at now, but I still don't know where he is. Why must he hide?

"I am here to use my past as a path to *him*. He hides there. He told me himself."

A splash, and a croak. "Mister hunter, I sees you'se returned! Although who is himses?" The kappa was behind Kael croaking with joy. The morning light coming over the horizon glittered on the stone. "The stones! You'se founds it!"

A flash came and a blade protruded in the dense shell. Only the tip was stuck in it, creating a small crack. The kappa shook, staring at Kael. Amid his wild hair, the kappa could see the faint burning of embers on Kael's neck. A moan rumbled out of Kael as his eyes glared at the beast, his pupils dilated.

"Anyone who stands in my way will be reduced to ashes. I cannot forget. I must find the sorcerer." He was no longer a man, but rather a vessel for his own dark desire, for vengeance. "Those who oppose me will be swept away by the flames."

The kappa shrieked and jumped, spinning into its shell. The protruding blade spun and smacked Kael in the head, jostling him and knocking the stone out of his hands. He could feel the heat dissipate and the burn on his neck cool.

Kael stared at the kappa shell. "Kappa." He reached his hand out but stopped. He saw the crack in the shell and noticed his knife laying on the ground. He ground his teeth. "I do not remember—"

The kappa shrieked, "You are a monster! I saw it in your eyes, the bloodlust and hate!" Several more incoherent balling continued. Kael stood and his gaze hovered over the stone. He could hear it whisper his desires, calling for him to pick it up. He averted his gaze then kicked the stone over to the kappa.

"Take the stone. It is the least I can do after this." He began to walk away. The kappa's eyes peeked out of the shell.

"The stonses—what about the shiny youse seeked?"

Kael stopped. "I dinnae ken if I deserve it anymore." He resumed and walked off.

Kael took Jorunn and retreated into the tree lines nearby. He built a small fire and tended to it, cooking a small stew. The rays of the sun peered through the green leaves, throwing green, bubbled shades onto the ground. He leaned against a tree and consumed the stew, drinking the broth from the small bowl like it was a cup.

He stared blankly as the embers still kindled within him. He knew the feeling well; the embers do not leave him, not fully at least. Not since the day the sorcerer faced him last, holding a blade at his throat.

Not your time, he said, and that fate decreed I was not ready... I wasn't ready. I was powerless. I watched as he... why was I spared? Why did he say to 'look within, look to the past, and you will find me.' Where will I go?

He could hear snarling. His vision was black, but he could hear it, vibrating deep within him. There was a *hunger*, too. The insatiable hunger to consume and be consumed. He wanted to be stronger.

But why? To kill a being that took everything from him? To blindly make him follow behind his antiquated footsteps, even as a child, places he once visited have borne fruit of malice. Everywhere he visits now, the corruption is there waiting for him. Is it chance, or is it fate?

He can feel his haunch bristle; he feels like a beast. He stared into the darkness and saw a puddle. He goes to it to drink it, but he can't use his hands. He laps it up like a dog.

No, he sees in the reflection he isn't a dog. He is a *beast—a large creature. A monster, even.* Red eyes peer back from the reflection. He can see the whipping of several tails behind him. It's all black, his fur is black. No. It's not all black. He can see a shimmer of Crimson on him. *Blood, it's blood. Whose? Is it mine? Or is it those who were in my way? I don't want to be a monster.*

Now there's a warmth. He can feel it rising in him. *What's this light?* Below him is a tiny animal, like a cat, or maybe a dog. It's a white light and has golden eyes.

"You're not a monster. You are just a lost soul." It spoke. It felt pure, and it washed over him. He felt more at ease. He then heard a croak and a weight on his palm. He could feel the vibrations from it and from his side. A fog lifted him out of the beast in the darkness and into light.

II

Ijos stared at the lake momentarily. He examined the area and found the remains of the kappas that Sarreif told in his story.

"It looks like the dwarf was right, Kael. You can see where he smashed their shells. See here—" as he pointed out large cracks in the shell of one kappa, "it almost looks like he cracked stone." Kael nodded as he examined the corpse, tracing his fingers around the wound.

Ijos stood and surveyed the area for clues about where the family would have gone. He walked over to the west and examined the surroundings for any tracks, broken twigs or anything else that could be disturbed.

He found several faint tracks from animals, but nothing big enough to fit a human. He was worried about that, too. *Maybe too much time has passed,* he thought. He glanced at Kael for a moment, who was sitting on the shoreline.

"Kael, be careful. You don't know what is in the water—"

But he was not quick enough, nor was the water the danger. A scaly tail wrapped around the boy's torso and yanked him backwards. Ijos shot up and sprinted towards Kael. A body sprung from the tall snowclad grass, attached to it was the scaly tail.

Ijos noticed immediately that this is a lamia. Its face was serpentine with large mandibles, its torso bare and its feminine breasts pale and blued from the temperatures. It hissed at him as its tail wrapped around Kael tighter, choking him.

Ijos unsheathed his blade and lunged, the lamia dodging the attack and swiping at him with her claws. His shoulder was ripped open by one of the talons. Kael struggled as the two danced around the other, his blade not able to connect with the serpent.

Ijos watched Kael turn blue. He took a small knife from his side and threw it at the lamia's tail, striking it and wounding the monster. It loosened its grip enough that the boy could breathe. Ijos resumed his fight as Kael caught his breath, still struggling his arms against the constriction.

The boy could not reach his own blade to help, his arms pinned to his sides. He attacked in the only other way he could; he chomped down on the scaly tail as hard as he could and bit off a chunk. The lamia hissed and coiled away for but a moment before the body lunged at the boy.

The lamia wrapped itself around the boy and watched Ijos with its piercing, yellow eyes. "Go ahead and try to attack. I will inject my venom into this boy before you strike," she hissed and smelled Kael. "He's just too tempting to let go. Ah, I can taste the shadows inside him. So rich. So tempting."

"What do you want?" Ijos demanded, pointing the blade at the lamia. "Is it the boy?"

A raspy laugh emanated from the lamia's chest, then a serpentine hiss followed. "What keen eyes you have. Yes, I could smell him from miles away—so much darkness wrapped around such a small, helpless thing. Delicious."

Ijos grimaced and clenched his sword. In the sunlight he saw a gleam of red in the sky, and his face twisted to a crude sneer. He almost chuckled as the lamia stopped for a moment, shaken by his abrupt change.

She leaned closer to Kael and caressed his cheek with one claw. The point opened a superficial cut that oozed a little blood. She licked it off with a narrow tongue as she side-eyed Ijos. His face maintained a blank slate.

"Does this boy not matter to you? No matter, he's good as dead anyway."

Her fangs protruded and closed on Kael's neck. Before they could rip the skin, a high screech pierced the still air and the lamia's eyes were being pecked out by a bright red bird.

"Nuria!" Ijos called upon his companion as he wicked his sword behind him, trailing the tip close to the ground. The bird retreated from the lamia and became a ball of fire that was consumed by his blade, igniting it. He lunged and spun, slicing the lamia in two right below her breasts. It hissed and screeched, flailing from the burns.

"You will not kill me so easily!" She exclaimed, using the last of her power to latch onto Kael and bite into his neck.

"No!" Ijos screamed. He thrust his burning blade straight into the lamia's skull, detaching from Kael before the flames exuded from every orifice with a hiss. The body slumped and Kael was free. The boy slumped to the ground and started breathing heavily and grew pale.

"Kael!" Ijos knelt and cradled the boy in his arms, shaking him and feeling his face. It was hot and sweaty. The bite marks were swelled and the veins protruding. He knew that venom had spread, and fast.

The boy held Ijos' hand and stared at him with glassy eyes. "Da'..." The boy said. "Where... da'... mommy... Ilith..." Tears began to stream down his face. His eyes flickered as a coughing fit ensued.

"Kael, can you hear me?" Ijos shook him harder. "Answer me, Kael. What do you see?"

The boy's tears kept streaming. "Where is mommy, da'? Why is the house on fire? I dinnae wanna die..." His eyes shifted behind Ijo and his face contorted into fear. "Who is that man in black behind us?" Ijos turned sharply, but nothing was there. "Why is fire coming from his hands, Da'?"

"Kael, no one is here..." Ijos could feel wetness on his face as he wept for the boy. "What did the man in black do?"

"Why do I have to hide, da'? What is this man here for? What is the piece he is talking about?"

Ijos stared at Kael oddly through tears. *He must think I am his dad.* "Am I talking to the sorcerer about something? What do I say?"

"Da', please no! Dinnae this! Dinnae die!" A soundless cry from his lips, acting like he was in pain. His eyes were in shock. He began to pant and grind his teeth. "I hope you die!" A gasp and he examined his chest. He grasped it and cried. "We are not the same..." he whispered. "W-we cannae be the same." He convulsed and flailed about. "Help me, my daddy—"

Ijos shushed him and had pulled out an old bronze coin. He was juggling it with his free hand with the fluidity of water. "It's alright, Kael. You will not remember the trauma of your past. You will be—" But he stopped.

Kael snapped out of the trance and stared directly at Ijos with hatred. The eyes fazed, flickering between yellow and blue. Ijos could feel a trickle of warmth in his side. Kael had taken his sword and stabbed him. Ijos fell to the ground, holding his side. Kael was still in his lap. His hands shook as he cradled Kael.

There was a faint trace of black running through the veins of Kael's face.

"You have failed, swordsman. This boy is mine. I have already infected him even before you met him." Kael ripped his own shirt to show a pulsating red aura from his chest. "His bloodline and mine are intertwined; fate has decreed it."

Ijos looked at Kael with pain. The sorcerer spoke through him and wondered what the red aura is swirling around the boy's heart.

"The latent hate and bloodlust within the boy that has been sparked since that day is the catalyst, and my mark will see it will come to fruition. You cannot stop. You are much too late—"

Ijos had enough of the sorcerer, imbuing the magic of a chant to place a block on this aura. He strained, his veins popping and the coin started turning into the color of a smoldering ember and he kept up the spell. The scent of burning flesh filled his nostrils as the coin burned his hand.

Nuria perched on his shoulder and screeched, her power draining into the coin as well. He kept chanting until he placed the coin onto Kael's bare chest, burning a disc shape into it. Kael gasped and out of his mouth came black fog. The cloud loomed over their heads as the voice filled his ears.

It is not over, swordsman. I will return one day. Fate will not be stopped by such meager magic.

The fog dissipated and Ijos tended to Kael. He was still sweating and was burning with a high fever. His breathing was shallow, and the blue of his veins were spreading up his neck and down his chest.

"Aveline." Ijos stated as he got up, ignoring the pain in his side from the wakizashi. Kael had not stabbed it far enough to damage any organs. He held Kael in his hands as he rushed northwest.

III

Midday. Kael awoke sitting against a tree. He felt hot and sweaty despite the shade. He regained his composure and tried to process the memory that was brought back.

What does the sorcerer want with me? What does he mean by we are connected? He was more confused than before, and he worried about the feeling he had before the memory.

He lifted his right hand, the hand that has slayed so many beings, and wondered if he did it out of justice or his own malice. He clenched his hands and felt a sturdy object in his left. He held it up against the glistening sun peeking through the trees.

It was a knurled brown coin, tarnished over time with some patina. There was a square hole in the middle.

His breath caught in his throat when he had some recognition of the coin. "A tumen. They dinnae make these coins anymore, Ijos told me it came from his homeland."

He turned it over several times, realizing that it was the coin of the past. He moved his tunic to the side and traced old scars, two pinpoints on his shoulder. He then took the coin and placed it on a faded scar on his chest. The scar was larger, mostly misshapen as he aged, but it was similar. Similar enough to confirm the memory. He leaned his head back and took a deep breath. He could almost smell a faint tinge of burning flesh. He opened his eyes as he thought on the last word Ijos said in the memory.

"Aveline, huh?" He gazed northwest, past the trees. He couldn't see far, but he knew his path would continue that way. He got up and mounted Jorunn, pulling the reins to his next destination.

Sealed

Embers

I

The sun's glare created a heat wave over a castle town, the perimeter towers wavering like a mirage. The silence that filled the gap between the stronghold and the invading army was fragile. It waited for the singular break of sound to entice the chaos that followed.

The invaders stood a sea of red, their colors covering the frontward grassy fields of the castle town. Then the noise broke with trebuchets creaking to life, giving out the whine and grating as a death call. They hurled flaming projectiles that pounded against the stone walls, shaking the very foundation of the town's defenses.

Within the castle walls, the defending army braced themselves for the onslaught, shielding their eyes from dust and debris being knocked loose. The men atop the walls shielded with large metal barriers while those in the towers used slits in the stoke to shoot at the oncoming horde.

Then the sun was blotted out by a cloud of arrows, raining down on the steel barricades, striking those unfortunate enough to stand too far out of the shield. The defending retaliated by raining boiling oil down upon those who dared to approach the gates.

The civilians of the castle town were barricaded in their homes, fear plastered on their face and weighing heavily on their souls. Arrows struck inside the gates as another cloud formed over the town.

The invading army broke into the town in a matter of hours by climbing ladders onto the wall. The fortress fought back with more boiling oil and torches, burning several to the bone.

Pikes were jammed down the ladders, piercing eyes and arteries that were not covered by armor. Alas, the invading army's numbers were too great, as with one soldier dispatched, two more took his place.

It was chaos on the walls, bodies flying off the edge, whole or in pieces, and the army broke through. A skinny soldier was among its mass, weaving through the fight and slicing either the axillary or jugular of the opposing soldiers.

The small soldier ate their way through, their metal shining in the sun, the insignia of a horse with two heads on their chest contrast to the sea of the defending army's owl crest. The soldier broke through and reached the gates, stabbing a straight sword into the skull of the men barricading the gate. Men behind this soldier rallied their help, guarding their back and slaying waves of the enemy.

The gate was open. The soldier broke the contraption and the door fell. The town was open to the invading army.

"Come! Take the head of the Lord of this town! Take this town for the crest of Erria!" A shrill, dainty voice shouted.

It pierced the air like a hawk, and like a hawk, the soldier's piercing eyes saw all. A quick reflex and the soldier spun, jabbing their sword into an enemy's neck, blood pooling down the blade. The soldier stood for a moment as the crowd of its allies rushed past to take hold of the town.

The soldier's helm shifted a little and there was a gleam of green eyes underneath, locking onto its prey as their own eyes faded. They released the blade when the enemy was limp and lifeless. The soldier wicked the blood of the blade and moved with the crowd towards the castle.

II

The siege continued. The soldiers inside the castle walls barricaded any door or window as best as they could, using tables or any wood they can break apart. The center of the castle was an elegant main hall and in that was a man, barking and raving.

"Hurry! You must protect the castle at all costs!"

His voice threw spittle in every direction as he whipped his head to bark more orders of the same. His greying beard was covered in spit and sweat. His purple gown whipped swirled around him as he turned and walked to a large throne.

As the chaos ensued in the castle, men and women running with wood in their arms, the man sat down on this throne, reaching with his ringed fingers to reposition a wiry crown on his bald head.

Another man came to his side. He was spindly; his robe was draped over his body like a sheet and flowed with no hint of the body underneath.

"My lord, we must surrender. The opposing army has breached the walls. It won't be long before they enter—
"

"I know!" The Lord barked. Sweat beaded down his brow and his eyes flickered, watching the soldiers carry any piece of wood. "I know. But what will they do when they find me?" He had a fearful look on his face.

He went to open his mouth again when there was a loud crash at the main door. There was a momentary silence and then another crash followed.

The soldier started yelling and piling in from of the door to keep it from opening, but it was no use. The invaders used a battering ram, large and crude in its misshapen metal glory, and knocked all the shielding soldiers aside. Another team behind the battering one slipped through and dispatched the fallen men.

As chaos ensued, the servants fleeing, the small faction of soldiers ran their course down the hallways and into the main room. They were met with the final guard for the Lord, surrounding him as a shield. He squirmed and shivered on his throne. His voice became shrill and his face red as he barked orders.

"Guards! Protect me at all costs! Protect your lord!"

The small band stopped and dispersed, allowing the small soldier to pass to the front. They held out their arms and glanced at each of the guards.

"Do you really want to die for such a coward?" Their eyes locked on each of the guard and then to the man that stood by the throne.

Their gaze continued past the man. "You don't have to lose your life over a man who would throw yours away in an instant. We just want to dispatch him. All for the land of Erria. And someone else will have to be appointed here as vassal of sorts. Something this man has denied and sent his own troops out in retaliation."

"What says it?"

They exchanged glances with the guards. There was no shift in allegiance. They sighed. "I see. I really did not want to do this by force."

They unsheathed their sword and braced themselves to attack when the wiry steward of the lord started pulling him out of the throne.

"What are you doing, Escar?! Are you defying me?" Escar continued to pull him off the throne. He began to drag the lord across the floor, his determination emboldening his strength despite his wiry stature. "I will have you executed! You!" He pointed to one of the guards, "Kill him or you will be killed too!"

The guards stood still as they watched the two fight. They were silent; but they started to move out of Escar's way as he dragged the lord over to the enemy lines and left him. As Escar walked away, the lord turned around and spat towards him.

"Escar, you bloody traitor! I'll have you beheaded, all of you beheaded at the end of this!"

He then felt a tap on his shoulder. He turned to see the leading soldier had taken their helmet off. A woman's face peaked out of the armor. A thin face of ivory skin, only barely sun-kissed, was framed by hair that was long, wavy and nearly black. And the eyes were a bright green, piercing the lord and silencing him.

A smile crept on the woman's lips before she swiftly swung her blade, the only trace of it moving was the sheen as it beheaded the lord. Escar watched from the throne.

The green eyes followed to his gaze and locked on again. Her voice was much calmer now, more akin to a cat's purr.

"Thank you, Vassal Escar."

III

Ragged breathing accompanied the dull glare of light through a burlap sack. Both the sight and fear were owned by a man pulled along by a lead. He knew what he was being led to, who was pulling him, and he feared when that trek ended.

His legs felt weak; the muscles worn thin from fleeing in this town he once called home. Why? What was the purpose of an uprising? What was there left to reclaim?

Things didn't change after the trading of hands, but he—and several other men—could not stand idly by as the soldiers who killed neighbors and loved ones to ransack their home from the lord.

And it all culminated when they attacked the soldiers when they were off duty, championing in the taverns like a spoil of war. They knew the faces of the invaders well, plastered in the seats of those who gave their lives to defend Belford.

They knew the consequences when they tailed the leader of those soldiers—if you could call them that, they're really mercs—and tried to stab her in an alley.

But it all backfired, and he could hear the others breathing and praying under their breath. *Oh, Dagda...*

The long walk pulled them through the throes of town, hearing the gasps and whispers of their neighbors.

Oh, that Irin—shh honey don't speak too loudly. They'll hear you. The muffled cries of kin as they watched their da' or uncle dragged out of town. And the noise all persisted until they heard the gates open and the light shone through the sack. He could see the vague shape of the field.

One by one the sacks came off. The sun glared in their eyes, facing southeast over the vast, lush field in the mid-morning heat. If he wanted to die, he would have picked a day that wouldn't have been so hot.

A voice cleared their throat behind. One man next to him turned around but received a blow from the soldier nearest. He eyed him out of the corner of his eye as he saw red appear on the other's face.

"We stand here," the voice boomed, albeit shaky, "To charge the accused of treason on the hands of Erria."

Another clearing of the throat. "I, Vassal Escar, hereby charge Orus, Scot, Bihl, and Irin, all of Belford, for treason. Witnesses hereby gave right to the charge, unnamed for their own safety."

The soldiers behind the men released them by cutting their rope ties and pushed the men out towards the field. He watched as the other men turned their heads, gasped, and sprinted out in the field.

The glimpse of fear in their eyes made Irin want to run forward without looking back, but he did anyway.

The same fear chilled every bone in his body. He ran despite the numbness washing over him.

Escar's voice faded as he ran, but he still heard it well. "For these actions, the accused are hereby sentenced to death by a hail of arrows."

Irin and the others tried to run, but all of them stopped when the sky was blotted out by a dark cloud overhead. They collapsed to their knees as they prayed (*Oh Dagda*) while they were skewered by a hail of arrows.

IV

The interior of a tavern was in an uproar of jovialities as many drank into a stupor. The noise was a sharp racket, the greatest noise coming from the corner of the bar as a group of off-duty soldiers rallied in a small crowd. Many of the locals side-eyed this but kept silent, drinking their shots to burn their fears away.

The crowd was jeering as the woman soldier was chugging a pint of alcohol alongside another soldier. The man slumped down in the corner as she chased down more, finishing off her glass with a loud uproar of approval by the crowd. She laughed and slapped him on the back.

"Come now, Jude, are you gonna let a girl beat you at a drinking game?"

Jude groaned and dry heaved. "Ain't no ordinary girl, are ye, commander?"

The crowd laughed and drank some more. Jude ended up passing out in the corner and the rest of the party continued. The commander moved on over to the bar and flagged down the bartender.

"Aye, can we get some more pitchers? We are runnin' a tad bit dry."

She peered to her side to see a man sitting at the bar. Beside him were two swords leaning against his stool, the leather straps tied tightly around them. They were large, both with fairly standard scabbards—though the top near the locket had wide slits on the sides to allow easier unsheathing—but one of them caught her eye. It had a unique hilt, fashioned much like an unlit torch. There was something dazzling to her in the folded patterns of the blade. In her drunken stupor a smile crept across her lips.

"I haven't seen you around 'ere before. A traveler, I presume?"

The man leaned back and turned to look at her. His rugged face was covered with a short, dark brown beard but accented by piercing blue eyes, enough to startle her.

"Aye, just passing through," he rasped. "Just stopping long enough to wet my throat and to continue heading Northwest."

The bartender delivered the pitchers, but she ignored them, climbing onto the stool next to the man. Her eyes were glazed as she shook her head.

"That ain't no good. I gotta tell ya, ain't nothing northwest, 'cept for the Dark Forest."

The man chuckled. "'Tis a pretty good name. Very unique and descriptive."

She ignored his interjection and stretched her arms as wide as she could, swaying slightly before balancing on the stool. "It spans *this* much of the northwest. The only thing you're fixin' to find there is getting lost."

She stared into his cold blue eyes for a moment, her eyes swimming in them. She pulled herself out of a dazed and fiddled with the pitchers.

"What's yer name?"

His eyes didn't shift, keeping them on her and he grabbed his tumbler.

"Kael." Kael swirled the drink before taking a swig again. He felt the bourbon burn down his throat. He only broke his eye contact tour gauge how much liquor he had left.

"Y'know, I've heard that name before...." She leaned back on the stool with a puzzled brow. "Ah, well, it can't be helped. The name's Azalea." She peered over his shoulder at the swords. "I take it you're a swordsman?"

"Just a vagabond passing through is all," he said as he cocked his head toward his swords. "The bigger the monster, the bigger the weapon needs to be, right?" He smirked.

She smirked back. "Ain't that the truth. I've gotta say though, that one sword is pretty interesting." She began to reach past him to the torch sword. "Do ye mind if I take a look—"

Kael grabbed her wrist before she got too close, holding it so that she strained to stay in the stool. His blue eyes pierced through her and stopped her dead in her tracks.

"I do mind. I'm not one to let someone examine my swords." He glanced over her shoulder to her company, who was beginning to agitate at the sight. "Even if you happen to be a soldier, I have no cause to show you my weapons."

"It's alright," she said. She took her hand back and shook it slightly. His grip was stronger than she would have thought. She furrowed her brow, "Kael... Kael...." She shook her head a few times. "Ah, no use. So, vagabond, do you have any stories of your travels?"

Kael shook his head. "Not any worth talking about right now. It seems, though, that this town has seen some better days. "

Another smile crept on her lips, though Kael thought it looked more sinister.

"Aye, we just took Belford under control of the house of Erria. It took us a while, but we were able to breach their walls. Of course, we got paid handsomely for taking the head of the lord." She smiled. "What a surprise it was for him to have his head lopped off by a girl."

Kael took a swig of his drink. "It shouldn't be. Man or woman can swing a blade. There really shouldn't be any surprises anymore. I heard there have been monster sightings near towns and cities as of late."

"That's true," she said. "I heard of merrows swimming in the Ofria near Shropeshire, and some have sighted ghouls in cemeteries close to town. It's almost as if—"

"—there's nothing left for them in the wilderness?" Kael glanced at her as he completed her thought. She nodded and he sighed. "I've seen it as I've traveled, too. Usually, these creatures stay away from civilization, but they've grown emboldened. Maybe the winds have changed, maybe they have tired of the food they've eaten out in the wild and seek something more fulfilling. Only they know their reasoning."

The two continued to talk about trifling subjects, about swordplay and battle scars. The conversations led into the night and Azalea's group left, leaving the two to stagger out in the moonlight much later.

He had a room at the only inn in town, and she ended up in his bed. Their breathing was in tandem as they slept together, the sheen of sweat dripping from his skin in the candlelight in the summer heat. She twisted her

183

hand into his hair and pulled him in for a kiss and entwined with him for half the night.

When they were done, he laid beside her and stared at the ceiling, closing his eyes every now and then for a long spell. She laid her hand on him in such a gentle manner, unlike her commander role. The hand was calloused, but it still felt soft to him. She traced scars on his chest, scars of assorted sizes and shapes. Some were clean and some looked like they had been ripped through his skin.

"What did you do to get so many scars?"

Kael opened his tired eyes and stared at her. Her face was sobered, the glassy expression gone. It had a mixture of curiosity and worry.

A weak smile came across his face. "My father taught me how to be a monster hunter since I was young. It was a way to make money, I suppose. There's no shortage of monsters."

She nodded absentmindedly and continued tracing the scars. She would examine it as she traced them, then she stopped for a moment and glanced at his face. "So, what kind of beast would cause a scar like this?" She traced a large puncture wound on his bicep.

He studied the wound and furrowed his brow. "A harpy, I believe. It was some job that he heard from one of his friends, how there was a forest near Durecht in the south that was overrun by harpies. They couldn't get any wagons through the forest without being attacked."

He took in a deep breath and turned to the window. It was still dark despite their lengthy endeavor, with no trace of sunrise coming.

"I remember that the nest was up high, on a large cliff in a mountain close to the forest. I followed a lot of trails and scents in the area to reach the cliff and nearly died while scaling it. The nest was in a cave in the mountains. It was dark and I was young, but I lit a torch and threw it into the nest."

He took a deep breath. "It burned and screeched, not sure if it was from any harpy burning or just the nest itself. But once it started burning, all the harpies came at me at once. I've got some other scars from them—" he pointed on his side and pulled his leg out to point at another, "—but as I was fighting them, one of their talons pierced through my arm and it began to fly out of the cave."

He traced the bicep scars himself, his face blank as he was lost in thought.

"I was barely hanging on, trying to hold myself up so that it didn't tear through my arm and drop me. It couldn't fly too far, as I was heavy with all my weapons, and the other harpies were behind us. We both dropped from the cliff and the harpy was able to slow us down enough that the ground didn't kill us, but I broke several bones."

"Ijos heard the commotion from afar and as I was fighting the pack he dispatched them with a crossbow. After that, I started to carry a crossbow with me. Swords dinnae make for good weapons against flying beasts." He chuckled a little.

Azalea propped herself up on an arm and gazed at him. Her pale skin glistened in the moonlight from sweat. Kael took in the beauty of it until she snapped him out of his thoughts.

"It seems like you were close to your father. Ijos, right? That's what your father's name is?"

He stared directly into her eyes, his own quivered slightly. Was it fear? He seemed a little reluctant to talk about the man. He sighed and little and averted his gaze.

"Yeah, Ijos was his name. He used to travel with me to these jobs when I was younger. At least, until I was about sixteen. Then I would go on my own and come back with money and food."

She rolled onto her back and stared at the ceiling. He did the same, the darkness blurring as sleep began to blanket him.

"Ijos. It sounds familiar..." She pondered on the name as she began to doze off, and so did Kael.

Eissizir Weald

I

The sun rose and dew evaporated with the oncoming heat, creating a rising fog. Kael awoke as the sun crept over the horizon with Azalea still slumbering heavily. He clothed quietly and slipped out of the room without making much sound, though she did not stir when he did.

He closed the door behind him and paused as he gazed at her peaceful face. A part of him wanted to stay, but his resolve won in the end.

He left the inn without breakfast to retrieve Jorunn from the stable. When he tied his belongings to set out, he tipped the stable boy with a Quek, a small bronze coin that was the base coin of most of the kingdoms.

He left Belford at a trot and headed northwest to the Dark Forest. Jorunn trotted faster once they left the walls, and he examined the landscape change from a grassy field to jagged outcrops as he passed the base of a mountain range.

The expansive forest was still far off, and the mountains overtook most of the landscape for now. He could strain his eyes and see the darkness that the tree lines offered.

The noise of Belford faded as he pushed onward, the rocky foothills of the mountains proving· to be a challenge for Jorunn. Kael urged her on not by spurring her but by patting her neck to encourage her to take her time.

Kael turned in his saddle as he heard hooves behind him, only to see the mercenary band led by Azalea tailing him. Their gallops caught up to his careful gait quickly with Azalea's smirk leading the pack.

"You didn't think you could fuck and run, did ya?"

Kael grunted and averted his eyes. "Kind of. What do you want?"

"Well, we've finished our job in Belford, and this seems interesting enough. Right, boys?" She turned her men.

All the men agreed to their leader with a controlled, quiet rally. She turned around and smiled at Kael.

"Besides, the Dark Forest is dangerous. You might need some allies."

He pulled Jorunn back around to face his goal and began to trot away. "Suit yourself. Just dinnae get in my way or distract me."

Kael picked up his gait as the rocky land evened out. The distance between him and the group lengthened little by little as he passed through the foothills. Gravel would occasionally roll down the hill and he would watch for anything, though it always ended up as nothing.

The group reached the looming tree lines as the sun neared its peak. The shadows cast by the tree line were cool to their sun-heated skin, making the sweat that coated them even cooler.

The trees were much larger in this area than Kael has ever seen before, some nearly as wide as a castle tower, and most of the roots were large enough a man could fit inside them if they were hollow.

The mercenary band murmured quietly behind him, reveling at the size and mystique of the forest. Kael stared inside the canopy of trees and saw that the distance blurred due to a fog that enveloped the dense foliage.

Kael moved Jorunn forward when he heard some whispers or protest behind him. He stopped and turned to face them.

"Not coming?" A smirk plastered his face.

Azalea snapped out of her awestruck stare of the massive trees to return with a mocking smirk of her own. "Of course. Let's go, boys."

Kael and Azalea were the first to enter the forest. She caught up to his gait quickly and matched it, but both were struck by the green tinted twilight cast by the ceiling of leaves.

The forest felt different than the foothills of the mountains; even the temperature was much milder, much more that to a cool spring day. Rocks were replaced by gnarled roots that grew more plentiful as they trekked deeper inside, coating the floor and exuding a feeling that they pulsed like veins.

The horses felt uneasy, and their steps were flighty. But Kael kept Jorunn under control better than the rest by soothing her. The deeper they went into the forest, the more Kael felt uneasy himself.

We are being watched. He scanned the vast entanglement of trees, at the enshroudment of shadows cast by the dense foliage. His ears pricked up and focused on all the noises, from the chittering of small mammals to the chirping of the various birds, but he could not hear any suspicious sounds.

He focused his hearing a little more and heard the babbling of a small brook in the distance, to their left. His attention was diverted when Azalea guided her horse closer to him.

"Do you hear anything?" She turned to him "I noticed you was focused, and it seemed like you were trying to hear something.

He straightened himself up in his saddle. "Nothing out of the ordinary, just the wildlife of the area. There is some running water nearby, though."

She sighed quickly. It came out more like exasperation, but her face was that of amazement.

"How did you learn to do that? The enhanced hearing, I mean. I can't really hear much in here, and I definitely don't hear any creek or river."

Kael guided Jorunn over a clump of roots, tied almost like a knot.

"When you live in a forest and hunt for a living, you become accustomed to listening to nature. You can tune to certain parts of the area better and separate the noises. That's what Ijos taught me."

"What kind of man was your father?" Azalea asked. Kael shrugged and stretched his shoulders.

"He was quiet. He had a bad leg and couldn't fight much anymore, or at least not like he used to, so he taught me instead. He looked somber most of the time, like he had lost something. But he loved me, or so it seemed."

He furrowed his brow, his face showing discontent. "We lived in a small, secluded village in the mountains further east. There were others, in the village, I mean. The mountain may be part of the same range as the one we passed, since it extended behind Belford and to the east. I think we were closer to the plateau that enters the Vrall territory."

"He told me that he was a monster hunter himself in his youth, that he saved me from some monsters that attacked a village. Apparently, he had been tracking them for weeks and their patterns were sporadic. Our home had a vast collection of books on monsters and fighting styles, and he would regularly take me down to the forest at the foothills of the range to train."

191

"He seems like a good man." Azalea said.

"Yeah, he was." Azalea watched as he turned his head away. She caught a small glimpse of his face as it turned to see it contort in pain.

They continued in silence for some time before they happened on a small river that ran through the forest. Azalea stared in bewilderment as he raised his eyebrows. Kael then dismounted and walked by the river, pulling out a map and examining it. Azalea peered over his shoulder from her horse.

"That map is outdated." She dismounted and pointed at some places. "These towns are no longer there anymore." Her hand hovered over Caede for a second before she pulled it away.

"It was just a map from home that I took with me. I have no idea how old it is." He shrugged. "It doesn't have any details on the forest, though. It has it as a different name on here, though. Eissizir Weald."

One of the men walked up to the two. "I've heard that name. When I was a wee lad, my ma' would say that the Eissizir Weald was where the witch of the world lived."

Kael cast him a sideways glance. "Witch of the world?"

"Aye, you heard right. The story goes that it is an enchantress that has lived here since the beginning."

Azalea shifted her feet and said, "My dad used to say that humans came to this land a long time ago. By the time we came here, the Dwarves and elves had already been here for centuries."

The man nodded his head. "I've heard that too. I also heard that dragons used to be here as well. Large, magnificent beasts that were intelligent. They used to teach their ways to the foreigners that came here. The witch, though, was said to have been here long before them. She was said to have given life to the animals and plants of the land. She was called the mother of this land."

"When the foreigners came, she greeted them and gave them shelter and food. Her only desire was for them to give to the land as much as they took. And they did that, cultivating the land and raising animals, only killing to eat what was necessary. She would walk amongst the towns they built, tending to the humans, and teaching them her ways."

"As time went on, though, man began to take more than give. Greed set in, and they would steal from one another and kill for sport. The mother was unhappy, casting plagues on the people who defied her. It wasn't long before man began to fight one another, murdering and pillaging not only their own kind, but that of the elves and dwarves, too. They developed weapons to kill dragons, and the mother feared they would one day destroy the lands."

"Amongst those who pillaged and killed, there was a man who was consumed by his greed and hate, and he rose up and ended up leading a massive army. They say he was so consumed with bloodlust and violence that he became a monster himself, and his men were the same."

"The lands were awash in blood and flames, and the mother's fear was coming true, so she did the only thing she could do. She cast a curse on these men and banished them to another dimension, one that was already burning. Ruhe'll, as they called it. The curse sealed this dimension shut with all their weapons and malice, bound by magical chains and a magical key that was broken into seven pieces, and given to the elders of an ancient race for safekeeping."

Kael sighed and laughed. "What a great bedtime story. I bet you wouldn't sleep all night thinking about it, huh?"

Azalea laughed too. "Just a kid's story. Right, Thopps?"

The man, Thopps, laughed too. "Aye, I was always wondering if those pieces really existed. Maybe my ma' told me that so I would be more mindful. She used to say she would take me to the witch for her to put a curse on me too."

They all laughed. But then a large groan echoed in the forest. Kael unsheathed his claymore and poised for an attack. A flock of crows broke the canopy, cawing as they fled in the sky. The forest was silent, save for the crashing of small waves in the river.

The silence broke as there was a thud in the distance. And another. The noise became a rhythm and a large being appeared in the distance, moving towards them. It was covered in vines and had a human-like face, but its eyes were black with a speck of white light in it. The group scurried to dodge a large vine the giant used as a whip.

"What the fuck is that?!" Azalea yelled as she tried to calm her horse. Kael had already mounted Jorunn and whipped past her, towards the giant.

"A golem!" Kael yelled. His sword was still in his hand, using it to cut stray vines that whipped the ground. The mercenary band was in chaos, the men being whipped by the vines, leaving large cuts on their skin.

"Keep your distance!" His voice was barely heard over the chaos.

He evaded vines as he maneuvered through the battle on Jorunn, men slicing at the vines. Kael watched as the vines regenerated after they were cut, their efforts fruitless. The vines slammed down in chaos, shaking the forest floor and causing the men to topple over or fly into the air. One man had his sword stuck in a thick vine, causing him to pull up into the air as it retreated. He fell from a decent height into another man.

Kael slowed down to a gallop as he tried to rationalize. His eyes darted over the golem, inspecting it for any flaw. The dense foliage of its body squirmed like snakes over one another, creating a near impregnable armor. Its head was square and stony, though snake-like vines covered most of it.

He thought that if he was alone, he could take his time to scour a weakness. But these men followed him here and he did not wish to bury anyone today. He could feel his chest tighten and a vein pulse in his head as he grew irritated that he could find a weakness.

He then felt a *whoosh* as Azalea passed him at full gallop. One hand held the reins, but another was outstretched with a little torch pointing away from the airflow. It glowed bright in the dimness of the forest, basking the cool green in the warm orange of the fire.

Azalea evaded a few vines as she closed in on the golem—who, guided by the light of the flames, now focused on her—and flung the torch like a javelin as she got close enough. A vine slammed down close to her jolting her horse, which bucked her off under the golem.

The forest burned brightly of fire as the golem was consumed by it. A grating sound came from the thing, jarring them slightly as it grew louder. The sound was accompanied by a barrage of thugs as the golem hit itself with its vines, putting out the fire before it spread too much further.

The fire had spread far from the torch and fast, creating a gaping hole in its chest. Seeing this gave a jolt to Kael, giving him an idea. He kicked Jorunn back into a gallop as the golem resumed its rampage, then men fleeing and fighting.

Kael swooped close by and pulled Azalea behind him, saving her from a stomp from one of its stone-laden leg. He then circled back around and bound straight towards the back of the thing, its attention diverting back to the swarm of men in front of it.

I need to get close to it, then I can use it. He
spurred Jorunn faster, pushing her to gallop faster amidst
the battle. As he got close to the golem, he pulled the
other sword from his back, took a deep breath, and
muttered. He stood on the saddle and, when he got close
enough, he leapt, spinning in the air towards the golem.

His swords began to smoke and then ignited,
flames coating the blades as he cut through the body of
the golem. The flames whipped out as he lunched in the
air, forming two whipping tails.

He cut through the body and rolled as he landed
and turned as the flames spread. The golem staggered and
dissipated into ash before too long, the vines burning away
as well.

Kael felt a shiver run through him, a chill that took
some energy with it. His heart was pounding in his ears
for a few seconds, but his inner voice was screaming. *I did
it! I was able to do it again!* He then heard a faint voice
calling his name, but it ebbed off as the men and Azalea
crowded around him.

The men murmured as Kael stood up and rotated
his shoulder some, working out the soreness. Azalea came
up on Jorunn with her own horse in tow. He rubbed one
of his shoulders as she beamed down at him, discounting
and handing over his reins.

"What the hell was that?" She was awestruck. "I
haven't seen anything like that since..." She shook her
head in bewilderment.

"Ijos taught me ancient arts that was passed down in his clan. While I cannae use it like him, I still have some power to it." *Is that right? Ijos used to say that a deity would grant power if you asked for it. But it was, in some ways, and bond...*

"It looks pretty useful to me." Kael stared at Azalea and then averted his gaze to the river. The fog was still thick in the distance. He had no idea what was ahead.

"We shouldn't stay still long. Whatever this was is likely just the start." He mounted Jorunn. "We should follow the river upstream. We may find something that way."

The group only stayed long enough to patch up the minor wounds the soldiers had before they began their journey again. Kael glanced back at the pile of ash as he pushed away the buzzing in his head. His mind was trying to focus on the feeling he had when he conjured the flames and the voice calling to him. It seemed familiar, just like the time with the bandits.

He brushed it off and thought about the golem and its attacks, furrowing his brow as he analyzed what he recollected of the battle. *It wasn't trying to kill us,* he thought. *It could have, but the largest vines just hit around us. It was just trying to drive us away.*

II

198

The group trekked deeper into the forest and followed the river for quite some time. The shadows were beginning to darken and the group stopped and made camp at sunset. The men huddled close to the fire, almost flinching away from the encroaching, mystical darkness.

The air changed to a near constant sense of foreboding, the darkness beyond the glare of the fire hiding any possible threat. The men were spooked from the golem and every noise made them jump.

A rustle in a thicket of branches caused some of the men to moan out of fear and jump before a silhouette parted the bushes and came towards them. The orange glow illuminated Kael walked out of the darkness holding an armload of branches. He scowled at the group as he dropped the wood on the ground.

"Dinnae piss your pants, boys. I'm sure you dinnae have a change of clothes. Of course, you could just wash 'em off in the river." He smiled crookedly and thumbed back to the babbling water. "That is, if you're not afraid of what may lurk in there. Maybe you'll get lucky with some merrows."

"Fuck off!" One man said. "We aren't some baby who pisses their knickers."

The men rebounded in agreement but shook out of their skin when they heard a wave crash behind them. Azalea laughed as she threw another stone into the water.

"Cowards," she said, laughing again. The men murmured amongst themselves as Kael passed the group towards Azalea. She was perched on a moss-covered stone, staring into the fire. He noticed her stare pierced through.

Kael sat down beside her. His hair was wet, and he wore a black shirt that clung to his wet skin. He held his claymore and popped the blade out a little to inspect it.

"Earlier, you said you haven't seen a skill like mine since some time, but you broke it off. Have you seen it before?"

She furrowed her brow, fiddling at a small twig. "I... I can't really remember. It seems familiar to me, but I don't know how."

Kael leaned back onto his elbows. "It disnae matter now. You've seen it now. Where are you from?"

"I lived in the capital for years with my mother and my uncle," She bit her lip and averted her eyes. "But I ran away a long time ago. My uncle was a terrible man. He... he did a lot of horrible things."

She glanced at the twig and then threw it in the fire, the light catching the glistening tears on her face." I was born in a town in the northeast, though. A town called Caede, but that town was—"

"Destroyed," Kael interrupted. "I saw the ruins myself. I was born there, too." Azalea eyes shot up to him, and he smiled. "Maybe we knew each other then."

"Maybe you're right. But my dad was the Lord of the town. He died protecting it." Kael glanced at Jorunn and the other sword that he got from the rubble of Caede.

"My mom protected us as we traveled to Mynheir, to my uncle, Haskell. He was my dad's older brother." Her lips quivered. "We lost my brothers while on that path. Some highwaymen... they killed them as they took us."

Kael grimaced. He felt a pain of familiarity with her words, but he wasn't sure either. He laced his fingers with hers slowly. "The world is cruel," he gazed at her solemnly, "and war knows no boundaries."

The words resonated hard within Azalea, racking her brain loose a shard within her mind. She could see a worn-out swordsman who told her the same words after losing her brothers, losing her innocence within the world. Kael had the same tired expression. He released her hand and laid down, rolling over away from her.

"I feel like tomorrow will be more exhausting than this one. We should get some rest."

She nodded and laid down herself. The fires burnt down to embers by the time she slept, but she had at some point rolled towards his back, his hand resting on his opposite side, and she laced her own hand within it. They stayed that way as they slept, not as lovers, but rather like children who found comfort within one another, to ward off the harshness of the world.

III

The morning brought dew from the canopy, extinguishing the flames before they woke up. It proved to be helpful as they did not have to worry about grass or trees catching fire, like the forest watched for itself.

Azalea was patting her horse down and making sure her tiedowns were snug when Kael came up her astride Jorunn. He wore his red tunic and battle armor again, but she could only look at the peculiar torch-esque sword that peered over his left shoulder.

She smirked as he helped her into her saddle, despite being able to do it herself.

"Y'know, the black shirt was more fitting for a hunter. Plus, you looked good in it as well."

He chuckled softly. "Maybe so, but I'm not trying to hide while hunting." He examined his clothes. "Oddly enough, most beasts see in monochrome anyway. The cannae tell the difference between green and red."

She pulled a strap tight, but her brow furrowed with realization. "Red really suits you more, anyways. Especially after seeing you control fire."

Kael exhaled sharply though his nose. It was ironic to think that he could control fire when his attempts paled in comparison to that of his mentor. Ijos made it appear so effortless while he had to focus and audibly chant an incantation for it to work. Maybe this is what Ijos meant by divine power is not inherent, but rather brought to fruition by persistence.

The group continued their aimless path for something after they packed their camp, riding alongside the river for hours with no interruption. That is, until one of the men yelled for the group to stop.

"I can smell cooked food!"

The group sniffed the air, and it was as he said. It felt familiar and unknown at the same time. A soup, but with an underlying scent that could not be placed. The scent itself sat like a stone in your stomach, emanating an insatiable hunger from it.

The group sniffed the air as they wandered, searching for its source. The scent was stronger coming from a faint wind from the north, which permeated the forest despite the density of the trees. The group galloped through the forest, led by their noses, until they could see a small stone hut breaking the landscape in a clearing.

Kael was at the side of the pack when he noticed the river bubbling. Azalea was galloping beside him when he grabbed her reins and pulled both their horses to a stop.

"Halt and heed!" His voice echoed in the clearing that they had not yet reached.

The group did not stop, nor did he want to stop. It was by sheer willpower that he could stop himself, even more so to stop Azalea, not without some protest. She tried to pull her reins free to no avail, all while he repeated his warning several times.

The rest of the group was in a frenzy to find the food, such a frenzy that they did not see the water pour out of the river and onto the land until it was too late. The water took form like a whip and knocked the group off their horses as they entered the clearing, then it slithered onto land. It assumed a slender, rope shape and its heads split into three, each turning into an amorphous shape of a serpent head.

"Hydra!" The men yelled in unison. The water serpent shot streams of water at the group, sending any who were hit sliding across the grassy meadow. Kael squeezed his legs into Jorunn and hiked her into a gallop.

The serpent turned its amorphous heads to him and shot several streams his way before swiping its body at him. He evaded the attacks and once again perched on the saddle, unsheathing both blades. He took a deep sigh before he murmured again, waiting until the last second to jump.

The serpent did not have enough time to sling its body again, leaving it vulnerable. His blades hissed and ignited as he jumped, the flames roaring in the air. He aimed for the base of the heads for his attack, and he sliced in an x-pattern. The water hissed as it evaporated, and the heads severed.

But as Kael landed on the other side, he turned to see the heads were back with another added to it. It sent four jets of water to him and knocked him off his feet, sliding across the meadow near the river side.

He felt dazed as his blades hissed from the steam. He stumbled up as the serpent shot a stream again, only evading the water as he sidestepped slowly. He noticed its tail was still submerged in the river. The serpent shot several jets of water again, Kael dodging them as he closed the distance.

He held his blades close, taking deep breaths as he ran, igniting his blades again. This time he could envision the whipping of white tails in his mind allowing the flames to strengthen, imitating those tails in orange form.

The serpent sent jetstream after jetstream, but Kael narrowly missed them. It lunged the midsection of its body out like an outstretched arm, a desperate attempt to pluck the warrior from his path, but it was to no avail.

He reached the base of the beast and pivoted his blades into the ground as he somersaulted, plunging both blade on the return into the tail, severing the link between the serpent and the river. It let out a screech, like the hiss of evaporating water, as the flames of the blade bubbled up the body and out the mouths of the heads.

The flames protruded and whipped, only at the last moment did it seem to take some ethereal form. Kael could have swore it looked canine in nature, all coupling with the same whispering of *Kael* in his head that seemed to accompany the flames.

The water dissipated from its form and dropped to the ground in puddles, absorbed by the lush grass of the meadow. Kael surveyed the disheveled group and saw no one was severely injured. At most, he saw some people were bruised, but no broken bones either. He was not surprised.

Thopps gaped at the meadow. He was soaked from head to toe. "What the hell was a Hydra doing in a forest?"

"That was not a hydra." Kael flicked his blades before sheathing them. He flapped his arms to get some of the excess water out of his tunic. "I don't know what the hell it was."

"That was a Vatnmur," a voice echoed.

It was like a whisper right into your ear, ephemeral in the stillness of the meadow. A slender figure appeared at the door of the cottage in the meadows. A flowing, faded dress cloaked most features, save for a dark porcelain face that looked both old and young at the same time, accented by long hair the color of bright light.

"A guardian of the lovely Eissizir Weald." She walked across the meadow to the group, her gait a flow much like water. She stopped in front of Kael.

"The child, aye?" Her eyes pierced through him like a knife. "Yes, the child of fate. I should have known the first time you exhibited the skills passed from Ijos."

On his face bloomed a blank realization as a name jutted from his tongue. It felt red hot and warmed his whole body.

"Aveline." A smile crept on his lips as he embraced her, surprising himself as he felt the warmth of familiarity.

From the Veil

I

The inside of the cottage was larger than the outside, housing many plants and artifacts of nature. The main room felt less like a room and more of an extension of the meadow; the supporting beams were covered with moss and there was a consistent light within the home, like the sun was glowing effervescently.

In the center was a throne made of vines like the one the golem was made of, moving slightly as if alive. In the throne sat Aveline, who invited the group into her home from the meadow.

They all sat on the moss-covered ground in awe of the tranquility of the cottage, with its everlasting spring weather in an enclosed space. Kael stood close to the throne and observed the meadow-like structures for a moment before turning to her.

"This all seems surreal." Kael stared at Aveline with disbelief, scratching his rough cheek absentmindedly. "Like it could be a painting or a dream."

She smiled at him, her flawless face showing no wrinkles or blemish. "Reality is often more surprising than dreams. You have seen this before, child."

He cocked his head for a moment. "I suppose so." He furrowed his brow and rested at the throne base. His stature kept their eyes aligned. "I cannae remember, but I know I came here.

Aveline did not stir in her seat, returning the intense stare that Kael was giving her. He felt like she was reading his mind, knew it in a way, but he continued.

He rummaged in his pouch and returned his hand outstretched with the tumen in his upturned palm.

"This coin held something to me. A memory, and a memory block all the same. It showed something that happened to me when I was younger, and how Ijos—" he stammered for a moment, "—uttered your name as he examined an illness I had. I came this way to search for you, for your help. Maybe to make sense of it all."

She closed her eyes and nodded. Her eyes flicked beneath her eyelids like she was examining a book, rolling from left to right several times. Her eyes opened as she exhaled slowly.

"I knew you would. You have a dark veil over your past, Kael. I put another over top of it to protect you when Ijos brought you here."

She stayed in her seat and placed her hands in front of her, displaying them like a rose blooming. In that he could see a vivid picture of the forest, though he could feel it was different. Older.

"It would help if I told you how you came to this forest the first time. You see. When Ijos brought you, you were succumbing to a potent poison from a lamia..."

II

The meadow in Eissizir Weald was basking in the pure light of day while Aveline harvested some of the wildflowers in the meadow. There was a faint wind that weaved its way through the dense foliage and into the meadow, bringing with it a chill. The meadow was fixed in a spring temperament compared to the brisk, chilly winter the rest of the world experienced.

Aveline felt no shiver from the cold, but her body shook as she felt a presence enter the forest in a fervor. Nature transmitted to their master that it was two souls; one in a state of fatigue and fear, the other was a swirl of darkness, like a toxic swamp.

There was a mixture of chaos within the soul, slowly cracking it from the inside out. There was still light within it, but where there were cracks, a darkness had seeped through.

Aveline stood in the field and focused on those two souls. Focused not with her mind, but with her connection to the forest. She knelt and placed a hand on the ground and a pulse moved the blades of grass away from her hand.

She signaled the golem that patrols the dense foliage through the vast root connections to protect the forest from these unknown beings. Through the forest, the nerve-like roots transmitted the order to the golem, which stopped and traveled towards the invaders immediately.

The two humans who entered the forest were Ijos and Kael. Ijos was carrying the child in his arms, cradling as he ran. Nuria was flying overhead, dodging thickets of branches that created the canopy. Ijos' gait was staggered like a wounded animal, his panting echoing off the gigantic trees that inhabited the forest. The forest had no markers for a trail and the trees and dense foliage made the environment appear the same in every direction. There was a light fog, too, that perpetually covered the forest.

He did not stop, instead he closed his eyes as he ran. His feet did not stumble, and he evaded the trees as he passed them. The underbrush caught his legs several times and ripped at him, cutting through the cloth of his pants and cutting his legs, but he continued.

He focused on his hearing while he closed his eyes, listening to the vibrations of the trees so he could move around them, but that was not his goal. In the fare distance he could hear the breaking of waves, a body of water that is within the dense forest. That was where he was headed to.

Ijos sprinted with light feet despite his wounds, barely touching the ground as he traversed the foggy space, reaching a small river enshrouded within the dense copse. He stopped at the riverbank and scanned left and right. He turned right and followed the river.

He heard a thud in the distance and pushed himself to run faster. He did not need to be stopped by anything, not with Kael in danger. He opened his eyes to see the boy's pallor had turned ashen.

His breathing is shallow now. I need to hurry. He patted Kael's face, wiping away a thick coat of sweat. Although the air was cool in the forest, they were both drenched in sweat for different reasons. "C'mon, Kael. Stay awake."

The boy stirred only a little, letting out a faint moan. His eyes opened and rolled back into his head, then closed again.

"Fuck." Ijos pushed himself harder and ran faster, following the river.

There was a crash as a vine slammed down right behind him. Amid his worry, he had lost focus on his surroundings. A huge green golem stumbled towards them on the right. Its gait was jagged and broken—like a puppet. Like its extremities were being pulled by invisible strings.

The vine that slammed down retreated and repositioned, slamming down again close to the duo, though Ijos' lunged away from the attack each time.

213

Ijos' gait was still broken by the wound on his side, where blood was still seeping slowly. The sharp movements he contended opened the wound more and more.

Nuria screeched in the distance as she swooped down, divebombing towards the retreating vine. Her body was engulfed in flames as it connected with the vine, catching the green whip on fire. The vine was inundated with the fire, spreading up the length of it and towards the body.

An audible sound akin to metal being shredded poured out of the mass that is the golem, its movements turning robust as it flung itself into the river. Waves crashed wildly as it accepted this offering, like a mouth opened wide for food, flooding the shoreline. Ijos jumped further back to avoid the crashing of water from the river.

Steam poured from the section of the river where the golem submerged. It bubbled as the mass was swallowed whole before the waves seized and became calm once again. Ijos stood at the river briefly before he ran. His gait returned as staggered as before, though the wound was more apparent this time.

He sprinted no more than fifty feet before the waves crashed again, giving rise to a resurrected golem. The flame was extinguished, but the scars present on the vines were present. Singed sections of the vine caused it to wildly flail as it exited the river, the vines barely holding together by a few strands.

Ijos cursed under his breath. He leapt wildly like a wounded animal, creating enough distance from the golem in the densely wooded area.

He knew he could not escape it for long, so he found a downed tree and laid the sick Kael in a hole in the trunk and turned around to face the golem. It had struggled getting out of the river and onto the banks proving the river was deeper than it seemed. Now it was tumbling towards him with fervor, almost humanlike in its gait.

Ijos whistled and began to run towards the giant. He could sense Nuria flying by his shoulder as he ran towards the golem, taking a deep breath as the phoenix spiraled into flames and coated his blade again. He felt his muscles tense up and swell with the newfound strength, his wounds numbing as he was consumed by the magic of his deity.

His gait strengthened as he lunged at the golem, his red blade slicing through the legs and crippling the giant even more. Flames came from the embers born by the cut and began to spread up the golem's legs.

It slammed one of its long arms down at Ijos but missed—the man imbued with magic was faster than before. His breathing was more ragged as he felt consumed by the flames, but he paid no heed as he swung down and severed the resting arm, then severed the other as it swung it down in childlike retaliation.

The golem lay on the ground like a baby learning to keep its head up. It dull, glowing eyes peered at Ijos. A rumble came from the empty shell it called a body. His eyes were calm as he cut the head of the golem, severing it with the flames spreading and eating away at the vines that it was made of.

Nuria exited the blade, and with her she took that immense power. Ijos could feel it sucked out of him like a strong wind, taking his breath away at that moment. Then the pain began to flood back, bringing along with it a new pain of strained muscles, some the torn fibers of muscles strained too far.

Nuria perched on his shoulder for a second and cooed at him before she flew off to the downed tree trunk and sat beside the hole. He hurried to the trunk with his damaged body.

He held Kael and checked for a pulse. There was still a faint pulse, and his skin was a little cold in some places and scorching hot in the other. Ijos took no time to ponder or fret and started off again, trailing the river. His movements were a lot slower and more forced, but he still covered ground quickly.

When he felt like he could not go on anymore watching the trees pass in blurs, closing his eyes as his lungs were on fire, he stepped into a clearing and into a meadow of perpetual light.

And there she was, staring at him with wide eyes.

"Aveline." His own voice sounded distant, or like it was spoken through a wall.

That was all he remembered as he blacked out.

III

Aveline felt a shudder racket down her spine as she heard a crash in the forest. She still knelt and was peering through the eyes of the golem, whose sight was drowning in water.

Get up, ba'nashei. She could feel a humanlike shudder ripple through the golem as it forced itself up through the water and back onto land. Its eyes wavered as it emerged from the river, flailing its vines to retain its balance.

The golem lunged onto the riverbank and trudged through the forest groaning. Its vision could see the faint trail the Intruder had left, following it as it continued to flail its vines. She could see the vines were singed well, with many of the vines barely hanging on by few fibers. The embers still glowed despite the water—a glow nearly prismatic. Like the fire was magic.

I've seen this fire before. Her midnight raced as she dug into her endless memories before it clicked. *Golem, I need you to cease now, for your life.*

But it was too late. She could see the man through the golem's vision, and saw the prismatic flames engulf him as he charged the golem one last time. Aveline felt the heat through the connection slice off the limbs of the golem before the man stood directly in its vision.

Then the connection was severed, and the vision was black. The forest was quiet as Aveline stood and scanned the meadow. She closed her eyes to search for the aura of the man. At first it was dim, like an ember was fading out, but she could feel it spark again and then it was rushing.

Then it was here. The ember was at the meadow in the blink of an eye, blazing with fervor and fear in front of her. She opened her eyes to see the man and saw the face looked the same as before, with the red bird perch on his shoulder.

He still looks so tired.

The man took a deep breath, and a small smile crept on his lips.

"Aveline."

Then he fell. He fell so that his shoulder hit first and the boy he was cradling rolled safely onto the ground, rolling to her feet. She could feel the dark aura coming from this young boy. She knelt and felt the clammy skin, both hot and cold.

She then gasped as an influx of magic shocked her, like it was a whip lashing out. She could see an ancient face in that shock, causing her to redouble a recoil. She shuddered and ran to her cottage, returning in a swift manner with an old blanket.

She wrapped the boy gently enough, so she was not touched again and carried him to her cottage. She returned and began to drag the man there as well.

IV

Ijos woke to the smell of soup over a fire with dim sunlight in his eyes and warmth on his cheeks. His eyes focused on his surroundings in muted awe.

He was not outside but in a meadow encapsulated by a wooden dome and wooden beams covered by vines supporting it, but there was a warm, but soft, light that shone from every direction.

He was laying on a bed made of vines in this field. He tried to pull himself up but felt a distant pain on his side and remembered the knife that Kael shoved into him. He then panicked before his eyes settled on the boy wrapped in a blanket on a bed of vines close by. He eased a little.

Memories of this place flooded back. Memories of when he was a boy and stayed here for a portion of his childhood. A childhood, though that had been faded and worn before its true time.

He then flashed back to cherry blossoms falling amongst fire and felt his normally dry eyes well up with tears. He pushed it away and continued to get up.

"I wouldn't do that." A voice rose from the nature-covered home, though he did not see her. "Despite my capabilities, that wound has not fully healed. Too much movement and you will open it back up."

Aveline rounded the corner of a wooden wall , which he assumed was a hallway or another room. Flowers and vines covered the wall almost to the point that you could not see the wood.

In her hands were large acupuncture needles and gauze. She waltzed over to a pot suspended over a fire in a fireplace that stood in the middle of the home, the fireplace having three large openings from each side. She stirred the pot and pulled out a ladle of soup to rest into a bowl. She brought the bowl to him and knelt.

"It has been a long time, my child."

He took the bowl and drank the soup like water. The properties of the soup warmed him well as he drank it, numbing his wounds more than the leaves that were wrapped around his side.

"It has, Mother Aveline. I cry for your forgiveness for such a rude intrusion." He briefly averted his gaze. "And for your golem."

"It is no matter, Ijos. The ba'nashei can be made again. Normally it does not attack so ruthlessly at invaders—" she glanced over to Kael, "—though I suppose it may be because of the sick one."

Ijos shifted on the vine bed gently. "What of him? He's been bitten by a lamia, and the poison is spreading. I need your help—"

Aveline clasped the man's hand gently and patted it. "I've already extracted the poison and given him an antidote." She flashed a small vial with green liquid in it.

"The problem now—and what drew the lamia in the first place, as well as the golem—is he has a large swirling darkness within him."

"He has a vortex of dark, evil magic within him. It is not natural, but rather much like a curse. Bloodlust and hatred are just a small part of this magic. I think if it stays within him, it will consume him. He would become a monster in every sense."

Ijos could not find the words. Why would the boy become a monster? What happened to him?

"The sorcerer." His voice sounded hollow with despair.

Aveline nodded. "I do not know why he cursed this child, but he did."

"Can you do anything about it?"

Aveline took her hands away and held up the acupuncture needles once again.

"I can certainly try to extract it. It will take a lot, and I cannot do it alone."

Ijos and Aveline knelt over the boy with the needles in her hands. She took a deep breath and braced herself.

"He needs to be still the whole time. If these needles are even a little off, he will die."

Ijos nodded. The sweat gleamed on his face in sheets as he leaned over the sick child. Aveline plucked one of the needles out of the pile and held it like a quill.

She then hovered it over his neck and with one swift movement, plunged it into his skin.

Kael shot awake as the needle turned red from heat and began to scream and thrash. Ijos held him down to prevent him from moving.

Aveline was stone faced as she plunged another needle into his neck, and another. As each needle was stuck into his skin, his screams became louder, incoherent words that sounded like a foreign language.

A guttural roar emanated from him on the fourth needle and his eyes began to roll back in his head. Ijos began to struggle after the fourth needle, like the child was imbued with the strength of a monster.

Ijos used all his body to hold Kael down. "How many more?!" His voice was raspy, and he had to say each word with effort.

Aveline did not look up at him. She was concentrating on the needles. "Three."

The fifth and six needles were plunged into the skin in quick succession. Ijos could only see the tips of the needles sticking out of Kael's neck as he held him down; he could only steal a glance before Kael swatted him off him with immense strength.

Ijos flew across the room and hit the vine-covered wall, cracking it. Aveline was knocked out of her trance as Kael stood up and grabbed her by her throat, choking her as he lifted her high above his head. Her knees dragged the floor, her legs tried to kick free, but she could not move away.

"I will not be banished again, *iridach'u.*" The voice warbled in and out of Kael's mouth, like it was coming from a distant land.

Kael then threw Aveline across the room, past Ijos and into a throne made of stone, shattering it. Ijos stared, but it was not Kael's eyes staring back.

Instead of blue, they were black, and the sclera was bloodshot. The bloodlust coming from him was stifling, nearly palpable and crushing to Ijos. He felt like he could not move. But then he heard the clink of metal beside him, and he turned to see an acupuncture needle. Aveline coughed and rasped.

"T-the needle! It needs to be plunged into the center of that mark on his neck!"

Ijos took all his strength and grabbed the needle and got up. Black smoke swirled around Kael as a low growl emanated from his chest. The boy held out his hand and shot that same darkness at Ijos, who dodged it by rolling on the wall. The smoke hit the vines, and they wilted and died immediately.

Kael shot the darkness at Ijos again, and again, with Ijos dodging them in the same manner. Ijos then grabbed soil from the ground and threw it in Kael's eyes, blinding him.

The possessed Kael scrubbed at his face and yelled, shooting darkness in several directions out of anger. When he regained his sight, he went to attack again, but Ijos was gone. He eyed Aveline and raised his hand to her, focusing a large amount of darkness and red malice into his palm. His eyes burned with hatred.

Then Kael stopped. He felt immobilized as his eyes shifted to see Ijos behind him. The needle was plunged directly into the center of the mark, and the other six surrounding the mark, and all seven needles glowed red. A faint, ghostly thread came from each of the needles and traced back to Aveline, who knelt beside the broken throne and began to recite ancient words.

The eyes in Kael's head began to roll back as he wavered and collapsed but did not hit the floor as Ijos caught him. Kael's face turned to Aveline with hatred.

"You may curse me yet again, may seal me once more. But I will return one day, ancient one, and your head will be the first to roll."

Then the darkness was sucked into the seal like a cyclone. Leaves rustled in the cottage, and some were torn completely off the vines. Ijos held on to Kael as he saw the mark fade into a scar. Then the needles pushed themselves out and onto the floor and melted into a silver puddle.

Kael became limp in Ijos' arms and Ijos began to panic. He started to panic so that he didn't see Aveline come up and she rested her hand on his.

"He is just asleep, Ijos. He was fighting it while he was possessed."

"How do you know?"

Aveline pointed at the dead vines. "If that thing wanted you dead, it would have shot you even while you were rolling. Kael made sure to throw its aim off."

Ijos smiled at Kael before his vision blurred. He felt pain and warmth on his side. Blood seeped from the wound.

Aveline grabbed Kael out of his hands before he could collapse and winced out of expectation to see the malicious face again, but it did not come. The seal she placed seemed to have worked, and she noticed the boy was not covered in sweat nor was he hot or cold.

She placed the boy down and then helped Ijos back onto the bed and tended to his wounds once more. Her hands began to shake just ever so slightly.

V

"What was the darkness?" Kael looked at her with a stern face, "and was it extracted?"

Aveline averted her gaze. Kael saw minute rubble from the old stone throne. "I tried, but I did not expect to see what I did. The curse that was placed on you opened a portal. You were to be used as a host for something more ominous."

"My people were the first to come to these lands, preceding the elves and dwarves by several centuries. We lived peacefully and lived with the land, sharing with it instead of taking. Then the elves and dwarves came, both by sea. They came from a distant land wishing to start anew, and so they did. They learned our ways and lived alongside us for centuries more.

Then the humans came, too, from the sea. They came to us, and we offered to show them our ways, and they did, for a time. But as time passed, some would quarrel with others, and some would take more than they would give.

My people were not pleased; the lands we shared a life with were scarred and hurt from these newcomers, and so we originally shoved those who did not abide to our rules to the south. The south, as you know now, is a barren land. And for some time, we knew peace again. Those who abided lived with us peacefully."

"Then, a monster came from these barren lands."

The group stopped and exchanged glances. The soldier Thopps shook with excitement and began to talk before Azalea elbowed him in the side.

"He was once human, like you. But he was consumed by his own goals: total control of all kind. He amassed an army and, through dark magic, was able to transform into fearsome beasts. The lands were awash with blood. My people watched as people of every race were slaughtered by this army. We decided that we had to stop this."

226

"I should tell you about my people first. We are an ancient race called the iridach'u. We have an exceptionally long lifespan, but our race does not spread quickly because we can only have one child every 300 years. Our numbers are small, but we are well attuned to nature, therefore we can connect to it and use magic to use it to our aid. Our magic is old and does not involve killing or taking, but rather a mutual relationship with nature. We feel the pain of those that we connect to, like the golem."

Kael opened his mouth, but Aveline held up her hand. Her flawless skin was scarred with the smallest hairline cracks.

"It is not your burden to bear, child. This is the way of my people. Since we did not populate very often, we numbered in few. At that time, we were only about a hundred or so of us. We do not have a violent disposition, either, but we had to do something."

"It was here, in this forest that we lured the army to decide their fate. As they pillaged the lands, they were drawn here, where we used golems and other magical creatures to bring them to the center of the forest, this meadow. It has its own magical properties, as you can see here. Always temperate, away from the harsh elements of the outer world. It is a connection to the astral plane, and it holds a thin veil to other worlds."

Her hand began to shake, but she kept it up, moving so that her palm was facing upwards. Threads began to release from her fingertips and intertwined above them, creating a funnel.

227

"From the Veil, we used our magic to open it and create an ethereal funnel to another dimension, one of fire and darkness. It took everything we could, but through our magic and our legion of magical creatures, we passed them through the vortex, cursing them to another dimension."

"The veil was closed, and a lock was placed on this vortex to keep from opening again. But as it was done, many of my people had perished. They gave their life to subdue this man and his followers. "

Her hands shook as the threads dissipated into fog and a single tear streamed down her face.

VI

"I KNEW IT!" Thopps jumped up and yelled amidst the silence. "You are the Witch of the World!"

Azalea tried grabbing him, but he did not seem fazed. Aveline smiled.

"Such a name. I've heard of the stories, but they are not entirely true. My people were here before the others, but I was not the only one."

Azalea let go of Thopps and turned to her. "You said many of your people died. Were there any left?"

"Yes, but only a few. The lock that closed this vortex had a key, and the remainder of our people decided to break that key and keep them from falling in the wrong hands."

Kael stood up and dusted his tunic. He walked to Aveline and held her hand. "Thank you, Aveline." His face contorted into a sad smile and his eyes were glossy with tears. "I had no idea I caused such trouble. This mark—" he gestured with his hand, "has been burning for a long time and I did not know why."

Aveline replied in her own sad smile, overlapping his resting hand with her other. "My dear child, you carry a great burden with that curse." She grasped his hand tightly then, pulling him closer so the others did not hear. "If you do not relinquish this path you are on, you may yet be consumed by it."

Kael pulled away and shook his head. "I do this for Ijos. And I would not stop even if I was swallowed whole."

Aveline stood up and walked to the fireplace. She tended to a soup much like in the past, portioning out a serving for each one of the party.

She handed them out before she sat back down. "I know you have gotten what you seek from me, but I must ask you to stay long enough to rest and fill your stomachs. It is the way of my people to offer this soup to travelers, at least that was how it was long ago."

The group gave many thanks and ate their soup. Most of the group ate and talked to each other, but Azalea and Thopps ate in silence. They ate and watched Kael, who did not touch his soup.

He examined the wall covered in vines, which had grown back in time, though he could see the vines did not grow back right. The ones that had died by that darkness were ever so slightly mutated, the leaves pronged, and the stems had thorns where they shouldn't.

He clenched his hands as he saw the wood was still cracked beneath the vines, too.

Eidolon

Light

I

It blurs. Time is only one path that we follow, but one we cannot escape. We are all prisoners, like a bloodthirsty beast that will consume all.

The river flows beside Kael's campsite as he reflects on his own fate.

"'The beast will consume me before too long,'" he jammed a sharp stick within the fire as the last fires of the sun set. "'If I continue this path, that is,' is what she said."

Two weeks have passed since he met Aveline and she revealed a dark part of his past. The mark on his neck was a curse. He was consumed by darkness and hurt Ijos during it.

Why can't he remember that part? Each memory he relives, he can remember it in some way, like a blindfold being taken off. This one he could not remember. The way Aveline told the memory, it was like he was not himself. But who was he?

He tossed the sharp stick into the river, watching it surface and float away. He and the mercenary group left the Eissizir Weald with the guidance of Aveline the next morning. They parted ways at the base of the mountain.

"Are you sure you won't come with us?" Azalea stopped as the group continued back towards Belford and turned to Kael, who was heading south. "We were going back to see if any mercs in the town heard of new jobs. I'm sure we could use your skill on the battlefield.

Kael brushed his hair behind his ear and squinted against the rising sun. "No, I dinnae really have an interest in fighting for other people. Let their war be their own." He rummaged in his pouch and brought out his fist, holding it out to her. "I'm sure we will cross paths again one day, Azalea."

Azalea held out her hands and he dropped a coin into her hand. It was one that she had never seen before, a knurled brown coin with a patina on it.

"It's a tumen. Ijos told me once that his lands had its own currency. Keep it. Maybe when you look at it, you'll remember our time together."

She looked down at the relic'd coin and clasped her hand into a fist over it. Kael turned to walk away but she grabbed his shoulder and turned him around to her and embraced him. He returned the hug with a tight embrace of his own before letting go, patting her shoulder, lastly holding his hand to her face in a more intimate embrace.

"Take care, Azalea."

She held his hand onto her face for a moment longer before letting him drop it away. "You too, Kael."

He walked away and so did she. But as he was beginning to saddle on Jorunn, he heard her yell. "You know where we are! Don't forget, you aren't alone!"

He waved as they left the base of the mountains, and he left in the opposite direction. He had no path at this point, no answers as to where he was to search next.

He wandered aimlessly in the countryside for some time before he ended up beside a river that his map called Einir, though it seemed to be of old tongue. He camped there several days and dwelled on the words that Aveline told him.

He slept for a while, but it was restless. He instead stayed up all night, alternating between staring at the stars and their reflection on the water.

As morning came and went, he took out the old, worn toy of his youth and twisted it in his hands again, hoping it would give him any answers, but it bore nothing for him. It was like this for days, camping at the same spot as he dwelled deeper into his own thoughts.

On the morn of the last day, he packed up his gear and retraced his path back north, hoping that chance or fate would align again.

II

Belford was lively as post-battle casualties and damaged were swept under the rug. The inn and tavern owners let their disdain for the outsiders dwindle, treating them as old friends after they bought out their stores several times over.

War always paid handsomely for several occupations and liquor was always in demands after a hearty win. The tavern at the junction of 3rd and Elmore was lively just like the night before and the nights before that.

Azalea was hunched over on her stool at the bar despite her troops partying in the far corner. She turned the tumen over in her hand several times, not touching her drink nor talking to any of the barflies close to her. Jude came up to her and began to speak, but it was muffled by her own thoughts. He stood there a moment before tapping her on the shoulder, startling her from her daze.

"What do you think, Captain?"

She blinked her eyes to push away her cloudy thoughts. "Think about what?"

"There has been word that mercenaries are needed down south, towards Aisha. We could take the Lyndis path and through Mynheir—"

"No!" Her shriek caused the bar to become silent. Everyone looked at her before the normal jumble swelled again. She panted for a second and took a deep breath through her nose.

"I mean—mean that there's no reason to go through Mynheir. The capital is always busy, and it would take just as long to clear the guard posts than if we skirted around it."

Jude shrugged and then nodded. "If you say so, Captain."

He walked off to join the rest of the group, and moments later Azalea got up and left. She returned to her room at one of the inns in town, undressing and lying in bed bare.

She still held the tumen in her hand and flipped it over in the moonlight and dim candlelight of the alleys until she fell asleep. The coin was still clutched in her hand as she slumbered in her inn, unaware of the magic pouring from it and vibrating up her arm and into her mind.

III

I remember how the snow crunched that year. How our breaths seemed to rattle as we did all we could to survive. After everything fell, we ran. After it all fell, we did all we could to keep ourselves together...

The weeks after the fall of Caede were arduous. Isabella led her children through the barren, snowy scape and it took a toll on her resolve. She was near a breaking point, though she did not let it show much in from of her children.

She felt like they had been running in circles since they had parted with Sarreif at Duris Lake, had actually run a circle once, and ended up back at Duris Lake long after Sarreif disappeared. The panic of that realization was almost enough to crumble her if not for the dependence of her children.

That felt like a lifetime ago, and they finally found the Lyndis path after traversing through the brush and woods of the wilds. She knew it was the Lyndis path. There was recognition by the nearly iron-colored packing of the dirt of the wagon road.

Finding the path was a great relief to her, a faint glimmer of hope as she knelt and felt the wagon grooves as hard as steel. They kept on that path for days, hoping to run into a town or inn, anything out of the elements.

The cold was bitter, and they brought so little with them as they fled. Sarreif was an immense help when he was here, but he was gone, and their food was reduced to nothing but crumbs. They began to live off any berry or leaf they could find, and in the winter, it was not much. The sparse forests they found shielded them from the freezing wind enough for them to huddle together and survive for the night.

As they walked the path, though, they did not find anyone. There were no wagons or travelers as they walked the path, but they came upon an abandoned inn by sunset one day. The windows had been broken, and the door was shattered, but it was better than sleeping in the snow again.

Isabella walked in first to make sure there was no one else in it. She did not hear any sounds save for the wind, so she brought the children inside. She saw the wood on the floor was black with dried blood and she had to hold back a gasp. They crowded around the hearth and Isabella was able to make a crude fire for warmth, though it took her several times and about an hour to get it going.

Night crept upon them and as the kids slept, Isabella stayed awake and kept the lookout, though she would often glimpse at the dried blood and her mind would go back to Caede.

It would replay in her head over and over, seeing Baldock close the secret passageway behind them, not knowing if he was alive. Her heart hurt, feeling that he was dead, only a dried bloodstain much like the ones here.

It was here. I remember writhing in my own sleep when a noise woke me. It was a muffled choke, and I felt a chill even despite the warmth of the fire in the hearth. I got up and saw Mama by a window, swaying back and forth. Mama...

She began to fall when she felt a hand grab her in time and helped her to the floor. Her head cleared and she saw Azalea holding her hand.

"Azalea, what are you doing awake? I can manage watch by myself."

Azalea patted her hand and sniffled. The girl had been crying. "I had a bad dream about daddy and woke up. When I woke, I saw you bobbing and choking on your breath."

It was the dream that daddy was being stabbed by a man in a robe. I could hear his anguished screams, but what scared me more was the yellow eyes.

Isabella felt ashamed to let her daughter see her like that. She bit her lip and averted her eyes.

"It's okay, mommy. I know you will take care of us, but I know you're hurting, too. You don't have to hide it from me."

Hearing those words was like cutting a taught string. Something snapped and her façade fell fast, tears streaming as she silently sobbed, Azalea crying with her. They cried for Daddy the night before Azalea fell asleep in Isabella's arms as she fell asleep herself. The sun woke them up and they continued the path, not speaking of what happened the night before for the next couple of days.

The family found an abandoned town a few days after they left the inn. The sign on the outskirts of the town has 'Einmir' (*The name puts a pit in my stomach*) written on it. It was not large by any means, much smaller than Caede, but it was still large enough to have a couple of taverns. It was quiet with only the wind howling through the empty roads and alleyways between buildings. Einmir was once a busy highway town, but through war, it was reduced to nothing.

The family found a small home that suffered the least amount of damage to board up for the night. It was cramped, only having one main room and another small room to the side, with furniture overturned and scattered, so Isabella moved the furniture around to allow them to rest on cushion rather than on a hard floor.

She tried to light a fire, but after an hour, she gave up and started to search the house. She pulled some tattered drapes and used them as a makeshift blanket for her children.

The night was cold without the fire, but the warmth of the huddle of the family kept them warm enough to sleep deeper than expected. Isabella was going to keep watch but ended up falling asleep herself due to exhaustion and the warmth under the blanket. She jolted awake when she heard the door hinges creak in the still of the night and darted her eyes towards it.

A large shadow loomed in the frame, the moonlight barely accepting any features. The only thing Isabella could make out was the sinister eyes in the head of the man that stood there. He walked forward into the room and brought the bitter wind with him, like a ghost on his back.

"Well, lookit wat we 'ave 'ere, boys!"

From the behind the shadow came two more, though none were as large as the first. One was stout, the other almost as tall as the leader, but much lankier. As they came forward the shadows became men, the heinous kind that you can see their intentions by their soulless eyes and their rotten gum, racked grins.

They bolstered weapons; the two smaller men had a sword and large knife each, but the largest man had a primitive weapon, which looked like a cross between an axe and a mace, like it could be brutally effectively in subduing its target. Isabella began to panic and scurry, yanking her children out of sleep to run to the next room, screaming as they were pulled out of their dreamscapes.

But the large man was faster than he appeared, blocking their way in a blink of an eye. His smile continued in the dim moonlight, twinkling like piss-colored gems.

"Don' go, the fun's aboutta start." He turned to the other two men. "Jarn, Arrold, take care of the kids."

The two men flanked Isabella and despite her frantic fight, clawing at the men and using all her strength, the men pulled her children away from her grasp. She fell to the floor in the struggle and release. The large man stood over her with his piss grin. He then looked at the kids, who were split between the two bandits.

The lankier man—I think it was Jarn—held me down as the stout one held my brothers. He clasped them both by the throat to the point they were gasping. I remember the weight crushing me. He really pressed his body into mine and there was a bit of shaking, too.

All I could do was stare at my brothers before Mama made a noise. She turned and bit the man holding her tight, so much that he yelled. I watched as a black ooze came from a chunk missing in his hand, then Mama was flying across the room to the other wall. Her head hid with such a dull thud; I thought she was dead.

Isabella's head blurred and ached. Her vision was blotted but enough to allow her to see the large man come towards her and yanked her by her hair towards a clear part of the floor. He ripped at her makeshift fur clothing and exposed her pale abdomen to the cold, causing a shiver to ripple through her. He tore more and her breasts became exposed, and his men began to laugh.

"She's pretty supple, eh, boss?"

The man named Jarn squeezed me tighter to him, and I felt something hard against my back, throbbing with a sickening heat. I couldn't suppress the fear as it bubbled out of my throat.

"Shut up, you cunt." The boss snarled at him and both the men stopped laughing. He turned back towards Isabella, who was flailing her arms in front of her. "Ya think ya can get away, 'uh? Ya took a bit outta me, now I'm gonna take sumtin from ya."

His smile came back more bastardly than before, showing his blackened gums. He shifted and began to pull his pants down, splaying a prick that was not too long, but was thick and scarred. He wasted no time and paid no heed to her struggle as he thrust it within her.

She screamed and flailed, trying to get away, but he flipped her over and pushed her face sideways. "You're gonna pay for what ya did to me," he said breathlessly. "Jarn, Arrold, have your way with the kids."

Mama dug her face and nails into the floor, noises coming out of her mouth guttural and broken. I didn't know what was happening until I felt it, too. A burning sensation as I felt like I was being torn, the heat and pressure. The jagged swaying.

All I could think about was a red-hot poker being shoved inside me. I screamed. It was unbearable. He told me to 'shut yer yap,' and it was 'ruinin' it' for him. All I wanted was something to end it. That or end me...

The stout man groaned. "Boss, do I really have to...?"

The boss laughed in between grunts. "Are you a dolt? Just kill them if you want. Ain't no use in wasting your prick on some young boy meat. You can have a turn with the girly there after Jarn is done."

Stop... please. My fingers were bleeding from digging into the wood. Mama screamed for them to stop; I watched as she tried to claw away. I focused on her hands. Not on her face, covered with dirt, or that the man violating her was pulling the hair out of her scalp as he made her watch.

I did everything I could to avoid watching what the other man did to my brothers. But my eyes betrayed me, I locked onto their fearful, pleading eyes...

Arrold took a knife and slit both the boys' throats at once, their screams and pleads drowned by the rush of blood from the wounds. Their hands dropped from their heads as the light left their eyes. Arrold wiped the blood from his hands and turned to Jarn with a scowl.

"When you gonna be done with the young cunt? I want a turn too."

He walked no more than a foot and in front of the door leading to the next room when he stopped and Jarn gaped at him. Arrold turned to his boss and the side of his head had a large knife protruding from it. His mouth bubbled with blood before he staggered and slumped to the floor.

The two remaining men stopped and held their own weapons, grasping at their trousers so they did not trip on them. Jarn stood over Azalea with his sword sticking straight out much like his prick in his pants, but that did not prepare him for a small figure climbing him like a tree and stabbing a small sword in his neck from behind. He yelled and swung wildly, barely missing Azalea as she scurried away.

The figure took the sword out and thrust it through Jarn's skull, the blade coming through his eye, and he staggered and fell. The figure was muted by the dark night, but they could see it was a young boy.

A warrior. A hero, even. The wild hair. Even in the moonlight could I see the blue eyes, piercing the dark. Those eyes saved me, ended my suffering.

His face was blank, but his eyes shone in the dim moonlight as a breathtaking blue. The boss gripped his makeshift mace-axe tight and crossed the room in two strides. His free hand was grasping for the boy as the weapon swung from the other side hoping one would catch him in some way.

245

"Come here, you little cocksucker—" followed by a hard swing that barely missed the boy. Isabella used the commotion to get to Azalea and began to retreat from the house, only to be stopped by another figure in the doorframe. This one was tall, but thin, and was wrapped in a torn robe.

He did not stop to look at the girls and instead let them pass. Isabella glanced back as the man silently walked behind the boss and thrust a katana the color of the night through his chest, twisting it as the boss yelled. His yells began to gurgle as the blood came out his mouth. He body fell toward after the man used his foot to release his blade from the corpse. The boy moved to the side, so he was not caught.

Isabella watched in silence despite the danger, despite there being another stranger who he did not know. She was even more alarmed when a bright red bird perched on a small post beside her in the snow. She looked back at the man to see he was in front of her.

"Lady Isabella." He was holding out a small piece of paper, causing her to flinch and shiver. "My name is Ijos. I have been sent by your brother-in-law, Haskell, to escort you safely to Mynheir."

He glanced back at the corpses and even more so at the bodies of Gareth and Zareth. He lingered on them for a moment. When he turned back, he had an incredible sadness on his face.

"I am sorry that I am late."

Mama shook and we fell. I don't know if it was from the cold, or the shock, or the trauma. It May have been all three. But the moonlight glistened on the tears and blood as we collapsed into the dusting of snow.

IV

Azalea woke up in a sweat. The summer was hot, though the night was cooler than usual, but she was drenched from head to toe. The dream she had was vivid and opened old scars anew.

She reached up to her face and felt it was hot and swollen. She began to recall it all again and the trauma was beginning to weigh back on her, like she could feel that bandit still in her and could still see the corpses of her brothers.

Her heart was pounding so hard that it almost drowned out the sound of the pounding on the door. She peered out the window to see it was breaking dawn and wondered who would be seeing her this early. Her men would surely be passed out with some whore or another at this time.

She walked over to the door and opened it to see Kael and inaudibly gasped. Her thoughts immediately flashed to the vivid blue eyes from her dream. The same blue eyes that stared at her now.

"You... you were the little boy."

Kael cocked his head to the side. "What?" His hand was still outstretched to knock again. "What do you mean?"

She grabbed his hand and pulled him into the room without a word. She collapsed on the bed as he stood by the door, her mouth opening and pouring out the vivid memory she dreamed. She took careful time explaining the brutal attack of the bandits, choking at the details like a bone in her throat.

Trudging up past trauma made her stick a little at recalling the minute details, often glossing over a sizable portion of it. She did, however, put more detail in the boy in her memories and how he dispatched the man named Jarn. She put even more detail in the man that accompanied him and recalled that his name was Ijos.

Kael scratched his head at this and racked his brain for a moment. He leaned on the door. His eyes pierced into her.

"I suppose I do remember this... but just barely." He shook his head. "Fuck, I wish it was simpler than that. How did we end up there after Eissizir Weald?"

"I don't know either, but you saved us." Azalea yawned and batted the sleep from her eyes. "And Ijos said you were sent by my uncle. Why?"

Kael stared at her with a stern face. "Why indeed. Ijos didn't really do tasks for other people, unless it was to for a monster post."

They spent the rest of the morning talking about the events with no avail on the reasoning. It was not before too long that there was knock on the door behind Kael's back, and he opened it to see Jude.

"Ah, Kael," Jude's gaze flicked between him and Azalea long enough to convey doubt. His eyebrows arched as he noted the sweat clinging to her skin and disheveled hair while Kael was cool and composed. "I was not expecting you. Is everything... okay?"

Kael glanced back and shrugged. "I came to accept the offer on accompanying your troupe for a while." Azalea looked up and smirked a little. "If for no other that my path has led to a dead end."

Jude grimaced and glanced at Azalea. "I see. Well, boss, are you ready?"

Azalea got up and picked up her ready-packed bag from the bedside. "Aye, I suppose." Kael had a puzzled expression.

"Oh, I forgot to tell you," she chuckled. Her memories took present over anything else. "We were about to head to another job close to Aisha. We were going to take a detour east around Mynheir and head towards the badlands."

"Sounds good to me," he replied as he surveyed her face. *Why not Mynheir? Why does she seem apprehensive at the name alone?*

The group recouped at the gates of Belford after the rest of the troops gathered their things and worked off their hangovers. Kael was situated close to Azalea at the front, noticing that Jude was side eyeing him most of the time. When the group was ready, they set off. The fields surrounding Belford were quiet once again, the battle becoming a distant memory already.

They passed several merchant wagons on their trail before they entered a small town named Einmir. The name felt like a cold brand, sending chills down her spine.

Azalea noticed many of the structures from the past were completely rebuilt, some were torn down, and the town did not look even remotely the same as on that wintry, violent night.

When they passed where the house she was violated in and her brothers killed, she gripped her reins hard at the sight of a small field in its place. She remembered so well watching the swordsman and young boy bury the bodies and mark the graves with a stake. But those stakes were gone, long withered by time.

Before she knew it, she had dismounted her horse and left it. The gentle wind picked up as she felt herself walking to that field. Her hands trembled as she dropped to her knees.

The stakes were gone, but in time someone had replaced them with gravestones. They were small, but they were a physical thing she could touch. She caressed the stones with her hands, trying her best to remember her brothers as they were at home, not on that violent night.

She was so lost in remembering them that she had missed the writing on the stones. Both the gravestones were etched the same thing: IN TWILIGHT'S EMBRACE, TWO STARS REST, THEIR LIGHT UNDIMMED BY WAR'S SHADOW. Azalea was silent. She didn't notice herself weep or her chest heave.

She didn't hear Kael come up to her and crouch beside her, but she watched him place a flower in between the stones. A lily, which was lavender in the middle and black on the edges.

He held out another to her and she took it, holding it to her face for a minute while she prayed. She didn't know who or what to pray to, but she asked for something to watch over her brothers in the next life, and to give them a longer life than they had here.

She laid the flower in between the two stones on top of Kael's and returned to her horse. As the group went on, she glanced back one more time, noticing she did not see any of those flowers nearby at all.

The span of land after Einmir was uninterrupted for a long time. They passed through bogs and close to a loch, but other than small homesteads, they did not pass by any other towns.

After a couple of days, Kael looked around to see they were back on the Lyndis path, heading eastward, knowing that Duris lake was not too far from here. He thought of the kappa and the crack in his shell, clamping his teeth down for a moment before moving on.

They ended up setting up camp near a grove on a small hill at sunset. Kael scanned the path ahead and noticed it entered another forest in the next day or so. The group talked jovially as usual, though Azalea was not part of it. She was eating in silence under a large tree that stood out from the rest. Kael left the rest of the group to sit beside her, looking up as she did. They watched the stars twinkle amongst their backdrop of darkness.

"Do you ever wonder what is beyond the stars?" He stared up at them, the stars reflecting in his eyes, nearly black in the night. "Are there Gods above us, watching down and controlling us like a child would with their toys? Or is it nothing?"

Azalea didn't reply. She gazed at the stars and pondered this herself, but no answers came to her. She then reached into a pocket and pulled out the coin he gave her.

"Here." She flipped the coin at him, and he caught it midair. He examined it and began to hand it back to her, but she shook her head. "Nay, I don't need it. No use in remembering you now if you're in front of me."

She sighed. It was shaky, rattling in the stillness around their tree. He continued to stare at her, but she had to take a few breaths before she returned his gaze. Her eyes were unsteady, ready to break at any moment.

"I couldn't believe you were the boy who saved me and my mother. The... things that happened have always been in the back of my head, and I knew they happened, but I couldn't remember how. I remembered the faces of the men well, and I remembered my brothers died, but I always remembered it as a sickness."

Kael flipped the coin over to her despite her protests. "Take this, then. It's imbued with magic, apparently one that helps memories that have been suppressed by magic."

"Why would my memories be under a spell?"

He shrugged. "Maybe due to the traumatic nature of these events. You could have been put under some repression spell so that you did not have to live with it."

"Who could do that?"

"Ijos, maybe. Some of the memories I have attained on my journey had him put me under a spell when I was troubled with my past. It seems it had its side effects, though. Mostly with speech."

She didn't speak about this. She understood why she would forget the trauma; that part was easy to digest, especially for something like that to happen to a young girl.

But why would she forget Kael and Ijos? She still remembered parts of the rape, and her brothers dying, but not being saved or the causes of their deaths. It weighed heavily on her mind.

Transfixion

I

Kael studied his map and noted that the forest did not have a name, at least not at the time the map was made. The group of mercenaries did not know the name either, just knew they were on the right path. It was a large forest with a serene calm not unlike Eissizir Weald, but it had a path through it that was well traversed.

They traveled through the expanded copse for some time before they heard a rumble in the distance, dismissing it at first since it was so far away. Azalea rode up next to Kael and matched his gait for a few moments before talking.

"I had another dream about our past," she glanced at him, "not long after the incident."

Kael grunted a little but glanced over at her as well. "As did I. It was while we were on the road to Mynheir."

She nodded, her gaze intense on him. She felt like he had the same dream, too, by the way he kept glancing at her this morning while they were breaking down camp.

She didn't hesitate in describing the memory in full detail, and he didn't stop her, letting it play in his head again.

II

The group was in a forest when the first rays of light crept through the canopy. Ijos had already been awake for hours, unable to sleep much since he rescued Isabella and Azalea in the abandoned town.

He thought back about how he buried her two sons while the snow was falling, using a rusty shovel that he found near a small garden nearby. He considered burning the bodies of the brigands, but he decided they didn't even deserve that kind of rest.

He hoped their souls would feel unrest as their bodies were ripped apart by scavenger animals.

He jolted awake last night as Isabella screamed in her sleep, followed by the girl not long after. Neither had spoken much since that night, and for good reason, he thought. Both were skittish of any physical contact; the girl would flinch if he looked at her.

They were less wary of Kael, though, since he was so young. He would often help Ijos by handing them items—mostly food—so they did not have to interact with him much.

Kael was still asleep when Ijos had an odd feeling. The forest exuded a sense of calm, but he felt there was an otherworldly aura as well. He remembered when he was taught by Aveline that there were celestial spirits that had supernatural powers.

It was the same feeling he felt when he met Nuria, too. The bird was perched on a branch on the outskirts of their campsite, and she, too, felt the presence. Her beady eyes loomed over the vast forest as Ijos shifted and began to sort out breakfast before the fire burned down to embers.

The group woke not too long after Ijos was done, since the warmth was gone and the smell of cooked meat was in the air. Even Nuria left her perch to partake in the food, and Ijos spared some of his rations to feed her. Azalea avoided his eyes during breakfast, but Isabella began to look at him more. As Ijos folded up the pelts they used for bedding, she came up to him and stood a moment. He stayed crouched as he looked up at her, softening his movements so he did not startle her any.

"I wanted to thank you for saving us. I- I mean back there." She shifted her eyes away several times. "I know it's not your fault that it happened."

She pulled out the letter a held it out in front of her. "How did Haskell know we would need to be escorted?"

Ijos finished tying the pelts together. "He didn't. Lord Caedmon sent him a letter the morning before expressing that he felt an ill omen for Caede. He was sending the letter to have someone come as an escort back to the Capital so he could feel at ease."

Ijos stood up slowly with the tied pelt and slung them over his back a little too swift. It caused her to flinch.

"I came to Caede as it was burning. I've known both Haskell and Lord Caedmon for a long time, and they know I am experienced in fighting creatures. I was already out... when I got the letter from a familiar that knew how to track me."

Ijos looked away for a moment into the forest. He thought he heard a noise. It was in the same direction as earlier, but he brushed it off as just the noises of wildlife.

When he turned back, Isabella was a couple inches away from him and she embraced him. He could feel her steel against him, trembling for a moment before she let go.

"I still want to thank ye." She forced a smile, then turned around and knelt to Kael.

"And you, you brave warrior, I want to thank you for saving my daughter."

Ijos could see the smile on her face was much more genuine, and the hug that she embraced him in held much warmth. Ijos couldn't help but smile a little, then he glimpsed over at Azalea, who glared at her mother with cold eyes. The smile fell from his lips.

Ijos finished packing their camp, despite it being only the pelts and a small portion of rations, and the group started to set out. Ijos only paused when he realized Kael was still sitting in the same position as before, staring out deeper into the forest in the same direction Ijos thought he heard something. Ijos knelt beside him.

"What is it, Kael?"

The boy did not budge, transfixed on whatever he was watching. Ijos could feel it, too, like they were being watched, but he did not feel any danger.

"Maybe a spirit is watching over us as we pass through this forest." He clasped Kael's shoulder, which moved the boy out of his trance. The boy smiled at him but glanced back again. Ijos eyed the same direction and saw a small shadow disappear in the distance. "Let's go, Kael."

The boy got up and followed Ijos to the rest of their group. They followed the winding path for the duration of the morning, only stopping once to eat some of their rations, mostly rabbit meat that Ijos had hunted in the days after the abandoned town. They were salty and it burned the sores in his mouth, but it was better than an empty stomach.

Kael ate nearly the same as him, which was not too surprising since he was still growing. Isabella ate a few pieces of it, but she mostly helped Kael, telling him not to eat with his mouth open or wipe the grease on his clothes.

Manners, Ijos snickered, *at a time like this.*

He turned to Azalea, who had not eaten at all. She stayed as far away from Ijos as she could at any camp site they made, but she didn't stay close to her mother, either. She only allowed Kael to get close enough to her, but he did not do it too often. It was, again, only to hand her food and other items needed for survival.

The path in the forest led out to a large, grassy plain. The grass was mostly covered in snow, where this side of the continent was temperate, having hot summers and bitter cold winters. Ijos thought of his homeland and remembered how little it snowed.

But that was ages ago, he thought. *Those lands probably don't even look the same anymore.* He watched Kael walk next to him and thought about how their pasts are similar in ways. He smiled when Kael looked up at him and they went on.

The group could see far enough ahead there was a town. When they got closer, they could see it had intact walls and there were guards atop these walls. Very few inhabited towns remained during the war, either pillaged by invasions—in times when there was a fight for power—or the more recent forces of monsters controlled by the sorcerer.

The town of Gormsey was still far from the capital city of Mynheir, but since it was situated in a rural area meant that it needed to be well guarded, even more so since it did not have any advantages such as a waterfront or hillside. Since it was in the open plains, it boasted large stone and wood walls to protect from any invaders. As the group neared the walls, a man atop the wall in a tower yelled.

"Stop where ye are!" He had a crossbow loaded and pointed at them. "State yer business!"

Ijos spoke up, clearly articulating his words. He is well versed in the customs of war and the precautions people take. He gestured towards Isabella and Azalea. "I am a Knight of Kyndis, escorting survivors to the Capital. We are just passing through and staying to rest and replenish our resources."

The man slightly lowered his crossbow, his face blocked by a helmet and face mask. "A knight, eh?" The man mumbled something to himself, too low to be heard by the group far below him. "I suppose we will allow it." The man turned and yelled. "Open the gates!"

The giant wooden gates cranked open; the contraption used grinded and created an indescribably horrible grating noise. Isabella and Azalea clasped their ears, while Ijos covered Kael's to protect his hearing.

The town could be described similarly as the gate; dreary and filthy. Many of the building walls were piss stained, flecks of blood and vomit splattered them as well from the people who have contracted disease. The buildings were poorly built with many of the structures containing gaps between the wood used. The people of the town were dirty and tired, most of which looked like they were refugees themselves. It was a common occurrence; other towns would have flocks of refugees that survived the massacres of other settlements.

The group traveled through the town, searching for an inn to rest safely for some time. The inn they found was nearly full, so the group had to stay in the same room. The inn consisted of a main building and then smaller buildings that connected via walkways.

There was a small bookshelf in the room, though it was sparse, containing only a couple of tattered books. He watched as Isabella pulled an old book, sat on the edge of the bed with Kael, and read him the book. It was a collection of fairy tales. He listened as she recounted an old legend that was turned into a kid's story, about how an invulnerable manticore was defeated by a man.

He leaned against the wall and watched as Kael was engulfed in the story expressing childlike awe, hanging onto the words like he was living in it. When the story was over, Isabella took the bed with the children, holding Kael tight, and Azalea was curled up by herself. Ijos slept on the floor, using the bundle of pelts as a pillow. They had been on the road for a few days and were exhausted, so each of them slept deeper than usual.

In the late hours of the night, Ijos awoke to the noise of a door shutting softly. He sat up and noticed that Isabella was absent from the bed. Isabella had left the room, walking outside, and watching the moon hide behind the clouds. In her trance, she did not hear Ijos exit the room and accompany her to the rail, leaning and staring off into the night. His heart dropped as little as she withdrew from his presence.

Ijos continued to lean on the railing. He spoke in a very calm, gentle voice. "I was born on the other side of the kingdom, in the west amongst the land of lilies. Unlike the east, the west stayed warmer than cold, and the Sakura trees were always in bloom. I used to love watching the cherry blossoms fall with my mother."

Isabella did not respond. She stared at him, her fears still present, but she felt a calm within him and a warmth of safety as well. She felt bad that she flinched when she was around him, but she could not forget the face he made as he stabbed into the bandit, either.

"I watched the cherry blossoms fall amongst the embers when my mother died as well. My village was attacked by another nation who wanted our land for themselves. I was just a kid then."

"My mother hid me as the men broke into our home and raped her before stabbing her in the chest several times. Even after all that, my mother wanted me to take her outside to watch the cherry blossoms one more time. The scene is still imprinted in my brain."

Ijos stopped and cleared his voice. Isabella could see his eyes glisten in the moonlight.

"A mother's love is unconditional. I see how you feel for Kael, and I'm sure you felt the same for your own children, since you protected them in the wilderness for so long. However, I see myself in that child as well, especially after all that he has been through. I see that death has taken its toll on him, but he stands under the pressure well for someone so young."

He paused for a moment and glanced at her. "When we reach Mynheir, I plan to take my leave, and Kael with me. I want to raise the child as my own and pass along what I know."

Isabella did not have any opposition to this plan, as the man was strong and could protect Kael well enough.

One question had been persisting in her mind since they arrived here. It came out before she could stop herself.

"What are the Knights of Kyndis?"

Ijos seemed to smile at the question. "Think of them as the old King's answer to the war we are in now, but you will only hear of them now, and never again. Few people know the extent of the sect."

Isabella felt confused by the answer but felt that the answer she got was the only answer she would get. It seemed that talking about the subject was like a call, as a bird—his familiar, it seemed—flitted down to them and perched on the railing.

Isabella watched as the bird held out its foot, which had a small roll of parchment attached to it. Ijos opened it and read what the in it, scowling as he read. He turned and smiled.

"This is Nuria, my companion. I had sent a letter to Haskell about the details of Caede, and he wrote back. She tends to find me quickly."

He paused as he read the letter again, grimacing in some parts before he resumed a blank face and stowed the letter away.

"Come, let us go back inside and rest. We still have a long trek ahead of us."

Isabella turned her eyes back to the moon and sighed quietly. "You go on ahead. I can't sleep."

Ijos turned and leaned his back on the rail, propping himself up with his elbows, patting Nuria some. She crooned at the affection.

"I understand how it feels to be restless, especially after what you have been through. Unfortunately, it does not get better. The world is in a state of chaos right now, the war creating widows and orphans more every day. This town has its fair share of those that survived any attacks through Hera and possibly even some from other areas."

He turned to her and paused. "The only thing we can is do is stay strong for the children while we travel to the capital."

She quietly sobbed in the moonlight, aware that Ijos was looking at her. Not with judgment or pity, but rather with understanding. She understood that now that she knew what he had been through. Nuria crooned again in the silence.

He propped himself back up on his feet and walked towards their room, Nuria gliding to perch on his shoulder, and paused a moment as he reached for the handle. His sword was still on his waist, glistening in the moonlight.

"Don't stay up too long. Like I said, we still have a long road ahead of us. But I understand you need some time."

Isabella stayed outside for some time, staring at the moon, and letting her mind digest the events that had happened. She sobbed and tried to remember her time with Caedmon.

When dawn broke the sky, the group headed out of town. Isabella awoke and saw that Ijos had tied another letter to Nuria and released her into the sky, watching as she flew into the foggy distance.

The town did not have much in the way of equipment or food, which is understandable with the refugees. The town was crowded enough that it took some time to get to the westward gate, which was in no better shape than the east gate.

The scenery changed little as they walked; there were fields of scorched earth and forests decimated, either as collateral damage through battles or used as material for any faction or town to create barricades. In the far distance they could see outposts for soldiers, but they stayed far enough away, knowing that they would be full of any survivors as well as the wounded and sick.

They continued to walk through abandoned battlefields and remnants of forests, focusing on surviving as they traveled to Mynheir, the Capital.

III

Azalea became quiet after she retold her dream. She remembered very well how she felt after the incident in the abandoned town, how she could not digest the

266

violation. She sighed and stretched in her saddle as they continued the path.

The rumbling continued in the distance. She tried to think if she saw any storm clouds in the sky before they entered the forest, but she couldn't remember. The rumbling stopped almost as suddenly as it started, and she focused again on the memory.

"I still can't be around my mother."

Kael glimpsed at her from the side. She was still looking forward, but she was fighting to avert her eyes. He surmised it was shame or guilt.

"I know it wasn't her fault, you know. What happened to us, and what happened to Gareth and Zareth. She did the best she could in her situation. But I still felt like she let it happen, despite the fact it happened to *her* too, and I couldn't be around her after that. I folded inside."

"I left her when I was still a teenager. I ran away because I couldn't take it anymore. I felt like I could watch myself better on my own." Her eyes glistened with tears. "All the stuff that happened... on the road, in Mynheir, we even moved out back to a small town in Hera for a while... it was all too much. I never felt safe with her."

"And what I realize now is I only felt safe by myself, except for you. I didn't feel threatened or anything with you, even as kids. Maybe it's because you saved me and killed the man who... did that to me. Or maybe it was because you treated me normal afterwards and didn't push yourself on me or ignore me."

Kael opened his mouth to speak but nothing came out. He had no words of solace. He saw the child she was then. He felt himself transported back when he was a child, too.

At that time, as a child, he didn't feel like he was doing anything. He remembered knowing she needed saved and acted, nothing more or less. And she had to survive afterwards, so he did what Ijos said to do. She was a child like he was, and they were both living through the same hell. He didn't see her any different.

Azalea filled the silence with her own words. She didn't want a response. She needed to further her monologue as a catharsis. A necessary outlet, and Kael was that outlet she needed.

"Since then, I've been on the road. I fell into the mercenary job when someone noticed my swordsmanship and wanted me to fight for them."

She let go of her reins and looked at her hands. "I've killed so many people, taken their lives. And every time I've done it, their face would look like those men, or Haskell, even sometimes my mother. And the last one always made me feel guilt."

"They were always the most important targets, too. I would hesitate, but then I would be filled with such a rage and do it blindly. Then I would drink myself to sleep."

She was going to continue, but the distant rumbling became an avalanche of noise. It sounded like a crack of lightning had hit close by, though the forest was lush without damage.

The whole caravan stopped and had to soothe their horses, spooked into a frenzy. They drew their weapons and watched the forest for anything. Some murmurs began about a golem or hydra, chittering of their past encounters in Eissizir Weald.

Kael moved from the caravan and surveyed at his surroundings. The forest seemed unremarkable, but on closer sight, he could see things were amiss. In the distance, he saw trees that looked older than the rest, or at least what remained of them looked old.

It could have been chalked up to age, but the remains of the older trees were broken, with no log on the ground to accompany it. He examined the trunk and noticed it had a pattern that looked like something had torn the tree away from it. The rumble continued off in the west of the path they were following.

He felt a surge, his hairs standing on end under his clothes and he spontaneously spurred Jorunn in the direction of the rumbling. He could hear the protests of the group and Azalea yelling his name. All of it faded into nothing as he delved deeper into the copse.

IV

He felt it, *heard it.* Hushed whispers as he passed similar broken trees, ripped from their stumps. Their voices echoed the same sentiment: *save the sacred one.*

Save the heart of the copse. The echoes grew louder the longer he and Jorunn delved deeper into the forest, further off the path and enveloped in a fog that was denser than normal. It all culminated in a loud uproar in his head of whispers before it was dead silent.

He came upon a shallow pond, glimmering in the soft light of the canopy. It exuded a sense of calm—but within it was a sickness, a plague gnawing at flesh. He looked at the rippling of the water as his mind came back from the uproar of the whispering trees. When his mind came to, he heard *it*—the sickness he felt come to life.

A sickly chewing sound came not too far from the pond, the shallow waters circling a singular tree. It was much larger and much older than the rest of the trees in this forest, and he could feel the vibrations coming from it, the calm he felt before. But with every chewing sound came a disruption of that vibration. The jolt was like a metallic bar striking each vertebra of his back.

The fog was dense, but a monstrous shape clung to the tree. He dismounted and stepped through the ankle-deep water into the grove. The fog cut through as he walked onto the next land and he saw what it was: a scaly, putrid beast with pus running down its back.

He knew it was the embodiment of the sickness he felt. It had its back turned and was chewing on the ancient tree, eating its bark one piece at a time.

Kael heard a noise coming from the feet of the monstrosity and his eyes followed. There he saw a small animal, bloodied, biting at the monster's legs to no avail. It was a fox, small and primarily white, though it still had splotches of orange and brown.

Help me! Kael heard reverberate through his head. It was high, but not head splitting, nor did it sound worldly. *If this tree dies, so does this forest!*

The monster paused its chewing long enough to finally notice the fox biting at it. In a blur the mass swung its foot, and the fox flew away from the grove. It landed in the shallows, its blood seeping from the blunt trauma into the water.

Kael reacted instinctively, his body moving on its own as he unsheathed one sword and swung heftily at the leg that kicked the fox. He cut it clean off the body, the appendage rolling down the gentle slope. He lunged toward it, not understanding why, but he couldn't let the severed leg touch that water. He stuck his sword into it and held it up. Its weight was immense, requiring both his arms to lift his sword with the leg stabbed through like a hog on a spit.

The leg wriggled and writhed, pulling him back towards the beast, who had stopped munching on the tree. Tendrils reached from the leg towards the stump it once called home. Kael knew it would try to reattach, although he did not know why he knew this. He used his strength and spun around, flinging the leg far into the woods and away from the grove.

His hesitation after was a mistake.

The beast was in his face, its own a mix between a rodent and a bear, with all its sore open and pus running down it. He had no time to react as a paw came crashing into his side, sending him flying into the shallow water as well.

He rolled with arms overhead and his sword clattered away from him. He landed beside the fox, who was barely breathing. Kael put his hand on the fox, who shivered from the touch. He felt a warm, vibrating sensation come up his arm.

Save... save the goddess. She lives in the tree.

Kael struggled to stand up, the blow knocking him off kilter for a moment. He got up and grabbed his fallen sword, unsheathed the other, and muttered his incant under his breath. The air distorted slightly as he felt a pull towards the fox. His words ended with a weight to them, and he felt the air funnel to his blades, igniting them.

He used a small rock on the slope to jump, gaining enough height to see the beast's neck. He swung in a wide arc, spinning midair as the first blade cut through the nape. The second blade stopped—the flesh began to heal—and the flames dissipated.

The flesh held Kael on his back despite his efforts to put the sword free. The monster then grabbed him and slammed him into the tree, knocking the air out of him. It threw him on the opposite side of the shallow pond, his swords cluttering away from him.

Kael could hear his heartbeat in his head with each breath. He could feel warmth from his chest as lacerations oozed into the water.

He stumbled upright and over to his fallen swords. The wet blades glistened in the dim forest light. His eyes drooped, shutting tight as he dropped to his knees. He heard the monster stomp away—and then the chewing resumed.

Why must I be so useless? I can't do anything right. I can't even save this forest! Must I always fail?

He buried his face into his hands, feeling a burn in his eyes, hot and painful. *I couldn't even save Ijos when he needed me most.*

He felt a warmth brush up again his arm and opened his eyes to see the bloodied fox lying beside him. It was breathing heavily and peered at him with blue eyes like his own.

There was an understanding there, like it could read his thoughts. There was a red flash across his vision, like a red bird flying into the distance. It crooned, an all too familiar sound. *Nuria...?* But it also felt like a fire.

I can lend you my powers, it said telepathically, *just so we can beat this monster and save the goddess. You've used it before, calling upon my aid in battle. I heard you—praying for power. Kael, let me lend you my power once more.*

Kael breathed heavily and nodded. The fox stood up and howled, turning into a mist and entering Kael's blades. His blades ignited, turning red, then blue, and then finally white; the heat was extraordinary.

But it did not harm Kael. The flames touched his hands but did not hurt. He turned and felt the flames pull energy into his body, strengthening his muscles and dulling his pain.

He sprinted towards the beast and before he left the shallows, he jumped high. He cleared the canopy of the forest and descended on its head. He used the blades parallel to stab downwards and pierced its skull with a loud *crack* resonating through the forest.

The monster tried to pull its arms up to grab Kael, but it floundered, the white flames pouring through its body. White flames roared out of its mouth, eyes, and ears as its body was burned from the inside out.

Kael stood on a pile of ash and the white flames were gone. He felt the energy sap from his body and the fox was beside him, still bloody, but much less injured this time. He collapsed on the pile of ashes.

Kael, the fox came up and brushed his arm, and a warmth resonated through him. His wounds closed on his chest and his muscles relaxed. Exhaustion fell over him like a wave.

We are bound by fate, Kael. I have been watching you for some time in the celestial realm. Bind with me, much like Ijos bound with Nuria, the phoenix spirit. I am Kinaa, the Kitsune. We are two parts of the same soul. Let our soul bind.

Kael felt in a daze, picking himself up and leaning again the elder tree. He chuckled, but it came out more like a wheeze. "I would rather die than bind. Fate doesn't dictate me..."

He faded into unconsciousness as Kinaa laid beside him, her words distorted through the fog of sleep. As he fell into darkness, the one thing he remembered was her saying *at the brink of death, will you still refuse fate?*

V

Azalea found Kael leaning against an ancient tree unconscious. She hurried to him and checked to see if he was dead, but his breathing was heavy with sleep.

There was a large pile of ash in front of him as well as some smeared on his clothes. There was blood in the shallow water surrounding the ancient tree and she opened his clothes. There was no wound, not even a bruise on his skin.

Kael woke when he felt Jorunn nuzzling him, pulling his hair on accident. He sat up in his deer skin bedroll. He realized he had been changed into the black shirt and spare pants he kept in his saddlebags. Jorunn nuzzled him again and he patted her before standing up.

"I wouldn't try that yet if I were you." Azalea was sitting beside his bed, eating a small bowl of stew. "When we found you, you looked pretty pale, though you had no

275

bruises. Your clothes were soaked and dirty. I searched your bags to find those. Hope you don't mind."

Kael shook his head to clear the fog in his mind. *The monster, that was it. And the fox... fated to bond? Is it the one I saw in the drawing, hearing when I use fire?* He grunted as he shifted on the bedroll. There was a dull ache deep within him, but he pushed through it. "There was a monster eating some ancient tree. I think it was the heart of this forest."

Azalea nodded but focused on her soup. "You were leaning on an ancient tree when we found you. And that pile of ash, it must have been the monster. I can feel it, the heart, or at least that something's different. The forest feels much safer now."

"The men noticed it, too," she gestured towards the troops. "They were worried that ominous rumbling would return, and we would be attacked by some monster, like a golem. But it never came again."

Kael glanced over at a tree to see his clothing hanging, dried and mostly clean. "How long have I been out?"

She stirred her soup, but she finally looked at him. Her eyes seemed puffy and heavy. She hasn't slept. "'Bout half a day. It was getting close to sunset when you broke off, so some set up camp and some searched for you."

Kael got up despite her advice against it and walked over to retrieve his dried clothes. His belt bag and baldric were draped over the branches as well, and the pouches were still heavy with his items.

He opened each pouch and examined to make sure they were not ruined. He pulled out the map he had, and it was still wet; the ink had bled and smudged. He walked over to the fire and threw it in. It hissed and sizzled, the edges curling and turning red with fire.

He watched it for a second before he returned to his clothes. His tunic had dried enough and the ashes were washed off. He returned to his former battle wear and stowed away the other clothes.

He strapped his belt on before returning to his bed roll. His weapons were laid beside it, so he tied the baldrics back into the scabbards and slung them over his back. His hunting knife was strapped to his right leg like usual.

He picked up a small katana and held it in his hands for a moment, turning it over in his hands. He pulled the blade from its sheath and examined it. It glistened like it was new. Azalea shifted closer to him.

"That's the one you had as a boy, right?"

"No," he croaked. His gaze fixed through the steel. "It was lost a long time ago. No, this one was a gift." He turned the blade in his hands. "A very special gift."

He sheathed it and stood up. "We should get moving. We don't have too much further in this forest, and we should leave it before sunset."

The group picked up their camp and as Kael sat in his saddle, he glanced back once in the direction of the Grove. How he knew it in was in that direction he did not

277

know, but he felt certain it was, and he could feel that Kinaa was watching him as well.

He clucked Jorunn on, despite feeling a strong pull back, but he did not concede to fate—not yet.

The Capital

Parting

I

Kael was right, after all, that they would exit the forest by sunset. The orange and pink gleam of the sunset bore down on them. The encroaching dusk cooled the heat that greeted them from the coolness of the forest shade. The forest gave way to the town Gormsey, nestled in a sprawling field.

Maybe it was post-war expansionism, or maybe it was just the predictable march of civilization, but the large field was smaller now due to an expansion of the town. The original town itself still had remnants of a wall long since torn down.

War was less present in this area, less so than the north or the south; the eastern side was relatively civil. Refugees from wars past fled from less fortunate towns and rebuilt their lives here.

Even though the field was smaller, it still boasted plentiful crops for the town and for trade, as the group passed by rows upon rows of different harvests. Wheat and barley were always the winning crops, but there was also corn and potatoes, pumpkins were beginning to grow large, and there were some other stalk plants like sharpscane.

They passed by the newer homes and into the older part of town, where they picked out a tavern that was as good as any to lodge at. The men reveled in glasses of mead and beer, Azalea joining in, but not drowning herself in it like usual. Kael seated himself at the bar when he felt a hand grab his shoulder. He glanced over to see Jude beside him, holding two glasses of beer.

"Join us." Jude held out a glass at Kael, nearly spilling some. His face seemed placid, but not fully genuine. "I know we've not spoke much, nor have we always seen eye-to-eye about—things," his gaze glossed over to a corner. He cleared his throat and continued. "We have all been through a lot together in that short time. Join us."

Kael nodded and walked over to the tables that the group occupied. Half were already hammered, and the other half were on their way. Azalea watched as the men happily drank and sang, slurring the lyrics to near incomprehensible gibberish. She smiled at them until Kael sat down beside her, which she turned her head, and her smile dropped a little. He kicked his feet up on the stool opposite of him.

"They're a merry bunch, eh?" He said as he followed the words down with a gulp of beer. It was watery and bland.

"Aye, they're always ken to drowning their worries in the devil's juice with good company." She swirled her own drink but didn't lift it to her mouth. "What do you say we leave them to their merriment and have some of our own?"

Kael upturned his glass and drank the rest of the watered beer in two gulps, then stood up and let her out. He followed her to a small room in the tavern that served as a boarding room, and they quickly became undressed and intertwined again.

The summer heat had dissipated since the last, long before the events of the forest and the realization they were traveling partners in their childhood. The coolness of the late summer, nearly autumn winds prevented them from sweating too much, not sticking to each other as they lay in bed afterwards.

Kael laid with his arm over his face and Azalea studied the ceiling afterwards. She sighed and turned towards him. He could still sense her stare.

"You're leaving again, aren't you?"

He pulled his arm off his face and stared at the ceiling. "I feel like my path is heading towards the Capital, and yours does not. There will come a time, and soon, that we will have to part ways again."

She bit her lip in the faint darkness. "Why don't you come with us instead? Is this so important?"

"It is to me," His voice came out in a sharp exhale, betraying his own guilt. It shook with every word.

"I must find what I am searching for, and it seems the only trail is from the past. And our past goes to Mynheir."

She stood up in the darkness, the moonlight glistening off her bare body. He could see there were scars, too. He noticed a good many were around her hips. "Mynheir is a dark place, Kael. The things that happened there... it was awful. I remember it all now."

She sat on the bed and faced the window. He could see the glistening of tears streaming down her face. "I don't want to lose you to that forsaken place, too." She turned to him. "Even then, you held me together. You were like the brothers I lost, but so much more."

She spoke through the night. Kael listened as she told him what happened to her while she lived in the capital. His story in hers was short, but she told it as if it was the only important part of the story.

He listened to her talk about her rebellion, how she would run from her mother and hide in the slums of the city. How she would play with the poorest children and fight with the noble kids. How she threw a knife at Haskell when she was a teenager, and how she started sleeping with older men in the dirtiest bars in the lower districts.

She felt disgusted with herself, but she felt a missing part of her in these men, the low-lifes who reveled in the young. She talked about her self-depreciation and her acts of rebellion against her mom and her uncle.

It all culminated in her fleeing the capital and joining a traveling band of mercenaries. They used her, of course, but she did not care as long as she could fight and let out some of her anger. War was grey, and she wanted to be grey, too. She did not care if she took a life, or one thousand lives, as long as she could turn grey.

When morning came, she had fallen asleep against Kael, who held her tightly. The stories folded into silence, carrying them to where their lives once again coalesced. His hands rested over hers, interlocked like they could not bear to be apart. Their skin pressed with no space between—like even the air might pull them apart. They looked more like lost children than lovers, who only took solace in one another to fill that loneliness.

II

The road beyond Gormsey forked atop a small hillock. At the fork there were two signs. To the left was a sign with AISHA and an arrow pointing left, while the right sign had MYNHEIR with an arrow to the right.

Kael turned Jorunn towards Mynheir and the group stopped. There were some murmurs amongst them, but they hushed when Azalea glanced back at them. She turned to Kael after they stopped.

"Are you sure about this?" She eyed past him, down the slope and along the road. In the distance was the city of Mynheir, its stone towers like swords thrusting into the sky. Her eyes turned vacant for a moment before she came back to reality. "Your path can always diverge."

Kael shook his head. "This is my fate, if there is such a thing. I'm sure of this."

They both dismounted and hugged, the longing between them almost palpable. The men dismounted, too, and they all said their farewells, some shaking his hand, some hugging him awkwardly. Jude was the last to say goodbye, shaking Kael's and bringing him close. Jude's mouth was close to Kael's ear.

"I will keep her safe. Just know that your absence will leave a mark on her."

Kael furrowed his brow and nodded, acknowledging the possible consequences. He watched the group mount their steeds and leave the hillock, the late summer winds blowing leaves that turned early in a small whirlwind. The group became specks before he moved, taking the right path down. The road continued for miles, and he passed a merchant wagon or two on the way, but he did not see much in the large plains surrounding the capital.

Kael came upon a large lake in the field when he was close enough to start seeing tiny specks of soldiers moving in the large walls surrounding the city. He watched the sky turn dark. The lake was surrounded by small cliff sides; the water embedded much lower than the road.

What started as a few drops of rain quickly turned into a downpour. In the midst, Kael found a small overhang of cliff on the shore of the lake and led Jorunn down to it. The overcast sky made it hard to tell what time of day it was, but Kael did not bother with a campfire just yet. He sat on a rock jutting from the sands and watched the rain pour onto the lake, creating a fine mist that hovered above the waters.

He watched this for some time before he observed some of the mist take shape of a man hovering, the features blurred by the fluid form of the mist. From it came whispers, lulling him into standing and walking to the shore.

The form came closer, holding out a hand towards Kael, bargaining for him to leap into the water with it. He walked without a thought, intrigued by the spirit, unaware of the slimy tentacle wrapping around his foot. He heard the spirit whisper to him again.

"Come, warrior, this is your fate. Your home rests at the bottom of this lake."

Then a laugh and the tentacle yanked him underwater. He struggled and kicked to no avail; the pull too strong for him to grab a sword off his back. The light of the overcast sky was replaced by the darkness of the water.

He felt the burn in his lungs; he knew he would need to inhale soon—either air or water. In the depths came a gleam of one giant eye attached to the tentacle, and he felt several more tentacles starting to wrap around his body.

He clasped at his leg, seeing the rims of his sight turning red. He fumbled, his hand raking against the cloth and then leather, finally to the handle of the knife, and pulled it jaggedly.

He felt the sting of the water on the cut, but the pain in his lungs took precedence. The blood suspended in the water as he cut a couple of the tentacles lashing at him before he freed himself from the one around his foot.

He felt the rumble of a scream underwater and the eye disappeared. There was silence only for it to return with a chopping jaw below it. It clenched and chopped at him, inching closer. He retreated slightly before anchoring himself on the edges of the maw with his feet. He then thrust the knife into the eye of the beast, and it squealed then descended into the depths.

Kael's vision was nearly gone at this point, and he could feel his lungs about to explode. His vision blackened long before the surface came, death grabbing as his feet to pull him under.

But he breached the surface and gasped for the burning breaths his lungs so desperately needed. He clamored and fought back onto the shore and watched the misty form approach him, cackling again.

"Well done, warrior, but do not revel in this. Your path will be littered with trials more arduous than this beast. Some you may never hope to slay, just like the sorcerer you seek so fervently."

Kael stood and unsheathed his sword and swung at the mist, dispelling it with a loud hiss. In the loud noise he heard a *clang* and looked down to see a knife, green with gold ornamentation. The mist began to recede on the water away from him and heard the voice one last time.

"For the monsters who prove most difficult, even with your expertise."

The rain had stopped and the mist was gone. Kael picked up the knife and unsheathed it. The blade was a magnificent ivory color, pristine and polished to a mirror sheen. It had a faint inscription on it in a language he had not seen before. A new voice rose up from the blade and spoke to him, deep and distant, as if from the depths of the water.

At the same time, the artifacts in his pouch began to tremble. He sat down on the rock on the shore and closed his eyes, breathing deeply. He willed himself into memory—not to escape, but to understand. To reaffirm his path is the right one.

III

The road to Mynheir was long. The group reached the top of a hill to see the dazzling city in the distance, a true marvel in contrast to the countryside. The outskirts were lively with wagons and people, some just traveling, some were refugees that were seeking solace in the city.

The group managed to hitch a ride onto a merchant wagon, a young boy who had just begun the trade. He and Ijos talked while they passed the refugee camps, consisting of either makeshift tents or drab homes made of leftover wood and scraps. There were many small camps in the area with people huddled around fires, cooking small portions of meat, and sharing scraps of food.

Soldiers guarded the gate, so the boy had to show papers that proved he was part of the Merchant's guild, who let him pass alongside the group. The city itself was massive: the roads were cobblestone even on the outskirts, with shops on every corner as well as taverns at every stone's throw.

The merchant headed beyond the outskirts and entered through a second gate that separated the city into an inner and outer section. Inner Mynheir was elegant, with its paved roads and buildings made of finer stones, its streets lit by everlasting torches, and the taverns clean and sophisticated. Brothels were still aplenty, but they exuded elegance like the rest of the Inner Capital; the women were blemish-free, and they did not cake their faces with powder and makeup. The capital Mynheir truly was distinctly different from the rest of the world, almost as if they were disconnected from the gruesome war.

The group went their separate ways from the merchant when he arrived at his own guild; a massive structure that resembled a bank in the market that surrounded the castle grounds.

The market was livelier than whole towns in the countryside, busier than any port Ijos had been. He tried to avoid the capital as much as possible and he felt like he could never get used to its pace, so his pace quickened through the market.

He wanted to reach the castle as soon as possible, but everything mesmerized Isabella and Azalea they passed. It was the first time they looked bemused since the incident on the highway, so Ijos backed his pace back down so they could sight see. The two would gasp and stare at many objects; dolls from the west that looked like they were made of porcelain, scarves that emitted warmth and heat for the bitter cold of winter, and much of the market sold magical items to the masses.

What was delegated to sorcerers in the country was available at hand here, where potions were sold in bulk that could help you regrow hair or change your eye color. There were remedies for stomach aches and for gout. Most seemed superficial at best, aimed to enlarge the already bloated ego of the wealthier class that lived in this part of the capital.

In the market the group was encumbered by the crowd and Ijos looked around to see Kael was gone from his side. He searched frantically, pushing several people out of the way, yelling his name.

"Kael!" The people eyed him oddly and some ignored him outright. He had retraced his steps enough and ran into a priest, dressed in a white robe with his face covered. Ijos noticed Kael beside the priest, clasped at the robe.

His eyes did not look the same despite peering at Ijos. The priest clasped Kael's shoulder, the other hidden by a long sleeve.

"I found the young boy wandering by himself. I could not bear to think that he was lost and would not find his father." The priest's cowl shifted in what Ijos thought was a smile. "I was helping him search when you found us."

Ijos feigned a smile back and held out his hand for Kael. "Thank you, father. Your kind gestures are appreciated. Come, Kael." Ijos stared at the boy, who still had a cloudy expression, like he was far away. Ijos grabbed his hand and pulled him away from the priest's grasp.

"Kael!" He shook the boy and his eyes cleared. His gaze shifted between Ijos and the priest. He grasped at Ijos' robe and turned away from the priest.

As they departed from the priest did he notice Isabella and Azalea behind them. Isabella watched him with concern, but Ijos walked past her with Kael in tow. "Let's go."

The marketplace bustled without missing a beat. Ijos glanced back after, but the priest had dissolved into the crowd, unable to be located. It was as if he turned into thin air. Ijos was tired of this place already.

Hoping to make haste to the castle at once, he tapped on Isabella's shoulder. He gestured to the sky—the noise of the market was too overbearing for speech. The sun was on its descending path, indicating that sunset would be coming before too long and there would be plenty to tend to once they have met Haskell.

It was then that they resumed their trek to the castle, passing the remaining shops and carts in the market to pass through the upscale part of the city, home to the lower officials of the court. Ijos watched the people pass and scanned the alleyways. He felt like the priest would show up again, and he felt an odd presence of the man. He felt more at ease when they passed through the upper district and into the castle grounds.

The castle itself was guarded from the rest of the city by large, iron-wrought fencing that blocked the view inside, with the only way into the castle grounds was by a large metal gate guarded by several soldiers.

As the group came close to the gate, one of the men spoke up in a clear, commanding voice.

"Halt! State your presence and identity!"

Ijos motioned for the group to stop and pulled a metal pendant from his neck. The pendant bore a red shield with ancient writing on it.

The soldier contorted his face into confusion then to a blank, but stern, expression. "Is that supposed to mean something to me? I do not recognize such a crest as a red shield! State your business!"

It was then that a deep voice rose from behind them, "That is enough, soldier! I know this group. They are with me."

The group turned to see a large man clad in armor, save for his head, which was topped by dark hair swept back revealing a face that was rugged but elegant, clean shaven and accented by emerald eyes.

The face was brightened even more by a smile that blossomed at the sight of the group; a smile infectious as Isabella and Azalea bloomed smiles as well.

"Haskell!" Isabella turned and yelled. "It is so good to see you!"

Haskell walked to embrace Isabella and Azalea, but they both withdrew. Haskell stopped, confused over the reaction, but he smiled anyway.

"It is great to see you, Belle! And my, Azalea, how you have grown!" Haskell boomed, but then he quickly cut it short. "I heard about the massacre. But where are Gareth and Zareth? Ijos notified me that you made it out of the town safely with the children."

Isabella broke down at the mention of her two sons with Azalea looking hollow. The joys of seeing the spectacle in the city had been a good enough distraction for a moment but she went back to the numb stature she was accustomed to now. Ijos stepped up and told Haskell about finding the girls attacked by bandits and the boys dead.

"For fuck's sake... why were you not there?" Haskell roared at Ijos and slammed his fists on the ground, denting the gauntlets with the force. "You were supposed to protect them! That's why I hired you! Your order is supposed to protect..."

Haskell cut his anger short, quelling himself and became dead silent. Ijos regarded him with blank eyes, knowing the man was right. His mission was to bring the family back safely and he failed.

Ijos withdrew a dagger from his thigh and stabbed himself in the left shoulder. He raked the blade down to tear the muscle. He had full intention on ripping his body apart until he died when he snapped back to reality by the familiar tug at his sleeve.

Kael was worried but did not stop him. Isabella, however, ran to Ijos and pulled the dagger away from him, only to slap him in the face. Her face was pale, but her eyes were burning.

"Don't you disgrace my boys' memory with this. You avenged them and saved us. It is not your f-fault," her eyes began to pool. "You did the best you could."

And maybe it was the best he could do. But for him it wasn't enough. He tried to grasp at the dagger, avoiding her eyes. She pulled her hand further away, out of his reach, then tossed the dagger near Haskell. It clattered against the cobblestone, blood dropping from the force. Haskell hesitated before picking up the weapon.

She then hugged him and gave him a kiss on the cheek. "I should have thanked you from the beginning."

Ijos nodded his head and thanked her. In the back, Haskell glared at the embrace between Ijos and Isabella and the dagger twisted in his hands.

IV

Kael twisted the dagger in his hand. Normally the memories had something to do with the object he found, though he did not see the object during any of the memory.

He studied the blade again, then stowed it away in his saddlebag for the time being. The sun began to creep out from the clouds, so he mounted Jorunn and set back on the path.

Kael rode Jorunn across the plains, following the well beaten path that led to the Capital Mynheir. The outskirts of the capital were surrounded by makeshift homes and small farms tended by peasants.

The outskirts looked like a small village, full of life separate from the walls it leaned on. Kael passed by the village with minimal attention.

He entered the city's outer walls with relative ease; the only issue was the wait to get in through the guards stationed at the outer gate. Kael traveled through the outer wall, the lower tier of the capital, not pausing to look at the sights.

The inner wall was smaller but more populated; the market of the capital was the prestigious gem of Mynheir, save for the castle of the King. He dismounted Jorunn and walked while in the inner gate, walking slowly amongst the busier streets.

The market was busy as usual. Kael noticed the vendors and the shops, each selling more ridiculous items than the last. He caught glimpses of potions that could cure baldness and a talisman that would grant luck.

He thought it was all ridiculous. He noticed a small clock shop with clocks of varying sizes as he passed into the noble's district. His passage went far enough to pass a small cemetery, noting that he felt it was for the nobles that lived in the city.

Kael paused when he saw a familiar house to his left. It stood out amongst the other homes, and it was built of a redder brick than the others. He stood in front of that home for some time before he tied Jorunn to its fence, walking up the steps, and knocking on its door.

The old oak door stirred something inside him. He could see two sets of green eyes, one darker than the other. One holding more malice, and the other pain. Kael knocked once more, his heart demanding he see one of those eyes. There was a momentary silence before he heard a shuffling, the door unlocking, and Kael meeting eyes with a man.

V

"Come in, I have plenty of room for everyone." Haskell's home in the inner district was massive; a perk of being a commander in the royal army. The home was accented with plenty of gold and silver, and the walls were bright white—so bright that it was blinding. "I can have the servants get you some clothes, but in the meantime, there are two baths here. Take your time."

The girls giggled and reveled in the idea of a bath. The group began to separate to bathe, but Haskell stopped Ijos.

"Ijos, may I speak with you for a moment?"

Ijos glanced back at the group and Kael, who held onto his sleeve. Isabella redirected Kael's hand and smiled at Ijos.

"I can take him. Don't worry."

Ijos nodded and smiled at them before they left. He turned to Haskell, whose disposition changed to something more severe.

"Walk with me, if you please."

Ijos followed Haskell down a hallway opposite the way the girls and Kael went, which led themselves outside into a small garden filled with flowers. At the center was a cherry blossom tree. Haskell had his back to Ijos, but he could sense the strain on the man's face.

"Do you like this place? I tend to come here when I am deep in thought. Just like now, when I am trying so hard to figure out how you could just abandon that family and let them suffer. Even the fact you let my brother die—"

He walked over to the cherry blossom tree and gently touched it.

"Do you remember this tree? I had it brought here a long time ago. I always thought that the falling blossoms were so serene. Don't you agree? Or does it

298

remind you of something else, like loss and hopelessness?"

Ijos tried not to respond, but his face betrayed him with the twitch of a grimace before it returned to its normal calmness.

"Haskell, if I may, I tried my best to save everyone. My mission was to escort them to the capital safely. I had no idea that there would be an attack on Caede. Do you really think that Lord Caedmon would abandon his people?"

Haskell observed the sky in silence.

"No, I suppose not. My brother was always the type to throw himself into danger. I was hoping that would have changed when he had a family." A petal floated down, and Haskell caught it. He rubbed it between his index finger and thumb, enough for the petal to tear.

"But the twins..."

"When Caede fell, that boy—" Ijos gestured towards the inside of the house, "was orphaned. I took him in and as we searched for Isabella, there were complications—"

The sharp thud of Haskell's fist connecting with Ijos' face echoed in the garden. Ijos fell to the ground and blood poured from his face. There was a slight breeze, and the cherry blossom tree wavered in the wind, causing petals to fall.

Haskell was seething, standing over Ijos, and pumping his fists tighter. "I don't care about your excuses.

I sent you on a task as your superior and you failed me. I saved your life all those years ago, when my father invaded your village, and this is how you repay me? I should have let him kill you."

Ijos said nothing as he stood, walking out of the garden in silence. Haskell stared at him as he went, still crushing the petal between his fingers.

Malice

I

The door opened and a frail, old man was standing in the doorway, staring back at Kael.

"May I help you?"

"I may have the wrong address. Is there an Isabella that lives here?"

The man gawked at him. His eyes were murky brown, dulled by age. "No, sir, you may be mistaken. I have lived in this house for the past twenty-some years by myself. No one has lived in this home since the late commander used to live here."

"I see, thank you. I apologize."

Kael left the doorway and untethered Jorunn. He felt that the capital was a dead end, leaving the void to encroach upon him again. He wandered the alleyways aimlessly for some time.

Then it pervaded his mind; what was dark seemed to turn to a peaceful, purple cloud. There was a lull to the feeling that seemed to yank into him. That feeling was stronger in a certain direction, and—like bait on a line—it led him.

What it led to was an old house somewhere on the outskirts of the market. The outside was drab, with paint peeling and rickety posts. He tethered Jorunn to one of the posts and walked into the home. Inside was dimly lit by candles, reminiscent of that purple cloud. The fire was purple to him. A very attractive young lady was at the desk and smiling at him.

"Welcome." Her smile widened. "What services would you like today?"

Kael cocked his head and turned around. He did not see a sign outside the building and the room appeared normal, but it had no notion of a business. "What services?"

"This is a brothel. What service would you like today? Sensual massage with happy ending? Maybe a blow job? Or would you like the full package?"

Her eyes flickered for a moment. It was purple, an overbearing purple that consumed him. The candles danced and he felt like he was swimming in them. Then came a twitch in his body and a heat that was uncontrollable. He felt something wet and noticed he was drooling, too. And then he felt the more surprising urge that he would dry hump her if he could not be with her immediately. Red flags were alarming in his mind, but his body began to move on its own. "The full package, and now. Please," his voice begged. Deep in the cloud, his own inner voice was screaming. *It's a trap! Don't do it, you idiot!*

The woman smiled and held out her hand and he took it like an impatient child. She led him through a dim hallway and into a small room that was fashioned with a single bed. She pushed him onto the bed and before he knew it, he had undressed himself. He felt the throbbing sensation down below and it was nearly painful.

This is magic, his inner voice said. *A succubus, and if I don't get away...*

The voice drowned out when the lady lunged onto him and began to ferociously kiss him. She had undressed rather quickly, and he smelled the scent of cherry blossoms and old leather mixed with the metallic taste of iron. He felt him enter her and then a wave of paresthesia radiated from there.

The clouds consumed him. As it was transitioning to darkness, he heard a voice. A man's voice ('Does Nuria pique your interest?') and the faint clash of swords came through the darkness.

II

Months had passed since Ijos, Isabella, Azalea, and Kael had arrived at the capital. Winter was gone, too, and with it spring had arrived. The trees were dotted with pink and white, some red, and the courtyards were in bloom and vibrant amidst the growing war outside the walls.

Ijos did not spend much time in Haskell's home after they arrived. He eventually started renting a small home in the middle district, which had two bedrooms so that Kael could have his own room.

Kael still did not speak, rather he used his actions to convey. Ijos opted to stay either in the aviary where Nuria resided or training with Kael in the training grounds of the castle, that is, when he was not away on missions.

It became apparent after they arrived at the capital that Ijos was a part of the royal army, though he would not explain what role he had. Isabella would often keep Kael when Ijos was away. This time, though, Ijos was home, and he and Kael were in the training grounds.

The sun was at its zenith while he sparred Kael, teaching him how to pirouette as well as proper footwork. Nuria was perched on a nearby post during this, calmly watching the session with her sharp eyes.

The air was hot. Both Ijos and Kael were drenched in sweat, so they rested for a moment in between sets. Ijos noticed that in the months that passed, the boy had grown a bit more. He was taller, and the training had shaped his body with definition.

Ijos was no longer sure of the boy's age. At moments he seemed around five. But when he wielded a sword, Ijos could see remnants of the man he will come to be—the stern, ferocious expression that made Ijos worry for his future.

For now, though, he was still a young child, and Ijos could not push him too hard yet. So, they rested in the shade of a tree on the training grounds, sipping from a leather waterskin. Ijos noticed Kael would sneak glances at Nuria often.

"Does Nuria pique your interest?"

Kael nodded. Ijos knew the day would come when the boy would be interested in Nuria. It is only natural, as many people do not see such mystical creatures, at least not ones up close. Ijos whistled, beckoning Nuria to perch on his shoulder. She was nearly three feet tall—large for a bird—and looked comical perched on his shoulder.

"She's a phoenix. They say phoenix can create and control fire. They are also immortal, as when they die, they combust and rebirth from the ashes."

Ijos pats the bird, who nuzzles his hand.

"I bonded with her a decade or so ago. There are some people in this world who can bond with creatures like her. Creatures that control elements and have immense powers. No one knows why, though."

The bird hopped on his shoulder and landed beside Kael. The boy stroked the bird, and it let out a croon. Ijos smiled.

"They eventually called these bonded creatures totem spirits. It used to be a ritual, a coming-of-age for some. The previous king, though, saw there was potential in this. He watched soldiers in his ranks rising quickly due to these bonds; their companion gave them powers that could not be recreated artificially."

"But there are few of us. In a world like this, where everything is changing, even this art is lost. My village used to hold rituals for warriors who showed the gift."

It seemed like he watched the clouds roll by for a long time.

"My father was the chief of the village, but he never bonded with a spirit. My grandfather, though, was a great warrior. He was bonded to an Amarok, a large, monstrous wolf. He was one of the greatest ones to come from our village. They say, though, that each deity is unique and will amplify the skills of the host. Passed down in my line was the way to control fire through swordsmanship."

Ijos stood and unsheathed his katana. He took a deep breath and clenched his sword tight. As he did so, his sword became encased with embers and a small flame surrounded the blade.

"The fire itself is an extension, almost a tangible expression of the fighting spirit inside. We can control it and use it to aid us in battle. A normal slice may be able to cut through skin and bone, but with this—" he swung in a large arc, releasing a cascade of flames out in front of him, "we can cut through metal and stone."

Kael watched the dissipating embers with fervor. His eyes licked at them like they were water and he was parched. Ijos saw the potential the child had, saw the latent strength that he could mold. A smile crept up on his face in anticipation of the next moment.

"With Nuria, I can expel so much more. These flames can turn into an inferno."

Ijos turned to Nuria and the tone shifted. Nuria crooned as she leapt into the air and circled him several times. He thrust his blade into the ground, and Nuria disappeared into it.

The air sucked into the hidden blade and Ijos pulled it out, causing a huge inferno as he leapt into the air. The flames formed into a phoenix as he came back down, the fiery bird dive bombing alongside the blade.

The impact let out a huge burst of flames and Nuria was released into the air again. Ijos stood amongst the flames. The flames were widespread but contained, concentrating the power at the impact.

Kael was left untouched and his eyes shone, a smile creeping up on his lips. Ijos felt pride as this child watched him. He wondered if this was how a father felt raising a child and seeing him look up to him, or like a mentor seeing his pupil look at him with reverence.

Ijos coughed a little and reminded himself of reality. He walked over to Kael and sat down. "It does come with a price, though. The world is balanced; power will always have some kind of tradeoff. This power comes at the price of your own health. We weren't designed to withstand the power of these deities, so our bodies wear out faster. I would not rely on these attacks unless I absolutely needed it."

He let out another cough, this one ending in a rough wheeze. He felt the rattle in his chest; the same one he felt after Caede. It worried him. He feigned a smile.

"Come, let's practice some more. You need to learn stronger footwork."

III

"Caede was decimated by the unknown Black sorcerer. This is not the first town in the kingdom to suffer such casualties. While the army is at war with the Vralls to the north, towns have been torn to the ground and loyal subjects have been mutilated."

King Alrich scanned the roundtable of his most trusted men. The faces that stared back at him were stone, betraying no emotion to the news. "What good is a kingdom without its people? The war is not more important than these towns."

There were six men at the table, some were dressed in golden surcoats while some wore ragged clothes more suited for a brigand than that of the King's court. Ijos was among the latter, seated on the left and two chairs down from King Alrich, next to Haskell. Alrich leaned forward for a moment of contemplation. He then leaned back and slumped into his chair.

"The knights of Kyndis were formed when we saw some people could harness the power of their totem spirits." He glanced at the tattered garbed people at his court, resting his eyes on Ijos last.

"So far, it has helped tremendously. We've been able to wipe out dangerous monsters and claim lands we could not before." He regarded a larger man with a black beard. "Cormac, you have been able to reclaim the lands closest to the Wastelands."

Cormac nodded. "It was troubling, indeed. There was a den of vampires nested in the Erris ravine. They had been kidnapping people and livestock alike for years, even miles from their nest."

The King nodded. "And with that, we were able to claim the lands to be used for more crops for the Kingdom. The soil there was especially useful for that of the Orichus tree. I hear a group of druids occupies it now, teaching the medicinal properties of the fruit."

He turned to the others. "Elris, with the chimera plaguing the villages of the northwest, and our commanders of the royal army who have helped with the ongoing war with the Vralls, reclaiming villages and land invaded by those savages as well as subduing revolts of the Outcasts of the Wasteland, the prisoner lands."

"But this army—those monsters," he paused, interlacing his fingers, and sighed. "Those monsters are nothing like we have seen before. What do we do?"

The table was silent. No one responded to his question for some time. Alrich looked weary, born from the weight of a dying kingdom. His once lustrous hair was brittle and dry and his skin tighter against his face.

"We need to do something. We need something."
He rested his hands on the table and bent forward.

Ijos cleared his throat. "When I was at the massacre of Caede, I saw him. The man who leads that army. I even spoke to him."

Alrich peered at him, not entirely shocked by this news, but he did not speak.

"He mentioned that the endless night is nigh. That Balaal will be resurrected and our ambitions of protecting the shards are fruitless."

The room was silent. The men instinctively held their necklaces, each wearing one on their neck, save for Ijos. The air grew heavy for a moment before they all released their necklaces. The King stared at Ijos solemnly.

"We must consider the idea of peace with the Vralls and focus our efforts on the other issue at hand. If we have more forces in our own land, then maybe Caede would not have fell."

Haskell stood up at this notion. "No, the issue is that Caede fell due to the incompetence of these Knights. If Ijos was capable enough in his task, then we would have not lost as many people, and I would not have lost my brother."

Haskell glared at Ijos. "Baldock was a shardbearer as well. We should have kept someone there. Had I not sent him to retrieve them prior and had Baldock not had a feeling this would happen, then we could have lost a shard."

Ijos stood up as well and stared at Haskell. "The sorcerer and his army move sporadically. We did not know why he was moving around. We know it now. I did my best in reaching Caede in time, but I was too late. We need to protect the shards. This army seems to be hitting the towns that are isolated enough that maybe the shardbearers will come out."

His eyes flickered to the King before continuing.

"But I still went, guided by the pretext you had given me. The apprehension that Lord Caedmon had detailed in his letters did not point us towards him. We have only been able to dispatch the remainders after the massacres."

Haskell stepped in close, his face inches from Ijos'. "And yet, even with the information, you failed. Then you failed to protect his family on the highway. There is no room for failures in the King's court. There is no room for you here."

Haskell glared at all the men proclaimed as the Knights of Kyndis. "None of you belong here. To think that such lowborn people could attain knight status, even sitting at the roundtable of the King. My father would be disgusted, even more so that you cannot complete your task."

One of the other noble men in a surcoat clasped Haskell's shoulder. "Haskell, these men have been on the field just as we have. They have proven time and time again they are capable and have led several battles themselves. If your father believed in Ijos, then you should as well."

Haskell grunted at the notion. "My father would have killed him if it were not for me, Warrix. Ijos owes me his life, and this is how he repays me and my family. These vagrants have no place in this court."

Ijos left the room in silence, the objections of the men deaf to his ears. Haskell only stayed for a moment longer before he shrugged off the hand and exited the room in the opposite direction with no objections for him. The King did not speak the whole time, lost in his own thought about the issues at hand before he silently dismissed everyone.

IV

Dinner was eaten in silence. Kael was sitting at the dinner table, too, though Ijos was not present. He often came to eat with them when Ijos was gone for a mission.

Kael and Azalea took well enough to each other that she would entertain him often, playing small games and making him laugh. It was a stark departure to her otherwise nature, where she was quiet and reserved. When he was present, though, she seemed to lighten up some.

Isabella and Haskell did not speak for most of it, both focused on their food. Isabella glanced at the door often. Haskell grew weary from the silence after some time.

"How are you liking the capital, Belle? I'm sure you have gotten acclimated to the city lifestyle after these months?"

She turned to him, which filled him with a warmth he had not felt before.

"The city is wonderful, Haskell. Me and the children went to the market today and enjoyed ourselves well. All the stuff there was overwhelming; so many things I could not imagine their uses. I'm still not used to the loud noises and the constant sounds even through the night."

She smiled and he felt the warmth rise again. He felt like he could burst, but he remained cool.

"Yes, it does take time to get used to the sounds, but I am glad you enjoyed yourself. I'm sure you will adapt well and eventually like living in the city."

Her smile faded. "Maybe so. We shall see."

The rest of the dinner was eaten in silence again.

That night, there was a rasp at the door. Isabella opened it to see Haskell. It was late and the children were asleep. Haskell stared at her without uttering a single word. He continued to be silent as he tried to lean in and kiss her, his mouth puckered and tried to pull her in by the waist.

That was when she caught the strong stench of alcohol coming from him and she instinctively pushed him away. She apologized and closed the door, gasping and fighting back tears on the other side, hidden away from him. He stood at her door for a while, like stone, unsure how to react to the act of rejection.

V

The night was still as two bodies intertwined in silence. Ijos and Isabella made bed together, as they have for some time. Isabella often used the excuse that she could not sleep and roamed the upper district, but it always led to her going to Ijos' house.

The sheets turned and folded, the two silently panting in between kisses. They laid together for some time after they were done, their skin still electric from their embrace. As they laid together afterwards, Ijos thought about how it came to this.

It must have been during the first month after they arrived at the capital, before Ijos and Kael moved to their own place. Ijos spent a lot of time during the day with Isabella and Kael, though Azalea still kept to herself most of the time. As they got closer, Ijos and Isabella began to spend time without the kids.

Ijos knew it was wrong, but he needed her, especially since Haskell made sure to either shun him or talk to him condescendingly, even at meetings. It was while Ijos had stayed in Haskell's home, in a small room closest to that garden with the cherry blossom tree.

It reminded Ijos of his home, or what was once home. There was a light rasp on that door one night and Isabella was in the frame, lunging on him as soon as he opened the door.

It was fervent, gluttonous love, where it could not be satiated until both lovers were exhausted. Ijos knew it was wrong. He felt the wrongness as she grabbed him with passion and locked his lips onto hers, nibbling his lips and gasping.

He knew better as he began to feel his hands betray him, tracing her body through the outline of her thin shear of a nightgown, feeling her hips and her breasts and growing bolder with his touch.

He knew it was wrong when they closed the door somehow quietly amongst the passion, and his hands betrayed him again as he took off her nightgown, seeing her glisten in the dim moonlight.

It felt like forever to him as he basked in her love, melded with her several times that night, and just about every night since. He remembered seeing the cherry blossoms fall like they always do—casting a dance of shadows as they passed over the moon.

Then he remembered the night of his town and he turned his face away. Isabella stirred and turned to him.

"Ijos, what's wrong,?"

He laid his arm over his face and gave a weak chuckle. "Just thinking about how something so beautiful can live alongside something so destructive." His somber eyes fixed on her. She could have wept for him without thought.

"Like how embers can float with cherry blossoms in the sky."

She volleyed him with kisses and held him tight, like she was trying to keep him grounded at that moment. She pulled back for a moment and pulled his chin up so he met her gaze.

"Embers don't always burn. They can provide warmth, and maybe those cherry blossoms are falling because it is winter, and they are frozen."

Their gaze turned them back into passion, where they intertwined once again.

Outside the house, a large figure leaned against the wall smoking tobacco rolled with a green leaf. He contemplated about the forbidden love he had heard for months. He accidentally stumbled into it one night, watching as the shadows of the cherry blossoms danced around him, concealing his own shadow. He hated Ijos with all his body, loathed him for his mistakes and incompetence.

He hated that his own father, who would have killed him, held him in higher regard as Ijos excelled in school. He claimed him as a son despite the past, and Ijos let him. He hated him for the attention he got when he became the youngest war general at sixteen, preceding

Haskell's own at twenty. Ijos was always better than him, on the field and off, in academics as well.

And yet, even when he fucked up like he did at Caede, which Haskell secretly hoped for, it never blew up for Ijos. When Belle was raped because he played pretend father to an orphan, she still confided in him and trusted him. Even Baldock was close to him; his younger brother was not there for the siege on Ijos' home, so he did not understand why he was inferior. Haskell hated him. He should have died a long time ago.

He drew on his cigarette for some time as he pricked his ears for any sound in the house. He did not care if he was caught outside. He hoped he was caught, hoping he could give any reason to oust Ijos for adultery. Even just to kill him, to protect Belle's honor.

But that time did not come. The night grew long, and they did not stir. Haskell abandoned his post and retreated to his own home. He turned around one last time to see a small figure in one of the windows on the second floor.

He could see the raggedy hair of the orphan staring at him—staring through him with his blue eyes.

Contrition

I

Haskell spent most nights drinking heavily until he could not stay awake. One night, when he was still on the beginning of his binge, he heard a knock on his door.

He did not stumble much in reaching the door, opening it to see a priest. The priest had his face covered except for an opening large enough for his eyes to see. The cowl that concealed his face shifted in what Haskell assumed was a smile.

"Good evening, Commander Haskell. I'm sorry for the late interruption."

"Good ev'ning, Father. It is no problem, no problem at all. What may I help you with?"

The priest leaned forward and touched his forehead. Haskell watched this odd action with foggy eyes, but he paid no heed. "May I come in? The King sent me."

Haskell was perplexed, but nodded his head and led the priest in. He walked with the priest in silence to his study, where, moments before, he had been drinking himself into a stupor like every other night. His desk was messy with a small pile of scrolls, a few bottles of bourbon, and a few empty bottles to the side. He poured himself another glass and took a sip. He then raised his glass towards the priest, raising one brow.

The priest shook his head. "My faith does not allow us shepherds of the word to partake in such human desires."

Haskell continued to gulp down the spirit and set the glass down. "So why would our majesty send a priest at such an hour of the night? It is not of him to ignore the hands of the clock."

The priest got up and walked over to the empty fireplace. Haskell poured himself another drink and saw the gush of green light in his peripheral. He looked up to see the fireplace ablaze with green flames. In the back of his mind, he felt a cold tingling, like the buzz of flies or the pins and needles of a sleeping limb.

The priest turned to him. Haskell had forgotten about his drink almost as soon as he poured it. "The King thinks, through the divine grace of our savior, that we are a desperate need of cleansing within his inner circle. Those who are not borne to be in the circle should stay out of it, you see."

The priest walked over to a candelabra on a small table, touching his fingers on the tips of the candles. Each

320

touch left a small green flame eating at its wick. "But he is not sure of how he can exclude those who are already there and whose positions have overstayed their welcome.

He walked over and stood in front of the desk. The buzzing in Haskell's head grew, overbearing and blocking out everything except the priest's voice. "And I gave him the idea that you, my dear Haskell, are the perfect person to lead this endeavor. For you see, if a certain person leaves, then I believe that all those who don't belong will leave."

Haskell watched as the flames flickered and licked at the air above them. The green glow gave his face such contrast, aging him with heavy lines. He shifted his focus to take a long swig of his drink.

"You want me to drive Ijos away."

The priest's eyes glimmered in the green fire. Haskell noticed that the priest's eyes were the same color, though he was not sure if it was coincidence or not. "Without Ijos, who has been the de facto leader of the 'Knights of Kyndis,' the rest will surely fall apart."

"So how do we do it? I assume the King does not want him dead."

The priest shook his head. "No, at least not by your hand. It has been under my discretion that we use someone close to him. What about his paramour? I think she goes by the name off Isabella..."

Haskell slammed his cup down, breaking the glass to the point that the shards went flying.

"No. She is much too delicate for this."

The priest's cowl shifted in what Haskell assumed was a smile. He gritted his teeth. Then he had an idea, and his grinding shifted into a chuckle.

"What about the orphan that he is taking care of? A small child, but I have watched him train with Ijos, and he is strong. I think his name is Kael."

The priest echoed Haskell's chuckle. "Kael, huh? An orphan saved by a man, only to damn him in the end?"

The two traded laughter as they went over details of their plan, Haskell's own turning to near howling when he thought of the dramatic irony, all while thinking about how to console Isabella when this was over.

II

Days came and went without much event, Ijos training with Kael and Isabella visiting him in the night. Haskell would attend meetings pertaining to the warfront.

The news was grim as they faced severe losses against the forces of the Vralls, whose war tactics were the use of berserker fighting styles. Men who left the battlefield were often missing appendages, if they left the battlefield at all. Haskell was in a good mood despite his overbooked schedule of war councils, where he held a high commander position.

The day was warm as summer crept closer; a short spring was present this year. Ijos had left the capital once again on a small mission in the south, close to the Wastelands.

Isabella, Azalea, and Kael were in the market, browsing the multiple vendors that crowded the large market. It was early enough that it was not packed within the area, but Isabella held Kael's hand, who, in turn, was holding Azalea's hand out of instinct. He was one of the few who she allowed any form of touch.

They passed by several stands before Kael had stopped at a small stand that sold magical items. A lot of it was lights powered by crystals, which was a new technology that the academy of alchemy and wizardry was inventing. Crystals were a strong foundation of magic, though the strength of magic was highly dependent on the quality of the crystals used. The Wastelands had proven incredibly useful in crystal mining, though the continuing revolts had slowed down progress.

Kael looked over the trinkets when he landed on a small, circular object that had a face with different symbols on them. The merchant peered over the stand at Kael and smiled.

"You like that, boy? The wizards from the academy at Rildenfell called them watches. The symbols are the times that the sun will rise and set as well as the moon. Pretty neat, huh? It's like a pocket sundial, without the need for the sun!"

Kael picked the watch up and turned it around, watching as the crystal at the center gleamed in the sun. There was a metal hand that pointed in between the two symbols for sunrise and the zenith of the sun. Small, archaic numerals were etched around the metal outline of the face of the watch.

Kael examined it for a moment before he reached in his pocket and pulled out a small pouch of coins. He counted out the coins—a task that Isabella taught him during his academic time with her—and bought the watch. The merchant wrapped it and handed it back to Kael and they continued their browse of the market.

Isabella glanced at Kael clutching the object close to him. "Did you really enjoy the watch that much, Kael?"

"Ijos," Kael said as he held the watch up to her. "Ijos." Kael was still not able to talk much, save for the names of Ijos, Isabella, and Azalea. Isabella smiled at Kael.

"Ijos will love that." The trio continued to peruse the market, though they did not buy anything else. They finished their market visit by ending in the city square, a vibrant area that was often the center of attention for entertainers.

When they entered the square, they heard a traveling band playing a fast melody that ran multiple arpeggios, some of the instruments playing an ascending and some playing a descending tune. They watched as the band played dancing and working up a sweat in the heat.

Kael especially enjoying it, his eyes dancing much like the band. But then his eyes fixed down an alleyway. A buzz invaded, feeling the vibrations shift in his head and fixate on that darkness. Isabella and Azalea were so engulfed in the music that they did not notice Kael leaving their side and down the alley.

III

It was dark, too dark for daytime in the buddings of summer, but that was the only way to describe it. The heat seemed to dissipate in the alley and with it came a cold that chilled your bones, but your skin still felt warm.

Kael walked in a daze, his head feeling blurred from the buzz that kept pulsating inside. He would twist and turn in the alleys, not aware of his path until he was already inside a vacant home in some part of the city.

His vision cleared enough to see that it was devoid of furnishing, with the only thing breaking the dull, aimless was a small spark in the fireplace in the corner. He felt it calling him, bribing him with the sweets only a child would understand—like the lucidity of a daydream that washed away nightmares.

He sat in front of that fireplace and watched the spark: a small, green buzz like a bee. Was this the noise he heard? It filled the box with the same noise. It began to bounce around in the firebox, dancing like the band that he left. It grew with each bounce, and the buzzing wavered and trilled—almost like laughter.

When it was done, it stopped in front of Kael. The green spark was now a flame. He examined it and thought he saw eyes staring back at him—beckoning him. He clapped, though he did not know why. The fire shook with what he thought was glee.

"Come with me," the green flame said. "Let's be friends."

A flame stuck out like a hand and Kael instinctively grasped it, then flinched. It was cool—cold even, cold as ice—and that wispy hand pulled him up and into the throat of the fireplace.

It spun over and over, racing his eyes around in his head before he landed in a shadowy field. The sun was dim and dull; the moon was present and interlocked with its twin in a sky of purple with red clouds.

Kael stood up and walked around. The field was home to multiples of the green fire sprites, all frolicking and dancing with the faint wind that blew consistently.

"Let's play!" The little green sprite that guided him here was still holding his hand, its eyes more visible in this light. He thought they looked hollow.

The child in him felt a sense of wonder in this world, wanting to dance amongst these sprites for as long as he could. The warrior that has been trained in him, however, was alarmed. His eyes would shift as the two halves fought within. His child side began to frolic with the sprites involuntarily, a heat rising in him as he danced and a foreign laugh escaped from him.

The sky would darken for a moment before it came back, and his vision would blur constantly. He could not control the laughter that rose from his throat, all while the fire sprites were chanting in some foreign language.

Deglis. He was sweating and the heat was becoming painful. It scorched, but he couldn't yell past the laughter. *Deglis.* The sprites were laughing and dancing with him. Were they burning him? They weren't touching him, but he felt a fire burning his groin. *Deglis.* His mind held nothing else but the burning.

Then it was released and all he could envision was Ijos, but he was not relieved. No, he felt something new. A hatred for him, the perception that Ijos was a failure and must be killed. Why? Why did he feel this way? He couldn't shake it, and thinking about it made him giddy, laughing more and dancing harder. He danced harder and harder and laughed until he blacked out.

In front of the fireplace in the abandoned house was the body of Kael, unconscious on the floor in front of the dark, empty firebox. Standing over him was the priest, his cowl pulled down to reveal his face, which was accented with sharp features.

He grinned maliciously at the unconscious child. In one hand was a green-hilted dagger, the other drawn into his robe. The then-orange blade ebbed and shifted to ivory.

The priest stopped and admired his work: a magical sigil etched into the groin of the boy. The sigil cooling from an orange glow to a faint scar, it linked the boy to the emotions of Haskell by that of an old magic. In the center of this sigil was the written language for Ijos, latching the emotional hatred of Haskell to the boy.

He put the knife away and pulled the boy's trousers up. He then hoisted the child over his shoulder with one hand. He walked to the door and left the house, his footsteps making no noise despite the uneven flooring.

IV

"Kael!" Isabella shouted in the alleys connected to the square. She had turned away just for a moment to watch the traveling band play. She had his hand in hers, so why did she not feel him slip away?

"Kael!" She shouted it again. Azalea echoed it as she searched too. The two were beginning to feel frantic. The boy acted mature for his age, but he was still a child, and a mostly nonverbal one, too.

They ran up and down several alleys before she rounded a corner to see Kael leaning against the wall of a house in a small alley. He was not awake. The two ran to him and checked him out, feeling his face and checking to see if he was breathing.

"Kael? Kael, are you okay?" Isabella was shaking him, and it stirred him awake after a moment. "Oh, thank the gods. Are you hurt?"

He had a distant look on his face and before his eyes sobered, a small chuckle came out of him. Isabella did not like those eyes; they were not the boy's eyes. But then he came back and looked around, like he was searching for something.

"No." It was the first time he said that word, but he said it clearly and with such a serious tone. Isabella nodded and they got him up, but she could not shake that the boy had changed.

Later that evening, Ijos was back. Isabella greeted him and did not tell him that she lost Kael, afraid that Ijos would be upset. She only said that Kael was acting a little off.

Ijos took Kael home, where the boy did not walk close to him at all, or even look at him. They ate dinner in silence. When Ijos was getting Kael ready for bed, Kael did not want to be touched by him at all.

"Kael, did I do something? Are you mad at me?" His tone faltered at the end.

Kael stared at him for a moment and Ijos saw the same that Isabella did. Though, Ijos saw a gleam of green in the normal blue of the boy's eyes for a moment before the boy walked away from him and went to his room. Ijos stood there for a moment as he tried to grasp what he saw.

V

Kael's demeanor continued through the next week. He could not stand to be around Ijos and he would push Ijos away if he got too close. Ijos was not sure what to do, training day came up, and it was hot like usual outside. Ijos deflected Kael's attacks like usual, parrying them or using the training sword to deflect into either side of his body. The blows seemed harder than usual, and Kael had a dark look on his face. Ijos was beginning to see the blade chip from the attacks.

"Easy, Kael. It's just practice—"

But Kael yelled and swung hard, cracking the blade and staggering Ijos. He was caught off guard by the ferocity of the attack, and he was even more surprised to see the boy move with such speed afterwards.

In an instant he felt the warmth of his blood as the blade pierced him. Had it not been instinct, it would have pierced his heart. His hand moved fast enough to stop the blade, though the blade pierced his hand and the tip was protruding from the other side. Kael was huffing, breathing heavily as his head hung.

Then came a *clink* and something felt onto the dusty ground and hit a rock. Kael stared at the object with his head hung. A shudder echoed through the boy's body. Ijos reached down with his free hand and grasped the metal object. It was the watch with the crystal at the center.

Kael dropped his hand from the blade and slumped to the ground.

"Ijos." The boy uttered the single word and brought a shaky hand to the watch. "Ijos." He raised his head, and his face revealed itself from the dense mask of hair. His face was wet with tears.

Ijos pulled the blade out of his hand and embraced the boy, who began to sob. "Who did this, Kael? Who made you do this."

"Burns," Kael choked between sobs. "Burns." He patted his groin and then pulled his trousers down slightly to show the sigil, which was like a scar, but it was red with inflammation. "Haskell."

"Haskell?" Ijos choked the words out himself in disbelief. *How could Haskell do this? Why would he do this?*

"Haskell," Kael said as he pointed at the sword. Ijos thought about the action and then about Haskell's own hatred for him.

The boy cried in Ijos' arms in the training grounds for some time. Later that night, Ijos laid awake in his bed thinking about the event. He thought about the mark on Kael and him saying Haskell, pointing at the sword.

He could only think that Haskell hired someone that used dark magic to use the boy, and it angered him. It angered him so much that he was out of bed before he knew it.

He paced the house quietly as he thought on it, wondering what he should do. He paced for several hours before he came to a conclusion.

He must kill Haskell.

He must do it before something like this happens again, but it did not ease his mind. No, it would not be easy. What he will be doing is treason to the court.

He did not sleep that night. He walked onto the balcony of his room to smoke a grass cigarette, which made his cough worse.

VI

Burns. Kael could feel the mark burning him on the groin, and he felt frozen in the moment. His mind returned to that of the man he is—not the boy he was in the memory—trapped inside the body of his youth.

All he could do was feel overwhelmed with the guilt and pain of that moment. But he relished in the tactile embracing of Ijos he so missed.

The air distorted in the memory and darkened. He felt a chill run up his spine, unable to move as he was caught in the memory. A gasp and moan came in his ear from behind.

Then he was plunged out of the memory and into darkness. He fell onto a soft, squishy ground and stumbled to his feet. He was no longer in his child body, but back to being an adult again.

He walked in the darkness for some time, hearing whispers and moaning, agonizing screams in the distance, too. Then a dim light was ahead, and he rushed for it. He passed through a jagged, soft crack in the darkness to a grim path.

The sky was a sickening purple with green clouds; the landscape jutting rocks with a narrow path ahead of him. He followed the path—slippery with streams of dark, thick fluid—through the jarring landscape. Jutting rocks cut him as he slipped several times in dark puddles.

He walked into a clearing, and in the center was an amorphous blob, writhing. Then it changed, forming into a shape of agonizing pain.

"Kael, why would you do this to me? What did I do?" The shape was an exact replica of Ijos, young like he was in the memory. But his hand wasn't pierced, it was his chest. His face contorted, turning the expression of pain into malice. "I should have never saved you. You let me die. You."

Me. I did let you die. Kael walked up, his face wet from tears, but he was numb to feeling them. He had no control over his body anymore, just the overwhelming guilt and pain. He wanted to be embraced by Ijos one last time, to be able to save him this time.

"Ijos," Kael breathed out slowly. But then he saw Ijos face shift slightly and saw the woman's face, saw the smirk and lustrous gluttony feeding on his pain.

The instinct battled his own guilt and attachment to the illusion that he went to draw his sword, but it wasn't present. Then he felt his side and pulled the green knife from his belt. He watched as his mind yelled to stop as he stabbed the illusionary Ijos' head.

VII

Kael cut through the illusion with Ijos' scream piercing his ears. The illusion faded from the warmth of skin to scaled and old blood.

His screams were replaced by the shrill of a woman's—the creature that was on top of him. Her gash puckered around Kael's prick before she tore off, with tendrils hanging from it.

The woman had transformed, showing skin that was scaly and paler than the flesh tone she had before. She had small wings fluttering viciously on her back while she clawed at the knife in her head.

The knife exuded a dim, greenish glow, and the glow spread from the wound to the rest of the woman's body. As it spread, her screams increased in agony. Her screams faltered, collapsing into guttural moans.

"You still are not ready for the sorcerer, lost child," the woman spat.

He leaned over and gripped the hilt. He yanked it, forcing the succubus to look him in the eyes. They were cold, calculating warrior eyes searching for an answer.

"What do you know of it, succubus?"

The succubus screamed one last time before she slumped over, blood pouring from the wound. Kael leaned over and pulled out the blade. He didn't bring it in with him; it had been stored in his bags since he obtained it. He strapped it onto his belt.

As he exited the room, he saw the house with a new lens. It was dusty, coated with old bloodstains. A shiver raked up his spine as he realized he was deceived so easily.

He exited the house and untethered Jorunn, patting her snout. His attention was diverted by a loud, roaring sound close by. He guided her as he went down the next alley, winding deeper into the city.

Struggler

I

Kael entered the market as the roaring stopped. The normal jovial crowd of the market had stopped and was centered around a wooden structure, large enough to tower over the crowd, and at the center there were gallows.

On the structure stood a man in a robe wielding a cross and clutching a book. His eyes penetrated everyone in the crowd as he smiled. Behind him were three people with burlap sacks over their heads.

"Come ye, come! Witness the judgement of sin! The due punishment for heretics, spreading their blasphemous words against our God! May they be washed and warmed by the flames as they enter the next life!"

The crowd roared and raved, the echoes of the words 'heretics' and 'blasphemous' resounding in the marketplace. The priest held up his hand, palm facing the crowd and they went silent.

"Witness the heretics!" The sacks were ripped off by guards standing behind the prisoners. The eyes of the accused were full of fright, searching around for a miracle to save them. Their struggle was in vain as the noose tightened around their neck.

One, a woman, loosened the gag over her mouth long enough to yell 'Long live the old gods,' before the guards gagged her once more. The ensuing silence was only momentary before pillars of 'heretic' shot out of the massive crowd. An uproar followed .

Kael locked eyes with another, a boy no older than seventeen. He could see that the boy did not know what he did wrong.

Kael then shifted his eyes to the priest and met his gaze. The priest smiled, and silent words filled Kael's head.

The endless night is nigh, lost one. You see before you the effect of the darkness, already permeating your capital. The day will come when Balaal will rise and wash this land in flames.

The priest smiled at him as he waved his hand and the floor gave out beneath the prisoners. The woman's neck snapped, the crack echoing in the market.

Kael watched as the boy's eyes lost their luster amongst his struggle, staring at him with hope that he could save him.

The crowd roared at the spectacle. For them, it was like festival, like a celebration of life and not death. Kael ignored the crowd's reaction as he watched the priest exit the scaffolds, heading towards an empty alley.

Kael pushed his way through the crowd in a feverish manner. He was close to the answers he so desperately needed. Jorunn trailed behind him, nickering as the crowd became more active at the dangling bodies.

People would sway and pull others; some would flop on the floor and convulse. He had never seen a spectacle before. The crowd was so engrossed in the false act of divinity that they ate it up, engorged by the idea that those who spoke against their religion were punished with due judgment.

Kael began to elbow and kick through the crowd as they became more aggressive, some pulling on him and Jorunn. He swiftly exited the crowd and followed the priest into the alley, thinking he was a bit behind and would not be seen.

He did not expect that when he rounded a corner that the priest would be standing, waiting for him. He saw the smirk on the priest's face, like it was cut out crudely by a child.

"Welcome, lost one, to the Capital Mynheir. As you can see, faith in our God is to the most importance. We oppose the old faiths of the gods and goddesses here. Tell me, have you been cleansed by the flames of our God?"

Kael was silent, staring at the man. The priest cackled and danced a little.

"Come now, don't make me ask again."

"What are your motives, sorcerer?"

The priest cackled. "Oho, sorcerer? I am just a lowly priest, a vessel for our God and prophet for the people. Am I a prophet to you, lost one?"

"You're nothing but a stain on my life." He unsheathed his sword and held it out in front of him. "It is time for you to pay for your *sins*, priest, as you call yourself."

The priest pouted his lip at this but quickly grinned afterwards. "Shame. I was hoping we cleansed the capital of all the heretics. Oh, well." He snapped his fingers and laughed. "The just people will rid the capital of heresy."

Jorunn neighed and Kael turned around a moment too late. The crowd that was raving earlier was behind him, grabbing for him, pulling at his armor and hair. Jorunn began to kick and flail.

Kael turned around and saw the priest walking away, laughing loudly over the commotion. He watched the priest's figure leave the alley, turn left, and head up the steps of an ornate building.

"No," he yelled, though it was drowned out by the crowd. They swarmed him tighter, blocking the alley from his vision. They began to kick and punch him.

Kael was driven to pull out his swords and hack his way through. He started to revel at thinking of the delight in seeing the blood, but Jorunn's struggle brought him back. He examined the people surrounding him as he struggled to move away. Their eyes were glassy—cloudy—like they were under a spell.

He instinctively held his sword to attack but stopped himself again, though the lust for blood was trying to draw him back.

They're still people. Maybe they could be saved. He threw his fist into the first person, hitting them in the chest and knocking them back. The crowd did not stop, not when he hit them with his studded glove nor the kicks of his metal-clad boots.

His only other option was the pull Jorunn out of the crowd and escape. With a strong tug of her reins Jorunn jumped over the crowd that surrounded her and landed beside him, pointing towards the exit of the alley. He vaulted on her and they galloped through the alley with the crowd in tow.

Kael rounded the corner and into a side alley, the deranged crowd on their heels, nearly climbing over each other. There were bystanders in the alley that moved out of his way as he passed, only to be consumed by the mass of pharisaic maniacs. They slammed each other into the wall, unaware of broken bones or the people crushed by the mass. Blood spewed across the walls.

The chase continued through the outer alleys before he exited to the main inner gate, then the outer walls and away from the crowd. He gained speed in the outer wall before he exited the capital altogether.

He strolled the perimeter village of Mynheir as he digested the events that just unfolded. He hung his head as his body shook.

I was facing the sorcerer and I still could do nothing. He climbed out of my grasp so easily. He ground his teeth hard. *Why can't I do anything right? I'm powerless against him. Even after all my training and fighting, I'm still no match to him. I'm back in the same position as I was then...*

Kael was in his head for so long that he did not hear the man beside him. He turned his head to recognize the man well.

"Cormac? What are you doing here?"

Cormac was an older man that wore tattered clothes and had a sword strapped to his back. Beside the man was a large wolf, calmly walking, its shoulders almost matching Cormac's. Its soot body was marked with faint ancient writing. It held no notion of malice in its eyes as it walked alongside them.

"I see Duff is still with you," Kael patted the wolf on the head. "Hey there, Duff."

The wolf closed its eyes momentarily. Cormac cleared his throat.

"It isn't safe here, Kael. Come with me and I will explain everything."

Kael nodded and they exited the village, heading towards a large rocky outcrop in the distance. He knew that place very well. He was returning home.

II

The pair made their way out of the small town surrounding the capital Mynheir, not saying a single word as they passed the few straggler homes of the perimeter. Kael dove deep into his mind for the ride in the outskirts, retracing the events of the capital as well as the illusions of the succubus.

The picture of Ijos being stabbed in the heart by his own doing was shaking him, even if he knew that the succubus used his memories to feed on his despair. His hands shook with the thought. Then he saw the pain in Ijos' eyes and he gripped the reins tight.

He had been so wrapped in his mind that he had not noticed the sparse trees appear in the fields. It was not until the sun was blotted out by a blanket of leaves, with several beginning to change in color.

Fall had come before he knew it—creeping its way since he left Gormsey. It took him a week or so to reach Mynheir, and in that time he hadn't really noticed the trees.

He blinked his eyes and settled them on Cormac, who was scanning the area ahead. He stopped and glanced at Kael before continuing, letting out a sigh.

"So, what happened back there, Kael?"

Cormac was sitting astride Duff; the wolf was the same size as Jorunn. Their gaits matched and they paced themselves at a center, allowing for talk. Kael recounted the events in the capital, pointing that the priest had to be the sorcerer, in which Cormac looked down for a moment and nodded.

"I see. To think the priest... and to sentence those who did not agree ." Cormac muttered to himself. He looked lost in a pile of memories, searching through them like a pile of loose parchment.

"These hangings, the public executions," Kael's words shaking Cormac out of his past, "why doesn't the King put a stop to them? Doesn't he fear the people will turn on him?"

Cormac screwed his face into a distorted grimace. "The King has lost his head. He lost his son recently and he delved into religion, just like the rest of the capital. The fracture of the kingdom consumed him. He wants to cleanse the lands of any ideas that oppose the faith of the flame."

A holy war. The lands were awash in a religious war that was eradicating any old faith and relaxing it with a new one. Kael scoffed at this notion, but then he thought about the events of the capital and then how the people looked.

The people were willing to grasp anything that gave them hope. The lands were so steeped in bloodshed that he could see why people would search for a new religion that promised change.

"What does this mean for the kingdom?"

The wind blew, bringing on the smell of ash. They were close. Cormac looked up and then back down, exhaling slowly.

"He has sent out his own people to retake the provinces and 'eradicated the heretics'. The west has already been affected. The army has been focused on invading and eradicating the Vralls, a move from the King to 'cleanse the lands of savages'. The king is not who he was."

Kael would not know who the king was before. He does not remember ever meeting the king, and Ijos never talked about him. He stared at the looming range through the fog. The foothills of the mountains were close.

He knew they would be there before too long. His stomach felt like it was turning inside out.

The ridge of the mountains loomed overhead as the pair enter the montane forest at the foothills. They passed several rock outcrops as they got deeper into the forest, the slope of the land pulling them higher up the range.

The trees persisted for a while as they ascended the mountains high enough that the air was opaque with fog. The only way they stayed together was by listening for each other's movements.

The forest broke and in a large, rocky clearing stood a tiny village. The homes were built out of timber from the forest and did not support any frivolous adornments and there was a small waterfall that crashed into a river which ran through the middle of this town.

There were no more than ten homes, all clustered together around the center. Most were black, missing the roof, and some were only a wall or two. The ground had spots still coated with ash.

It was quiet in the twilight of the sunset, marking an otherworldly tone to the setting.

"I still feel the dead walking amongst us," Cormac said as he paced past Kael. "It has been quiet since that day, since everyone..." His voice trailed off as Kael looked around.

They trudged through the abandoned village, the winds wailing past the walls and stirring up memories for Kael. He could hear the voices of those who long departed this place, their voices intertwined with the wind, but they are gone.

As they passed a small bend in the river, Kael glanced at a particular pile of ash. Silver, sparkling even in the dusk. A cold chilled his spine as he remembered. Green eyes, full of pain—to empty, soulless windows. And black flames, the flames that caused this.

The pair stopped and dismounted at one of the homes; the outside was drab and withered by the weather. Before Kael entered the home, he glanced back at the village and past it, to a home that was in a wooded area just beyond the clearing.

"I have been trying to track the sorcerer for some time." Cormac pulled out some papers as he was waiting for the soup to cook.

"After the Battle of Caede two decades ago, he seemed to disappear. No other attacks, nor was his army found. There had been some isolated members of the army; roaming the countryside, often finding a town and ravaging it until monster hunters dispatched it."

"After some time, and after a dozen or so of these incidents, the monster hunters named these beasts: *Stökkbreyta.* The word for mutation."

He stirred the soup some.

"Fitting, right? They all look like some mutation of various things. Some look bearish, boarish, deerish, but they all have that scaly hide, and their features take on the elongated snout of a rat. Not to mention the claws."

"Long enough to be daggers," Kael replied, "and sharp enough to cut through steel. Aye. I remember very well. Not to mention the beady, soulless eyes."

Cormac nodded as he stirred the soup some more. "The sorcerer himself has been missing, but the events in the capital make sense. It all lines up, when he stopped attacking villages and when the priest showed up in Mynheir. But why?"

Kael pondered on it, too. "Causing mass casualties of war and then stopping suddenly makes no sense, and for so long. Why now, of all times? Could he be searching for something again?"

Cormac instinctively put his hand on his neck. "... Maybe you're on to something, Kael. Maybe it is time for you to understand what happened in the capital so many years ago."

Kael looked at Cormac inquisitively. "What do you mean?"

Cormac sat down with two bowls of soup and handed one over to Kael. They both took a sip of the broth, then Cormac sat his down.

"As you can see, the 'kingdom' is nothing more than several provinces governed by different Lords. Once upon a time, these Lords were under the King, and Mynheir was the capital of the kingdom. It was supposed to be the central hub for everything."

He brought out a coin. It was a quek. Cormac placed it on the small table between them and spun it with two fingers. The spinning coin dazzled in the candlelight.

"Now, each province has its own currency and trading, though the trades do overlap, but that is the nature of trade. Merchants will go to the lands of the Vralls, too, as well as the other towns and cities. The Merchant's Guild has headquarters in Mynheir as well. The provinces though, are split and governed by their own Lords."

Cormac took a sip of his soup before continuing.

"The lands west of Mynheir are governed by two people. Warrix controls the towns and villages in the Northwest, from Ilah—on the border of the Dark Forest—to Broun that sits on the north side of the Merce estuary. Harlow governs the lands south of Merce, which includes the town Merce on the south side of the estuary and all the way down to Ogier, one of the border towns of the Wastelands."

"The central north and south provinces used to be ruled by a lord each, but they have since fell due to constant warfare. One lord does not rule Hera either, but they are fairly peaceful in controlling their own respective towns."

Cormac got up and refilled his soup. He had been drinking the broth in between sentences, though Kael had been engrossed in the history lesson. He wasn't aware of the political state of the world, nor did he really care. When he was younger, he would just report to the burgomaster of the town for monster hunting jobs. They would typically have a bulletin of all the jobs offered.

"So where does the priest come into this?"

Cormac sat back down.

"Right, the priest. See, when the kingdom was still united, there was a roundtable of the supreme commanders of the royal army that held council with the king. Believe it or not, Ijos and I were part of that, as well. We were more or less a special operation force of people who used supernatural powers to help with the war efforts, and then our efforts were focused on finding the sorcerer as he gained power."

"The battle of Caede wasn't the only attack he had; he was storming different areas for a few years prior. His patterns were erratic, often having us come as he had already demolished a town. But this roundtable was a council on both the warfront with the Vralls as much as ideas on how to combat the sorcerer's forces."

Cormac sat the bowl down. His demeanor changed, hardening with the next words.

"The last war council was months after you and Ijos came to the capital. Haskell and he had been at odds since he returned with Isabella and Azalea. Haskell blamed Ijos—and you to some degree—for the deaths of the twin boys of Caedmon and Isabella."

"There were several war councils after you arrived, but most ended with Haskell stating that our special division was incapable of the task handed to us. He also stated the presence of our lowborn birth was a disgrace to the table. The other commanders tried to calm him down, but Ijos often left after Haskell took things personally. Then one day, Ijos attacked Haskell."

Kael was alarmed. "Ijos wouldn't do that, not without being provoked."

Cormac tilted his head down and peered up at Kael.

"You're right. Ijos claimed Haskell attacked you and did something sinister. When Haskell refused to acknowledge it. He then said you were laying with Caedmon's wife, stating the infidelity was enough to imprison him, Ijos attacked. The table was divided."

"Of course, I was with Ijos, and so was Elris. But the commanders sided with Haskell, stating that Ijos was a savage and so were the rest of us. The King did nothing;

neither stop the fight nor did he stand with Ijos or Haskell."

"The roundtable broke that day, and the commanders left the capital and most went to claim land for themselves. The King became jaded as time went on, focusing his efforts on the war with the Vralls. I heard the priest became his advisor..."

Kael stared into the broth, trying to process everything he had just learned. "So, the kingdom fell apart because of internal strife?"

Cormac nodded. "Yes. The unity we once had was shattered. Trust eroded, and alliances crumbled. It seems the sorcerer exploited our weaknesses so easily. To think he would infiltrate the capital disguised as a priest..."

Kael took a deep breath. "And now, we're left with fragmented provinces and a looming threat. What happened after the roundtable dissolved?"

Cormac's eyes softened. "After the roundtable broke, we decided to leave the chaos behind. Ijos, Elris, and I were followed by a few followers within the army, those we fought alongside on the battlefield, as well as their families. We formed this village in the aftermath, a sanctuary away from the wars and politics. People came and went over the years."

Kael nodded slowly but then shook his head.

"Why cannae remember this? I just remember waking up in this village one day, like I had been here for as long as I could remember."

351

Cormac frowned.

"Ijos wiped your memories clean, again." Cormac watched as his face contorted. "I know. I know about the times that Ijos wiped your memory clean with the *kiokatsu.* It's an ancient technique passed down from Ijos' village. He only did it to help you. When the roundtable collapsed, the city was in chaos. Haskell and Ijos fought again in the city, and you were injured during that. You were in a coma for some time after we left."

Ironic, Kael thought, *how I'm always incapacitated at key moments. I'm incapable of anything.*

Cormac cleared his bowl a second time.

"This village was a haven for all of us. There were even some who found solace here from the turmoil of the insurrection afterwards. The capital always stood strong, but the rest of the lands... it was surprising that there were any towns left. There were battlefields in the fields between villages. Many people died. You've seen the stones."

Kael nodded. There weren't very many fields that didn't have the littering of gravestones throughout them. Kael clenched his fist. "We need to find the sorcerer, and soon. He needs to be stopped."

Cormac placed a hand on Kael's shoulder. "One step at a time, Kael. The road ahead is perilous, but together, we can face whatever comes our way. Come."

Cormac walked over to a table and Kael followed. On the table was a large map of the lands. Marked at the top in heavy writing was the word *Lothanac*. Kael examined the map to see some areas circled and some crossed out. Some had some small, nearly illegible writing. "What is this?"

Cormac leaned over the table and wrote something beside the city of Mynheir. "This... this is what I have been doing since the last time we saw each other, Kael. Since that day, since Ijos—"

Neither spoke; Kael thought he saw a tear sparkle in Cormac's eyes.

"—Since the village was destroyed. We thought we were secluded from the world, but the sorcerer found us, somehow. Since then, I've devoted my time to tracking him again. I've only come here to collect my thoughts and try to make sense of it all. This is what I've found."

Cormac pointed at several marked out towns.

"These towns have been affected by some spell. The people there do not act normal anymore; they act like puppets. These areas have high concentrations of hangings and executions, and I've noticed the wildlife in the area is sparse. Monsters tend to patrol these areas more, too, like they are attracted to whatever magic is cast."

"That would explain why there have been less jobs in the other towns," Kael replied.

"Right. As of right now, I did not see any difference in how monster hunters are treated. A necessary evil, I suppose. However, most of the corpses I saw were branded with a sigil of an undying flame, often accompanied by the words 'Balaal' or 'the endless night is nigh,'."

Cormac shifted his hand to a circled town, situated between Mynheir and the provincial border of Hera. He recognized it as Gormsey. "I just came from this town. As I arrived, I noticed that only one person or two were acting odd, like a puppet. As time went on, more and more were affected, and had I not been aware, I could have, too."

Kael cocked his head. "What do you mean? I was just in Gormsey a few weeks ago. There was nothing odd about it."

"Aye, you must have just missed it. But those who were acting oddly began to preach about the undying flame, they had an odd smell to them. I think whatever is affecting them is transmitted by a gaseous spell."

Kael stretched a little, becoming stiff from leaning over the table. "Interesting." He then moved his hand over to the last two circled towns. "What about these?"

Cormac tapped them then slid his hand back to Mynheir, then moved his hand in a semicircle. "There is a pattern to this. As you can see, the towns that are marked out are closest to Mynheir, mostly in the south and east areas. Gormsey is on the border of the Hera province and the last of the east towns to be affected before Hera. The closest town in the Hera province is Maju and Anju, which are the ones circled."

Kael nodded. He can see the pattern easily. "But why not move to the west?"

"The west is controlled by Warrix and Harlow, and they have an iron rule on their lands. I'm just assuming, but the lands surrounding Mynheir as well as Hera are not governed by any one person. The armies of Warrix and Harlow are much larger than any lord within these areas."

"Makes sense," Kael replied. It does, after all, make sense to engulf the smaller towns before trying to provoke an army. *But what is the sorcerer's motives...*

"I was going to check these towns out next," Cormac said, pulling Kael out of his thoughts, and scratched his face absentmindedly. "You being here, though, may be fate. Maybe we should each take a town and check them out."

Kael nodded. It seemed like a solid plan. "Which town do I go to, then?"

Cormac scratched his face more, the stubble on his face resounding a dry scrape sound. "Maju. I suppose. It is a small town that doesn't really have any real strategic value besides its crop yield. You could scope it out for a day or two and then meet with me in Anju."

Kael lifted himself away from the table and began to walk towards the door. "Aye, I can do that. You be careful until I get to Anju, Cormac."

Cormac walked towards him and put his hand on his shoulder. "Kael, it wasn't your fault. I just want you to know that."

Kael shrugged the hand off and silently exited the house. Cormac did not object, instead continuing his preparations. The door closed, the latch echoing in the empty village.

It had turned dark in the time that Cormac and Kael palavered. The stars' reflections glistening off the river and waterfall like diamonds—a stark contrast to the embers that fell the last time Kael was here.

III

Kael grabbed Jorunn and pulled her reins, guiding her past the cluster of homes and to that isolated home in the thicket of trees. He hesitated at the perimeter and stopped at the first tree. The trunk bore faint slashes that were healed from the passage of time.

He took a deep breath and walked through the thicket and to the cabin. Its roof was covered in fallen pine needles and dried sap coated the wall. The door was slightly ajar, and Kael unsheathed a blade as he swung it open, expecting to see something.

His face was pale, and he was shaking slightly, like he saw a ghost. The cabin was empty. It was an unorganized mess inside, with books and parchment on most tables. There were two adjacent rooms off to the left side.

The fireplace was dark and dusty from disuse, much like the rest of the cabin. Kael walked into the first adjacent room and stared at the four walls, at the window that overlooked the smaller wooded area and beyond that was the village. There was a bed, neither small nor large, and a small stand beside it that had several wooden figurines.

He sat on the bed and picked up one of the figures—a swordsman, with a long, curved blade—and smiled. He placed it back and walked over to a dresser that was still full of clothes, most of them too small for him now. He took one look back at the room before he took a deep breath and walked into the next room.

It was much more filled than the other room. It was a bit bigger too, but it had to accommodate a desk and bookshelf, as well. The bed and dresser took up the same space, but the desk and bookshelf had nearly twice as much space. A window was behind the desk, overlooking a drop that gazed upon the wild landscape of the Hera province, which would be breathtaking in another set of eyes at another time.

Kael walked over to the bed and dresser, raking his fingers on them lightly, like he was afraid they would shock or burn him. On top of the dresser was a hunting knife much like the one he lost, so he took it and strapped it to his thigh. He then trailed a semicircle back to the desk and stared at the chair and drawer side of the desk, really examining the details.

"Ijos never allowed me to look in his desk," Kael said as he sat down in the chair. A childish smirk appeared on his face. "But I suppose he winnae—"

The smirk was gone, in its wake was the following loneliness he carried.

Of course he wouldn't know if I looked through it.

Kael opened the drawers one by one, seeing masses of parchment in the bottom drawers and plenty of ink wells and quills in the top drawers. He then shut them hard, the *smack* sound echoing. He got up and went to the bookshelf and started throwing the books off, grinding his teeth.

"Of course he winnae know, you dumb bastard!" He threw more books, leaving one shelf bare, and moved to the next one. "It's your fucking fault, yours!"

Amid the dull thudding the books Kael heard a metallic noise. He turned around to see a false book on the rest; its chamber open and a small medallion had fallen on the wood floor. It was a gold locket attached to a sturdy chain. Kael bent down and picked it up, opening the locket to reveal a small shard of labradorite.

In the hollowed-out book was a piece of parchment with the word *Kael* written on it. Kael picked it up and walked to the window so he could read it in the moonlight.

Kael,

If you are reading this, then I am gone. It could be days, weeks, or even years until you read this. You are a son to me, regardless of our circumstance. I might have saved you that day, but you are the reason I'm still alive. Every day since then, I have felt a new purpose, and that purpose was to raise you to be the best you can be.

I have watched you grow from a lonely child to an eager teenager to the man you are now. You still act so unsure of yourself, but you are destined for greatness. I will always love you, and I'm proud of the man you have become. You have overcome so many hurdles in your life.

The medallion enclosed with this letter is a shard. There are seven shards, and they are very important to this world. My time has been dwindling these past couple of years, and that is why I have not gone with you on any monster hunting job, and I am sorry for that.

The years of overusing Nuria have taken a toll on my body, exerting my muscles and breaking them down much faster than I expected. But this shard needs to be protected, and I know you are capable. The sorcerer will come for this, and you need to keep it safe. Always keep it safe, guard it with your life. I have faith in you, son.

Ijos

The tears had welled up in Kael's eyes long before he finished the letter. Some of the tears that fell stained the paper, some running small parts of the ink. Kael walked over to Ijos' bed and laid down, clutching the shard and paper tightly, even as he slept much later.

Kael woke in Ijos' bed the next morning and walked out, still clutching the letter and shard, staring at the chilly morning gleaming on the abandoned village. The quiet was only broken by the roar of the waterfall and the streaming water in the river.

Jorunn neighed softly from a patch of grass under one of the nearby trees. He mounted his steed and trotted over to Cormac's home, but he was not there.

When Kael opened the door, the house was silent, but on the table with the map was a letter addressed to him. He opened the letter, but it only contained two sentences: 'See you in Anju. Be safe.'

Kael stuffed the letter in his pouch and exited the house to mount Jorunn again, draping a dark cloak over his shoulders to warm himself from the chilly air. He left the isolated village, once his home, and resumed his path to the sorcerer.

The Sacrifice

Crimson Squall

I

The cackle of the crows echoed on the hill. A large dule tree was positioned at the top, the leafed branches swaying in tandem with the body hanging in the decaying gallows below it. The hill was silent save for the whispering of the bitter wind, which swayed the corpse back and forth.

Two days ago, the corpse was once a man. He had stumbled into a small village, planning to rest and head on his way. The man was not tall or brawny, nothing was extraordinary about him at all.

But he stayed at the small tavern of the town and drank all the same, an outsider to their customs. He had drunk too much with a man in a black robe that he did not remember the night. All he remembered was waking up as he was dragged to the gallows, the town chanting incoherently and ignoring his pleas.

He pleaded for his life with the townspeople right up to the moment the floor dropped and his neck snapped. The last thing he remembered seeing was that the eyes of the people looked like they glowed red, even in daylight.

The silence was broken by the clomping of hooves, and a man in a hooded cloak atop a horse appeared on the slope. The horse stopped in front of the weathered gallows, and he turned towards the corpse, lowering his hood.

Kael had traveled from the mountains towards the town of Maju, using a map he took from Cormac's home to guide him, a trek of several weeks. He held his hand up to his face to shield him from the chilling late autumn winds and examined the corpse in the process.

The corpse was bare save for torn pants, the hair on its head pulled out from the root and its eyeballs eaten from the crows. The skin was picked at and most of the flesh was gone except for its chest, where the skin was bright like canvas. The corpse's chest bore writing, carved into the skin in sharp writing, stating 'the endless night is nigh'.

The corpse continued to sway back and forth in the wind as Kael became a silhouette, leaving the hill and back to civilization, trotting past an old wooden sign with the words MAJU written upon it.

II

Dawn breaks on Hera. The kingdom contained many abandoned towns in the aftermath of unending wars over generations of time. These rubbles were left to nature, with many yielding to the vines and trees, intertwining with nature, providing a home for the animals of the area.

Lonzo did not pay attention to such towns. He had no care for the relics of the past, nor the massacred or the dead. He had a job that needed to be done. As a traveling merchant, he ventured all over the lands, selling his wares to the Vralls, the warriors of the Northern lands, all the same as that of the Ciallians in the center as he does to the Herans.

He picked up goods in the North to sell to the others for a higher price, knowing he will sell things they have never seen before. Mushrooms, fish found in freezing waters, clay pots that hold endless volumes of fluids, so many things he could not keep track of at times. His wagon was always full and so was his money pouch.

He was heading to the town Anju, positioned on the east bank of the river Aquia, which ran parallel to the greater Oquia. Lonzo would be traveling through some forests, and, dangerous as it may be, through fields of graves.

Lonzo was not old, but he was not young anymore either; he was closer to his mid-thirties, sporting mid-length brown hair with speckling of grey to show his age. He kept a cropped beard that framed his round face well, and his beard showed his age more than his hair, but his face showed lines weathered by the elements of nature.

He wore a typical traveling merchant's clothes: wearing a common grey tunic with some leather padding and braces, in case bandits ambushed him, with cloth pants and boots. He often kept a short sword and crossbow on him to protect himself. His clothing fit him well, but it seemed a bit baggy as his line of work often kept him on the road, and he often forgot to eat.

Lonzo packed his wagon in a small village called Maju, an unremarkable place with a penchant for farming ordinary crops and a small lake for fish. It was about a day and a half's ride to Anju here, so he needed to ensure his wares were packed well and he was well prepared.

The morning was quiet and the inn he stayed at was only now just starting to wake up. Some people were walking the roads, with local merchants selling produce and other food at a small market.

Once he had his wagon settled and his wares sorted in a way that was acceptable to him, he sat on the wooden perch and snapped the reigns to urge his horse on. He passed the small market and as he moved, he passed a tall man in a dark cloak with long, brown hair.

Their eyes met, and Lonzo shuddered. The man's face bore such intensity that he felt it in his soul. His exit of the village was swift as he urged his horse on to a trot, hoping to create distance between him and the man. What lay ahead of Lonzo past the village was a sprawling field.

As Lonzo surveyed the dawning landscape, he noticed plenty in his environment. The road was bumpy, as the rains had eroded some of the pathway. This side of the village was reclaimed by nature, so there are no people working in the fields or hardly any traversing between towns.

In fact, the landscape of the area north of the woods was peppered with graves. Whole fields filled with unmarked tombs due to the massacres that occurred decades prior, as well as the continuing warfare after the fracture of the central kingdom. Lonzo could throw a stone and hit a grave on either side of the road he was on.

He has traversed this area before, and he would only do so in the day; at night, monsters such as ghouls, kubikajiris, and black dogs would roam these lands at night, eternally hungry, eating corpses and preying on any unfortunate traveler who got lost or traveled too close.

The village was guarded by walls, and many of the people believed in superstition, so they would clutch onto talismans or place ofuda on their doors to ward off evil. But the day was safe, and Lonzo knew his way.

The clop of the horse and the creaking of his wagon repeated, and the birds of the morning were singing their songs. Lonzo grabbed his water skin and took a drink, but his thirst was not quenched. It was mead he desired.

Despite having stayed at Maju, where he drank his fair share of mead the night before, the trek through Hera's upper area was long and it often took him past a few abandoned towns, where he would often stay since the buildings supplied adequate shelter for the night. Maju was the first town since the Northern lands, so he reveled in the bed and warmth that given to him, but one night did not feel like enough.

The monsters that lurked in the wild could be repelled by a concoction that was made by mixing daggerwood and wormshot, which he ground into a paste and smear it on the doorframes and walls of abandoned home so that the monsters would not come near.

He did not sleep much, however, since he still stayed alert for other things. Thing like animals that would not be repelled, or bandits, who would loot his goods.

Lonzo scratched his face and yawned. The morning sun was above the horizon, and it hurt his eyes, but the warmth was nice in the winter weather. A week ago, Lonzo had been in the snowfields, leaving Gorm, the Vrall capital, and he was bundled up in many garbs, some fur, and some leather.

This weather was much milder, but the skies looked dull, and he hoped it was not going to snow here, too. Lonzo was beginning to get hungry, and the tree lines of the forest were in sight. He held off stopping to eat until they broke the tree line. He did not want to eat by graves; that would bury his appetite like the dead.

He reached the forest, and in it there was the rustling of leaves, the chatter of squirrels and snorting of deer. The birds flying above the treetops would chirp, as if having a conversation with one another, and the winter breeze was blocked by the trees. He made camp using some fallen twigs and branches, picking ones that were not too damp so the fire would light.

He struck his flint several times, cursing slightly as they did not spark well. At last, he had a fire going, subtly basking in the warmth, and cooking some soup overtop the flames. The sounds of nature gave him a calm tune to relax to, enjoying his soup as his horse, Pruna, grazed on the grass. Lonzo began to delve into his thoughts, talking aloud, as he often did when he was alone.

"These lands are not kind to a merchant, eh, Pruna? It seems there can't be an era of peace. Monsters, humans, it's all the same. We are always watching our backs. Its either a claw or sword is aimed for it."

Lonzo paused, sipping on his soup. He swirled his jar of mead and took a swig to chase down his soup.

"'War is eternal,' they say," he sighed. "Be it from nation to nation or humans to monsters, both or anything in between. What curse was placed on us to deserve this? At least that *sorcerer* and his army disappeared."

He then stared at his clay bowl, still half full, steaming with soup.

"Even then, some areas are as dangerous as ever. For a while, monsters would stay secluded in uninhabited areas, far off from civilization."

"But ghouls have been spotted far from the graveyards, kappas and kelpies found in rivers and lakes close to towns, and a chimera was roaming the streets of Vrall's capital! I could not believe my eyes, a monster

369

roaming a city as if it were the wilderness. It took several Vrall men to take the beast down, some people got hurt and few killed. The beast looked sick, like it hadn't eaten in ages."

Lonzo sighed. It made him wonder why monsters were moving closer to towns. Was there no more food in the vast wilderness? Did the beasts eat too much, or do they think that humans offer more? The lands were changing; people were becoming more violent, warring over territory, and the monsters were coming too close to people, killing because they cannot find anything else. Their hunger cannot be satiated by deer or fish, but blood of man, much like the greed of the nations.

Lonzo pondered too long, for the day was becoming short, and his shadow thrown by the fire was reaching far. He took dirt and threw it on the fire, then he crouched and gathered his tools. While standing, he heard a noise. A noise unlike he heard in the woods before. A crack like the sound of breaking a bone, followed by a low growl and a feline hiss.

Lonzo unsheathed his sword, holding it out in front of him, as if he'd done this before. He cannot remember the last time an animal attacked him, but it had been too long, and he was out of practice. The sword felt far too heavy in his hand, and he was shaking slightly. He scanned his surroundings, searching for any sign of movement.

He heard a rustle to his left, then to the right. He feared he was against more than one, but the rustles kept shifting, confusing his perception of space, and it caused him to lose his balance. As he slammed into the ground, he could hear his horse whinny, and he felt a *whoosh*.

A warmth spread on his stomach. In a daze, still delirious from vertigo, he looked down at his abdomen and saw blood bubbling and gushing out of him. He tried to utter out a gasp, a yell, any form of noise.

The noise was muffled as a scaly, claw borne hand grabbed him by the neck and pulled him deeper into the woods. His wagon was left and his horse, tied to a tree, was kicking, and pulling at its reins, to no avail. Through the treetop snow began to creep through, cascading above.

Winter had begun, and the dull sky wept cold tears for Lonzo.

III

The morning frost still hung in the air in the small village as Kael watched a merchant pack his wagon.

Maju was quiet in the early morning, the villagers not fully awake and only beginning to sell their wares. The merchant boarded his wagon and as he passed, their eyes connected. The fear in the merchant's eyes was something Kael has seen before; although the world was in ruins, people still looked at him as if he were a monster, too.

The wagon sped up and left the village in a hurry, but that did not concern him. He watched the village for was any signs of change—of magic or darkness hiding in the shadows.

It looked normal on the surface, but he could see that the people acted almost *too* normal. They moved like they were going through the motions, their voices were flat. If there was laughter, it sounded like it was forced, like an unnatural bubble coming from the throat.

In the center of the town stood a wooden crucifix, a contrast to the rest of the village in how elegant and new it was. It did not seem like it was from here but rather brought from somewhere far away. The wood would have been found in a warmer climate, not the pines or beech or maple of the area. No, it was smooth and a pale pink.

Kael decided to walk around and scope out the town some more. He walked up to one of the local merchants and browsed his goods. The merchant smiled, the edges too far up his face.

"You are not from here, are you?

Kael continued to browse.

"No. I'm just passing through."

The merchant waved his hand, steady, but jagged in movement.

"Well, do you see anything you like, traveler?"

Kael looked over the produce, which was dingy and small. It seemed like the harvest was not good for this town. But he still picked out some items and gave the man a couple coins. After, Kael nodded towards the center of the town, towards the large wooden crucifix.

"The crucifix seems new, I dinnae remember it the last time I was here."

The smile grew wider, almost like the snarling maw of a gator.

"Ah, yes. A priest from the capital came and enlightened us with the words of a greater being. The promise of eternity in bliss if we followed him, and a blessing upon our crops, too! Our harvests have been less fruitful the past few years, and we have tried everything. We prayed to the old gods and tried to give offering to then, but the product was worse with each year."

The man danced a little behind the stand. To Kael, it reminded him of the Capital. The dance the priest did. "Then he came, and our crops began to grow more! The promise of a bountifully harvest and an afterlife, who wouldn't want that?"

Another smile breached, the cracked lips parting to show rotting, stained teeth. "But those who still followed the *old ways* were heretics and must be punished. The old gods did not help us; we were condemned by following them. Even after the proof, some still clung to the old ways. And the priest said, 'Those who did not follow the one true leader must be shown what awaits for them in the afterlife if they do not repent,' and so we did punish them. Just like how we are punishing her."

Kael followed the man's hand and saw a woman restrained in a pillory in a small fenced yard. She was bent over like she was deflated.

"She is a vagabond, caught with sacrilegious objects in her pouch. The innkeeper found them one day when he went to change her sheets. Old tomes of monsters and mythology and potions. Just like the druids, she dabbles in the dark arts. She is being punished in the hopes that she will repent and join us."

Kael turned and walked to the bound woman while the man was still talking to him dully. The man watched Kael walk away with vacant eyes before he stopped talking and glanced at some of the other villagers nearby.

Kael entered the yard and to the woman, who was staring blankly at the ground. He stopped in front of her and stood, waiting to see if she would talk. The villagers began to watch, gathering behind the fence quietly. She was muttering quietly, indistinct save for the word *Dagda* near the end. Was it a prayer?

"Do you pity me, vagrant?" The woman spoke. Her voice was hoarse and dry. "Do you wish to release me from my shackles, amongst those who bound me in the first place, or do you condemn me as well?"

She sighed, shakily and coarse. It came out more like a cough.

"I will not beg for my life. I will not renounce my faith in the old gods." She glared at him. "They can tear me limb from limb, and I will not pledge to their *so-called* god."

The crowd behind them began to murmur. One person shouted *heretic,* and others began to join in. Before too long, the entire village was out at the fence, shouting and cursing in tandem. Children began to climb over the fence and into the field and Kael knelt to the bound woman. He unsheathed his sword and broke the lock on the pillory with a strike of the pommel.

"If that is the case," he said as the rusted latch broke and she was freed, slowly moving her arms and neck as she looked into his eyes, "then would you kill these soulless puppets to save your own life?"

In his hand he held a katana. It was wrapped in blue-dyed leather and had a dark wood sheath. She took the katana and smiled, unsheathing it to see the blade glistened like silver. The edge was sharp enough to cut fog. A snarling smile crept on her lips as she began to see the red of revenge cloud her eyes.

"What are they?" She asked as she swung the sword a couple times to gauge its weight and balance. It was light and felt more like an extension to her than a weapon.

"Humans." Kael grunted. She saw the sorrow in his eyes as he unsheathed one of his swords from his back. "They're under a spell, and a strong one at that."

Her face dropped and she furrowed her brow. "Just a spell? Can they not be saved?"

His face contorted into a grimace. "Either we kill them or they kill us. I dinnae know how to break the spell, and we dinnae really have the time to figure out how. That is, if there is a way."

The crowd of villagers stomped down the fence as they yelled *heretic* in waves, sounding much like the cawing of deranged birds. Their eyes were blank, and they moved like they were on strings. Most wielded weapons of some kind, be it old rusty swords or farming equipment. The crowd lunged at the two in the yard. Kael looked at this mass with sorrow, but he knew they were lost.

The two warriors began to cut through the crowd, cutting the chattering down as they ran though. Their swords hacked the mass, blood spurting through the air as well as limbs. A small child scowled with malice as it chirped *heretics* repeatedly, not stopping to scream when Kael cleaved it in two.

Two men flanked him as he did this and cut him with a pitchfork, while the other nearly hit him in the face with a sickle. The woman cut the arms off the sickle-wielding villager before he could strike again, his words cut into a gargle as she slit his throat.

The yard bore resemblance to a battlefield afterwards. The two warriors stopped to catch their breath in the aftermath.

"Who would do this to innocent people?" The woman asked.

"What's your name?" Kael asked.

"What's it matter? Who would do this?"

"It disnae matter," he said as he held out his hand for the katana. She eyed him for a moment before she sheathed it and handed it over. "I'm just asking before we part ways."

"Samera. Are you going to answer my question?"

"I cannae really answer it. I dinnae have the answers yet, but that's what I'm looking for. My name is Kael, though."

"I see. Well, Kael, I thank you for helping me."

He snorted softly. He didn't look her in the eye this time. His face had turned ashen, and a grimace plastered it. He knew this feeling. It was guilt, knowing things might have been different. But he also knew the other truth, too. The truth in survival.

"I dinnae see any point in anyone dying over something as trivial as religion and faith. I would suggest you find a weapon and provisions before you leave."

There was a rumble in the ground and Kael turned to see the severed bodies squirm and writhe, sliding on the ground towards each other. The bodies coalesced into a blob of decaying flesh, the corpses already rotting from the inside out with surreal speed.

The flesh would turn to mush to be able to merge with the others, creating a rigid body, with some faces protruding out of what would be the chest and stomach, and its arms and legs were made of the corpses' appendages. On top of this horrendous mass was a head

377

made of many heads, creating a massive helm of comical proportions, like it should topple over any moment.

Kael handed back the katana to Samera and unsheathed his blades once again, taking a deep breath despite the overbearing stench of rotting flesh. "Go right!" He yelled as he ran to the left, flanking the monstrosity. Samera followed his advice and went right, but he glanced back to see that her eyes were wide with fright.

"*Heretic! Blasphemer!*" The monstrosity roared, each of the faces of the fallen villagers sounded these words like echoes. It stomped and flailed its arms, noting that the arms ended in a volley of heads that began to exude out smoke.

Kael jumped back and pulled the cloak over his face. "Dinnae breathe the gas, Samera!"

She was trying to dodge the other arm and the gas, covering her face as she rolled. Kael exuded his flames again (*Kael, use my power*) and went left. He danced under the body and hacked away at its legs, toppling it in a couple seconds. The arm flailed, and the gas spewed in every direction, but Kael covered his face. He retaliated with a volley of hacks, cutting the faces until they stopped.

The head of the monstrosity began to inhale and Kael ran, jumping as the body exploded in a gush of gas. The body exploded on itself and the body parts flew, the faces in a surprised expression as they splat the ground and rendered into bloody masses. Kael watched as the gas subsided in the center of town.

He waited to see if the flesh would reunite, but it didn't. The walls of the houses and the roads were covered in bloody masses. The crucifix was covered in blood, too.

Kael took a deep breath and began to walk, examining the remains as he walked through the town.

"Samera!" He scoped out the town to see if she was hiding or if he would find her body. He couldn't find anything. He even exited the center of town and through the smaller roads connecting the other homes, but there was nothing.

He had lost hope and gone back to Jorunn in the inn's stable when he found his katana laid next to her stall. The stall next to hers, which had a young black stallion boarded, was empty.

He eyed the gate to the stall to see two words etched into the wood: STAY SAFE. He smirked a little and exhaled a long breath of relief as he gathered Jorunn and exited the town.

In the distance loomed a massive forest. A forest that separated Maju from the next town over, Anju.

House of Carnation

I

Separating Hera into the Upper and Lower is the Liela woods, one of the largest forests in the lands of Lothanae. Winter had begun for the province of Hera, where snow falls more than the rest of the lands, and the snow was heavy on the trees and blanket edges the forest floor.

The woods were quiet, save for the rhythm of the horse and the ragged breath of a man. The wildlife was gone; there were no prints in the fresh snow nor were there any broken branches or foliage eaten. The forest exuded an aura of death and dismay.

As Kael continued along his path, he listened closely to the sounds of nature; the trees waving in the wind, the soft thud of snow falling from a branch, the movement of the river, the crunch of the ground underneath the horse's hooves, and the breathing of his horse.

Softly, in the far distance, did he hear sounds of life, but not what would normally be heard. Instead, it was teeth gnawing into flesh and the muted cries of the prey as they struggled to get away. Kael slowly approached the area in which he heard the noise, and as he headed into the clearing, he gazed upon the monstrosity that had been feasting upon the animals of the woods.

It had big, bugged out eyes, with scaly skin and fins along its pointed spine, as well as humanlike hands that were home to three claws as big as large daggers. A Stökkbreyta. The body was no bigger than a normal man, with a frame that was anthropomorphic, but hunched over quite a bit too.

The beast was too focused on its food to notice him approaching, so Kael quietly dismounted and approached the beast from behind. He unsheathed a sword as he approached, the metallic sheen echoing in the empty forest. A low growl emerged out in response, gurgling with blood, which was followed by a hiss that was both snakelike and feline at the same time. Kael was unfazed and took another step towards the beast.

A voice rose from the beast's throat. It was unnatural, like it did not belong.

"*The time of man has come to an end. The flames of Balaal will consume all.*" The voice was deep and nearly incomprehensible due to the gargling of blood in its mouth.

Kael stopped in front of the beast and spoke, clearly, in a rusty voice, "Where is he, mutie? Where is the sorcerer?"

The beast responded with a vibrating snarl, displaying its blood-stained teeth.

" The era of the endless night is n—"

The beast's words were cut short by the blade swiftly swinging down and severing its head, instead ending the speech in a sharp exhale, followed by bubbling of blood leaving its mouth and neck. Kael stood over the body and slowly exhaled. His eyes drifted from the corpse of the beast to the prey that was subtly spasming.

It was a small deer, older than a fawn, but not by much. Its guts were ripped out; the edges festered as if infection had already set in. He watched as the deer took its last breath and laid still.

He watched as the deer corpse trembled and mutated. Its hooves were turning more paw-like, with claws starting to emerge through the keratin mass. Its fur was becoming scalier, with the ridges of its broken spine starting to jut out like fins. The doe eyes were becoming cloudy with death, but they were starting to come out of its skull, bugging out like a fly's eyes.

Kael laid his sword on the ground and knelt, examining the corpse, when it exuded a gasp and rhythmic breath from its chest. Its heartbeat started up, picking up speed with its breath, which was so ragged it sounded like paper ripping.

The body started to convulse, and with that, the corpse was reanimated. The corpse of the deer uncovered its teeth. Its cloudy eyes were bored into him.

There was no time for shock. It was just another monster now. Kael sighed as he lifted his sword and at once cut off the head, ending the short second life of the

383

deer. He stood, brushed off the grass from his pants and walked to his horse. He searched in his saddlebag, pulling out a large leather sack and placed the heads in it.

Kael paused, though, as he heard the nicker of another horse nearby. After he strapped the filled bag on his horse's saddle, he scanned the area, searching for the other horse.

In the distance, he saw the horse accompanied by a merchant's wagon, with the embers of a dying fire. He walked to the abandoned campsite, searching for the person that would have made the camp, but all he found was blood painting the forest floor and some of the trees. The wagon held some wares, but nothing else on the shelves.

After scouring the dickey box, he found some parchment that contained an insignia. It was familiar, like a symbol he's seen before. For now, he stashed the parchment away. Kael untied the reins of the lonesome horse from the tree and joined his own.

Atop Jorunn, he led the second horse by the bridle through the trees. The path exited the forest and opened to a small riverside town named Anju. The woods behind were silent once again, haunted by death in the aftermath.

II

The town of Anju was busy despite the snow. On the west side of town ran a river, which held a port and a market that stayed busy in the summertime. The surrounding fields produced bountiful crops that were exported out to other regions, and a castle was not too far from the town, so soldiers often came to drink at the taverns and harass the townspeople.

The damage the soldiers caused were paid by the garrison, and the people were afraid of them, as the lord of the castle was a brute and could tear a man in two. No one liked the army; men often enlisted so they could abuse the power and were often intoxicated, fighting anyone who even looked at them the wrong way. Other than the market and the taverns, the rest of the town was quiet.

Kael entered the town riding his horse, guiding the horse he found by the reins. The side of his horse was dripping with blood from the leather sack that held the heads of the beasts, staining the horse's coat red. The townspeople that he passed glared in shock and disgust; the smell the heads of the beast and mutated deer was enough to turn your stomach.

The customs of hunting always led to the same place: the leader of the settlement. It didn't matter if it was a small village, a town, or garrison, the leader typically pays the job. Some may be contracted out, but most officials do the business. This led Kael to the burgomaster's office.

The building was at the center of town (as it usually was in most towns) and Kael took several small alleyways to get to it. The smell of the rotting heads were drawing a crowd, and that was the last thing he wanted right now. The clanking of metal follow the horse's gait, drawing attention to him from those nearby, who would take one look at him then quietly scurry away.

Kael reached his destination, a small run-down building made of stone. The porch was made of wood, more ornate and newer than the rest of the building, creating an obvious juxtaposition between the two. He unsaddled his horse and tied the reins of both horses to the elaborate railing and grabbed the seeping leather bag.

Inside he was met with an overweight older man peering at him behind a counter. The man looked as if he had been running for miles, glistening with sweat from the sunlight through the front window, matting what was left of the hair on his head and his large beard.

"May I help you?" The man had a husky voice that crackled, likely from years of smoking. There was an ashtray on the desk that overflowed with ashes to the point where there were some on the floor.

The man was startled by the Kael's appearance. He became even more startled when Kael tossed the leather sack in the air and landed it on the counter in front of the sweaty man, jumping back and staring at the mass. Blood began to seep onto the wood.

"What the fuck is this? You can't just come in here and throw your vile shit around you kno—"

Kael scowled at the man's ignorance. "This was found in Liela woods, not far from here. It's a Stökkbreyta, and it has been killing the wildlife. It also mutated a deer; its head is in there as well. I am sure some of the wildlife was mutated as well."

The man behind the counter stroked his beard, slowly opened the sack, and peered in. The heads were grotesque, covered in blood, and the jaws were gaping and showing the multiple rows of teeth in its maw. His mouth contorted into a scowl that demonstrated his disgust. "My name is Aurel, I am the burgomaster of this town. And you are?"

"My name is Kael, sir."

Aurel paused in his study of the dismembered heads and examined the swordsman for some time. His beaded forehead wrinkled in several ways before he turned back to the heads.

"Kael, huh? An unusual name."

Aurel huffed, coughed, and spat into a handkerchief he had in his back pocket.

"What do I owe you?"

"I am sure you can figure out a reasonable price."

"How does one hundred skells sound? Of course, if there are more of these things around, I would be happy to hire you to take care of it and ensure there are no more around this area. I can make it three hundred."

Kael pondered for a moment. Three hundred skells was a decent amount and the guise of hunting the Stökkbreyta should keep him in town long enough to see if the sorcerer shows up.

I wonder where Cormac is, though. Knowing him, he's probably laid up in one of the taverns.

Kael pretended to ponder the price some more, then nodded his head. "I suppose that will do, but I do not plan to stay long. I would like a room as well, so I can stay in town for a bit and track them down."

"I will make accommodations, if you give me time."

"Of course. However, there is another matter to discuss. An abandoned merchant's wagon was found in the woods. I found his horse and brought it here. I looked through and found an insignia if you can identify it."

Kael passed Aurel a rolled-up piece of parchment. Aurel unraveled it, revealing an intricate logo containing a treasure box surrounded by filigree. At the bottom of the parchment, it had a signature that Aurel knew immediately.

"This is Lonzo's signature; he was part of the merchant's guild from Mynheir, the Inner City in Ciall. He has been travelling here for a decade or so to sell and trade. Are you sure you got this right?"

"That's what I found when I searched the wagon."

Aurel read the parchment and sighed.

"He was a good man. He has family in Mynheir, so I will write them the news. Give me a moment."

Aurel walked through a doorway behind him, crossing a room and reaching an owl with curved horns perched on a window. He then disappeared behind the doorframe for a few minutes, reappearing with a rolled-up parchment that he attached to the owl's leg. The owl flew out the windowsill into the grey sky.

"They should know come morning. I will take his horse in and be sure to see it returns to his guild."

Aurel shifted and began to rummage through his desk.

"If you could give me time to search through my documents, I can find a place for you to stay."

Kael nodded and exited the building. He walked beside his horse and examined his belongings, of which were his two swords strapped to a sack on the horse's back. He made sure all his ropes were tied properly and then grabbed a piece of cloth, pulling out a skin of water and wetting the cloth. He then rubbed the blood off his horse. Her chestnut coat became visible again in those spots.

"Looks like we are going to stay here a while, girl. I'm sure wherever we stay will have a nice stable for you and plenty of hay for you to eat." He patted and rubbed her snout gently and the horse brayed in enjoyment.

Aurel opened the door and stared at Kael, who glanced at him from the side.

"I think I may have a place for yah."

Kael followed Aurel into the building and to his desk, standing bent with his hands on the top. Aurel sifted through some papers that he threw on the desk, creating a disorganized mess in the little time that Kael was outside. The man pulled out a handkerchief and coughed into it, examining the expectorated mass and placing it back in his pocket.

"This time of year, we typically have the solstice festival, so soon there will be decorations and people coming in from the countryside." He shifted through the papers, studying each one. "But it looks like the Lekr Inn has a room available. If you agree to the contract, then I can pay for the lodging. You will be doing this town a favor, we haven't had any monster sightings in ages, not since the leshy of my da's age. I suppose it's a blessing, with the way the world's these days."

Aurel took out a piece of parchment and wrote a letter addressed to someone named Anelle, rolled up the parchment and sealed the paper with a wax seal.

"Here, give this to the owner of the inn. It is just down the street to the west. It will be right next to the river. I will take and dispose of these—these abominable objects you brought me," Aurel spoke with such disgust at the end and paled.

Kael smirked a little, fully aware and amused the man was repulsed by the heads. "Thank you, Aurel. I will take my leave now."

"I wish you luck. I will talk to you again to see what progress you have made."

Kael went to exit the building, but his hand paused at the handle. It was nagging at him, and he opened his mouth before he could stop himself.

"You haven't heard of a man named Cormac entering town, have you? He would have been a monster hunter, as well."

Aurel narrowed his eyes. "A second monster hunter? Why, no, I haven't. At least, no one has come into my office today."

Kael said his thanks and slowly turned around, exited the building, and grabbed the reins of his own horse. He patted the snout of the abandoned horse and began his route to the inn, noting the unique aspects of the town that he had not noticed before.

The town was run down in this area; the roads were uneven, with stone missing out of the cobble, and the buildings were faded, and the paint was starting to peel away. He guided his horse to the west side of town; with the babbling of the river within hearing distance, he knew he was close. He rounded the corner and was met with a dilapidated old shack painted in the most muted shade of shit brown. Drunkards were sprawled on the terrace and the door was cracked from the bottom to the top.

Kael stared at the elegant pile of trash that the burgomaster was nice enough to lodge him in. He sighed and tied Jorunn's reins by the porch, gently patting her snout as he walked up the steps. The door screeched as he opened it, the hinges sounding as if they were going to break from the force.

Inside the inn was better, but only slightly. The main room was small, housing a small counter with shelves behind it. The walls were of cheap wood, with no decorations on the walls save for a couple rusty swords over a fireplace in the 'common room,' if the dreary sight could be called such. A couple wooden chairs were positioned in front of the fireplace and a woven rug beneath them. The room led into a hallway that would presumably lead to guest rooms. So far, the inn was unremarkable at best and was just slightly a step up from sleeping in the cold.

The only remarkable aspect of the inn was the woman behind the counter, who was thin with an angled face, her eyes slanted much like Ijos' were. She must have been young—close to, if not younger, than himself.

He stared intently at her brown eyes. He felt a pull towards her and didn't understand why, but he felt that he could get lost in those eyes. Lost in thought, he didn't notice he was still walking until his waist bumped into the desk, skewing it slightly. She scoffed a little under her breath and rolled her eyes.

"Aye, may I help you?"

"Yes, Aurel sent me here, with this." Kael handed the parchment over. "I was to be boarded here while I undertake a task from him. May I speak to the owner?"

She rolled her eyes again. It may have been condescending otherwise, but he didn't feel it when he looked at her. It was almost playful. "You're lookin' at her. The name's Anelle. And you are...?"

"Kael. The name is Kael."

Anelle broke the seal of the parchment and read the letter. Her expression went from a blank face to a slight contortion, obviously perplexed by the information conveyed in the letter.

"Well, Kael, I do not have many nice rooms, but I will look for one for you. Don't move my desk again while I'm gone." She playfully smiled at him and he felt something uneasy rise in his stomach, like it dropped and then was lifted higher.

She disappeared to the second floor, and he could hear footsteps quicken into each room, pausing, and scurrying back out, until it finally seized in one room. A faint shuffle of sheets could be heard and a clank here and there as stuff was being moved. At last, she came back down to the front, resuming her post at the counter, albeit slightly out of breath from her task.

"Well, lad, I found a room suitable enough for ya. It might not suit a king or even a knight, but you will find rest in it nonetheless."

"Ah, thank you. My horse, though, is still tied up to your terrace. Do you have a place to store her?"

"Aye, we have a barn out back. We can take her there now if it pleases ya."

"Yeah, I would prefer to do that first. My equipment is with her, anyways."

"Alright, follow me."

Anelle moved from behind the counter and past Kael and accidentally bumped into him. He felt an electric charge inside him from the touch and tried to brush it away, but he felt flustered and nearly fell. A small chuckle rose from her throat as she walked out the door.

Why did I do that? He felt dumfounded at his clumsiness, but he followed her. Jorunn greeted him and gently swayed her head left and right. Anelle was beside her with the reins in hand. Kael walked down the steps and held out his right hand.

"I've got her, she can be a bit finicky. She does not listen well to other people."

"I can manage her just fine, lad. I'll show you the way."

Perplexed, Kael followed Anelle out back, and he continued to be confused as his horse did not put up a fight in following, either.

The barn was more lavish than the inn, with fresh maroon paint without any signs of wear from the elements. The path to the barn was also clear of debris, a stark contrast to that of the inn, where drunkards had the ground and terrace littered with vomit and broken glass.

Whereas the inn was quiet, the barn felt alive with the sounds of animals: the bleat of goats, the lowing of a cow, and the nickering of horses. It seems that Anelle preferred the company of animals to that of humans and took care of them better. They came to an empty stall in the corner of the barn, which was kept clean and stocked full of hay.

"Here we go. Your saddle can be placed on the fence here, so she can rest her back. If ya don' mind me askin', what's her name?"

"Jorunn."

"What a lovely name." She pat Jorunn on the snout, staring lovingly into her eyes for a moment. She turned to Kael. "Now then, let's get you inside."

"Right. Let me gather my things."

He pulled a large, multi-pocketed leather sack off the saddlebags, then began to rummage through to transfer over to his bag. It seemed like he had endless amounts of items in that bag. He then unstrapped his two swords and placed them to the side.

Anelle noticed the swords were two-handed; one a claymore and another was a large sword with an intricate black hilt, possessing foreign writing, with the handle wrapped in black leather and an open basket pommel. She also noticed he carried a katana on his left hip, something she didn't realize before when she touched him, and a large knife protruded from his right thigh.

"Heavily armed, eh? What does a big man like you have to be so well-protected about?"

Kael continued to rummage through his equipment, letting out a rough huff in response to her question. *I don't know what to say. Why is my mind going numb?*

Only when he was done did he turn to face her, his blue eyes both intimidating and soothing to her. He opened his mouth then closed for a moment, furrowing his brows before he opened his mouth again. He softened his expression and tried to smile.

"I thank you for letting me stay at your inn."

She gestured to him to follow her, still red from embarrassment, and they headed back to the inn. Kael petted Jorunn one last time and left the barn.

As they exited, he noticed the sun was starting to set, but the town was becoming more alive. People began to traverse the streets, cheering and gathering at taverns, one of which was close by. He wondered if he would go get a drink sometime.

The room he was boarded in was not that bad, albeit empty. There was a bed with faded sheet and a pillow, stitched together from various cloths. The dresser was small but elegant, heavily scratched and the brass fittings were tarnished. Kael did not care, for this was better than wet grass and dreary caves.

He placed his bag at the end of the bed and began to take off his iron-clad boots. The door was closed, so he began to undress, first beginning with the mismatched leather and steel armor over his chest and shoulders, then his studded gloves and boots. He took his tunic off next, leaving his back exposed, showing the multitude of scars on his back. His chest was no better—there were punctures near the ribs and thick, heavy gashes across his abdomen.

The last thing he remembered was staring at the ceiling as he drifted off to sleep, wondering how long he would be in this town.

III

Kael awoke in a gasp, the morning sun beginning to warm his feet as the rays peeked through the curtains. The streets outside were filled with people; travelers from out-of-town were visiting for the festival. He stretched and assessed the room.

He felt hungry, so he might visit a tavern to acquire some food before beginning his task; he will be tracking any infected animals within the area and see if anyone has seen anything strange.

He took time dressing, recollecting his thoughts. Time had passed in a blur, the seasons melding together. In fact, he hardly noticed when they did change. But it was winter now, the frigid air all too invasive. But time did not stop him. This town will be the end of this, where he can finally face the sorcerer and win.

He was so immersed in his thoughts that he knocked the nightstand. It rocked, with a clatter of metal following. On the ground was a key, and beside it a note. He opened the paper and began to read it: *Dinner is at 7. Don't be late. Anelle.* He smiled and placed the paper and the keys in his pouch. *Did she put this in here when she found me a room?*

He pondered on it for a moment before he left. He locked the door behind him and proceeded to the stairs and down to the main room. The counter was empty, save for a vase of white carnations in full bloom—an odd notion for the beginnings of winter.

He stood for a second, hoping he would see Anelle. But when he thought about it, that uneasy feeling in his stomach came back. He turned and exited the inn in a hurry, crossing the street to the nearest tavern.

The tavern was busy, bustling with the laughter of many people. Kael surveyed the crowd for any familiar faces.

Where is he? He continued to look at the faces of people as he passed them, but there were a lot for a small tavern. It seems the festival started early with the arrival of the outsiders, so Kael sat at the bar, where there were fewer people. The bartender approached him and said, "What you want?"

"I'll have a rye bread with eggs and cheese, and some mead as well."

"Gotcha, I'll be back."

The bartender disappeared for some time; there was a kitchen behind a door. When he reappeared, he had a dish of bread and cheese with two fried eggs and a large pitcher of mead.

Kael felt eyes on him, despite the many eyes in the tavern. He noticed there was a band of rough individuals in the far corner of the building, watching him closely. He ate his food quickly and paid the man eight skells, since he did not have a knuckle to compensate for six of them, and he left. He did not plan to get into any fights this soon.

Kael walked the streets of Anju for some time, hoping he would run into Cormac. He checked each of the taverns in the town to no avail; every tavern was packed already and the sea of faces was hard to distinguish anything at this point. He returned to the stables and retrieved Jorunn, heading to the outskirts of town.

I suppose I might as well hunt in the meantime, he thought.

Even if it was a ruse, Kael could not stand the idea of any underling of the sorcerer being alive.

The trek to the woods passed the crop fields, where people would work to bring in the harvest, but that time had gone. The last crop, sharpscane—a vegetable often used in stews for its hearty flavor—had been harvested before the snow set in.

The tree line held a shadow despite the brightness of the snow, and with it was an ominous aura. Jorunn started to resist a little as they got closer to entering the forest.

"Easy, girl." Kael leaned forward and patted her snout, calming her down immediately. She only gave a faint whine of protest afterwards.

Kael crossed into the forest and dismounted at once, scouring the area for tracks. He did not see any signs of life the first time, but this side of the woods contained more evidence; broken twigs, small prints in the snow, and dried droplets of blood were sparse in the area. He was unsure how many animals have been mutated, some may have fled—but there should still be some in the area.

Over time, Kael traveled the span of a few miles of the woods, tracking one trail down to a larger deer that had been mutated. The deer was large, standing about five feet to its back, and had 8 points.

It was at the stage of mutation where it was closer to that of a Stökkbreyta than its previous life. The area that had been mutilated upon death was healed and heavily scarred. It moved sluggishly—succumbed to its hunger and weakness. Kael approached behind it in hope to catch it by surprise and behead it quickly.

The snow, however, hid a fragile branch, and he stepped on it. The break struck through the silence and the deer turned. Its eyes were bloodshot and its breath was flaring out of its nostrils.

It reared its head, initiating its frenzied attack and began to hurl its body at Kael, who rolled to the side at the last moment. The deer became a whirlwind, charging at Kael and turning as he dodged, snorting heavily in the midst.

After a few dodges, Kael rolled clockwise, positioned his feet on the ground, and sprung towards the beast before it could turn again, knocking it into a nearby tree.

It squealed and gasped for breath as Kael pulled a knife from his thigh and slit its throat. Blood poured from the wound, the animal staggering with cloudy eyes fixating on him. It staggered into a half charge but fell into a pool of its blood. It stilled in mere seconds, steam rising from the puddle.

Kael bent over and huffed, trying to catch air in his lungs. He then spat into the ground as he examined the corpse. He used his foot to tilt the head and examine the wound. Steam rose from it as well.

"Fuck. This is going to take some time," he said. "There's more of these. But how many? I dinnae have time to track them all down." The tracks into the forest were faint but there; his honed eyes could see them. There was several all muddled together and he had no idea how many that may mean.

He did not think that he would have to, but he now knew he would have to lure these mutations towards him. *It's an old skill, and Ijos taught me how to use herbs for this.*

He stood motionless for some time, scanning the woods, and determining the supplies he needed. He then gathered some plants in the area. First was bark from a specific tree, an ash-colored wood. The skin was humanlike, where it was slightly squishy but resilient. The bare tree beneath it oozed a clear sap when he pulled it off.

Next was some peculiar purple berries from nearby bushes. Their texture was coarse, much like sand had coated it (*Xachoiu, Ijos said*).

The last was brown weeds that had hexagonal blades. They frayed at the end into what would be a flower in spring or summer. It had a pungent smell that was hard to describe.

Returning to the clearing with his ingredients, Kael pulled a gray flask and small bowl from his pouch. He sat and placed the ingredients in the bowl, using his thumb to crush the berries and meld the bark and weed together to form a paste. He then pulled out a skin of water and filled the flask halfway. He filled the rest of the flask with the paste, then corked it and shook it vigorously.

Once mixed, the solution was an off-gray liquid. It was slightly viscous—like grey snot—but it was thin enough to drink. Kael examined the mixture with disgust, turning the flask upside down to see the solution seep with gravity.

He downed it in one gulp like a shot of spirit. It was cold and clung to his throat, an earth taste tainted by the bitterness of bad meat. A cold chill vibrated down his spine as he felt the slime seep into his stomach. His vision began to pulse in tandem with his heart, which was quickening.

It always does this at first, Kael grimaced as the wave of nausea swept over him. *And then comes the scent of molten metal. 'Like biting a hot sword,' Ijos used to say.*

The only thing left was an attraction. As putrid as it was, burning flesh always draws attention. Kael took his knife and carved out a slice of meat from the deer corpse. The acrid stench filled his sinuses, enhanced by the elixir.

He held back bile from rising as he used the resected meat and some dry twig to start a small fire. The smoke smelled sickly sweet, burning the putridness and replacing it in a worse way.

He crouched beside the fire with his swords drawn and crossed in front of him. Now he waited. He should become the hunted.

He stilled in that pose long enough for the sun to be on its descent to the horizon once again, but not enough for the skies to turn pink. Even with his heightened sense of hearing, he was still ambushed by the pack of wolves.

Deadlier with the mutations, and numbered about seven, the wolves had snuck up behind him with a predatory silence. The snow didn't crunch under their paws the same, surrounding him as he waited in a trance, unbeknownst to the threat behind. Only as one lunged did a snarl betray it. Its newfound hunger had bubbled through it newly formed rows of teeth.

He acted instinctively, the surprise masked by years of training. He crossed his swords in front of him and the mutie wolf was cut in two, sliced through the deadly sieve of blades. He followed with a low sweep and avoided the next wolf. It clasped its mouth shut overhead in its attack, muffling the yelp when he dug his sword into its stomach and ripped. Steam rose as its entrails tumbled out and coated him.

The warmth of the blood and guts were soured by the smell of putrid, rotting flesh, but he had no time to wipe it off before a third wolf clamped down on his thigh. He cursed as his blood pooled out of the wound. He retaliated quickly and cut its head off.

He had no time to tend to the wound, which was seeping down his leg. Kael focused his attention to the remaining four, surrounding him whilst he was focused on the others. He took a stance with one sword in front and one sword behind him and bent low to the ground.

At this time, the wolves lunged in tandem—to the point of eerie mimicry down to their snarl—and Kael exhaled and spun in a circle. The weapons igniting from sparks to embers, at last becoming a small inferno that incinerated the wolves midair. The burnt bodies fell back to the edges of the clearing, melting the snow beneath them from the heat.

He stood up, heavily breathing from the stance he took, and sheathed his swords. He was tired, beyond tired. The effects of the elixir had worn off. His eyesight dulled, his eyes adjusting to the approaching twilight slowly. His muscles ached and the pain from the wound came back tenfold. The pain and weakness pulled him to the ground, where he grasped his leg to stifle the bleeding some with one hand.

His other hand shot to his pouch and pulled a paper packet. He ripped the packet open with his mouth and spread a white powder on the wound. It sizzled on contact and he ground his teeth—it burned. He knew a primary ingredient was salt, accounting for the burn. The other ingredients helped to close the wound faster, and it did. After the sizzling, the bleeding stopped and the wound was a week-old scab.

It was still tender—why they never added an analgesic, he didn't know—but he got up and returned to

Jorunn in a thicket. She stomped at the ground with a forehoof, snorting heavily. It took him a moment to calm her, and even then, she jolted with any noise as they exited the forest.

The sun was at the horizon. It basked the fields in a red glow. Much like blood—blood spilt for him to be at this moment in time. He watched as the sun slid and disappeared as he passed into the town limits. The paths were lit by the street posts, candles adorning the small homes along the town limits. The farmhands retired to their homes, into the warmth of fire and family.

It was something that Kael never really knew, except in passing a window. He stopped once, staring into a home. Seeing the hearth ablaze, a mother and father in the glow with their children. He stared into that window until a flurry of snow landed on his face and pulled him out of it. He moved on, despite glancing back a few times.

It was always just Ijos and I, he reminisced. *We always just ate together but never celebrated any holidays; it was always training.*

The town was still lively currently; both the villagers and the visitors were littering the pathways, the commotion present due to the festival taking place. Kael had heard of these festivals, often they would be a weeklong and culminate in a large bonfire.

People would stop mid-conversation, gawking before whispering like they had seen something forbidden. He was used to being an outcast. He was raised in the mountains; although he had the village, it was cut off from the rest of the world in ways.

He stuck to the alleyways the rest of the way, traversing from one side of the town to the other, the back alleys less populated than the others, which was more comforting to him. These back alleys contained more interesting shops anyway; there was a potions shop in one, and another had a bookstore that contained volumes he knew the normal townsfolk would not dare pick up.

He did wonder, though, who would purchase *Gretest's Feasts: A Cookbook of the Best Orcish Foods?* Kael snickered at the thought of Orcs existing. They're as likely to exist as a wampus cat.

Lekr Inn was busier than normal, but hardly as busy as any of the other inns. Kael returned Jorunn back to the barn, filling the feed trough with hay and feeding her an apple he had stored in the saddlebags. He stopped and gently patted Jorunn on the snout, picked up his bags and headed back to the inn.

Upon entering, he noticed the inn was lit differently than before. A soft, orange glow filled the room from the hearth and candles on the walls and the main desk. It was dazzling—the candles flickered like warm stars.

To his left was a dining hall—although it was far too small to be a legitimate hall. More so a large room with a table that could seat maybe twenty people. This room was well-lit, basking with the same glow from an elegant centerpiece. The room was otherwise unoccupied.

This was deeply saddening to Kael, who stood there staring at the table, which was adorned with food. It was a fantastic meal to his eyes with several diverse kinds of meats and breads, an amount that would be fitting for a Lord. He noticed some meats, such as quail, horxax (which was similar in appearance to a deer, but its meat far more tender), pork, and chicken. After the day he had, he was mesmerized by the feast laid out before him.

"Yer late."

Kael was startled out of his trance by the soft, yet rugged, voice. Anelle glared at him with her hands on her hips. She wore a grey button-up top and a light blue skirt that was a bit short and tight, but she was wearing tights underneath and a pair of long black boots. He would not normally feel like this would match, but it suited her well.

"I said seven o'clock, and it's nearly eight. Do ya not know how to tell time?"

What a weird question. Kael did not know how to respond; he was out all day hunting and was not worried about the time. He just stood there and gawked at her.

"Well, are ya gonna answer me? Ye have all this gear, but ya can't even be bothered with a wrist clock, it seems?"

It was then that it clicked to him. "A watch," he said, reminding him of the crystal-powered clock he bought for Ijos so long ago. He remembered people

407

taking about the city of Maruja and their advancements with crystals, how they could power with even a sliver of a crystal. *But how did they get the pieces so small?* He stifled a laugh and turned to Anelle. Despite her smaller stature, it could be intimidating to see her with her arms akimbo.

"I didnae realize it was getting late, I lost track of time and—"

Anelle interrupted him in a huff. "I don' need any excuses, and yer filthy too. Hurry up and wash up and come down in some clean clothes."

Kael wanted to argue—and would have normally— but he just nodded and walked up the stairs. He was astounded in his own behavior, since most people tended to fear him anyways and few tend to try to speak to him in such a manner. With Anelle, though, he opened more easily and tended to do as she said. It was unknown to him.

He returned to his room and undressed from his dirty clothes. He had his own bathroom, thankfully, and he walked into the small closet-sized room and saw that it did not have a tub like most places he stayed. Sure, Anju was more profitable than the towns he had been to, or—in some cases—less devastated by the warfare in the north and south.

Instead of a tub, it had a spout coming out of the wall and the floor angled towards a hole in the floor. He was amazed at such a contraption, examining the hole, which seemed to connect to a pipe of sorts, instead of opening to the floor below. He examined the spout as well, and noticed there was a knob below it, like a doorknob. He turned it, and water spewed from the spout above, ice cold on his skin. The water eventually warmed up, heating to body temperature. It was a pleasant change to the cold outside.

After Kael was done bathing, he dressed himself in normal clothes, a pair of black pants and a white shirt. The only remnant of his normal attire were his boots. He returned to the dining hall, which now boasted more food than before, with Anelle eyeing him from the end of the table. He sat down at the other end, nodding to her as he did . She nodded back, and they both picked food to eat in silence.

He continued to eat but would steal glances at her. Unbeknownst to him, she stole glances when he looked down, too. She watched him fold in on himself instead of talking. *What do I say?* He never really ate a formal dinner like this. Ijos always cooked what they hunted, but it was not on fancy dinner plate or requiring fine clothes. *Do I ask her about her day?* Quite some time passed as they ate and no words were spoken between the two, until they both went to eat some more quail.

"Ya were gone a lot of the day. How long do ya think you'll be around?"

Kael stopped and thought about it. "I'm not sure. I cannot be sure of the amount that I'll have to track down. I may not even be able to find them all."

"What will ya do, then?"

He threw up his hands. It was a strong possibility that there were more mutants out there. He wasn't sure how he could find them all.

"I'll have to talk to the burgomaster tomorrow, see what options we have."

"Ya reckon ye'll be here a while?" Anelle looked hopeful.

"Possibly, it might even take the winter. The snow will set in and it'll be hard to do much hunting anyway. The north tends to have impassable blizzards during the heart of it."

Anelle paused. "Where are ya from, anyways?"

"Further north. Far enough that the winters were long, and the summers were short. Very little of the year didnae have snowfall."

Kael stared at a candle burning in the middle of the table.

"But it is no more. My home, just like much of the north, was burned to the ground. The people, too, were either burned or torn apart. I dinnae have a home. Not anymore."

Anelle stared solemnly. He looked up from the candle, and the fire reflected from his eyes. She felt like she could be enveloped in that warmth.

"What about you? Were you raised here?"

She picked at her food a little. "Nay, I was raised in the west. When I was young, my ma had to flee during an uprising. My da was lost in that war, and my ma was afraid she would lose me, too. We somehow came here, and my ma built this inn."

"I'm sorry to hear about your dad. War takes a lot of lives."

Anelle nodded. "Indeed it does. Just a couple years ago, my ma got sick. Demons in the chest, they say. She would hock up green sludge, her breathin' all shallow and harsh. She died in her sleep. I was left with this place."

"Do you really want to own an inn?" Kael noticed that talking about her mother and father brought great pain.

"No, but my ma loved this place. We were never as busy as the other inns, but my ma worked her hands to the bone to serve everyone that came through the door. I suppose I'm continuing her hard work and dedication."

"I always wanted to be a botanist. My homeland was home to a lot of plants, and I watched several be used to save people from the brink of death. I've loved plants since."

Kael saw flowers in every place—stuffed in corners, next to windows, even the desk had flowers and plants on top, beside, and behind them. And they all thrived—none wilted or dead. He really thought her love of plants showed in their growth, even in such wintry weather.

"I think the plants are beautiful," Kael blurted. He wasn't sure what else to say. He then murmured for a second and cleared his throat.

411

"Thank you for the dinner. It was the best food I've had in a long time."

His face gleamed into a smile and faded quickly. Anelle reached out and grabbed his hand and dropped it almost immediately, unsure why she did it in the first place. He stared at her for a moment, then turned and walked out of the room, to the stairs and out of sight. She sighed and sat down, covering her face.

Kael returned to his room and collapsed on the bed. He felt more tired now after his dinner and interaction with Anelle than he did after hunting.

He drifted off to sleep atop the covers, his feet hanging off the bed. The commotion outside did not awaken him, nor the jovial noises of the people enjoying the pre-festival happenings nor the various fights in the bars nearby.

Illusory Walls

I

Kael woke in the gleam of the morning sun in a panic. Jolted from a dreamless sleep, he lurched from the bed onto his feet. It was calm—the room was quiet and he was still clothed from the night before.

He stretched, pulling himself out of the momentary panic. He doesn't sleep deep—that was trained out of him at an early age. He took a few more moments to settle, shifting over to the window to gaze on the streets. It snowed more overnight, where there is now a fresh blanket of snow on the paths and layered over previous fall.

Amidst the chatter of townsfolk was the lyrical conversation of birds; something that was absent before. The few mutated wildlife he dispatched must have brought hope in the remainder, flocking back in the lessening dangers. It drove him to continue his complex task.

He doggedly continued to go out to the woods to hunt in the days after the dinner, though his efforts became more and more dwindling. His days were becoming monotonous—eating at the neighboring tavern, searching for Cormac (to no avail), and then staying out in the snow, maybe finding a small mutated rabbit or deer.

It seemed endless, and each day he would come home a little late, though Anelle did not scold him like the first time. They often ate in silence, but she eventually started asking about his day, asking if he was still hunting. The conversations eventually ended up more personal.

"So, how did ya get into the monster hunting trade?" Anelle felt the need to know him more, so she was determined that this dinner would be different. She had been questioning him about his job each day.

His replies were short and curt most of the time; he was sour with his less than par results. Even if it was a ruse, he was becoming more invested in it.

He pierced the meat in frustration, raking the fork on the bottom. "Ijos taught me how to hunt. He was a monster hunter by trade."

Anelle perked up a little at this. He did not often talk much about his past; these past few days he only answered questions about his day. "So was Ijos ya mentor?"

"More like a father. My family died when I was young and Ijos raised me. It must have been hard too, to raise a child alone."

Anelle nodded. "Aye, but I bet he is proud of ya. It seems ya are dedicated to yer job.

Yeah, he thought. *If only he could see how bad I am at failing—finding these mutations, let alone the sorcerer.* "He used to go on jobs with me until he got sick. This profession wears on the body."

Anelle examined him more closely. He was young; his face was youthful enough, even past the faint scar on his cheek. But his eyes were pocketed and weary. She felt a warmth in his blue eyes and averted her eyes.

"A-and is it something ya wanted to do with yer life?" Her stuttering came out as she dropped her fork. She tried to glance at him once more but failed again. Those eyes were captivating.

Kael leaned in his chair a little and looked up at the ceiling. "I... never thought about it. I never really envisioned doing anything else or thought about what would be fun."

Anelle raised her eyebrows. "Ya didn't enjoy anything as a kid? Nothin' at all?"

He thought about it. *As a kid? I mean, I trained with Ijos every day. Other than that...* "I always loved animals. Especially the magical ones. I remember that Ijos had this red bird and I would watch it fly over the village."

Anelle's mouth twitched and then spread into a grin. She wasn't looking at the man, but the boy inside him. "That's a soft thing to say."

"Maybe I could have taken care of animals. Maybe I could have been a rancher or shepherd." He paused. "I suppose it doesn't matter though. I hunt monsters, that's all I've been trained to do."

The rest of the dinner he thought about what his life could be if his home was never destroyed. Then he thought about how the sorcerer took from him a normal life. His resolve strengthened again to eradicate everything related to the sorcerer.

II

After several days of poor results, Kael succumbed to needing some kind of help in locating the mutants. In the morning, he quickly dressed and exited the inn. He left in stealth so he did not garner any attention from Anelle, as he did not have time to talk today.

He paused once at the door, though. His heart thumped for the hope that they crossed paths. He peered through the door leading to the back and didn't see her at all. Slightly disheartened, he closed the door behind him and down the steps.

His mission today was to talk to Aurel about where he can acquire magical means for tracking. He knew it would have made the past few days easier; despite that, he really did not want to use it.

The roads were covered in a fresh blanket of snow, but it was interrupted by several tracks, betraying the idea that it was early. Since his trip was town-bound only, he left Jorunn at the stable to rest today. He greeted her as he left, patting her down and giving her fresh hay.

"It's a rest day for you, girl." Her response billowed out of her nose in a cloud of condensation. She tended to her fresh pile of hay as he wound his way to his habitual breakfast stop.

The tavern visit was uneventful; the people were merry, and the soldiers of the local garrison were drunk early as usual. His meal was bland, and this morning seemed just as bland. He had small talk with the bartender, but he ate in silence otherwise.

He left the tavern and crossed the town to the office, wrapping his cloak tight as the winds whipped up. The hood whipped against his face, few tendrils of the frigid air brushing against his short beard as he climbed the porch.

The office door creaked open and gave way to the dingy inside that was lit by the fireplace. The portly Aurel was dozing behind his desk. His face and neck were beaded with sweat from the heat in the nearby hearth, and his droning snore masked Kael's presence.

After a minute or so passed, Kael cleared his throat to alert the man of his presence. The noise jolted him into comically falling out of his seat. Kael snickered under his breath as the man struggled to his feet.

417

"What the hell—what are you doing here? I thought you would be out hunting. What the hell do you want?" Aurel had a sharp tone in the voice, aggravated from being caught off guard and from Kael's presence in general. Kael dismissed any snide attitude and continued with the task at hand.

"I hit a snag in my plans. I need to know where your closest sorcerer is, as I assume you have a town sorcerer."

Aurel huffed at this, a tone he knew was very known amongst the idea or sorcerers. Although they garner high regards for their results, their methods are mocked and they are almost shunned, both out of fear and for the fact they are different. Most are elderly beings who seem to peer through you, with gaping eyes like crystal balls filled with smoke. But Kael needed results, so he knew the fastest tactic.

Aurel crossed arms at Kael with distaste for what he is about to say. "There is an old sorcerer by the name of Ignaz that lives on the edge of town closest to the forest, in an old, decrepit hut."

"I see. Thank you. I will be on my way."

It was then that Aurel unfurled his arms and placed them down on his desk with force. Aurel recoiled a little at his own action, though he continued to look Kael in the eye. "I do need to warn you, though, that he is an unusual fellow. He often speaks in tongues, talking of gibberish, and his eyes will stare straight into your very being."

Kael nodded sternly and left. Ignaz's hut was on the other side of town, which—although the town itself was not large like cities in the center of Lothanae—it did have plenty of roads and pathways that wound between homes and other buildings.

As he wandered an overgrown path, he heard a struggle of sorts. Closing in on the source, he heard a woman, angry and struggling, alongside the grunting of men.

"Didn't I tell ye, you have to business at my place, and you don't need to be hounding my clients."

A husky man with a drawl piped up. "We have business where we see fit, and it just so happens that you have some mighty fine customers staying there. So why don't cha tell us which rooms these ladies are staying in? We will make it worth your while."

Another man coughed and spat, then joined the conversation as well. "You look pretty fine yourself. How about you have some fun, too?"

There was a loud crack. Kael could only surmise she slapped the man's face.

"Fuck off, you bug-eyed git."

He heard a *fuck* and a shuffling as he rounded the corner. He saw the flash of clothes disappear as the men surrounded her. Her face was covered by one's hands so she could not scream.

"Now take it easy, and this will be over with soon enough. We are just gonna have a little fu—"

419

The commotion came to a standstill as Kael tore one of the men away, busting his face open with his studded glove. There was a total of three men, the first one was bleeding profusely from his mouth and nose, the latter broken.

The other two still had hold of the girl. He turned amid the fight to see it was Anelle. Her eyes were full of fright between the men. Seeing her was all it took.

He succumbed to it, the blinding rage—the ravenous darkness he kept at bay. The two men released her and flanked him with their swords drawn. Kael guarded from the blows with his gauntlets, ignoring the dull thud of pain. He grabbed one and thrust him into the other, knocking them both into a nearby wall. As they fell to the ground, he lunged on one and attacked.

More. His fists drove into the soldier's face. Blood seeped from the wounds left by the studs. *More blood.* He snarled. His eyes burned into the man's slack face, unconscious after the first blow. Kael did not let up. He could feel his hands aching, but he continued to beat the man. *I need more. More blood. More death.*

Anelle ran up behind him and screamed, trying to tear him off the man. Kael pushed her away and continued. *No one can stop me.*

A sword came down in his peripheral. Kael grabbed the blade and yanked the man towards him. He jammed the pommel of the sword into his chest with an echoing *crack.* The man dropped in an instant. He stood up and flicked the sword away from him with his foot.

Then—silence. He was motionless as he stared at the soldier. He gasped, trying to stop his neck from continuing. He heard the rumbling sobs behind him and feet shuffling. He reacted too quickly—pivoting hard, he almost fell down, his mind too occupied with reeling back. And then he felt a gentle thud into his chest.

Anelle sobbed. She buried her face into his chest and held him tight. He was frozen, still reeling from the voice inside for more blood. Her head blocked his view from the fallen men long enough for him to gain his composure.

He wrapped his arms around her as he came back and pulled her closer to him. He needed that warmth. He shuddered as he thought about how he felt in that moment. *But was it wrong? They deserved this.*

She mumbled and was breathing heavily, her eyes hot and flooded with tears.

"Please, stop. Please," She choked between sobs. "Not for me. Don't hurt yourself for me."

He blinked. *Hurt myself?* He didn't understand. Then he felt the blood on his face and hands. The aching. He wiped his nose on his sleeve and held her more gently this time. She sobbed harder. He hated the sound of it.

He didn't have the words to soothe her. He opened his mouth, but Anelle leaned away from him and stared into his eyes. He opened his mouth, but she closed it with hers. Her lips met with his and pushed any thought from his mind. The passion burst forth like fire, but only for a moment. She pulled away abruptly and out of his arms, turning away.

"I'm sorry," Anelle gasped as she gathered some things that fell to the ground in the altercation. She turned to him with red, swollen eyes. "I'm sorry."

She ran before he could even stammer a sentence out. He froze for a while trying to recollect his thoughts.

The hut. I was going to the hut. The realization thawed him and he examined the soldiers. They didn't move, but he didn't care. It was muted, but he felt the desire to beat them more. But the need for Anelle burned that away. It took a great deal for him not to turn back to the inn, but he walked towards the hut anyway.

He hardly noticed any of the scenery during his walk. *Anelle. Blood. Anelle. Blood.* His mind went back and forth until he smacked into an old, ruddy fence.

What the—

To say the hut was strange would be an understatement. It had five irregularly sized, differently colored walls, like a pentagon drawn by a child. The center held a chimney, billowing with white plumes. Then there was a crude porch that wrapped around the perimeter.

Kael's hand laid on the fence as he stared in a mixture of awe and suspicion. He took in the sight for a moment until he felt a sharp pain in his hand, retreating it away from the fence. He thought it was just pain from the injuries until he heard a bleating sound. His gaze settled on a small flock of winged goats—striped of black and tan—examining him with glee.

He took a few strides down the fence before jumping over the gate-less boundary. The goats flicked to him, nibbling at his clothes as he passed through to the porch. He ascended the steps—glistening with magic—and passed several rusty and dirty cauldrons.

All this piled up in his mind as he tried to recount other sorcerers he has crossed, all with similar "quirks,". Kael did not understand sorcerers, but he knew this was a necessity for his job.

As he approached the hut, the door of the hut shimmered and disappeared, leaving a small, lanky man in blue robes at the doorway. The man looked ancient, with long, white hair and a sparse beard, but with a massive mustache and a toothy grin that did not have quite enough teeth. The man opened his arms as if welcoming a son or daughter.

"Welcome, welcome! You are Kael, yes? "The sorcerer's voice was the squeaky dissonance of wet boots.

Kael was unconcerned by the wizard knowing his name—there was no need to question the anomalous.

"Aye, and I have some things I need to discuss with you. I need to locate a certain kind of beast."

Ignaz the sorcerer flashed a toothy grin and motioned Kael through the shimmering doorway.

"Come in, just do not mind the mess. I have been experimenting with some new ingredients and some have not ended so well."

As the two entered through the frame, Kael noticed there were singed parts of his robe and faint smoke coming from it.

In the hut, they began in a hallway with way too many doors for the size of the place. As they walked towards one door it disappeared and led to another hallway with more doors. It seemed like a maze, and Kael had a pit in his stomach.

III

The inside of the hut was massive. Stone walls filled the corridors, each alight with oddly colored torches, casting rainbow-hued shadows over them. The smell inside was just as unique—traces of vanilla and chamomile lingered in the air, whilst there were random whiffs of rotting remains and formaldehyde, and then that of cooking food, the smell of stewing vegetables. The strongest of all was the smell of piss-stained cloth and smoke—but Kael felt that it might be the sorcerer than the hut itself.

The sorcerer strolled ahead, winding through the maze with ease. A buzzy hum came from his mouth, his glassy eyes peering at the objects they passed. The hum bounced in a dissonant rhythm in Kael's ears. Only after a few minutes did it register it was an old folk song:

Issae was a boy who liked to have fun,

He would play pranks and run,

One day he ran into the forest,

He went too far and had to take a rest,

As he slept a bear ripped out his guts.

Kael did not understand why the sorcerer was humming this, but he did not ask. Sorcerers talk in weird ways, as if reciting poems. The men at last went through a doorway that led to a great hall.

Adorned with banners of ancient kingdoms and relic armor, it detailed the different factions that ruled the country in times past. Although there is one king over the whole land, there are those who ruled the lesser provinces. *There always had been Lords that ruled over parts of the kingdom that are out of the King's reach,* Kael thought.

Ijos taught him enough of the history of Lothanae. Even in past generations, these lords would often oppose the ideas and laws of the king, which led to violent battles that caused collateral damage to some towns. Thus, the lands were often stained by bloodshed. It was a constant tug of war of power by different factions. Contrasting ideals caused political issues better settled on the field than in a room.

King Sarroch, the previous ruler, had united the factions as well as he could, but he was frail in his old age. When the rule transferred to his son Alrich, war broke out. There was the Vrall nation in the north, whose treaty was brittle even during Sarroch's rule. Then there were rebellions in the Wastelands of the south, a slow explosion waiting to happen as lawlessness consumed it.

Then came a surprise—the one only known as the dark sorcerer. He appeared at the southeast boundary with his army of mutants, who many think to be the nation's bloodshed in physical form.

As of recent times, however, the factions have been fighting for boundaries. News comes from the west about the lords Warrix and Harlow sending their armies to reclaim from the other.

There is also a counterculture; those who wish to overturn the current system and enact a new Era of politics that gave people more choice. This faction is more radical and violent but is still in its infancy. These rumblings are mostly from the Wastelands, those banished from Lothanae and slaves for crystal mining.

Kael noted all the factions and followed the old sorcerer up a set of stairs at the end of the hall. Through the doorway was a vast library and sanctum. The sorcerer wandered over to a desk with scrolls strewn everywhere as Kael examined the room for a bit.

Books lined the walls, some tomes as tall as he; on obsidian tables were vials and crystal decanters of varying liquids. Animal skulls adorned the walls and in clear canisters were wormwood, arrowshaw, and many others he could not name.

Kael approached the opposing side of the desk. "Ignaz, I was led to believe Aurel about a monster issue—"

"I know what you came for, huehuehue." Ignaz squeaked. Ignaz pulled out the heads of the Stökkbreyta and mutated deer. "The burgomaster brought these to me after you 'violated his office with its putridity,'" Ignaz made a mocking tone of the burgomaster's voice and laughed at his own attempt.

The sorcerer then began to inspect the heads in an odd way, pulling at the skin and poking the eyes, pulling its tongue out and feeling the texture. "I have not had the time to examine them myself, what with my other important experiments," he flipped his robe to show the singed parts.

Ignaz leaned close to the heads and examined the Stökkbreyta for a moment. Although he seemed interested in it, Ignaz spent most of his time with the deer. He would stretch the skin further, slice off a piece and add something to it, then repeat. Some of these reactions would ignite, some dissolved into the liquid, and some turned the skin to ash.

With each test, Ignaz would write notes down on a scroll and murmur inaudibly. Kael was sure that Ignaz would end up taking a taste of the head by the end of it. He did not, though he did take the last sliver of skin and peer through it at a light.

"A Stökkbreyta is not natural, Kael. I am sure you are aware, but they are not naturally born, but created, and of that, through magic."

Kael regarded the heads, reflecting on all the previous beasts that he's slain. He thought about the various beasts and the origins of them, but the Stökkbreyta only had a known origin associated with the dark sorcerer. There may be some that roamed after his last massacre, like they had been set loose, but there was no den of them found, no mention of them in old tomes or fairy tales like other beasts.

"This is dark magic, indeed," Ignaz rumbled.

"You are aware of their origins, of their link to the *enbe'ach*, the dark sorcerer, as he is called in common tongue. Dark magic is forbidden at the academy," Ignaz peered over the head at Kael. " They were deemed forbidden long before I was born, which is ancient for you." He smiled his toothy grin again and resumed to the head. "So, if these creatures are created or of another plane, I do not know. Seeing this—" He poked the deer head," —means something new is brewing. I am afraid a dark time is upon us."

Ignaz gazed intently at Kael, staring at him with big eyes that almost bugged like the corpses'.

"And you, my dear Kael, are intertwined in these dark times. You must find the man missing in the woods. Such is the path of your destiny."

Kael froze and leered at the sorcerer. The fact he had not spoken a word about his intentions, yet the man knew, was off-putting. The sorcerer went back to working on the beast heads for a moment before he spoke once more.

"You may try to diverge, but fate will always guide you on the right path. This path you are on now will cause you much heartbreak and pain, but it is necessary to grow into the man you need to be, the man who will stop *enbe'ach*."

Kael, who turned his attention to some scrolls nearby, stumbled for a second. The dark sorcerer was his mission. Kael was haunted by nightmares of the sorcerer still. He had been on his path of revenge and yet he was no closer to him than when he started. He was face-to-face with him in Mynheir and could do nothing, but Ignaz—this scrawny, ancient old man—thinks he will stop him? Kael felt it too, felt like the sorcerer would be his end, but he felt driven to find him, and will find him again, even on his last breath.

Ignaz popped above the remains and cocked his head to the side. "I see. We are already out of time."

Ignaz appeared before Kael as if an apparition, holding his shoulders and gazing into his eyes. "When you leave here, you will face much pain, but you will grow stronger. Take this, as it will help you. But remember, find the missing man. He will guide you."

Ignaz cackled and dissipated into dust, forming a pseudo night sky in his castle. Kael was stunned. Shaking himself out of a stupor, he felt something hard in his hand. He opened it to see a small glass vial with a purple liquid in it, the liquid turning to fog and back to liquid in the vial constantly. He examined the vial for a moment.

He did not like the swirling, nor the faint vibration coming from it, but it felt important. He stashed it away, then he turned on his heels and made his way back through the door he came. He wasn't sure if he could leave this puzzle of a castle.

As he reached his hand out he heard an echo in the laboratory. *Do not refuse fate, for it could be disastrous.*

Kael opened the door to a blinding light and warmth on his face. The sun bore down on him the same as he left it—no time had passed while he was inside. As his eyes readjusted, it was then that Kael noticed that he was not alone.

The goats had disappeared, the yard empty and quiet. At least, he thought it was quiet.

"Where have you gone, you demon?"

Silence.

"Not going to answer us, yeah? Only suspicious individuals talk to the sorcerer, and you look like you're up to no good."

Kael knew this day would not end well.

Retribution

Throne of Duplicity

I

The inside of Carnigh Keep was dreary, sparsely decorated with animal heads upon the wall and aged red banisters with the coat of arms of the castle: a red lion wielding a large axe in its paw.

In the feast hall, atop a large, crude stone throne sat an equally large man. His body was covered in black leather under a black fur cloak, his head topped by disheveled peppered hair, and his face mostly covered by a large beard of similar color. His right eye was gone, the lid shutting the void from the world. The other eye was glassy, the fumes of strong liquor emanated from the figure and a barrel beside the throne.

A wooden tankard hung from his loose grip. The hall was empty, much like his stare. A large axe leaned on the throne, the metal tarnished from years of neglect.

The man would drain his tankard and refill in one motion, then resume his dead trance. He paid no heed to the rising commotion outside his walls, even when it came bursting through the main doors and sprinted towards him.

He was apathetic to the noise, to the pieces of shit that were his own troops. Not even if there was a group carrying three of their own, beaten bloody, towards his grace.

"My lord! We've been attacked! The town has attacked us!"

Uninterested, he drank his liquor and refilled it with apathy.

One breached the short set of steps to the throne. "My lord, please! These men were found in the streets, beaten until near death and left to rot. People said they heard the brawl but did not interfere, even when a man in red was pounding them to death! Sir what do—"

The lord jolted and fixated his one eye on the men. His voice rumbled with the next words, cracked from disuse and overconsumption.

"You are sniveling, weak, impudent cunts. You can't deal with one man? You bother me over some low life, who you should be able to deal with? Our name should strike fear in these people—and you let some ignorant fool best you."

He staggered out of his throne and towered over them, staggering as he glared at them. He leaned down to the soldier who spoke. The stench of liquor was a cloud, and the soldiers had to batter their eyes from the fumes. His heart was pounding.

The Lord belched and growled. "Bring this man to me. Find out where he is and place him in chains so I can swing down the hammer of justice."

The soldier timidly nodded. The Lord nodded in response and waved his hand at the wounded men.

"Take these men to the infirmary. I want them to be healed when I give my disciplinary action to them for their impudence."

With that, the lord staggered once more up the steps and onto his throne, resuming his binge, but this time with more emotion in his eye. He was silent as the men scrambled out of the hall before he uttered another word. His voice oozed with such hate and malice that it filled the hall.

"I have been waiting for this moment, Kael. The day I exact my revenge on you and your inept father."

A sinister smile crept upon his lips. He cackled and howled, like a deranged wolf ready for the hunt.

II

Kael was surrounded. The yard was occupied by a couple dozen soldiers, all pointing weapons at him. Kael heard the townspeople talk of the soldiers. They were brigands, thieves, whoremongers, and rapists—but it was done in the name of "justice". The town could not do anything to them; the mayor was afraid of the Lord of the nearby castle.

Kael slowly walked down the steps, keeping his eyes focused on any sudden movements from the men. Each man stood in a way that made them more menacing, their muscles flexed and poised to pounce.

But that was to the normal eye. Kael saw the skittish movements, shallow breathing, and sweat beading on their foreheads. He knew they were afraid, so he turned off the porch and across the yard. One yelled at him as his back was turned.

"You heathen fucker, are you not going to talk?"

"He must be scared, Raul. I would be too, surrounded by soldiers of Lord Haskell."

Kael paused in the yard. He recognized that name, but he wasn't sure where. It left a bad taste in his mouth as he tried to grasp it. The men kept talking to each other, and it clouded his thoughts.

"You think he's gonna piss his pants?"

"We've beat the shit out of men meaner looking than this cunt, boys. Come on, we have a job to do."

He ignored them and continued to the fence. Those closest to his path cowered as he passed, but none acted. At least, not until he got to the fence.

The raking of a sword unsheathed rang out and he reacted instinctively. His right hand unsheathed a sword from his back as he pivoted on the balls of his feet. A loud din of metal colliding filled the air as he blocked a downward attack. He peered into the soldier's eyes and thrust his left hand into the man's stomach. A loud retch came from the soldier as he vomited and crumpled to the ground.

The rest of the men drew their weapons, swords and crossbows alike. Kael had no time for idle footing. He pivoted again, drawing the other sword from its sheath. They piled on him as he blocked with both swords independently.

He was a blur, holding the blades to parry each blow and bolt. The fight was one-sided; in all their swagger, they were weak and inexperienced. With frail footing and poor aim, some of the men fell due to a stray blade or bolt. Kael knew he had to end this quickly or else there would be casualties, so he began to incapacitate them one by one.

Each parry he would send out a strong kick, jamming some of the men out of the chaotic circle and into another, making way for him to elbow or head-butt another. He made sure that he had the finesse to harm but not maim or kill them. The men could not contain him, and they were losing numbers quick.

I really didn't want to get into a fight in this town, he brooded. *If I keep this up, then I'll draw more attention, and maybe the sorcerer will know I'm here...*

Kael yelled and dropped his swords. They clattered as he held up his hands in surrender. The men hesitated. They eyed each other for several moments until one kicked his weapons out of reach and another tied his hands behind his back.

The ones left standing were still on edge, so that when he jerked his bound hands away, one punched him in the stomach. He doubled over to a knee jammed in his face, knocking him to the ground. The rest rallied around him, and they all began to kick him violently until he lost consciousness.

III

A wagon wheel creaked intermittently, accompanied by hushed murmurs. It was dark, but he was being moved. He felt the bumpy road and the crunch of ground beneath him.

He was blindfolded and his hands and feet were bound by chains. His head throbbed and he could not hold it up, either from pain or instability. He could hear people outside of the wagon—women and children—some in the distance and some close.

"See what happens when you confront us, eh? A gruff voice slurred, hiccupping afterwards. The vapors of alcohol seeped into the wagon. *I'm a trophy, a warning, it seems. They've already celebrated while I was unconscious.*

The men cheered and jeered, laughing as they passed by a group. He heard one snort and shoot snot, women screaming in disgust as they tried to evacuate from the line of fire. They would overturn things, from décor outside homes to items and goods outsides stores. They took their time parading him through town.

Don't let Anelle see me like this, for fucking sake. He repeated that line over and over in his head. He sat up and tried to keep his balance, but his head throbbed so much that it was difficult. He started to feel at ease when he felt the ground change to dirt, knowing he was out of the town.

Where are they taking me, and why me? Who is Haskell, and why does it sound familiar? He racked his brain for some time, deep within a trance until he got jolted out of it as the wagon stopped.

"Hey, open the damn gate, Sanson! We brought 'im back!"

The voice slurred but was coherent enough. Kael heard glass breaking high up—maybe he threw something to get the attention of the man named Sanson.

He could hear a faint rustle above and something came down and thudded beside him. He moved his leg and felt an empty cup. "Don't throw your fuckin' shit up here. So, ya caught the fucker? How'd ya manage that?"

"I'll do as I damn please to you, you cock sucker! And never mind how we caught 'im; I'll tell you later! Open the damn gate!"

Sanson grumbled and spat over the edge. The spit coated Kael's shoulder, warm and pungent. There was a

439

loud groan as the gate opened, massive in size and broken by the din of it. The wagon began to move again. It jostled him and knocked him over into the broken cup. He felt the warmth of blood on his cheek.

The man leading the wagon laughed at him. "I feel sorry for you, lad. You shoul'n have messed with us. Now you're gonna feel more pain than that knot on your head."

The wagon stopped once again.

Kael was dragged from the wagon across dirt and up stone stairs. The shift of cold to warm was evident, making him figure he entered the fort and into the related castle. They took several paces into the castle before the men him threw him on the floor like a ragdoll.

He then heard a clatter and large stomps of boots ahead of him getting closer until they stopped in front of him. A large hand grabbed him by his hair and yanked him up to his knees before another hand tore off the blindfold.

And there it was—a face he never expected to see again.

The name Haskell came back to him in an instant and his stomach dropped. The snide sneer that crossed the man's lips was sharp, cutting through his peppered, disheveled beard. He tightened his grip on Kael's hair, then he used his other hand to clamp down on his jaw, moving his head from side to side.

"Yes, it is you, isn't it, Kael? I can tell from those striking blue eyes. Ah, but you must remember the eye you took from me, huh? A green one, just like the other, albeit then it was a lot more vibrant."

He clamped down on Kael's jaw even tighter, to the point that Kael felt like it was going to break. Haskell released his jaw then threw him down on the floor. His face rebounded on the floor with a crunch, his nose busted open again.

Haskell turned to walk away, then twisted and kicked Kael in the ribs. He slid across the floor and into a wall. He rolled on his side, coughed and spat blood as he caught his breath.

Haskell knelt and examined the swords that the soldiers seized from him. Haskell picked them up and threw them near his throne before he walked over and picked Kael up by the hair again, then dragged him out of the hall and into a hallway.

"You are gonna regret fucking with me. You are gonna wish you did not get the attention of my men."

He dragged him towards a long set of stairs that led down to a cellar, which used to be a small armory. There was a bare table in the middle and Haskell threw Kael on it. Haskell then turned Kael around to face him. The last thing Kael remembers was Haskell's fist rushing towards his face.

IV

The sunset melded with flames of chaos. The city of Mynheir was in upheaval, facing a revolt against King Alrich as his lead commanders and his roundtable fissured.

The men of the former council roared and yelled, displaying their disgust of the capital, of the degradation of morals and merits under this king. With them rallied people, borne of nobility, who were tired of sharing class with those born of lower class. They thought the rising ranks should be limited by birth status.

But all that was naught important as Ijos stood in the chaos, flames of revolts swirling around him in the upper district. He had no thought on the matter except to protect everything he loved.

"Haskell!" Ijos roared over the flames and commotion, the looting and violence. "You will pay for this!"

Haskell had no words. He lifted his axe and lunged at Ijos, swinging in a wide arc. Ijos ducked, swinging upwards and slicing at Haskell's chest. He wore no armor today—he had no plans to go to war. His shirt ripped open and blood seeped, but he took no heed.

Just a fucking surface wound. Ijos gritted his teeth and tried again, but Haskell already had a fist flying toward Ijos. It landed on his chest and knocked him across the ground. Ijos rolled on his back as Haskell loomed over him with a baleful expression.

"You have taken enough from me, you ungrateful dog. Die a pitiful death."

Haskell laughed as he slammed the axe haft down, shattering Ijos' knee. Ijos screamed and swung his sword in a wide arc, slashing at Haskell's thighs. Dark blood gleamed in the fire light, gouged flesh rocking from the leg.

Haskell roared as he threw his axe to the side, climbing on top of Ijos. He pummeled him with a barrage of punches, each blow harder than the last. Ijos stabbed Haskell's side, but it did not stop Haskell. He was in a trance.

"Die, dog! Die, traitor! DIE, LOWBORN MUTT!" He continued to chant this over and over long after Ijos passed out.

Haskell stood up over Ijos' unconscious body, picking his axe back up and held it over his head.

"Die."

Before he could swing, Kael came out of the shadows and lunged. He scaled Haskell, pulled out a knife and stabbed Haskell in the eye. Haskell roared and flailed, dropping his axe in the process as he tried to grab Kael.

Kael pulled out Ijos' sword stabbed into Haskell's side and stabbed it into Haskell again. He pulled it out one more time before Haskell grabbed him, taking the knife out of his bloodied eye and stabbing Kael three times in the chest with it. He cast aside the boy as he screamed and flailed, throwing him into a nearby wall.

Ijos awoke to seeing Kael being thrown. Blood splattered as he flew through the air, the sheen reminiscent of cherry blossoms. His sword clattered next to him in the commotion. Haskell was distracted at Kael's trajectory and rest beneath a broken wall.

Ijos used Haskell's new blind spot to pick up his sword. He took two staggered steps and stabbed through Haskell's chest.

Haskell stared into his eyes as blood spurted from his mouth.

"Y-You dog... worthless piece of shit..."

Haskell slumped and Ijos withdrew and sheathed the bloody blade. As Haskell slumped, a gold necklace fell out of his ripped shirt. Ijos pulled at the chain and tore it away into his pouch.

He heard a scream and turned to see Isabella running with Azalea in tow, horrified at the scene. She saw Haskell on the ground and Kael against a wall.

"W-What the fuck... What did you do?"

Ijos stood up and leaned on his sheathed sword. "Haskell... he tried to kill me. He hurt Kael..."

Isabella ran towards him and caught him as he began to slide down. "Ijos, are you okay?"

Ijos nodded his head but began to cough. Speckles of blood splattered her face as kissed him.

"Don't die, please..."

At this time Cormac and Elris came up. Cormac rode Duff and Elris on his horse with a crow perched on his shoulder.

"Ijos!" Cormac stopped right beside Ijos and Isabella, dismounting and helping Ijos to his feet. "We need to go! The city is falling apart. Where's Kael?"

Ijos tried to run towards Kael but dropped, crawling the rest of the way. "K-Kael," Ijos flipped the boy over and put his ear to his chest. It was faint, but there was a beat.

Elris walked up and knelt beside the two, pulling out a small vial of clear liquid. Ijos held up Kael's head and Elris poured the liquid down the boy's throat. A few seconds passed before Kael rattled momentarily before he passed out again.

"It'll stop the bleeding and heal him, but it'll take time." Elris stood and examined the area. There was a buzzing noise that grew louder. "The crowd is coming. Ijos, we need to go."

Ijos nodded and turned to Isabella, who ran over to them in the process. "Isa, come with us. We can be a family."

Isabella looked at Ijos, beaten bloody, and Kael, who was unconscious in his arms. She turned to Azalea, who was huddled against her. Their eyes met and she knew. Isabella nodded and Ijos passed Kael over to Cormac so he could lean on his sword, then he put his fingers in his mouth and whistled.

A screech pierced the air and the roaring flames. Nuria appeared in the streets, followed by two horses in tow. She perched on Ijos' shoulder and crooned. Ijos and Elris helped Isabella and Azalea into the saddle of one of the horses then Elris helped Ijos in his, being mindful of his wounded leg.

As Ijos turned the horse around towards the nearest exit of the capital, he heard a roar amongst a flame. He craned his head to see Haskell was still alive, crawling towards them.

"Belle! Please don't go!" He crawled and scraped his way to her, the cobblestones ripping at his elbows and chest. His arms gave a few times and his face hit the ground. "Please... I love you, Belle. I've always loved you. Don't leave me to die."

Haskell began to sob, his face down on the ground. Isabella pulled at the reins of the horse to keep it still. Ijos turned his horse back and went to her.

"Isa, come with me. I love you, too. I don't know if I can't live without you."

Isabella's gaze shifted from Ijos to Haskell. She began to sob and grind her teeth, but she began to dismount the horse. "We are the only family he has, Ijos." She continued to choke through sobs. "I can't leave him to die... but I don't want you to go." Fresh tears continued to flow. She turned him with a defeated smile. "I don't know what to do."

Ijos felt a pain in his heart as he watched the woman he loved feel so torn. He knew that despite

Haskell's nature, he is family to her. If he had his own family, he would feel torn as well. She wouldn't be happy knowing she left him to die, and Haskell is far worse off than he is.

His hand trembled as he pulled out three smooth, round stones, and he leaned over the horse. "Isa, Azalea. Look at this."

He choked back every tear he could as he performed the spell, putting the two in a trance.

"You will forget me and Kael, and our journey together. Haskell was the one who saved you after Caede, and I was just a commander who came to see Haskell a lot. You will go to him and save him and he will keep you safe."

Ijos glared at Haskell with scorn, but the man did not move. *He must have passed out from his wounds.* Ijos stopped juggling the stones and the spell was done.

Isabella's face twisted in pain. She opened her mouth silently several times. The last time she opened her mouth, a frail 'Ijos' came out. It was a moan of pain as her eyes glossed, then her face went blank. She turned around and her face contorted in fear as both her and Azalea ran to Haskell.

Ijos pulled his reins and trotted over to Cormac, holding his arms out for the boy.

"Ijos, I can carry Kael." Cormac initially resisted, but the pain on Ijos' face muted Cormac immediately. He handed the boy over gently.

447

Ijos held Kael tight. It made him think of Caede and how he held him even then. But this time Kael was holding him together.

His face was stained with blood and tears as they exited the capital. He glimpsed back once as Isabella faded away.

V

It was dark in the cellar. Kael awoke bound tightly to a wooden chair. He tried to strain but to no avail, and he was hurting all over.

He stopped when he heard someone coming down the steps, and Haskell appeared at the doorway. Behind him was a petite woman with pale skin. Her skin was flawless, concealing her age. Her eyes were swollen and tearful. She stayed silent and followed Haskell to the table.

He motioned a large hand and she laid a large leather wrap on the surface. Haskell then moved her aside as he opened it. There were various tools that Kael could see, but Haskell chose some pliers for his task. He held them and leaned over Kael, inches away from his face.

"Where is Ijos?"

Kael stayed silent. He glared at Haskell. Haskell grimaced and grabbed Kael's jaw. His fingers pressed hard into his cheeks and made the bone ache.

"Let me ask this again: where is Ijos? More importantly, where is the fucking piece of shard he stole from me?"

Kael scanned his eyes before he spat into his face.

"Fuck you, you old codger." He cackled through the pain.

Haskell had enough. His fist drove into Kael's face. The chair tipped and his head hit the floor. His haw was hot and he felt it swelling.

In the aftermath, his tunic became untied at the top and a golden necklace spilled out onto the stone. Haskell sneered at the sight. He lunged for it but Kael lurched his head forward and bit a chunk from Haskell's hand. He spat the flesh back at Haskell and barked with mirth.

Haskell yelped and clutched his hand as it bled profusely.

"Fuck! Belle, I need a damn piece of cloth!"

The woman rushed to find a clean cloth to wrap his hand. The blood seeped through the cloth and she heaved.

"We need to sterilize the wound. The bite may lead to infect—"

"I know, dammit." He snarled and moaned as the blood dripped. He snapped at Kael's continued howl, which drove him into a rage.

"You snarky motherfucker—" He kicked Kael in the stomach several times. He stopped laughing and gasped. He folded and strained against the ropes as he vomited.

The woman named Belle urged him to stop and to hurry upstairs. He reluctantly agreed and stumbled to the stairs.

Kael began to flutter into unconsciousness when he noticed the woman had not followed the man upstairs and was kneeling in front of him. She was wiping the blood off him with a wet cloth. She spoke, but he could not discern what she said.

"I will find a way to get you out, Kael. Don't worry. I never forgot about you," She whispered once again before he heard incoherent yelling from above and she scurried off. Her eyes burned into his mind as he blacked out.

Desiderium

I

The solstice festival was in full swing. The people decorated the town in a frivolous manner, and the town square held the triangle-shaped fire lay for the bonfire. Music was playing on every corner; bards would frequent any and every place they could to play, intermingling and drinking.

Anelle was busy with the newest influx of guests. She was not particularly busy most times of the year, but with other places full, the people flocked to her. She stayed at her desk for the morning and tended to the animals afterward.

She was out at the barn tending to the livestock when she noticed Jorunn was still in her stable. Kael typically took her out with him when he went into the woods, and she did not notice him leaving his room today either. Anelle pondered this for some time while she did her chores. She decided she would ask Aurel after she was done, since he said he was going to talk to him.

She was cleaning the stalls when an owl perched on one of the walls. It gave out a long hoot as it cocked it head side to side. She gazed at the owl for some time before she went back to cleaning, noting that her grandmother said that owls during daylight were a bad omen.

What of it? It seems like everything is a bad omen these days, she thought. Sure, Anju was peaceful—save for the brigands of the Keep—but that does not compare to the news that came from the capital.

They say the King has delved into madness and has ordered for many people to be killed. More monsters are coming out from the wilderness and attacks on both livestock and people have spread. There may come a day when Anju isn't safe anymore, either.

Anelle's progress slowed afterwards, her mind preoccupied. Once she was done, she headed straight to Aurel. When she walked into the door, Aurel was asleep in his chair. She rolled her eyes and kicked the chair hard enough to move it. He startled awake in panic.

"What the fuck—" His eyes locked onto Anelle and licked his lips. "Anelle, what brings this pleasure?"

Anelle rolled her eyes again. "Keep yer eyes in your head, ya scoundrel. I am looking for one of my guests. Ya sent him to me. A man by the name of Kael?"

Aurel grimaced. "Ah, that savage. Yeah, I hired him to take care of some vermin in the woods so they did not come into town." His eyes darted out the window as he lowered his voice. "But he got himself mixed in with the soldiers of Haskell, so they took him. That poor bastard won't be seen again. And after the money I lost boarding him..."

Anelle picked up a large book from the desk and hit Aurel with it. The blow knocked him out of his chair and into the floor.

"Gods dammit Anelle! What did you do that fer?" Aurel rubbed the side of his head as he struggled to get on his feet. She smacked him again with the book and sent him back to the floor.

"Are ya fuckin' brain dead, old man? You're the mayor of this town, yet ya didn't protect a guest?"

He held his hands up for protection. "It ain't my damn job to protect fools who go'round picking fights!"

She raised the book again but stopped. "He wasn't picking fights, he was protecting me, ya sniveling coward!"

His face shot up with shock.

Anelle huffed and groaned. "Ya let these soldiers harass the people and turn yer back to us. Yet this outsider came in and fought back, only to be sent to his death."

She raised to book higher and he flinched. "You know retaliating is something a fool would do, Anelle. Lord Haskell is a ruthless man ever since he came here twenty years ago. I don't want to die, 'nelle. I don't want to die like the mayor before me."

Anelle glared contemptuously at him over her nose. "You don't deserve the ground you lay on."

She walked out of the building as Aurel muttered incoherent protests to her. She slammed the door to silence him and ran back to the barn. Jorunn greeted her with a soft neigh and welcomed the pats.

"Aye, lass, we will get back your owner. It's just me and you."

She mounted Jorunn once her saddle and gear was strapped. One click of the tongue set the horse to leave the barn. Anelle guided her through the town.

The keep was not too far from the town, but it was still about an hour from the town by horse. She took a small break so that Jorunn could rest a moment before finishing the trek. Their path led to the large iron gates of the barracks.

Anelle dismounted Jorunn at the gates and approached the gate. Above the gate, a man leaned on the battlement, the bottom of a bottle aimed at the sky. He did not move from that position for some time, emptying the bottle before he turned and threw it in the grass beside the road. He gazed around before he noticed her at the gate.

"Aye, 'hat bidness do ye 'ave 'ere, lass?" His voice was almost incomprehensible through the slur of words.

"I am looking for a man dressed in a red tunic. I was told he was here."

The man flitted a crooked smile. "We 'avn' seen anyone like that, so bugger off unless you want to service your troops in a different way." She flipped him off and he ignored her afterwards.

She picked up a rock, threw it at the man, and cracked him in the skull. He yelped in pain and rocked back and forth before he turned around.

"'ey! The fuck did you do that fer? What do ye want now?"

"I said I know he is here. I need to see the man that wears a red tunic."

About that time, another soldier appeared at the gates and tapped on the gate with his gauntlet. He looked more lucid than the other and he bore the ragged, grisly quality of a man who had seen battles before. She felt he might have been a higher-ranking soldier than a typical grunt.

"The man told you we haven't seen anyone the likes of the person you are talking about. If I was you, lass, I wouldn't inquire about him anymore and just go home. It would be for your best interests."

Anelle glowered and scrunched up her nose. "I ain't leaving without him."

The soldier shrugged, "Then you ain't leaving from that gate then. You can camp out here all you want, it won't change anything." The soldier above started cackling and the man at the gate began to walk away. "Just make sure you aren't blocking the road."

Anelle moved Jorunn to the side of the gate and sat on the grass, eye downcast. Jorunn nuzzled her face and Anelle patted her snout in response.

She sighed. "I'm sorry, girl. I can't help your owner. I don't know what to do."

She sat on the side of the road for a long time. She watched as wagons of soldiers left, catcalling her as they passed, but they continued to Anju so they could drink and harass the townspeople. The day went on and she still waited. All she had was hope that something would change, a miracle even.

The sun reached its zenith. Her head was between her knees when a pebble stung her neck. She turned with her hand on her neck and saw a woman peering behind the outside wall.

She beckoned Anelle to come, and Anelle felt intrigued and pulled by this woman. She led Jorunn quietly away from the roadside and into the small wooded area beside the fort. After she secured Jorunn out of sight, Anelle hesitated yards from the woman.

"You've came for him, didn't you?" For Kael?" The woman said in such a timid voice that Anelle had a tough time hearing her. Anelle skeptically nodded.

Tears welled up in the woman's eyes and she twisted her dress. "I want to help you. Haskell tortured him nonstop yesterday, but he's drank himself asleep now. Come with me, and hurry."

II

There was a secret door on the outside of the Keep, one that was hidden by stone. It could only be opened by a hidden lever behind a false stone in the wall. The passageway was dimly lit by cracks in the stones.

They shuffled quietly to keep silent, but it was not necessary. There were no guards nearby and the stones muffled their movement.

Anelle peered at the woman several times. She was small, diffident, and quavered at any small noise. Anelle stopped and put her hand on the woman's shoulder. A trembling racket went down her spine.

"Who are you, and why are you helping me?"

The woman stayed silent for a few moments before turning and continuing their path. But once they came to a fork in the passage, she turned to Anelle. "I knew Kael when he was just a little boy." She furrowed in deep thought. Was there a flash in her eyes too? "I helped raise him while he was living in the capital."

She resumed down the right fork. The passageway became darker as they descended deeper. The keep was much larger than Anelle expected. The passage sloped downwards and forked again; they took the left passage. They at last came to a wooden door. The woman paused before it and turned to Anelle.

"My name is Isabella, by the way." Anelle noticed Isabella was older. Her pale expression masked wrinkles and aging, but it was there. Her face was narrow and lovely.

She replied with a smile. "I'm Anelle."

Isabella stilled hesitated to open the door. "Thank you, Anelle. I do not know what he means to you, but Kael means a lot to me."

The door opened to a hallway that curved to the left. There were doors lining this curvature that they passed. The last door led to a spiraling staircase going up and down.

They descended further into the depths until they reached a sole door at the bottom. Behind the door was quiet save for heavy breathing, and Anelle could tell right away who it was. Isabella opened the door and Anelle rushed through. She nigh collapsed at the sight of Kael tied to the chair.

III

His face was bruised and coated with dried blood, his eyes black. His tunic was stripped off and his chest bare, exposing a new sheen of lashes across the front. His hands were tied tightly to the chair, and he was missing a few fingernails.

Despite all this, all this torture that he had gone through, Kael was still alive. His ragged breath fogged in as he heaved.

"Did you come back for more, you fucker?" His voice was hoarse, but when he opened his eyes, they were still fierce. "You can keep at it for years and I won't—"

He stopped when he saw Isabella in front of him. He noticed Anelle, and his eyes teared up.

"Fuck," He croaked.

"Oh, my gods..." She sobbed. Seeing him in this condition—this vulnerable—broke her to her core.

She dropped to the floor on her knees and yanked the ropes, but they did not budge. Isabella stood beside her and pulled up her dress to reveal a knife strapped on her leg.

She silently cut the ropes in quick succession. There were deep impressions from the rope. He exhaled sharply as he started to regain feeling in his hands. He tried to stand but instead collapsed and gasped in pain. Anelle held his shoulders as he grabbed at his chest and winced at the wounds.

"Kael, stop. You're weak."

Anelle tried to help him up, but he shrugged it off. He staggered upright for a moment, then slid down the wall beside the chair. He eyed his tunic on the table and stumbled to it. He grabbed it and knocked the tray of tools onto the floor in the process.

He struggled to lift his arms over his head to pull the tunic on, so Anelle helped him. She grabbed the tunic and pulled over his head, her hands running down his chest as she tried to keep it straight.

It sent a shiver down her spine as she felt his muscles underneath. She snapped out of her trance to realize he was still breathing heavy. Along her waist was a waterskin.

"Here, drink it. You're probably dehydrated." He took it greedily, nearly drinking the last drop in the skin, but he left a bit so she still had some. He seemed better after just some water, but he was still badly beaten.

His armor was on the table as well. Anelle helped him strap them on, and his scent intoxicated her. Even his sweat was making her falter, but her own trance kept her from feeling him shiver at her touch. Isabella watched all this with a sly smile, but she turned around by the end of it.

"Where are my swords?" Kael glanced behind the table to see it was empty.

"They are probably by Haskell," Isabella spoke without turning to him. "They are probably leaning on his throne. He hardly leaves his throne, only to piss or shit. He even sleeps in it."

The silence that trailed this revelation was palpable. Kael shifted from Isabella to Anelle, then fastened his armor tighter.

"Right, so I need to confront Haskell to get my blades." He flashed a nasty sneer and stretched a little. "It's time for payback for all the shit he's done anyway. Thanks for saving me—but now you need to get to safety yourselves."

Anelle went to open her mouth, but Isabella stepped forward. "We aren't leaving you. You're still badly hurt. And Kael—" she placed her hands on his shoulders, though she had to make him bend down to do so, "—Cormac is here, too."

Kael's eyes widened and he ground his teeth hard. "Where," he seethed, "where is he?"

"In one of the jails on the main floor. He was brought in a week ago, as the soldiers caught him off guard one morning."

"Where's Duff?"

Isabella shook her head. "I don't know. I just know that Cormac was brought in alone."

Kael gulped and nodded. So, it was a double rescue mission. Kael needed his gear back to save Cormac. *I'm sure Haskell won't let us just walk out of here, either. So, we will have to fight out.*

"Listen, I need to get my swords, and Haskell needs to be distracted so we can get Cormac out of here. So, I will get my gear and fight Haskell and you two will free Cormac."

There was no protest to this. Anelle wanted to, but she knew this was the best plan. She was worried about

461

Kael, though. He was pale and his chest rattled. "Let's go," he said.

The winding staircase led them near the main hall of the Keep. Isabella turned as they exited and Anelle followed her. Isabella turned and pointed at a door on the other side of the room.

"That door will lead you back to the main hall, right beside his throne." Her whisper carried well in the silence. "And Kael—be careful. He might have wasted away all these years, but he is still strong."

Kael nodded and approached the door. He felt a light touch on his shoulder and turned as Anelle pulled him in, his face to hers.

They kissed in the dreary by-room of the Keep, and though it was brief, it sent an electric surge through him. He felt an energy rush through him even after she pulled away.

He barely heard the 'be safe" that she whispered to him as her and Isabella fled to the cells further in the keep. Kael took a deep breath before he eased open the door.

The door didn't creak, despite looking like it would, and Kael peered through it to see Haskell asleep in his throne. He was snoring loudly and his mug was just barely hanging from his hand, inches away from the floor with some mead trickling to the floor. Leaned against his throne was his large axe, and beside that was Kael's swords and bag.

Kael snuck across the hushed hall to the back of the throne. His eyed darted around for any guards, but it was empty save for Haskell. He reached the back of the throne and slung his bag over his back.

Haskell snored loudly and twitched, causing the mug to drop and clang against the stone. Kael froze and peered around the throne to check on Haskell. His snoring stopped and Kael thought he was going to wake up. The snoring resumed and Kael grabbed each sword and silently secured them on his back.

Kael thought he might have to confront Haskell— a bitter blessing in his condition. He hesitated and considered slitting his throat. *It would be easy, and he deserves it. The fucker deserves to die.*

With a knife in hand, he leaned over the back of the throne. The knife was inches from Haskell's neck when he paused. *Why? Why do I hesitate?*

He couldn't do it. He slunk behind the throne, and his hand brushed the axe handle softly. He froze—but the axe did not move, and he retreated.

The door to the by-room was close when he heard a raking sound. The axe shifted and raked down the throne, clanging loudly on the floor. Haskell shot up in an instant on alert. His glassy eye focused on Kael crouched in the middle of the room. A snarl formed on his lips.

"You sneaky, heinous dog," he roared, stumbling to pick up his axe. "Those are my swords."

Kael stood up and unsheathed a blade. "These aren't yours, you bastard."

Haskell and Kael lunged in tandem and the blade and axe met. The din of metal echoed as the weapons bounced off each other. Words spoken through action as each blow was malice in form.

Kael swung low and sliced Haskell's leg. Haskell, unconcerned with the gash on his leg that poured blood, swung wide with his axe. When Kael dodged, he planted out a fist to connect with Kael's face. Kael fell, rolled backwards, and recovered. Each blow of one led to a retaliatory attack from the other.

Thus, their dance continued, the clangor of steel supplemented their strides.

IV

Isabella and Anelle paused momentarily. They had just entered the cell room when the fight began to echo through the main floor of the Keep. The clash of steel rang through the dense stone walls.

The sole guard paused momentarily before averting his stride to the opposing door. The two trailed him to the other side. Anelle picked up a fallen brick and bashed it into his head.

Blood bubbled from the gash as he collapsed and writhed. She let out a silent yelp and shook from the shock, then dropped the brick. She backed into a corner as the man twitched then stilled.

Isabella grabbed the cell keys from the body. He shook them at Anelle and then tugged her out of the corner. They locked eyes as Anelle stiffened, but she followed. *No time,* those eyes said.

They scoured the cells to search for Cormac. Most cells were empty—or at least devoid of life. Dead rat littered the floor. He was in the last cell of the block, stashed in the shadows.

Cormac's eyes snapped wide when he saw them. He scrambled and flapped his mouth silently before he mustered a word. "Isabella?" he gasped, his voice a hoarse whisper. "What in the world—"

The lock clicked audibly, and the door swung open with a creak. Isabella's gaze pierced through him. "No time for questions. We're getting out of here. Kael needs us."

V

The din of battle echoed as Kael and Haskell continued their battle. Haskell wheezed, his attacks haggard, and Kael could feel the aches of his wounds. Both were wounded—but Kael was weaker. The only thing he had left was determination.

Haskell swung wide and left his left side exposed. Kael had his chance and unsheathed damascus sword.

The blade whistled in the air as he thrust up and through Haskell's arm.

Blood gushed from the wound. The arm fell, and the axe clattered against the floor. Kael did not hesitate and incised the other.

"Fuck!" Haskell blared. Blood spurted from the appendages as he collapsed on his knees. He snarled and glared at Kael. "You fucking—"

Kael stabbed both blades into his chest and leaned close. He stared into the man's eyes for just a moment before he pulled the swords out. Haskell gasped and dropped to the floor. He was motionless as blood pooled underneath.

Kael stared at the body momentarily, his swords dripping with blood. Kael knelt and wiped his weapons on the cloak as he heard commotion of soldiers in the yard. Words peaked through the cacophony, such as 'Lord' and 'attack'.

Kael slipped into the by-room before soldiers piled in. He put his ear against the door to hear his victory.

As the noise grew louder he moved a large chest in front of the door, and then he turned around to see Isabella and Anelle rush through the opposing door with Cormac in tow.

He breathed a sigh of relief until he noticed Anelle was pale. Isabella cut him off before he could open his mouth.

"Where is Haskell?" Her voice wavered, but her eyes seemed fierce with hatred.

"Dead." Kael crossed the room and back to the door to the staircase.

"Come on," he said as he opened the door.

His eyes locked with Anelle's as she passed by, the tension between the two sent a shockwave down his spine again. Cormac paused and glanced at Kael before crossing the threshold.

They descended the staircase and through the hidden passageway. The chaos erupted in the keep and permeated through the stone. They winded through the hidden path before they got to the exit, where Cormac pushed past and opened the door.

The soldiers ran around the perimeter in a frenzy, and Cormac watched for an opening in their formation. When the coast was clear he motioned everyone to go as he followed up the rear. They crossed into the woods nearby to where Jorunn was tied. Kael ran to reunite with his trusty steed as the rest caught up with him.

"Cormac," Kael said as he patted Jorunn's snout. "Where's Duff?"

Cormac was rubbing his wrists. "I dunno. I sent him to retrieve you in Maju after I set up camp on the outskirts of town. A giant wolf doesn't really sit well with most townsfolk, you know? So, I was going to stay out in the wild with him, but then I got jumped by a group of those soldiers while I was sleeping." He rubbed his face. "Must've been the booze I had…"

Kael untied Jorunn from the tree and pulled her reins. "Alright. Isabella—you and Anelle should take Jorunn back to the inn. Me and Cormac will find Duff and meet you there."

There was a shuffle and before anyone could react. Crossbows and bows were knocked and pointed at them. Swords gleamed out of their scabbard.

"'ey boys, looks like we got ourselves a couple murderers and a traitor," One man said.

He walked past the line of soldiers and stood in the clearing with sword in hand. He was much older. A shining metal emblem pinned to his shoulder said he was a captain. "If any of 'em move, shoot through their eyes."

The line tightened their aim on the group. Isabella and Anelle stood beside Jorunn. Kael and Cormac covered them as best as they could.

"This is how it is gonna go," the captain piped, his voice booming in the thicket of the trees. "The girls can get on the horse and go, unless they wanna stay and service their army."

He smiled, surveyed for a response, and dropped it when there was none. "The older man will take his sword and plunge it in his stomach for all of us to see, rippin' out his innards."

"And the young man there," pointing at Kael, "Well, see, he's gonna have to come with us. Gotta pay for the crime of killing the lord, y'know? How's it sound?"

The group poised, but did not speak. Kael unsheathed one sword and held it out in front of him. He could see his hand shaking and the struggle to keep it upright. He was still weak from the wounds and the battle.

How can we win? He examined the line of soldiers, the tips of the bolts and arrows. He was pulled out of his thoughts when he felt a hand land on his shoulder. Cormac's face lined up with his and smiled. Cormac walked past the and into the in-between.

"I say," Cormac belted out, his gruff voice echoing in the woods, "that you probably yank your prick to the sound of your own voice, eh?" He continued to smile as the archers aimed his way, but the captain held his hand to stop the attack. "I suppose that's the ego of a man, hiding behind a line of soldiers, who can't fight himself?"

The captain sneered at the words and crossed into the space, sword drawn. "Aye, if you want to die by my sword instead, so be it. Men, do not interfere. Only if one of their group interferes may you shoot, and only at the offending party."

The captain lunged and thrust his sword forward. Cormac deflected it with his curved blade and followed up with a wide arc. The two danced within the small confines of the forest, around the trees and attacked in the empty space between.

The circle of the firing line acted as a boundary. Restricted in a tight space, they were forced to fight as even as possible. Only superficial wounds were sustained through the chaotic swordplay.

Cormac ducked a wide sweep but was unable to stop the trailing kick. The boot busted Cormac's face and knocked him down. The captain kicked his blade out of reach and loomed over him.

He thrust his blade into Cormac's shoulder first and twisted. He relished and laughed at his howls of pain. But then Cormac ripped the blade free of his flesh to the surprise of the captain, pulling the blade out with his hands and cutting them on the sharp edge.

The captain was stupefied by the bold action and froze. The sword pushed back into him briefly and made him stagger back. The stagger jolted him back and he snarled and thrust the sword back. The blade shifted and pierced Cormac's chest.

"Cormac, no!" Kael yelled, starting at the captain, but the women held him back. The archers armed at him, but held back to see if the women would stop him. He struggled and yelled, then slumped to the ground and dropped his own sword in the process.

Cormac's anguish melded into roars and snarls, an echo played upon themselves. The sound masked the beast that entered the line at the blink of an eye. A blur came and a sickening crunch belted over the screams.

The monstrous wolf Duff towered over the severed body of the captain. The headless corpse stance faltered and collapsed as the wolf spat out the head at the line of soldiers. The soldiers turned tail and left the group alone in the woods.

Seconds passed before they ran to Cormac. He gasped and clutched the wound with trepidation. Blood seeped through his hands.

"Cormac," Kael said as he ran and knelt next to Cormac. "What do I do?" Tears began to well up in his eyes as he held his hands over the wound. The sword had been pulled out when the body fell. "What do I do?"

Cormac laughed as he rested his hand over Kael's. "I'm fine, Kael. It didn't hit my heart. If it had, I would be dead already." He winced as he attempted to sit up. "Fuck, it does hurt, though."

Cormac pulled out the familiar white powder and sprinkled it on his chest and shoulder. The bleeding stopped immediately. He winced and cursed several times in the process, but he sat up after some effort.

"What a reckless fight," Isabella said. "You could have been killed. I mean, Captain Reid was known to be brutal—"

"I know, Isabella. I noticed who he was when I saw that blade of his. The red hilt of the Reid family has been known for generations, and they're all bloodthirsty. I didn't know I if would win, but I sure as hell wasn't going

471

to gut myself. Good thing Duff came in time." Cormac leaned back into the wolf and patted him.

A trumpet sounded from the keep, followed by a cacophony of yells. The ground trembled as they saw a cavalry exit the gate. The soldiers dispersed and headed for their hiding spot. Kael motioned for retreat.

Kael ushered the women onto Jorunn and helped Cormac onto the back of Duff. Kael jumped onto the wolf's back. He whistled and the tone set Jorunn and Duff to head deep into the forest. They heard the cavalry follow them as they were engulfed by the forest.

Bloodletting

I

The tumult of their pursuers faded as they went deeper into the forest. The forest engulfed them; the silence was broken only by Duff's footfall and their breath. The women were far ahead but within sight. They were still at a gallop to outrun their hunters.

As the sound of pursuit faded, so did their speed. Their gait slowed to a trot, then canter, and then a fast walk.

"We were lucky," Cormac piped. "If not for them two, we would probably be dead."

Kael nodded; his eyes pinned on the back of Anelle's head. It bobbed with Jorunn's staggered gait. Her head turned once and their eyes locked. She blushed and whipped forward. He averted his eyes to the ground as his own face grew hot.

"That girl has taken a liking to you." Cormac flashed a grin as Kael shot up. "I take it you like her, too. Your red face shows it."

473

Kael tried to stutter out something but couldn't. *Do I like her? What does that mean? She makes me nervous...*

Cormac didn't say anymore as Kael delved into his thoughts. He kept thinking of Anelle and about her smile, which made his face feel even more hot. He could hear Cormac stifle a laugh but paid no heed to it. He needed to understand what he felt.

Duff stopped abruptly in the woods beside the Jorunn. Kael looked up to see everyone else frozen and in shock. He followed their gaze and shook, too.

It was a grove, much like the one he had seen before, but the surrounding pond was frozen and snowcapped. The center tree was large—much larger than any other tree in the forest. But that was not the source of their shock.

It's like before.

A large, scaly monster wrapped around the base of the tree. He was so lost in his thoughts that he didn't hear the crunching. It took sizeable chunks out of the tree with each bite.

The monster was like a large Stökkbreyta, with the scales and rat-like tail, but it had more humanlike attributes. The head did not have a prolonged snout, and it had arms and legs. There were tatterings of cloth stuck in the scales on its back and hind side.

It paid no attention to its new audience. It was engorged in the flesh of the tree. It gnawed away towards a goal. Kael knew what it was.

It's after the goddess over this forest. Just like last time.

"Just like last time," he said. The others turned towards him, puzzled. He looked past them, to the monster. "It wants to eat the goddess at the center and drain the life of this forest."

Cormac dismounted Duff in one stride. He buckled slightly on landing, but his wounds were mostly healed now. He rubbed the healed wound gently as he pulled his sword.

"Aye, you're right. It's said that the vast forests of the land were always guarded and raised by goddesses." He exchanged a glance with Kael, still astride Duff. "You know what we must do."

Kael nodded and dismounted more gently. His body still ached, and his hands burned beneath his gloves. *It's nothing that I haven't felt before.* He arched backwards and stretched out the tightness in his back. But he felt there was a familiarity to this monster.

The two approached the monster, weapons drawn. As they walked over the frozen pool of water, the ice crunched underneath their steps. The monster paid no heed until they were within the circle of the grove.

The monster stopped its task altogether as they entered. They paused, braced for an attack, but they did not expect such a primal scream to come. It was shrill, piercing deep within their heads, and they fought all they could to drop their weapons to cover their ears. The women shrieked themselves and Jorunn kicked and neighed harshly.

The monster's tail swung out and knocked them off their feet. They did not have time to recover before it unwrapped itself and lunged. They quickly dodged the wide swipes of the beast's claws at the last moment.

It shrieked again and caught them off kilter and lose balance. The monster swung one of its grossly disproportionate arm into Cormac. A leg came out and kicked Kael.

Both men were knocked back to the frozen pool. The beast then scurried closer to the men. It ran in a staggered gait as its limbs flailed chaotically.

Kael propped himself up on his arms. He gazed into the face of the beast, a foot from his. He heard Cormac and the women yell in the distance, but he could only notice the eyes of the beast.

It didn't attack—but instead stared at him with the *eyes of a human.* There was a great sadness in those eyes, the sadness of a man who was lost. And then Kael could hear the echoes of a voice in his head. It was the echo of that wizard—Ignaz.

A Stökkbreyta is not natural, Kael, it echoed again. *Not natural...*

Kael took the glass vial he acquired from Ignaz's hut, popped the cork and splashed the liquid in the beast's face. It shrieked again, but it was much less shrill.

It grew less piercing, more so a yell. The yell of a man. Where the liquid splashed turned into pale flesh. What replaced the skull of the beast was a human head. Its mouth contorted into a face of pain; a permanent grimace, and furrowed lines. The eyes held sorrow but became clearer.

"Please..." The man said. His voice shook and racketed as the pain shuddered through his body.

"I don't... want to be... a monster... please... end my suffering."

The body trembled, its arms trying to claw at Kael. But there was an invisible force holding it back. The man's face twisted horribly as the pale flesh started to soften and turn back to the grey of the rest of the body. "Please..."

Kael drove the tip of his sword through the bottom of the skull. The tip protruded out with a mixture of red and black ichor. Tears welled in the eyes of the man and Kael could feel it in his own. The man twisted his face into a small smile as gazed at Kael.

"Don't... weep tears for poor ol' Lonzo... I don't... want to.. die as a monster..."

Kael gripped his sword tight. He forced his energy into it but could only feel a small ripple of flames. He pushed hard, but he was weak. Too weak for mercy.

He felt a hand cover over his and turned to see Cormac beside him. A rush of energy pushed his own through the blade. A vortex of flames exuded out of the skull as the eyes of the man blanked out. The body went limp and Cormac helped pull the sword.

Duff and the women came up the scene after the beast had succumbed and stopped at the base of the mound. The corpse quivered and exhaled as the grey scale-covered flesh turned. It shrunk and paled before finally resting as a human.

They buried him in the grove, to lay to rest as a human. Not a monster. As the pile of dirt was packed, Kael paced a small tower of rocks at the head. A marker—a human grave.

"For Lonzo," He croaked, then placed one last rock.

It was time to go. They all stood around the grave as they heard a crunch from behind. Kael and Cormac poised to fight but met with the unexpected—a white fox.

"Kinaa," Kael wheezed. He swayed, his reopened wounds seeping through his tunic. His vision blurred as he tried to concentrate. Cormac steadied him.

The fox seemed to nod as its blue eyes examined everyone.

"Kael, you have saved yet another goddess." Its mouth did not move, but they all heard her talk clearly.

Kael glanced at Kinaa, then back at the newly dug grave. He sat down in the snow and gazed into the canopy. No light peered through, but he squinted all the same.

"He wasn't a monster, you know. I couldn't let him continue like that."

Kinaa's eyes lit up. Was there a smile on her snout? "You have such a kind heart. Even after all you have been through, you still have compassion."

Kinaa started towards them and examined their reactions. The women seemed to flinch a little, but neither Cormac nor Kael moved.

Kinaa sat next to Kael and placed her paw on his lap. He felt a sensation dull his pain. He turned his head and they locked eyes.

"I beg you again to bond with me." She gazed past his eyes. Into him, into his mind.

"It is fate, as it was Ijos and Nuria, and Cormac and Duff," Kinaa said, shifting her eyes towards Cormac and then Duff, who perked his ears. They both exchanged glances. They seemed to talk, but the forest was silent. She then returned her eyes to Kael. "Bond with me before it's too late."

"No." Kael pushed her paw off and stood. He stomped over to Jorunn on the edge of the clearing. Kinaa followed him on his heels. He pivoted on his heels and crouched. He met her eye-to-eyes, his burning like blue flames.

"I willnae weaken myself to bonding with a spirit," he seethed. "I winnae allow myself to have such a thing happen."

Kael turned and grabbed Jorunn's reins. He pulled her to exit the grove. Kinaa sat at the edge and watched him leave, her ears pinned down. The reminder of the groups passed by her and glanced at her. Her eyes were wide and watery.

Cormac and Duff passed last. The latter stopped and stared at her, bobbing his head as if he was talking. Kinaa nodded her head and stood up, walking towards the damaged tree, then seemed to fade into nothingness before reaching it.

"Kael," Cormac said as he caught up to him. "I think you need to reconsider bonding with that spirit. I know you have preconceived notions—"

"I have nothing preconceived," Kael snapped back. He pushed past Cormac without a glance and picked up his pace. Jorunn whinnied but followed.

"I've seen what the repercussions are of a bonding. You dinnae feel exposed with a piece of your soul walking beside you?"

Cormac matched his stride and followed. "No. And I say that because I'm not exposed. Duff is his own, and so am I. But the link we have is like no other."

Cormac glanced at Duff beside him. The glance they shared said it all. They knew the other's thoughts and emotions, like they really were just two sides of the same soul.

"But he fills in my weaknesses, not exposes them. There's a sense of security with him."

The group continued for a bit longer. It was chiefly silent, save for the hushed conversation between the women. Despite speaking low, Kael could hear them well. It was mostly about what Isabella remembered of Kael as a child and Anelle listened with some awe.

She had a lot of questions about his speech difficulties as a child. Primarily it was how he overcame it, but Isabella was not sure herself.

"Look, I know you don't want to end up like Ijos," Cormac started but he trailed off. He tried to stutter through explaining the bond, but it was too intricate. "Kael, it's like—"

Cormac glanced to see Kael tear up at the mention of Ijos. He kept quiet for the remainder of their time in the forest.

II

They wound through the forest past sunset. They exited close to Anju as night blanketed over. They used the dark to sneak back into town.

Cormac was apprehensive about entering town with Duff, but he was not going to leave him. They followed the perimeter of town and entered on the west side closest to the river and used back alleys to avoid people.

When they finally made it to the inn, Kael boarded Jorunn as Anelle helped find a place to hide Duff for the time being. The barn was large, so they found a section of it that was hidden by bales of hay.

Anelle joined Kael as he was brushing down Jorunn. She seemed relieved to be rid of her saddle. Anelle patted Jorunn on the snout. But her attention was on Kael.

"How are yer wounds? Do they still hurt?" Her eyes examined his dirty clothes, where the cloth had been cut or punctured.

"I'm fine, thanks to Kinaa. The wonders of magic, you know?" He continued to brush Jorunn. He paused and stared off, then resumed. "I do appreciate that you came for me, but that was reckless. I mean—I'm a nobody."

"Yer not a nobody," she said, touching one of his hands, "not to me."

He stopped as he felt the electric pulse through him again from her touch. He had been done brushing Jorunn for some time but was watching Anelle help Cormac. He felt that upset feeling in his stomach again now that they were alone.

"Anelle, I—"

She leaned up to his face and pressed her lips onto his. He's kissed before; countless times since he was a teenager and boarded up while working a job. He could even remember the first girl he kissed: a young girl he saved from a pooka that was kidnapping girls in a village. She was the last one kidnapped and Kael saved her as the pooka tried to have its way with her right outside its den. The girl threw herself on Kael and kissed him in gratitude.

Even after then, after all the women he had been with, he never felt the pulse that ran through him when he was with Anelle. He felt like he could not breathe, his skin tingled and his stomach fluttered.

He kissed her back. His lips engulfed hers, and their passion only grew. She pulled away long enough to take his hand and guide him out of the barn. He could hear Jorunn snort, but he paid no heed. He dropped the brush in the yard as they hurried upstairs.

Anelle led him up to her room. When the door opened, Kael saw the room was covered in plants. The queen-sized bed was in the center, framed by two nightstands, but there were pots of plants he had no idea how to classify. Some hung from the ceiling and some had vines that sprawled to the floor.

He only had a moment to digest it. Anelle pushed him on the bed and jumped onto him. She folded into his arms as he landed on the soft mattress. She enveloped him in kisses. The passion grew between the two and they began to shed their clothes.

Both gasped when Kael entered her.

It coursed through him—a shock to his fingertips and toes. His hairs stood on end and his skin tingled. She moaned, writhing and clenched the sheets. They continued through the night until the morning sun began.

When they finally gave in to exhaustion they cradled in each other's arms. It was the first time that Kael did not dream about the past, or of nightmares. Instead, he slept peacefully as he cradled Anelle close.

Fracture

Digression

I

The following day was uneventful; they anticipated some kind of retaliation. Isabella and Cormac stayed in rooms at the inn, much to the latter's chagrin. He felt like Duff was cooped up and hidden for too long.

They did not venture out, either. But the other guests of the inn would bring back some snippets of news for them. Most was that the decorations of the town square were nearly complete, with the bonfire piled high with dry wood. Some guests said that the taverns have been abnormally calm lately, despite the influx of outsiders.

Kael and Anelle stayed in bed for a good part of the day. Their needs were insatiable. If they ventured even too far in bed, they would feel a chilling loneliness. It was love and lust. But it was mostly love—and it was addicting.

Kael felt a warmth in his head he never felt before—a calm that he relished. The nights that followed were free of nightmares or dreams of the hooded head of the sorcerer. His sleep was uninterrupted and serene. He felt secure for once, where he felt at home; where someone was waiting for him and where a dinner was available every night.

Is this what a normal life feels like? He once had a home. There was comfort with Ijos in the hidden village—but he didn't feel the warmth he felt here. The dinners with Anelle, Isabella, and Cormac felt like a family. He couldn't explain it, but it felt like a home.

But with this newfound sense of security, Kael felt a bloom of doubt within as well.

The next day, word spread that the Keep was deserted. The town had enveloped itself in a sense of calm and glee that they had never seen before. There were no fights in the taverns. No woman felt like they were being watched or catcalled, nor did they have to digest and deal with being groped at every turn.

On the morning of the third day after the Keep, Kael lay in bed much later than usual. The sun had already crept over the horizon and was high in the sky.

But he was still asleep.

It was restless sleep. His eyes flickered underneath the lids. His face contorted.

But there was no warble. No magic or blue aura. He was bare under the sheets.

He was back in the forest and Kinaa was in front of him. Her tails whipped back and forth as she spoke.

"You are falling into comfort," she spoke. "You are living your dreams of a normal life."

Kael opened his mouth but then shut it tight as she changed.

Standing in front of him was Ijos. Older and greying, but he still held the same silence in his eyes.

"This comfort is a lie," Ijos said. He held his arms open. Kael walked up and tried to embrace him.

"Ijos," Kael said, but his body went through him. He stumbled a little but then turned sharply to see Ijos staring at him.

"That life is not something you can lead. Fate won't allow it."

Ijos withdrew his sword and swung at Kael. Kael went to unsheathe and parry. He was unarmed. Ijos' blade went through him, but only a puff of smoke came from the slice.

It was an apparition.

"If you let yourself be enveloped by the comfort, you won't be ready. You can't become soft."

The apparition took its sword and thrust it through Kael's chest.

"Don't forget where your heart truly lies. Will you regret if you don't face the sorcerer again?"

Kael woke in a gasp. Anelle was in his arms. He stirred her with restlessness.

"What is it?" Her voice was thick with sleep.

"Just an odd dream," Kael said in a whisper.

He kissed her forehead as she snuggled back into him. This was the second day he had this dream. He had not told her about it on the first day, when he slept later than usual. He relished the idea that he did not have to get up at the break of dawn or earlier.

But it returned, and he could have sworn he felt the pain of being pierced this time. Was he feeling the pains of regret already seeping in? Did he feel like he could really forget his path of vengeance—the sorcerer—so that he could stay here with Anelle?

He embraced her tighter as his mind swam.

One side wanted to hang up his swords and to stay here forever. The other screamed at him to wake up from this dream.

Fate won't allow peace.

II

Kael laid in bed and stared at the ceiling. The early morning light filtered through the window. The rays hurt his eyes, but he didn't move.

It had been two days since the dreams had started, each one more vivid and unsettling than the last. Each night the blade seemed to pierce his heart, and the feeling became more and more real to him.

This morning, he could feel the burning and gushing of blood from his chest when he woke. He slipped out of bed and stole into the adjacent bathroom of Anelle's private quarters. Though it was feeling much more like *their* private quarters in the past few days. The bathroom was not so elegant but still held a tub and a mirror over the sink. And it felt right. He felt comfortable here.

He examined his bare chest for the wound, but it was devoid of any fresh marking. Scars plastered his skin, but they were old and faded. He stared into the mirror. His reflection gazed back at him. It held scrutiny.

The words of Kinaa and Ijos echoed in his mind. They were a constant reminder of the path he had chosen and the comfort he was beginning to crave.

He exited the bathroom and stared at Anelle still peacefully asleep in the bed. The warmth of her presence in his life, her warmth as he woke and slept, was a stark contrast to the cold dread that had settled in his chest.

He walked over and gently brushed a strand of hair from her face. His heart ached with the conflict that raged within him.

Unable to shake the feeling, Kael quietly dressed and slipped out of the bedroom. He left the inn and paced around the town. It had been busy with the upcoming solstice festival, but it was calmer without the soldiers. He paced the perimeter of town before he ended back at the inn with his head no clearer than he left.

Kael went around to the barn in the back. It was quiet save for the gentle sounds of the livestock. He brushed Jorunn some as he tried to make any sense of his conflictions. A sharp bark came from the back of the bark, followed by a hush. The sound had jolted him out of his thoughts for a moment. He went behind the hay bales stacked up for the livestock.

Cormac was standing next to Duff, who was picking a piece of fur on his haunch, or rather where fur would be. In Cormac's hand was a comb with a thick matting of fur entangled in it.

Cormac glimpsed at Kael before he untangled the matted fur off the comb and resumed combing the giant wolf.

"Did he startle you? My apologies, Kael. He had some matted fur and this is long overdue."

Kael was silent as Cormac comb Duff. The latter snarled briefly during the thicker parts of his fur. Kael decided he needed someone to talk to, and Cormac had a lot of experience.

"Cormac, can I ask you something?" Kael's voice was low, almost hesitant.

Cormac nodded and put the comb aside. "Of course. What's on your mind?"

Kael took a deep breath, trying to find the right words. "Do you ever... want to give up the fight? Like maybe there's a chance for a normal life, away from all this?"

Cormac leaned against the stable wall and considered his question. Duff eyed Cormac for a moment before he cobbed his haunch.

"It's crossed my mind more times than I care to admit," he said slowly. "But the thing about a normal life is, it's never as simple as it seems."

Cormac gazed at his boots for a moment. "Nor is it something people like us ever really experience."

Kael nodded, but there was a heavy weight in his stomach. "I've been having these dreams," he confessed. "Dreams where I'm told that this comfort is a lie, that I cannae afford to become soft."

He took a deep breath. "But when I'm with Anelle, Isabella, and you... it feels like home. Like something I could get used to."

Cormac's expression softened. "It's natural to want that, Kael. To crave peace and stability. You never really experienced what it was like to grow up in a normal home."

Cormac leaned against the wall. "But you must ask yourself, what would you regret more? Giving up your path of vengeance or giving up a life you never had?"

Kael stared at his hands. The conflict within him raged harder.

"I dinnae know," he admitted. "I just dinnae know."

Cormac put a hand on Kael's shoulder. "I—we—had it once, remember?." His voice was barely above a whisper. "It's not the same you feel now, but you had a home once. We both carry that weight, but we came here to track the sorcerer and face him."

He dropped his hand. His eyes were watery, but resolute. "And we both know he'll show up in Anju at some point. Whatever you decide, you might still have to face him here. After that, whatever you decide you will have to live with."

"The path of vengeance is a hard one, but so is the path of peace. Neither is easy, and both have their own costs."

Kael met Cormac's eyes and found a sense of understanding there. "Thank you," he said quietly. "I needed to hear that."

Cormac nodded. "Anytime, Kael. Just remember, we're here for you. No matter what path you choose."

III

The days after Kael talked with Cormac were calm. Their conversation had put Kael's mind at ease. This allowed him to prepare for the sorcerer's inevitable presence in Anju.

At night, he allowed himself to be enveloped in Anelle's warmth. During the day, he paced the town, searching for any signs of the sorcerer.

The town was much larger than at first glance. When he was focused on the job given to him by Aurel, he hadn't taken the time to truly see it. Now, without that cover, he wandered the town and took in every spectacle he could.

The others were often busy with their own tasks. Anelle was occupied with the work required at the inn and Isabella helped. Cormac often did the heavy lifting. He repaired anything that needed fixed. He also took care of the animals to Anelle's dismay. Kael would help with the manual labor from time to time. Cormac often sent him off, though, and left him with nothing else to do.

The town had a rich history. The first settlers had come here long before other parts of Hera were settled by those from the central Kingdom. They wove their faith around the gods and goddesses of nature, giving way to festivals for each.

The solstice festival, it seemed, was a rite to appease the goddess Daraliela. She presided over the Liela woods that encompassed a good portion of Hera. Her blessings were said to bring bountiful crops and births for generations. As such, Anju constructed a temple in her honor.

Kael's stroll ended at this temple. He stood before it and felt its weight. It exuded a force that stemmed from that history and the strength of faith. The temple was a testament to the power and reverence of Daraliela. Kael couldn't help but feel a sense of awe and respect.

It was a mix of cobbled brick and wood, though nature was intertwined with the structure as well. Any other structure would have looked in disrepair with vines and plants stemming out of the stone. The wood was discolored in places and the trunks budded out.

Despite all this, the temple did not seem like just a building. It held the aura that it was living.

Kael entered the temple to notice no pews or seating. Rather an altar with a stone statue took up the space. It depicted a woman with flowing hair, nude save for an ivy skirt around her waist.

Even though the stone was one color, Kael glimpsed a golden sheen in her eyes staring at him as he examined the base of the statue. He peered at the statue again and had the feeling he was being watched.

"Beautiful, no?" An elderly man rounded a side of the statue. He stood beside Kael and looked up as well. "Such is the beauty of nature, too."

They were silent for some time. At last, the man spoke up again.

"The goddess is said to give life in many ways, but it was only because she could never bear life inside her herself."

He placed a small flower on the altar. "The man she loved so dearly wanted a child, but she was barren. He left her for another woman, and she was in despair. So the goddess, then a mere woman, went into the forest and wept for days."

"When she came out, her home had been ravaged by war, as the lands have always been. She found her lover dying next to the corpse of his beloved. Despite her despair, despite his betrayal, she tried so hard to save him. But he died in her arms. She had to flee into the forest from the invaders, running as they shot arrow after arrow after her."

"She was wounded in the forest, still struggling to get away. She ended up at a grove surrounded by water. There, she drank from the water and passed, her blood spilling into the water and soil."

"But she was born anew as her blood mixed with the grove. She was able to give life, much like she had wanted to for her beloved."

Kael gazed at the statue and felt a pang of sorrow for the goddess. Why? It's just a story, after all. Even then, he felt like to lose everything you love hit harder now as he was dealing with his crossroads. Especially as he faced the idea that he may not be able to live a normal life.

Just like Daraliela, he may lose it all. One way or another.

"Thank you," Kael said, "for the story."

Before he left, he put his hand in his pouch and withdrew the small wooden statue from his youth. He didn't know why, but the wood felt like it resonated deeply with that of the temple. He placed it at the foot of the statue and left.

Solstice

I

The jovialities reached a peak on the night of the solstice festival. The town square was ablaze with torches and lanterns. Some were dipped in special powders that altered the flames' colors. Rainbow hues lit the square as people packed in.

The vibrant racket hushed when Aurel stood on a scaffold near the bonfire in the center of the square. He cleared his throat, then wiped some imaginary sweat from his forehead with a napkin.

"Welcome to the solstice festival!" Aurel's voice boomed as his eyes scanned the crowd.

"I bid thee welcome and many blessings as the year draws to a fold. Another year gone and another bountiful year for crops, for births, and for health. I say to the smaller towns that came as well—" he scanned the crowd, locking eyes with several people, "—that the goddess Daraliela recognized your work and faith. Your homes will be blessed too."

The crowd clapped and yelled. Aurel stood, his gut protruding out like a balloon, and held up a lit torch. "With this torch, we light our hopes and dreams so that Daraliela sees them!"

He threw the torch into the large stack of wood. The flames crept from the torch and engulfed the large pile. It roared, and the crowd echoed it back.

Kael stood amid the crowd and watched the spectacle unfold. Anelle was yelling, too. She grabbed his arm and wrapped around it.

He smiled at her; her face was lit with the dancing light. He watched her and was filled with sorrow.

I know I won't be able to stay, he thought. *I know he will be here.*

Anelle peered at him. His eyes were teary.

"What's wrong?" she tried to yell above the roar of the crowd. Isabella and Cormac watched the crowd, unaware of the conversation between the two. Kael just shook his head and leaned in for a kiss.

Then there was a loud crack in the distance.

II

The crack whipped the air like a lightning strike and echoed in the hills. The crowd hushed. Only the roar of the bonfire sounded. Another one came closer with the thudding of trees. Then there was silence again.

"Worship of an old goddess?"

A voice cut clear in the silence. It was loud enough for everyone to hear. It wasn't a yell, but rather barely above a whisper. The crowd whipped their heads around to find the source, but it was like an echo.

"Heresy is punishable by death."

"Kneel to Balaal, the flame that will cleanse this land," the voice commanded.

Aurel shrieked at the podium. Everyone turned to see the dark sorcerer beside their burgomaster. The sorcerer's hand rested on Aurel's neck.

"I said kneel."

A great wave of pressure came over the crowd and forced them to kneel. The sorcerer stood at the podium as Aurel knelt beside him, moaning and muttering.

Kael tried to fight the pressure—but he, too, was unable to move. He strained to see Cormac, but he was gone. Only Isabella remained. Anelle was folded into Kael and his arms wrapped around her.

The sorcerer stood at the podium, his free hand alight with flames. The crowd watched in horrified silence, unable to move under the oppressive force that held them down. Aurel, still kneeling, eyed the man with wide, terrified eyes.

"Burn," the sorcerer repeated, his voice warbling in and out of reality. He slowly lowered his flaming hand towards Aurel. The heat intensified as it drew closer.

Aurel's screams pierced the night as the flames touched his skin. The fire spread quickly and engulfed him in a matter of seconds. The crowd gasped and some turned away in horror. The smell of burning flesh filled the air and mingled with the smoke from the bonfire.

Kael's heart pounded in his chest as he watched the horrific scene unfold. His mind flashed back to seeing his own dad killed by this man. Then he thought of Caedmon that tried to save him.

He ground his teeth and tightened his grip around Anelle. She nuzzled into his chest to hide from the gruesome sight. His mind raced, searching for a way to break free from the invisible force that held him down.

The sorcerer watched impassively as Aurel's screams faded into silence. Aurel's body went limp and fell off the podium to the stone of the square. He turned his gaze to the crowd as his eyes pierced through the dark veil of his hood.

"Let this be a lesson to all who defy Balaal," the voice echoed through the square. "The flame will cleanse this land of heresy."

As the flames consumed Aurel's body, the pressure holding the crowd down lifted. Kael felt the weight ease off his shoulders and slowly rose to his feet. He saw fear and confusion take on the faces around him.

"We need to get out of here," he whispered urgently to Anelle. "Now."

He turned to Isabella and nodded. She responded the same. She knew what to do.

But before they could move, a chilling howl echoed from the woods. Dark shapes emerged from the treeline—the soldiers from the Keep. Their movements were stilted, and their expressions were vacant.

Behind them were the dark, sickly, scaly masses of the Stökkbreyta. They snarled and stomped their way into the square. The crowd erupted into panic and began to flee the square.

Kael unsheathed his swords and the familiar weight of the blades bringing him a sense of focus. It quelled the sorrow in his mind as the chill of sang-froid ran through him.

"Stay close to me," he told Anelle.

He stepped and cut down the first beast that lunged at them. The creature collapsed in two but more appeared around them.

He fought his way through the throng of beasts, his swords flashing in the firelight. Each strike was precise, fueled by his determination to protect Anelle and the others.

The crowd scattered, trying to escape the onslaught. But the beasts were relentless. Kael watched as left and right, the monsters and soldiers severed the people in tandem. The soldiers moved on as the Stökkbreyta gorged themselves on the flesh.

Kael rushed behind these beasts and severed their heads with the damascus blade. The razored edge cut through with no resistance.

Amid the battle, Kael glanced up at the podium. The sorcerer stood there and watched the carnage with a cruel smile. Kael saw movement below—Cormac climbing the scaffolding with his eyes fixed on the sorcerer.

Cormac reached the top and lunged at the sorcerer. His weapon clashed with a resounding clang against a dagger that the sorcerer produced at the last moment.

The sorcerer faltered. The soldiers seemed to stop for a moment when the sorcerer had to focus on defending himself.

Kael felt a surge of hope. With Cormac engaging the sorcerer, they may have a chance to turn the tide.

"Stay behind me!" Kael shouted as he slayed another beast.

He fought closer to the podium, determined to help Cormac. The beasts were relentless, but Kael's resolve was stronger.

He would not let the sorcerer win this time.

He hacked through several of the beasts and incapacitated some of the soldiers. He couldn't come to killing them. He hoped that he could free them from the sorcerer's hold.

Maybe it was the effect of finding home here. Maybe it was because he was so close to the sorcerer. But he felt like he could save them this time.

He cut his way through the beasts and soldiers out of the square to find a safe space for Anelle and Isabella. His mind flashed as he remembered watching Ijos fight to keep his safe as a boy in the massacre.

A grim chuckle exuded from him as he sliced through the skull of one of the beasts.

He eyed a Stökkbreyta behind them.

"Duck!" As they did, he swung his swords in a wide arc, scissoring the beast in two at the chest.

Its arms flailed and hit the ground. Blood pooled black underneath as it stilled. Kael chuffed and glimpsed up to see the temple. He knew that it would be the best spot for them.

He pushed the doors of the temple open and it was quiet inside. The sounds of the massacre were dulled to a whisper from the thick walls.

He scanned the inside to make sure it was truly safe when he heard a shuffle behind the statue. He held out his swords but eased as the old man came around.

"You will be safe in here," he said. "The sorcerer's dark magic cannot touch this place. Guide the people in here so they may be safe."

Kael peered at Isabella, then Anelle. "Help him." They both nodded. Kael glanced at Anelle one last time. "I have to go, I have to help Cormac—"

Anelle stole a kiss, heavy on his lips as he felt torn again. He didn't want to leave her, but she pulled away.

"Go."

III

Panic was rampant. The streets were littered with corpses. Kael added more as he dispatched every beast on his path.

The black sky was a grim backdrop to the light that the large bonfire put off, but the light acted as a beacon. He trailed down alley ways and cut down beasts until two caught him off guard. The beasts aimed to swipe at his head, but both were knocked off their feet as Duff lunged into them. He gnawed and ripped them apart in a matter of seconds. Kael nodded to him and they continued towards the square.

When he entered the town square again, it was vacant save for Cormac and the sorcerer on the podium. The clang of the weapons echoed as each strike rebounded off the other.

"Cormac!" Kael ran towards the podium. Duff flanked him but then stopped and growled.

Kael stopped a few yards from the scaffolding as a dark figure emerged beside the bonfire. The silhouette dragged its weapon behind it. A large axe, double bladed, scraped across the cobbled square as it came closer to Kael. Kael's sneered and took stance.

"I thought you died, o' gracious Lord Haskell." The figure continued to walk towards him. Kael laughed sardonically. "But I suppose you're not gonna talk now, you stubborn bastard."

The two lunged in tandem with Duff alongside Kael. The axe and Kael's blade met with a loud clang. Their faces were close and their eyes met. Kael could see the emptiness in his eye.

Duff bit Haskell's free arm off. While the blood spurted, the man did not stagger. He responded by slinging his axe flat into Duff with a crunch. The wolf rolled away with a weak yelp.

"You're not even really alive anymore, are you?" Kael's own voice felt hollow. The man was nothing more than a husk driven by hatred now.

Haskell swung wildly, the tendons tearing in his arm. There was no recognition of pain as the arm bled from the trauma. The haywire attack was unpredictable. Kael was pelted by blows that he partially dodged.

Haskell swung the with the flat side out into Kael with blunt force. Kael shot up his claymore rapidly. It guarded the blow and threw him over the cobbled stone.

He rolled and caught himself on the balls of his feet as shards scattered around him. He cast aside the claymore hilt and sheathed his other sword. He took a deep breath and stood as his eyes pierced into Haskell.

He felt the rightness in the katana around his waist. He pulled at the blue-wrapped hilt and poised the blade in front of him.

Haskell stopped briefly. The void in his lone eye cleared. The green hue came back and intense hatred flooded out of the socket. The man roared and rushed towards Kael, repeating the same word over and over.

Ijos! Ijos, Ijos, Ijos! repeated over and over.

Kael was no longer in front of him. The tatterings of Kael's tunic and the stance that he took—his hair pushed back by the faint wind. All was replaced by the familiar tattered aura of Ijos in Haskell's eye.

Blinded by hate, Haskell swung his axe too hard, severing his arm at the elbow. The axe soared as Kael dodged it fluidly like water and embedded itself into the ground. In one more swift move, Kael took the katana swung in an upward arc and back down in a diagonal arc with blinding speed.

Haskell's eye widened for a moment, his mouth trying to resound, but blood began to fill up its void. A croak came out as his neck slit in two. His head slid down the diagonal cut and fell to the ground. Its mouth continued to croak (*Ijos, Ijos*), but the eye did not blink. The eye strained open and followed Kael as he left. He wiped the blade clean and sheathed it, then ran towards the scaffolding.

The clang stopped with a flash of sickly light.

"Cormac!" Kael yelled. He climbed the scaffolding when Cormac jumped off and ran towards Duff in the distance. Kael glanced up for a moment before dropping off and following Cormac to Duff, who was trying to stand but kept falling.

"How bad is it?" Kael tried to inspect Duff. He was unable to get close as the wolf raved with pain.

Cormac was already pouring some contents of a glass vial onto the wolf's wounds.

"It's a broken leg. This should help with the pain."

Steam dissipated from his fur and he snarled a little at it. It soon faded and he appeared calm afterwards. Cormac then found an unburnt piece of wood that had fallen out of the bonfire and braced the broken leg with some ripped pieces of his clothing.

"Where did he go?" Kael looked around, but they were the only ones in the square. There were faint screams in the distance, but only the bonfire and their labored breathing were close.

"Dunno," Cormac scanned the area. "He could be anywhere."

Then a rush of wind came. High above them came a shriek.

Kael knew the voice.

He stared in terror as the sorcerer hovered above, Anelle in his clutches. Kael's heart was beating in his head and ears as he saw Anelle's terrified expression. All noise was blocked out by the racing of his heart.

He heard the sorcerer's voice as he breathed a purple fog down Anelle's throat.

You will only know loss and suffering, lost one.

You will never be able to escape this path.

Then nothing. The two disappeared as a singular flower mockingly drifted down to them. He picked up the flower to see it was a Carnation, its flowers blooming and dying constantly in his hand and the stem growing wildly like a vine.

Fuck.

He dropped the Carnation and sprinted from the square.

Fuck.

He kept repeating it, *fuck,* as he ran to the inn. He stopped in front of it to see leaves, vines, stems, and flowers growing out of every window and door of the inn. They curled outward and whipped wildly at the air.

Fuck.

He rushed in.

Bereft

I

Anelle. The vines. Anelle. Am I bleeding? It doesn't matter. Anelle—Anelle—please. Don't leave me.

"Anelle!" Kael's voice broke.

He burst into the house and pushed his way through the cancerous plants growing like pulsing tumors. The vines whipped at him wildly as he crossed the foyer. The plants overcrowded the floor and creeped up the fireplace.

A bloom on the desk erupted, releasing a mist of green poison. He masked his face and eyes with his cloak as he pushed forward and ascended the stairs. The vines cut into his skin, the wounds dulled by his desperation. He clung to the rail as he climbed the infested staircase like a sheer rock wall.

Anelle. Please be okay. Anelle. Fuck, why?

His heart pounded like a reminder of his helplessness.

The smell of the plants—a mix of earth and decay—filled his nostrils as he pushed through the wall blocking his way. No doors were visible underneath the sheath of green—except for one.

Anelle's (*our*) door at the end was visible, though the bottom of the door had vines swarming out like tentacles. The vines continued to lash him as he passed. He didn't feel the pain, dull compared to the emotional turmoil he felt.

The door seemed like a tombstone to him, an oak tombstone marking a grave. He held his hand over the knob before he turned it without resistance.

The color faded from his face when he saw the room.

His home was gone. Writhing plants that grew and died repeatedly in an eternal struggle infested and ate it away.

Plastered against the wall was the source of all the vines and plants. Protruding with bulbous, cancerous appendages to feel and lash endlessly was Anelle. Her face was green; her body protected in a cocoon-like structure of vines and poisonous plants. The brown of her eyes was gone and replaced with the eyes of night and darkness.

She shrieked as the vines lashed at him, but he did not attack. He ignored the pain as he climbed to her body suspended over the bed.

Her shriek left his ears ringing, his vision blurring. Still, he reached and caressed her moss-covered cheek.

He silenced her with a kiss as tears streamed down his face.

She closed her eyes. When she opened them again, they were brown again, lucid and calm. Kael had to force himself to pull his own lips away from her. He was already starting to sob. She tried to hush him, to pull her pinned arm and caress his face, too.

"I love you," she whispered, her voice trembling. "I will always love you, and I know I fell for you as soon as I saw you. Don't forget that."

He choked between sobs.

"We can figure this out."

He gasped and pulled at the vines that covered her body.

"We can do it. Please, I love you. I need you."

Her eyes filled with tears as she shook her head, though it, too, was pinned back.

"Nay, you don't need me. Oh, how I wish we could have lived a normal life. But that was not fate. It's out there, in the forest, and you cannot run from it. Not for me."

A vine stretched out and pulled the sword from his sheath and placed it gently in his hand. It wrapped around his hand tight so he could not drop it. He shook his head violently.

"N-no. No, no, no. I cannae do that. Please give me a chance..." he continued to choke and stammer incoherently.

"*I don't want to die a monster,* remember?" She smiled weakly. "Give me mercy and give me love as I exude my last breath."

A vine pushed his head to her as they locked lips again. His tears streamed and collided with hers as another vine moved his hand to guide the sword into the cocoon. It pierced it willingly and Anelle gasped. Kael could taste blood in her mouth, but her lips still locked with his.

Then she went limp. The cancerous plants dissolved almost as quickly as they sprang to life in their unending growth. Kael held Anelle's limp body in his arms. Her clothes were ripped to shreds and his sword protruded from her chest.

Her eyes still held love after she passed; her tears streaked down one last time.

Kael wailed as he cradled and rocked her lifeless body into his.

Then came the cackling in his head.

Oh, the woes of loss. Your path is only beginning. Cackling. *Come to the forest of dreams, of sorrow, of ashes. I'll be waiting.*

Kael's vision turned red. He had suffered so much at the hands of one man—but no more.

He gently laid Anelle's body down on the bed and pulled his sword out as he kissed her cold cheeks.

He ran out of the inn. He ignored the memories with Anelle in this place, of their homely dinners and the only sense of calm he has felt in a long time.

He kicked the door open and ran to the barn. He untied Jorunn and rode bareback towards Liela woods, through the wreckage of the massacre.

He skidded around a corner to the town limits and passed Cormac.

"Kael!" Cormac yelled, but he could only see the unbridled rage and sorrow plastered on Kael's face in the fleeting moment.

It was gone as Kael rushed to the forest.

II

It's dim.

Even in the darkness of the forest, it is dimmer than normal. The glow of the sparse moonlight on the snow did not shine as bright, like the snow absorbed it. Kael brought Jorunn down to a trot as he listened for any noises. There was the distant noise of the massacre cutting into the forest. There was nothing else.

He dismounted and left Jorunn briefly. Her whickering faded in his mind.

Where is he?

"Here." The sorcerer walked from behind a tree, dissipated, then appeared out from behind another.

"And here. I am everywhere—and nowhere."

Kael unsheathed his remaining sword. The ornate damascus blade. Its sheen echoed in the snowy copse.

The sorcerer laughed—howled even.

"Do you really think you can succeed? That your path of vengeance will end with you winning?"

His voice lost the surreal warble from the square. Kael noticed there was an odd accent to his voice, a trill in it he had not heard before.

In a flash, the sorcerer came at him. No tricks, no disappearing—just a lunge with a spectral dagger outstretched in front of him. Kael deflected the blade, but the sorcerer produced another in his opposing hand that glowed deep red.

Kael slid his sword down and blocked the next attack. The sorcerer responded with the other dagger. Kael instinctively tried to unsheathe a second blade. But the scabbard on his back was empty.

It broke. Fuck.

He didn't unsheathe the katana; the blade would break if he tried to guard with it. He then felt the heavy weight on his thigh: a reminder of the knife that replaced his own. He pulled it out and held it in his left hand—the ornate dagger of green and gold.

A chuckle rose and stifled in the sorcerer's throat.

"I see you've found my lost weapon. Tell me, does it feel right in your hand?"

No, it does not.

It is a finely crafted blade. But as Kael deflected with the blade, it almost seemed like it guided itself towards his own chest. It would inch closer with each parry despite his protests. The dagger was the sorcerer's, and it still was, working for him even now.

Kael tried to discard the dagger, but he could not let go. *It must be a spell—always some forsaken spell.* He was trapped and could not escape. He watched as the dagger got close to his heart.

Then the sorcerer dropped his spectral blades, grabbed the handle, and pushed it into Kael's chest. Kael groaned, but his eyes didn't falter. He thrust his sword into the sorcerer's chest and twisted. An inhuman shriek came from the sorcerer.

Kael chuckled. "I'll take you to A'Hel with me," he spat.

But the sorcerer's shrieks changed to that trill cackle. He moved closer, letting the damascus sword twist further through his body, all while pushing the dagger deeper into Kael. The sorcerer then held out a hand in front of him.

"Burn," the hand was alight.

He left no pause for Kael to pull away before he shoved it over Kael's heart.

The fire was different this time. The edges seemed darker than usual, the flame trying to turn black. And Kael felt it, too. The flames burned, but he could feel a weight within him trying to get out.

Then came an excruciating pain.

He felt like he was being torn apart, and with that he felt that darkness within him drawn to the fire on his heart.

It snarled. He snarled.

He collapsed on the ground and writhed. He could hear the voice, sensed that beast within him gnaw on his soul as it walked closer to his heart. His vision blurred. He could see clearly that a sigil was over his heart, the sigil of the sorcerer.

He laughed. Was it his own? He didn't think so. He didn't think it was even his voice coming out of his mouth.

The sorcerer leaned over him, sword still hanging from his chest.

"Come, Balaal. Use this vessel to leave your torturous prison," he tittered.

Then he gazed at Kael's desperate eyes and a flash of smile gave way from the artificial darkness under the hood.

"Your sorrow, your pain and suffering, all a means to prepare your body for my god. *Balaal.* You were nothing more than the sacrifice, lost one. And in exchange, he will rip your soul apart as payment from transgressing from his prison world to here."

No. A roar came from his voice. *No, I can't die. Not with you still alive.*

A roar and a moan escaped as Kael reached his trembling hand out to the sorcerer. Tears welled up in his frightened eyes.

But then he grabbed the blade of the hanging sword and yanked the sword down with all his force. The blade cut through the cloaked sorcerer and ripped the ethereal-like flesh in two.

The sorcerer shrieked in agony as black blood dripped from the gash. He staggered back before his trembling hands came up to his hood and slowly pulled it back.

Kael stared in horror at the face of the one that has plagued his life for so long.

A pale, sharp face stared back at him. Dark veins, like roots, encroached his face. His eyes were black, soulless, and bloodshot. On his forehead was a light scar of an eye, with red vein-like strings running through it. Kael noticed in fleeting that his ears were cut rudely at the tips.

"See the price of my path," the sorcerer growled.

The blood continued to drip profusely from the gash.

"We all suffer for a better cause; you will be the same. The cost of magic and my path to cleanse this world by reviving Balaal came at the cost of my own flesh. Your sacrifice will just be a drop in the sea of change and sacrifice this world needs."

The sorcerer stumbled towards him and knelt. "Let go. Let go of the suffering and this world. This is fate. Stop fighting fate."

No. He couldn't die. "No." His voice cracked. He panted. The burn surged through his veins.

He screamed. The fire pushed back. He writhed. He wasn't himself anymore. He was lost.

"No." the sorcerer grabbed a fistful of hair. Blood dripped onto Kael's face. The sorcerer yanked him upward until they were eye-to-eye.

He was grinning.

"Don't forget why you are here." His voice was like a knife. "This is all your fault. Remember."

No—

The village. The fires. The plume of smoke that choked the sky.

"Nuria!"

The wings that turned to ash. Wings that were supposed to be eternal.

Black flames.

He remembered screaming. It wasn't his own.

Ijos.

His green eyes. Then they were black.

Why did he face the sorcerer? Ijos said to wait. Ijos said—

It didn't matter. It was the fracture.

A roar came out of Kael like a volcano. He watched the sorcerer stumble upright and then disappear in a cloud of fog.

Kael writhed in pain on the snowy ground. He gasped and blood trickled from his mouth as he felt the darkness overwhelm him. His eyes darkened and he saw glimpses of his face, like looking in a mirror.

Face to face with this beast, he saw its monstrous form, scaly and reptilian. The eyes were red like fire, and tusks protruded out from its face.

This world is mine. You have suffered long enough, Kael. Let go. Your body will continue, ushering in a new Era.

The darkness encroached on him, and he could feel it almost fully consume him. He whimpered, his hands going numb as he tried to crawl away from something inside him.

Then they fell, landing on light fur. The darkness began to dispel, a light replacing it.

521

This is not your fate, Kael.

He's heard this before.

Bond with me. I can dispel him, I can drive the darkness from you and burn away the link.

Is it Anelle? He can see her face. A beacon of light to him. His cloudy eyes glanced at her face and new tears washed down. Blood trickled out of his mouth and the gaping wound in his chest. His body was covered in black veins that strained to take hold.

"Save me," he choked. "Please, save me."

A bright flame burned within him. He could feel the darkness shriek away from the white-hot flames. The threads within him singed and melted away, freeing his soul from cracking apart.

He saw the demonic face glaring at him with malice. Although it became more distant, he was still able to discern its whisper.

This isn't over. The world will be mine.

His breathing regulated as the pain subsided. The last few blots of his vision focused on a shadow. The moonlight shone through enough for Kael to glimpse the eyes of a man he once knew. They were no longer green, but black like a void. The man stared, but there was no recognition on the face. A face he loved dearly.

Ijos.

Then there was nothing, but it was warm. Kael sat in a field, green and bright. In it, he saw little fire sprites, but they were gentle. They giggled and danced around him, but they did not coerce him any. He heard a shuffle behind him, and someone leaned against his back. He knew this scent—the electrifying touch.

"Anelle," he said as tears streamed. He tried to turn but couldn't. He reached an arm back but was met with a barrier.

"It's not your time," she whispered. He felt her get up, but then felt her lips brush his neck.

"Stay strong for me."

Then he was alone in this field, the sprites far away. He slept on a mossy bed. The warmth did not quell the shivers in his body.

Ashes

I

"Your hair is greying," Kael said. Wind picked up through the forest and whipped their hair wildly.

Ijos sat beside him on a log facing the village past their cabin.

"That's what time does. What was once full of life will decay. We were born from the ground, and we will return to the ground."

"Seems pretty somber," Kael said as he peered at Ijos through a veil of his hair.

"Aye, but I've still got some time in me, son." Ijos smiled. "I'm sorry I cannot come with you this time. My knee has been bothering me," He flexed his bad knee and a crackle came from it. He winced in pain.

"It's alright. It's just a simple task. Someone said there were kappas coming on the Lyndis path and attacking travelers. They paid a good sum to take care of it."

Ijos chuckled. He patted Nuria on the head. She was perched on the log beside him. His eyes caught hers and his smile fell.

"I have something for you, Kael. It's your 24th birthday today, after all."

Ijos produced a crudely wrapped present, long and slender, from beside him. Kael tried to act surprised, but he saw Ijos trying to hide it as they came out here for some practice. It all seemed nonsensical, but Ijos seemed to enjoy it lately. He wanted to spend more time with Kael by trying to get him to practice more and giving him things. He adjusted the knife on his thigh as he remembered Ijos gifted it to him.

Kael smiled at Ijos as he unwrapped the present slowly. A glimpse of blue shone through and he tore it off at once. It was a blue katana. He peeked the blade from the Saya and examined at the white sheen of the blade.

"It's a katana from the west," Ijos said. "I brought it from my homelands long ago. It was my father's."

Kael remembered seeing this katana in Ijos' office, but only when he peeked as the door closed. He was never allowed in there. They did not say much afterwards; Kael stuttered a *thank you* and they hugged for an extended period.

Kael left soon after. The mission was detoured when a plume of smoke formed over the hidden village as he reached the foot of the mountains.

II

A pressure. No, not really pressure. But he felt like someone breathed life into his lungs. It radiated from his hips—a warmth that felt like the sun shining on his face. He could smell grass and, for a second, he smelled carnations. He felt pleasure, but it was involuntary, like a wet dream.

He dreamed repeatedly of the pleasure of being in bed with Anelle; her lips locked with his, her warmth intertwined. It was a recurring dream, only broken by periods of darkness and cold.

III

Liela woods. Snow blanketed the ground except for the grove that served as the heart of the forest. The pool of water that surrounded it was thawed and warm.

Little waves pulsed as a goddess, garbed in a vine skirt, straddled the bare, burned body of Kael. She took him inside her and gave him life through the intimate act. Her blessing guided from her directly into him through the physical contact.

She did this in periods, letting herself rest in between. It drained her ethereal aura each time. Color came back slowly to Kael as the black veins disappeared slowly and the burns healed.

Time passed. It always does. Time is like a river, unyielding to rocks or objects. Always fluidly wrapping around and continuing.

Kael woke up to the grass ticking his nose. He had rolled over on his side at some point and his bare chest heaved. He focused his gaze. It was the grove. The shapes became more defined, and he saw Kinaa sitting before him.

"Welcome back, Kael." He could feel her happiness and relief at his awakening.

There was a connection to the spirit he did not feel before. His body and soul felt like he could reach into her, and he could feel the overwhelming power she had in reserve.

It was warmth to him, but he knew it could burn at any second. He wasn't afraid of it—he felt it inside him, too. He studied his bare chest to see the wounds he suffered were gone. Just scars—a dull reminder of what seemed like just happened.

"Where am I?" Kael groggily spilled out.

He tried to sit up, but his muscles were weak. He felt Kinaa tense a little, like she was focusing, and then the tiredness in his muscles dropped away. He sat up easily, his body firm.

He gazed at the grove and saw the old tree he saved from that mutated human. *Lonzo, right? That was his name. He suffered, but he didn't want to suffer anymore. 'I don't want to die a monster'.* He felt a pang in his heart. He brushed it off and walked over to the tree. "The grove," he muttered.

"She's resting," Kinaa whispered as she stood beside him.

He should have been startled, but he knew, deep down, that she was there. He knew where she was at all times. Could sense her easily.

"The goddess Daraliela is resting. She used her divinity to heal your wounds. My powers saved you from succumbing, but you were still on the brink of death. She transferred some of her magic to heal the wounds. It took time, though."

"How long," he whispered. "How long was I gone?"

Kinaa seemed to calculate the time. "Three months."

Three months. Had he really been asleep that long? What has happened to the world since then? Where is the sorcerer? What about... what about Anelle's body?

Kael began to leave the grove, but his bare chest met with the chill of the air outside the waters. It shocked him and made him inhale sharply. He returned, grabbed his clothes, and dressed feverishly.

His mind flashed back to his last moment with Anelle. Tears welled up in his eyes as he saw Kinaa crying too. The suffering he felt, she felt it too. They were bonded.

Fuck, why are we bonded?

He heard a whickering. His eyes found Jorunn grazing on a patch of grass in the grove. His heart felt some relief for his companion.

Kael walked over to Kinaa. "I need to go," he rasped. His voice was hoarse from the long rest.

"I know. We need to go."

Kael mounted Jorunn bareback and Kinaa rode behind him. Jorunn did not seem fazed by this, having adapted well to Kinaa's presence while Kael was comatose. Kael guided her to the town of Anju and entered the surrounding fields it at a trot.

The fields were scarred. He could see black from uncontrolled fires still trying to heal. The fields had cleared spots free of crops where mounds of snow-covered dirt was heaped.

He has seen this before. Long ago, he knew what they were. Each mound had a small stone and some writing he could not make out from the distance.

The gates bore deep scratches and the roads were less populated. He still remembered the way back from the short time he was here. He found the shortest path to the inn.

He froze in the moment and forgot how to breathe as he gazed at the inn.

It bore scars, but they were masked. The stones could not fully erase the past, but someone healed them as best as they could. He dismounted and approached the entrance. He opened the door and through the open frame like a ghost.

And that is how Isabella saw him, like a ghost.

Her face welled up with tears and flushed as she passed around the desk (it had new wood to replace those broken). She embraced him with hushed sobs.

"I—We—I—We thought you died. Oh, Kael—" she brushed his hair and rubbed his back. He felt the tears welling up, but they didn't spill. She led him upstairs and into the room that was Anelle's. *No more. Not hers. You saw it. It was you.*

It was clean. It bore the same faded scars, but it was a normal room. The warmth was gone, though. The inn felt just like every other place he stayed; just a building with four walls to protect from the elements.

And then he noticed there were no plants. Not even in the foyer. They were all gone.

"Where is she," he croaked. His eyes were glossy and distant.

They walked out back to the barn. A snowcapped mound was nestled against the barn wall. A stone detailed her name. Nothing else.

Kael sat down beside the mound and placed his hand on the stone. His eyes stared at the snow, and he mouthed *I'm sorry* several times. He had no ability to speak.

Behind the stone was a singular Carnation blooming despite the cold. He knew it was her reminding him it was okay.

He got up and entered the barn to see his saddle was still propped up where he last had it, not touched at all. He carried it out to Jorunn and strapped it to her despite her muted protests. Kinaa jumped off Jorunn's back before he started and watched him work.

Isabella stood meekly beside him as he did it.

"When it was over," she tried to start, then stopped. "When it was over, I found Cormac in the streets fighting. He had killed all but a few of the beasts, and the ones left had fled at the sound of some horn. He said it was the sorcerer. He cried as he recounted you rushing to the forest, saying he thought you went after him."

Kael nodded. Isabella did all she could to hold back the tears again.

"We found her, too. He helped—Cormac buried her. He found a seed in her hand and planted it behind the stone, too. I didn't know what else to do—I felt alone. But then people still came here with the need to stay somewhere, and so I just did what I could. Cormac patched the place up as well as he could."

"But then we got this—" she handed him a piece of folded parchment. He unfolded it to see a sketch of his face and then, at the bottom: **WANTED: KAEL. FOR THE MURDER OF LORD HASKELL AND CONSPIRACY OF TREASON."**

"Cormac left not long after. He left me a letter. He told me it was for you if you came."

She handed him the letter and he opened it. It was sparse, but he knew what it meant.

Meet me in the Wasteland. He has a weakness.

Kael stashed the letter as he heard a sob. Tears streamed down Isabella's cheeks.

"Oh, Kael—"

He embraced her tightly. He pulled back and the sorrow on his face made her tears start anew.

"I'm okay. I will find him and we will finish this." His voice wavered a little at the end. "We will finish this and stop this terror."

Kael did not hesitate any longer. He mounted Jorunn and, with Kinaa on the saddle horn, he started to head out. Isabella had walked in the inn and came back with a sword. It was an old sword—a claymore much like his own—but darker. He examined it to see it had a fox head for a pommel.

"I found this one day while we cleaned. I don't know where it came from, but I held onto it. Now I know why." She turned to the kitsune as Kael strapped the sword to his back. "Take care of him."

Kinaa nodded and Kael gave her one last hug from atop Jorunn. He waved goodbye to the inn, glancing at the barn and grave as he did.

He went south and exited the town and followed the river until he crossed a natural bridge. In the far distance, past the snow, beyond the great fields of Hera, was the barren lands of the Wastelands.

He felt the tug of fate towards there, like a string or a compass.

"We are going to face a lot worse things from here on out," Kinaa said.

Kael nodded. He felt it too—a deep dread that crept up his spine. He spurred Jorunn towards the blanched lands ahead.

Afterword

    The road that Kael walked is much like the writing process. What began as a character evolved into so much more than I could ever comprehend. I had started this story in late 2022. I paused for quite some time after writing a prologue (which ended up as the 'Caede' chapter) and a small part of what is now 'House of Carnation'.

    As with most stories, I did not plan on the plot twists. I had the idea of a character that was bonded to a spirit since I was a child, but then it gave him the ability to shapeshift. I did not plan the obsession, the trauma, the pain. But, as always, the subconscious knows better. This story needed these themes. Part of my own issues bled onto the page as I obsessed and lived in the story.

    I had no intentions of releasing the story self-published. I had queried several agents with no luck. I still persisted until I was diagnosed with a low-grade chondrosarcoma in early 2025. The proceeding thoracotomy and rib resection made me rethink a lot of things. The story was already written, but that darkness I felt afterwards bled into the final stages of editing. It pushed me to take control as I released it myself.

The last few things I will say is that Kael's story is far from over. Things will change from here on out, and it will be darker and more epic. But we will still see a broken man wandering a world.

Thank you for reading *The Path of Ashes.* If the start of Kael's journey moved you, even in a small way, I ask you this: leave a trace—a review, a book recommendation, or an acknowledgement. Every bit of it helps bring this story through the noise and darkness of the publishing world.